THE
STORY
HOUR

Also by Thrity Umrigar:

FICTION

The World We Found
The Weight of Heaven
If Today Be Sweet
The Space Between Us
Bombay Time

NONFICTION

First Darling of the Morning

THE
STORY
HOUR

A Novel

THRITY
UMRIGAR

HARPER

Designed by Fritz Metsch

ISBN: 978-1-62953-334-6

For Dad
A million times over

"The truth does not change according to our ability to stomach it."

—FLANNERY O'CONNOR

"I am made and remade continually. Different people draw different words from me."

—VIRGINIA WOOLF

BOOK
ONE

1

I BEGINS.

Dear Shilpa—I writes. Belief me when I say not single day pass in six years that I not thought of you. How are you, my dearest?

Then I takes the paper, roll it like a ball of dough, and throws it across from the room. It land on top of the coffee table—why he call it the coffee table when in this house we only drink chai?—and I goes to pick it up to place in the dustbin. Shilpa never reading my note. He will never posting to her. Some things even stupids like me know.

I look at clock on the wall. Eight-forty-five, evening time. Husband be home by ten-thirty. Quickly-quickly I goes to the bathroom and open the medicine chest. I takes all the bottles out and carry them to the sitting room. I put the bottles in a row and for one minute only my stomach faints, as if the medicines is already in it. But then Bobby's thin face come to me and I see his sad blue eyes and the pain shoot my heart again. It was not my imagine. Bobby, too, look sad when he leaf today. I will miss you, he said, and his words was both honey and poison, sun and moon in the same sky.

I didn't say: Why you must go to the California? I didn't say: I wanting you to come to the restaurant every Thursday forever so I can watch you eat and feel the full in my stomach. I didn't say: In this cold country where I having no friend or relation, you are the only one who smile to me, who talk to me like I am person and not the garbage. I did not say: I have betrayed my husband twice—once to saves my family, second to save my soul. I didn't say, I didn't say anything at all.

Six tablets in the husband's My Grain bottle. Three antibiotic. Seventeen green tablets for relaxing the muscle from when he had the back pain last year. I remember something, and hurry from the room. In kitchen cabinet above microwave is big bottle of ibuprofen from Costco. I open. Hundreds of orange tablets. While in kitchen, I fill large pitcher of water.

I feels I should pray. Do pooja. Ask Bhagwan's pardon for sin I am doing. Ask husband's forgiving, also, for inconvenient I am causing him. Marry Rekha, I want to tell him. Rekha work in our grocery store next to the restaurant and I have saw how she look at him all flirty-flirty. Husband is good man, he work hard, eyes down, never notice Rekha or other ladies. Not his mistake he don't love me. Not his mistake I don't love him. Early on after marriage, I was hoping that slowly-slowly, the love will come. If my ma still alive, she could tell me what to do to make the love come. But Ma dead long back, and so I wait. When husband's father die three year back and he can't leaf business to fly to India, he so sad and griefing, and I think love will now happen between us, for surely. When I buy a new red sari for his friend's marriage and husband look at me and smile, I think that is love but it just the alcohol. Now I know. Husband love one woman. That woman not me.

I am not ascare to die. I am only ascare that after death I be alone. Maybe because of suicide, I go to the hell? If hell all hot and crowded and noiseful, like Christian minister on TV say, then I not care because it will be just like India. But if hell cold and quiet, with lot of snow and leaf-empty trees, and people who smile with string-thin lips, then I ascare. Because it seem so much like my life in Am'rica.

Bobby said he moving to the California to be near his sister. "I'm tired of being so far away from family," he say. "You know?"

"I know."

He listen something in my voice because he look up immediately. His eyes as blue as July sky. His long yellow hair fall like sunshine on his forehead and my finger burn from not touching it. "Yeah, I guess you do," he say, and then he smile, and I feels something hot and living move from my stomach all the way to my face. The husband is thirty feet away, sweating in his white undershirt in the too-hot kitchen, but he is nobody to me right now, a stranger on the bus, a blind man who never seen me. Bobby is the one who reading my heart, who knows my feets are in Am'rica, but that each night my heart fly like a bird over my father's fields, over our village square, over the stone house my dada build himself, searching, searching for Shilpa. Bobby—who never talk to my husband even though husband sometimes leaf the kitchen to come joke with his regular customer and say, "See you next Thursday, sir"; who sometime send an extra-special sweet from kitchen for him—Bobby can see that my husband do not let me talk to my relations, that he has made me a tree without root system, that he look at me and see the nothing. Sometimes when husband call me from the kitchen and his voice is sharp as the knife he holding, Bobby look up at me and make the face, the way children do when they taste a sour green mango from the tree. But something encourage in that face, also, like he say, "Go, Lakshmi. You strong woman. I knows you sad but the God will help you. Be brave."

For last two year, Bobby come for lunch every Thursday. Some week he on vacation and no show, and those week go as slow as the bullock-cart climbing the mountain. Then I hating myself for wearing good sari and putting Pond's cream on my face to make it more fair. Then I irritate with grocery store cus-

6 THRITY UMRIGAR

tomers who want to know where this-and-that is, and Rekha look at me with frown and say, "Kya hai, Didi? Go upstairs and take a nap for an hour, na?"

And now I am to never see Bobby again. Because he tell me today he is shifting to the California and although he say he come visit sometime, his eyes look down and his white teeth bite his lip when he telling the lie. Also, he wait till he finish his lunch, before to tell me. I say nothing, just nod my head, which feel heavy, like a mountain is sitting on top of it. I balance the mountain while I nods and smile, nods and smile. He is saying "job transfer," and "good weather," and "near my nieces and nephews," while I nods and smile. After a while, he stop talking and he lean back in chair and put his hands behind his head and breathe out. "But I will miss you, um, that is, this place," he say. And his lips become a half-moon, upside down.

I shake off mountain on my head. "Wait-a," I say. I rushes toward store. Another customer put hand out to ask for bill but I ignores him. I go into store and look around. Something I want to give Bobby. Something to carry on the aeroplane, something to take to the California. A memory from me. A memory of me. I look at shelves I have stocked—bottles of Pond's cream, Vicks VapoRub, Ovaltine, Horlicks, milk of magnesia, Kalvert's raspberry syrup, Patak's lime pickle. Nothing here to give. I go to next aisle and look—bhelpuri mix, fried moong dal, banana wafer packets. I grab a packet of gathias. He will snack on this on the aeroplane.

But I am not satisfy. I want something . . . more fixed. I moves quick to next shelf. Boxes of sweetmeats—halvas, pedas, jalebis. Cans of leeches, mangoes. Nothing, nothing.

And then I remembers. I go to front of store, behind cash register, where we keeps our boxes of expensive saffron. And behind the boxes is our silver tray, where each morning the husband lights a diva and says the prayers. In the tray we have small statues of our gods—a blue painted statue of Krishna, a wood carving of Hanuman, the monkey god, a silver statue of Lakshmi, goddess of wealth. Rekha is at the counter, checking out a customer, and I slips behind her and reaches for Lakshmi. But she having eyes in the back of her head because she open her big fat mouth and say, "Didi, what are you doing?"

Shut up, mind your own business, I want to say, but instead I say, "Nothing," and move to the door that connect restaurant to store.

But when I reach, the table is empty. Bobby has left.

Next to his empty plate, Bobby has kept twenty-dollar note. Lunch buffet is costing only $7.99. I grab the note in same hand holding the statue and rush to the front door. The brass bell above the door say ting-tong as I opens and shuts it behind me.

In parking lot, I look at bluegreenredwhite cars sitting neatly in a row, like tooths in the mouth. Quickly-quickly my eyes looks around the lot, trying to find Bobby. Has he driven away already? Without saying proper goodbye? My heart fall like the sparrow from the tree when I think this. The tears begin to burn my eyes, and then I sees him, far ahead of me. "Mister," I scream. He not look back. And so, for the first time since I am knowing him, I speak his name. "Bobby," I yells. "Mister. Bobby. Please." Without telling me, my feets start to move and then to fly, as if to catch his name before it leaf my mouth.

He turns around and his face look surprise as I rush toward him like the Rajdhani Express. He take a steps back, as if he thinking I will run into him, like train derailment. But I stops just in front of him and now my mouth feels dry and no wordings are coming to my mind.

"Yes?" Bobby say after a minute. He always look at me so kind.

"You leaf without saying the goodbye," I say, but his face turn red color like I pain him, and so I say, "You leaf without proper change back. Buffet only seven-ninety-nine."

He begin to laugh but not in mean way that the husband laugh when he make fun of me. "Oh well. It was only twenty dollars, Lakshmi. And it was a tip—for all the care you've taken of me these past few years."

The word "care" open a cave in my heart. In my old life in India, I takes care of so many peoples. Shilpa. My ma. Dada. Mithai the elephant. Here, I have nobody to care for. My husband don't want caring from me. Every time I nice, he just remember what he don't have. And what he do have—me.

I opens my mouth but nothing is living in it—no words. Still, I must try. "My pleasure," I say. "No extra tip required."

He smile again. "Lakshmi," he say. "It's okay. Really. No big deal."

At his naming me, I remember the statue in my hand. "Here," I say. "For you. A gift for the California."

His eyes grow big when I put the silver statue in his hand. And suddenly I not feel shy. "It's Lakshmi. Goddess of the wealth. Same name as me. Something to remind you of me in the California." I looks at him quickly and then looks at my feet. But still I am feeling Bobby's eyes on my face, making it hot like the sun.

"Wow. Are you sure?"

I nod. I see my feets in the dirty Bata rubber chappals I wearing in restaurant and then look at Bobby's feets in his leather sandal. All pinky-pink his toes are, like a baby's. I feel ashame and look up quickly before he follow my eye.

Bobby is staring at me, his head on one side like our old dog used to do when he puzzle. Then he smile. "Bye, Lakshmi," he say. "Thanks for this."

He put his hand out for me to shake, like I also a man. No man ever handshake me before. I unsure to do what. If the husband see, he will not like. But I see the hairs on Bobby's white arm, like golden thread. Soft, like a girl's hand. And then I think: I's in Am'rica now. I must shake hands like proper Am'rican. And so I takes Bobby's hand in both mine. "Good luck," I say. "God bless."

"God bless," he repeat. Then he pull out of my hand. "S'long, Lakshmi," he say. "I'll drop you a card from California."

I watch Bobby's blue car make left turn on main road. I knows Rekha, with her big eyes and long ears, counting the time for how long I absent. But still I standing, moving not forward or back, even though the sun strong on my skin, even though the breeze moving the pallov on my sari. I not ready to enter the hot, smelly restaurant. I not ready to serve the customers who is not Bobby. I wonders what would happen if I begins to walk, to leaf my life and just take one step, then second, third? I would go past Russian tailoring shop, liquor store, Dollar Store. But where I go once I exit plaza? Across main road is Shell station. But I don't drive the car—the husband say I too stupid to learn. I have twenty dollars in my hand which Bobby gave for the care. I have dirty Bata slipper on my feets. Not too far I can go on my own, I knows, but still, thinking of going inside store and restaurant makes a vomit in my throat. I hates my life, I thinks, and the thought give me the shock. Until this minute, I not knowing this.

"Lakshmi," I hears, and even without turning, I know who is calling. It is the husband and he walking fast near to me. He is without shirt, still in the white sleeveless ganji he cook in, and I notice the big arms with the dark hairs and the stomach that moves like a handi of water as he walk. He also breathe huf-huf-huf as he come to me.

"Are you mad?" he say when he reach me. "Going on a walk while the customers are waiting? Standing in the middle of the plaza talking to yourself?"

I say nothing.

He eyes narrow. "What's this?" he say, lifting my hand holding the twenty-dollar note. "You stealing from register? Rekha say you take statue with you. Forty-five dollar, statue is costing."

I let him take note from me. "Customer tip," I say. "I thought he make mistake."

"If customer make such stupid mistake, it's on his head," he say, and then smile, like he making a funny joke.

But I not laughing.

"Come on, stupid," the husband say. "Finish your work, you."

Sometime I think my real name Stupid. He call me this more than my own name.

He put his arm behind my neck and lead me back to store. If he could pulls me from my nose, I thinks, he would.

Rekha give me the funny look when we enter store. And then, in front of her, he say to me, "Now, where is statue you took?"

Rekha begin to wipe counter, as if she not heard. First time in her life she wipe that counter without me telling her to. "I tell later," I say softly to husband.

"No later-fater. I need to maintain inventory. Everything accounted for. That's what Suresh advise."

This year, the husband hire accountant for first time. One of the men he play cards with every Thursday become his new accountant. He feel very prideful about this. It make him feel like real Am'rican businessman, I think. Now everything is Suresh-says-this and Suresh-says-that. I not liking Suresh. I not liking any of the mens who my husband friend.

"I gave it to Bobby," I say. I turn my back to Rekha, so she cannot hear.

Husband raise right eyebrow. "Who Bobby?"

I feel dirty, having the husband say Bobby name. But he want answer. "Our best customer. He come every Thursday. He moving to the California. So I give gift."

Husband slap his head, like killing a fly. "Oh, you stupid. Who give gift to non-returning customer? You trying to bankrupt me or what?"

Behind me, I hear Rekha giggle. Chu-chu-chu, she sound, like mouse. My face feel hot as the iron. "You chup," I say to her. "Ears like open sewers you is having. Listening to other people's business."

Rehka get look of Hindi film heroine when she kidnap by villain. "Bhaiya," she say to my husband. "This is so unjust." Bhaiya, she call him, means brother. But way she look at him, not like sister at all.

Husband say nothing to Rekha. He only looking and looking at me, as if he seeing something on my face he not before see. "Lakshmi," he say quietly. "You thirty-two-year-old woman. Why you acting like some stupid teenage girl? Now, please, go faata-faat and wait on customer. We have job to finish."

I feel the tears in my eyes. But I am not crying when Rekha can see. In six years in Am'rica, I learn one trick—how to cry without tears. In my village, in the arms of my mother, I use to cry like baby. If I don't come first in my class, I cry. If Dada talk angry to Shilpa, I cry. If village children tease Mithai the elephant, I cry. When Ma get sick and I have to leaf my school in eight standard, I cry and cry till Ma joke we not needing monsoon that year. But in Am'rica, I cry from inside. Like singing song without moving your lips.

But now, as all pills are in the row, I don't feel sad. I feel relief. In Hindi film they always write letter when heroine do the suicide. But no one for me to write. Shilpa, I don't know address for. Better if Dada not knowing. The husband be upset for two-three days and then he hire new help for restaurant. Nobody here to miss me. Maybe Rekha miss me more than anyone.

At last minute, I get the husband's whiskey bottle and put on coffee table. The husband will be more angry over loss of whiskey than loss of wife. I smile to myself for making the joke. But inside the smile is thousand hot needles. Because in making joke, I making the truth, also.

I have never tasted daru before. Dada say good girls never drink the daru. But I pour some in glass now and drinks. Yah, bhagavan. It is like swallowing the burning matchstick. Maybe no need for pills, this alone kill me. But I swallow three My Grain tablets. I sit for a minute, looking at clock. Husband home from card game in two hours. Is the dying happening yet? Nothing happening, just room moving or I moving. Muscle pain medicine bottle is heavy in my hand. I pours out many tablets in my hand, like a maharaja pouring gold coins. I feel rich. I fills big glass of water and then swallow six or eight tablets. Then I drinks a little more of husband's whiskey. It tasting so bitter, I wonder if this is what making husband bitter all the time.

The room is going fast, like merry-go-round at the village fair. I pour more tablets into my hand but the hand so shaky that many falling on coffee table and then on floor. I don't care. I feeling lazy, happylike. I just swallows more pills. I knowing now that I am dying. I tries to think of my Shilpa's face, tries to remember her laugh, what her hands look like. I knows I should say the prayer, ask God for pardon for sin I am doing, but I don't. God seem very, very far away now. I wants Shilpa's name to be last name on my lips, my sister's face to be the last face I see before I am leaving this cold, empty life forever and ever.

2

SHE WAS ALMOST out the door when the phone rang. Dr. Margaret Bose groaned to herself as she glanced at the clock. Quarter to five on Friday and she was on her way to meet with Peter for a drink. Since they were meeting in Homerville, it would take at least a half hour to get there, and she was already late.

"Bose," she answered shortly.

"Maggie? Am I glad you're still here." It was her boss, Dr. Richard Cummings, head of the psychiatric unit. "Need to talk to you about a patient. You got a minute?"

"Actually, I was about to leave, Richard. Can this wait till next week?"

"Actually, it can't. We have a late admission. Came in directly from ER. Hard case. Immigrant woman. Attempted suicide. I can't get her to say a word. Husband says she understands English, but you could've fooled me."

Maggie wanted to cry with frustration. Sudhir was out of town only until Tuesday, and she had spent all week looking forward to seeing Peter Weiss again, ever since he'd phoned her on Monday and casually asked her out today, as if simply picking up a dropped conversation, as if he had not disappeared from her life three years ago with barely a goodbye.

"Can't Wayne see her?" she asked. "As I said, I was almost out the—"

"He tried. He can't even get her to look at him. Like I said, it's a tough case."

Despite her disappointment at having to cancel with Peter, Maggie was flattered. She felt a stab of self-hatred for being so susceptible to Cummings's flattery, after all these years.

She realized he was waiting for her to reply. She sighed heavily, cupping her hand over the mouthpiece as she did so. "Okay, give me five minutes to get there. What room is she in?"

"Room 745. Thanks, Maggie. See you Monday."

"Okay."

"Oh, Maggie? One other thing. For what it's worth, she's Indian. Just letting you know. In case, you know, it's helpful or anything. See ya."

Of course. That was the real reason Cummings had asked her to help out—because she was married to Sudhir. She should've known that after all these years of working at the hospital, of being the best goddamn psychologist on his staff, when Cummings saw her, he still saw a black woman married to an Indian immigrant who taught at the university. God, how she hated working in this lily-white town. What did Cummings expect her to do— walk into the patient's room and announce, "Hey, guess what? We're both married to Indian guys. So you can trust me, sister"? Did white people presume some primal solidarity between all people of color? Would Cummings be disappointed if she and the patient weren't soon bonding over cups of tea and trading recipes for samosas while watching Bollywood videos?

"Whoa, whoa," Maggie said to herself. "Where is all this hostility coming from? Cummings is a good guy, remember?" She and Sudhir had socialized with Cummings dozens of times, and she had never detected any of the reductiveness she was accusing him of now.

But she knew the answer to her question even as she posed

it—felt the answer deep within, where a spitball of disappointment lodged pungent and hot. Peter. She had so looked forward to having dinner with Peter. Ever since she'd heard that he was back in town, had been rehired as a visiting professor of photography at the university, had returned from whichever war-torn or famine-struck country he had visited most recently, she had debated whether to get in touch with him, whether to risk finding out if the passion that had flared so unexpectedly between them during his last time here was still alive. Her better angels had won. She had reminded herself how close to the edge of infidelity she had walked three years ago and told herself that choosing the sweet comfort of her marriage to Sudhir had been the right thing to do. So she had not acted on the knowledge of Peter being back, knowing that sooner or later she would run into him—it was a small campus, after all—anticipating and dreading that moment when she'd find herself face-to-face with him, at a faculty concert, perhaps, or on the bike path, or at a party. She had told herself that she would not be taken in by him this time—by that easy, relaxed gait, the lopsided grin, those green eyes that flitted restlessly in a face as malleable as clay, eyes that moved from one thing to another, restless, probing, watching everybody, always a little distant, a little guarded, always the observer. A photographer's eyes. Which was why she'd been so unprepared three years ago when those eyes had landed on her face and then stayed there, intent, focused, and lost some of their usual critical distance; they'd softened, and Peter had smiled, smiled so slightly that only she had noticed, not his usual one-sided grimace but a real smile that had made her flush violently.

Five days later, she had found herself in his arms, feeling his tongue deep inside her mouth, allowing his hands to hold her breasts, feeling the kind of surrender, the abdication, the setting down of a weight, that she had never felt with Sudhir. Like she was no longer responsible for her own breasts, for her own bones, her own will. She would not have expected it to be a good feeling, this loss of control, but it was, liberating and peaceful. And sexy. She had looked at Peter's big white hands, capable hands, hands that wielded a camera lens as skillfully as they were now handling her, hands that had pitched tents in the desert, changed tires on the side of dusty highways, handed bribes to informants in distant countries, turned over corpses in the killing fields. Sudhir was a whiz at math, but if a faucet leaked in their bathroom, it was Maggie who had to fix it. If they had a flat tire, he was as helpless as a baby while they waited for AAA to arrive. Maggie knew that in his lack of handiness, Sudhir was typical of Indian men of his class, and she had never held his ineptitude against him, had even found it endearing. But being in Peter's arms, knowing her body was being expertly manipulated and enjoying the manipulation, she felt for the first time a sense of loss. Not that there was anything wrong with Sudhir's lovemaking. It was just that Sudhir in bed was Sudhir in the world—quiet, efficient, competent, with no drama. He would never lose himself in bed because he never lost himself in the world. Whereas Peter was roaming her body with the eagerness of an explorer mapping a new continent. So it was with the deepest of regrets that Maggie had told Peter to stop.

A paperweight slipped from Maggie's desk, and she moved her foot out of the way with a small cry. Shit. She hadn't seen Peter in three years and already she was acting like some fool schoolgirl. This was why she'd never taken it any further with Peter, unable to bear the intensity of her passion.

She looked up at the clock again and then picked up her cell phone. Peter answered on the first ring. "Hi."

"Hey. It's me. Listen, something has come up at work. I don't think I'll be able to do dinner. I'm sorry."

He hadn't said a word and yet it came through, his acute disappointment. It flattered her, this unspoken need. Then he said, "Is this just an excuse? To get out of having dinner with me? Because you don't have to do that . . ."

"No. Really. We got a late admission. I'm really bummed at not seeing you. Honest."

"Well, why don't you just come by the house, then? When you get done. I'll whip up an omelet or something. Or we can go out for a late meal."

Her stomach lurched at the thought of visiting Peter at his home. She shook her head violently to rid herself of the temptation that was already forming. "Not a good idea, Peter. How about if I call you in an hour or so? And we can decide where to meet?"

She heard the chuckle, just the tiniest, faintest sound, heard the triumphant note in it, heard that he had caught what she had not said: I don't trust myself to be alone with you. It irritated her, that sound, but it also thrilled her, made the connection between them suddenly feel electric and charged. "I'll call you," she repeated. "Okay?"

"Okay, babe," he said, and there it was again, the feeling that he was taking charge of her, possessing her, reeling her in.

She ignored the screaming in her head that told her it was a mistake to see Peter Weiss, even in a public place, as she ran her fingers through her hair and prepared to exit her office. She caught the elevator to the seventh floor of the hospital and walked down the hallway past the nurses' station until she got to Room 745. The door was open—patients on a suicide watch were not allowed to shut their doors. She glanced in to see a hunched woman sitting on the bed, hugging her knees, staring at the blank white wall. Even though the woman faced away from the door, Maggie felt a stirring of pity. She had treated immigrant women before—the loneliness, the sheer isolation of their lives, was hard to fathom. Though the fact that this woman supposedly spoke English was a good start.

Maggie flipped through the chart, gleaning the basic facts. Taken to the ER at ten-fifteen p.m. last night. Was found slumped on the living room floor by her husband. Had to have her stomach pumped and was treated for a large bruise on her forehead. The MRI for an internal head bleed had come back negative. The woman was a thirty-two-year-old immigrant from India. Her name was Lakshmi Patil and she was employed at her husband's restaurant. Reason for suicide attempt unknown. Patient was generally uncooperative.

Maggie Bose drew in a breath, knocked perfunctorily on the open door, and let herself into the dark room.

3

I DOES NOT TURN around when I hear my name being called. They come into the room every two-three minutes, asking this-question and that-question. One wanting to know if I needs any-thing, another offer me water, one says he's Dr. So-and-so and can he look into my eyes and do this-thing and that-thing. All of them have the questions, all of them want to know why I do such a wicked thing, though nobody except my husband say to me what I do is wicked. At this hospital, everyone is nice and kindly, everyone's face look sad and sorry, like they all wanting to being my friend. But I is knowing the God-truth: I having no friends. Bobby is the only friend I had and now he is lost to the California. No, in this hospital, in this country, in this life, I's alone.

"Mrs. Patil?" the voice say. "I'm Dr. Bose. Maggie Bose. May I talk with you for a minute?" I know it is rudeness but I don't turn around. I am liking looking at this wall, which look like myself from the inside—empty and blank. A big piece of nothing.

"Mrs. Patil," the voice say again, and before I can think, this person come sit on the side of bed next to me. I am so surprise my head jerk up, and then I get the shock when I see her black face. I has never been so near to the black person before and I am so ascare I think I will do soo-soo in my gown. I push on my hands to move back in the bed, so my back resting on the wall.

The black's eyes grow big. "I'm sorry, my dear," she say. "I didn't mean to startle you." She get up from the bed and pulls the chair and sits on it facing me. I looks at the ceiling, floor, bed, her knees, everything but to look into that face again. My husband always say to never talk to the black. They liar and cheat, he say. Will rob cash register if you look away for one minute only. One time some college boys from place of Africa come to our restaurant, he give them such rude service, they complain. He look at them straight and say, "Then don't come back."

I knows they send this black woman here to make me ascare, to punish me from trying the suicide. I don't know what punishment for—for trying or for fail. "Please," I say. "I never do suicide again. Please, beg your pardon."

"Mrs. Patil, I'm not here to judge you. I'm here to help you. But I can't do that if you don't speak to me."

I remember what the husband say: The black will smile sweet like a baby before he stab you and steal your moneys. That is why she is talking about helping me and all. But I has no moneys. "I has no moneys," I say to her. "You go to the next room and try that patient."

"Nobody's talking about money," she say. "We treat people without insurance all the time. Please don't worry about this."

This woman making me angry. She think we are charity case. "We have insurance," I say. "My husband buy. We are having our own store and restaurant."

"Good. That's good. So that's something we don't have to worry about, right?" Her voice get tight, like we on merry-go-round wheel and she wanting to get off. "So now that we've settled that, why don't you tell me a bit about how you've ended up here?"

I am not allowing me to hear her words. This is a game I play when I'm not liking people. Instead of hearing their words, I allows myself to hear the silence between each word they say. Or, this is what I hear: Whawhawhawha. This is what she sound like to me.

She ask something but I make myself hear only the

Whawhawhawha. Her voice sound so funny to me, I begins to feel tickle with laughing. After few minute, she get up. Now I listens to what she say. "Okay, Mrs. Patil. Have it your way. I just want you to know, though, that by state law, we can't discharge you until we're sure you're not a danger to yourself. I hope you have a good weekend in here. I'll see you on Monday."

She move toward the door and now I feel ashame for how I acting. She put her hand on handle and then she turn around. "By the way, we have something in common. My husband is from India also."

"Liar," I say, and then I look at ceiling, so she won't know the word came from me.

But she hear me. She come back inside the room and stand in front of the bed. "I beg your pardon?" And when I say nothing, say, "Did you call me a liar?"

I say nothing, but I'm thinking, Indian man never marry the black. I will tell the husband this story when he coming to visit me tomorrow. I wants to look at her face, but I ascare. So I looks at her hand, which wearing silver bracelet and is pushing, pushing, inside her purse. She pull piece of paper out and take one-two step near me. "This is my husband," she say. "He teaches math at the university here. His name is Sudhir Bose. I'm sure he's shopped at your grocery store."

I keeps my head straight, but my eyes moving on their own to look at photo. I see Indian man, tall and handsome, dressed in a kurta-pajama and sitting on sofa, his face smiling. But then my heart go thap-thap because I see his arm is around a black lady who is wearing long gold earrings and red lipstick. She is also having big smile. I feel like I do when I looks at *Stardust* magazine and see photos of Abhishek and Aishwarya or Shahrukh Khan and Gauri—happy and empty at same time. My husband only look with love at a woman one time. That woman not me.

"Where your mister from?" I hear my voice saying. "Bombay city?"

"No, he's from Calcutta. We were there just two years ago, to see his parents."

My eyes grow big. They allow her inside Calcutta? And his parents know he marry the black?

"Where're you from? How long have you been in Burnham?"

"We not live in Burnham. We live in Chesterfield," I say. "Far from here. That is where husband business is. We live in the apartment above store."

She sit back on chair. I look at her knee, her feet, her fingers. But not the face. "Chesterfield, huh? I think I may have been in your store once, with Sudhir. He usually does the grocery shopping, since he's the cook in the family. Usually, he buys his masalas from the Indian store in Cedarville, where we live."

This lady make me crazy. First she insult me by telling me her husband does the shopping at another store, our competitioner. Then she tell me her husband does the cooking. Why the man must cook if his wife not dead?

I decide to lock my mouth shuts, but then I again hearing my voice say, "That man who owns grocery store in Cedarville is big fat crook. All extra-extra he charges. You want to waste hard-earn money, you shop there." I have heard my husband say exact same thing to customer.

She smile. I can tell from her voice. "I'll make sure Sudhir knows this, Lakshmi."

How she know my name? How? I feel panicky, like pot of water boiling inside my head. I turn to look at door, to make sure it still open and I can run out, and in looking doing this, my eyes land on her face.

Her face look so soft and welcome. Her face dark as the mud but her eyes light brown, like honey, same-to-same color as Ma's eyes, and Shilpa's. And kind and gentle-like, and suddenly I thinks of Mithai the elephant. How he used to get same look in her eyes when I sing to him.

The black lady's smile gets bigger and now she shows her teeth, white and strong, as if she grow up chewing the sugarcane that grow in my village. "Hello," she say softly, as if she just is walking in, and I feels shy. I look down at floor.

"What're you thinking, Lakshmi?" she ask, and I say, "About Mithai. How you look like him."

Her eyebrow goes up and she look at me crooked. "Mithai? I look like a sweetmeat?"

And now I'm knowing for sure she marry to Indian man because she know mithai is name for the sweets we sell in the store. She think I calling her a halva and this is so funny to me that a laughing comes out of my mouth, like a bit of soo-soo that leaks down there sometimes, and then she shake her head, and that make me laugh more. I try to stop but nothing happen. I have not eat since yesterday and now I am filling my stomach with my own laughing.

Then I see she is worry, so I stop. "Mithai is my elephant," I explain. "Not sweetmeat. In my village."

She still look worry, like she want to take my fever. "You own an elephant?"

I nods. "He belong to landlord of my village. But Menon sahib hire me to take care of him. Mithai is my best friend. "

She look at me close, like she interest. "Where is your village?" she ask.

I tell her and she nod but I know she never know where to find my village. Maybe she will ask her husband if it near to Calcutta. I feel good that she will talk to him about me tonight. "It not near Calcutta," I say. "Very far away from Calcutta."

"I see."

"I know where the Calcutta is," I say. "I was first student in my class until eight standard. And I very good at maths. Landlord also hire me to do accounts for his shop." I not know why I being show-off to this black lady, but it is as if the husband's liquor I drink the day before today is still burn on my tongue.

She pull on her lip. "Why did you stop being the first student in your class in eighth grade?" she wanting to know.

The shame and sad hit me so hard, it make tears to my eyes. God is punishing me for being prideful a minute ago. "I leaf my schooling in eight standard."

"Why?"

"My mother become sick."

She take deep breath. She look far away from me for a minute and then she say, "That's funny. My mom fell very ill when I was young also."

I feel interest. "How is she now?"

"Dead. She's been dead for many years now."

I feel like to cry. "My ma is also dead." And again my mind go to Shilpa. How she cry as we watch our mother burn on the funeral pyre. How I made promise to always give my protection to her. How I kept my promise.

We sit chup-chap for one or two minutes and then she get up from the chair. "I'm glad we chatted today, Lakshmi," she say quietly. "I'll be back on Monday to see you. You take care of yourself, you hear?"

I angry with myself for feeling alonely as she make ready to leaf my room. Monday not coming until Saturday and Sunday has passed.

She stand over me near the bed and then she touch my hair lightly. "Nothing is worth killing yourself over, Lakshmi," she whisper. "Every problem has a solution. I want you to remember that, okay?"

THE STORY HOUR 25

I feel as if it is the priest at the temple giving me a blessing. "Okay," I say.

"You promise?"

"Promise," I say, but I don't know what I promising. My heart feel soft, like it do when I was a young child and still had a mother.

"Good," she say, and then, like broken promise, she gone out of the room.

4

THE SHAKING STARTED as soon as Maggie exited the room and stood in the hallway writing notes in the medical chart. She steadied her hand on the edge of the binder as she wrote, stopping to smile at the two nurses who walked past. "Patient responsive," she wrote. "Eager to talk. Command of English and language comprehension passable. Need SEVA to do a home evaluation." SEVA was the regional social service group that helped Asian immigrants who were victims of domestic abuse. She had sat on its board when the group formed seven years ago.

She wrote for several long minutes and then flipped back a couple of pages to reread the psychiatrist's notes. Unlike many of the psych patients here, Lakshmi had not seemed fuzzy-headed. Maggie was relieved to find that Tom had not gone heavy on medicating her.

She was aware that she was still shaking as she took the elevator down to her office and was thankful that she was alone. It was a silly problem, this, but there it was. She had mentioned it to her therapist, Sophie Anderson, when it first started five years ago, but Sophie had shrugged it off. You can't be in this line of work, and be engulfed by human misery, and not develop a tic or two, Sophie had said.

Maggie had escaped it longer than most of her colleagues. For years, she'd been capable of detaching herself from her patients' problems, was able to enjoy her life with Sudhir—the home they'd built, the garden they'd planted together, the vacations they took, the friends from grad school whom they still visited, the visits by Sudhir's siblings and cousins from India. She'd had no trouble reminding herself that this was her true life. She'd come home from the hospital, take a shower, and let the running water wash away the tales of incest, domestic abuse, parental neglect, or child abuse; would compartmentalize the suicide attempts, the PTSD, the schizophrenia, the autistic younger brother, the borderline mother, the cigarette burns, the beatings with rubber hoses, the date rapes, the hoarse whisperings in the dark, the muttered threats to never tell or else, the guilt at having killed civilians at point-blank range. She prided herself on her ability to maintain the wall of separation between home and hospital.

Her confidence in her ability to keep her boundaries intact was so great that five years ago she'd convinced Sudhir to add a back porch to their house, where she could see clients in her private practice. It would be cheaper than the office space she'd rented all these years, she'd argued, and ultimately, the goal was to quit the hospital job and focus on her practice. The Cedarville winters were cold and brutal; it would be nice not to have to travel to the office after a day at the hospital.

And so, for her birthday, Sudhir had hired the brother of one of his colleagues to build the extension. They'd gone to Rome for two of the four weeks it took for the structure to be built.

Two days before she was to see her first client at the new office, her phone had rung. It was her day off, and she had just stepped out of the shower. She ran to pick up the phone, sure it was Sudhir calling to say he'd forgotten something at home and could she drop it off. "Hey," she said.

But it wasn't Sudhir. It was her father. She knew from the way he wheezed into the phone a fraction of a second before he said, "Baby girl? It's me, Wallace."

When had he taken to calling himself that instead of Dad? She knew she'd sometimes called him that during her angry college years, had said it deliberately, as a way of hurting him, punishing him for all the things she held him responsible for—for the four years when her mother lay dying of cancer, for the fact that she died despite the torturous, barbaric treatments and surgeries, for the fact that he had married Sybil Miller, a wealthy widow from Florida, and had moved to Naples with her soon after Maggie left for college, as if his years with her mother and her had been a mirage, as if all he'd done was bide his time, counting the minutes until she left home for the first and last time. And then there was the other business, but she never permitted herself to think of that anymore, the memory of it too dark and confusing.

Maggie felt a spurt of anger. Years and years of no contact and then a phone call out of the blue. The easy familiarity of calling her "baby girl," as if the intervening years of silence had never happened, as if he had not ceased to be a father the minute she'd entered college, leaving her to fend for herself at Wellesley. Her first summer from college, Sybil had invited her down to Naples, but after two weeks of staying with them in Sybil's sprawling home, of watching her father and a woman she didn't know frolic like lovesick teenagers in the pool, of catching him pinch his new wife's bottom when he thought she wasn't looking, of seeing her father—a man who had worked two jobs for as long as she could remember, one as a maintenance man at Columbia University and the other as a clerk at the neighborhood convenience store—dress up each evening in a Hawaiian shirt and freshly pressed chinos to go to the country club to play cards all night, after two weeks of being around a man who treated her as if she were a distant niece he was rather fond of rather than his only daughter, whose eyes were mysteriously unburdened by the weight of those dark years when his wife had lain in her bed growing pasty and skinny as the cancer ate her alive, who dabbed a little aftershave on his shirt just before he left for the club, as if to keep his nostrils from remembering the smells of rubbing alcohol and morphine and bleach, after two weeks of suffocating in Sybil's air-conditioned, museum-like home, Maggie bolted. Used the last of her work-study money to buy a plane ticket to New York. Their old neighbor, Mrs. Tabot, her mother's best friend, had taken her in, just as Maggie had known she would. She would spend all four summers during her years at Wellesley in Mrs. Tabot's brownstone in Brooklyn.

"Hello? Baby girl? You there?" Wallace was saying.

"Don't call me that." She hated how peevish her voice sounded and hated herself a bit more when she heard his chuckle.

"You sore this early in the mornin'?" he said. "Wake up on the wrong side of the bed, huh?"

She sighed. "What do you want, Dad?" she said. "Is everything okay?"

" 'Course it is," he exclaimed in the cheerful voice he now spoke in, which made him sound like an Amway salesman. "Sybil an' me are gonna be passin' your way tomorrow and thought we'd like to stop and see you, is all. We're drivin' to Oregon to attend her godchild's daughter's wedding. Thought it'd be fun to stop and visit with you and that husband of yours. You gon' be around?"

She'd ended up inviting them to dinner the next night. Wallace and Sybil had not been in their home even though she and Sudhir had lived there for over ten years. In fact, her father and Sudhir had met only twice. She had visited Sudhir's parents, who lived halfway across the world in Calcutta, more often than that.

The shock of seeing how old Wallace looked since she'd seen him last helped her to be polite to him for the entire evening. That and taking her cues from Sudhir, who, as always, was an

impeccable host, attentive and gracious. She noticed the effort
her husband made to play the role of the dutiful son-in-law, how
he drew Wallace into every conversation, how he frequently re-
filled the older man's glass with the single malt he was drinking,
how he was polite even to Sybil, who had only gotten louder and
sillier with age. At the end of the evening, he insisted on driving
the elderly couple's car to the hotel to drop them off, even though
Wallace swore he hadn't had too much to drink. Maggie followed
in her car.

Sudhir got into the passenger seat after they'd said their good-
byes and was quiet for the first few minutes of their ride home.
Then he asked, as if picking up a conversation, "Do you really
hate him so much? He seems harmless enough."

"I don't hate him." She took her eyes off the road for a minute.
"What makes you say that?"

"The fact that you flinch every time he touches you. Like when
he tried to hug you goodbye. I mean, God, Maggie. He's old. He's
probably worried he might never seen you again."

She was quiet, knowing he was waiting for a response but unsure of what to say. The blankness, the still whiteness, that always
fell on her when she thought about those years with her father,
covered her now.

"Mags?" Sudhir's voice was gentle, tentative. "Where did you
go?"

In response, she turned left into the nearly empty parking lot
of a shopping plaza and pulled into a space where there was no
one around. "I'm going to tell you something, okay? Something I
should've told you long ago. But I couldn't."

Sudhir shifted in the leather seat. "Oh God. Don't tell me
he—" he started.

She nodded. "Yes. I mean, not exactly. That is, nothing happened. Not really. He just . . . It began after my mom got sick. He

rented a hospital bed for her and put her in this little room we had off the kitchen. And then at night he'd come and get me. To lie in bed with him."

Sudhir made a choking sound, and she put her hand on his arm and stroked it absently. "It's okay. I told you. He didn't, like, do anything. He just, like, rubbed himself on me. He called it cuddling. He said we were comforting each other since Mommy was sick." The old, familiar coldness began in her stomach and moved into her limbs as she spoke.

"Bloody bastard. I'll go to that hotel and kill him," Sudhir swore, and she shook her head impatiently.

"Hey. Stop it. Like you said, he's an old man now. And God knows what he was going through, too, with Mom being ill and all."

"How long did it go on?"

"I don't know. I honestly don't remember. Those years when she was sick—it's all a blur, y'know?"

"So it stopped when your mom died?"

"Uh-huh. Before that. Odell was in college then, and he came home for a week. I must've said something that made him suspicious. I just remember him asking me all kinds of questions. Made me feel queasy, the look on his face. God. I still remember the look on Odell's face." Maggie gave a nervous laugh, the icy feeling now in her throat.

Sudhir undid his seat belt, leaned over, and pulled Maggie toward him. "Oh, honey. How could you have carried this with you all these years? Without telling me?"

She spoke with her head buried in his shoulder. "I wanted to. But I don't know—for years I told myself it was essentially meaningless. I mean, when I think of what horrors some of my clients have suffered, this is nothing. Know what I mean?"

She heard an uncharacteristic harshness in Sudhir's voice. "Nothing? Is that why you're shaking like a leaf?"

She half-heard him, remembering what had followed: Odell had confronted their father, threatened to expose him. "Listen," Odell had hissed. "You so much as look at Mags wrong ever again, I'll move her out. And I'll tell the whole goddamn 'hood you're a dirty old man. I'll expose you in church. I'll tell your boss and his boss. And then I'll kill you with my bare hands."

Wallace had been defiant, then defensive, and finally, defeated. "A man gets lonely, Odell," he'd said. "You too young to understand. Your ma bin sick for a long time. Besides, I ain't done nothing evil to your sister. We just cuddle, is all. I dunno what lies this girl is spreading about me."

Odell's hand curled into a fist. There was metal in his eyes. "You need a woman, you go to a whorehouse. But you leave my baby sister alone. You understand?"

"I do," Wallace muttered, but the look he flashed Maggie was pure hatred. Wallace had always worshipped Odell, his boy who was studying at Berkeley on a full scholarship. The weight of his son's contempt was more than he could bear.

"Odell helped me," she now said to Sudhir. "He made him stop."

"Then I'm forever in his debt."

"But Dad never forgave me," Maggie continued. "When Odell moved to Paris directly after college, I think Dad blamed me for it. Not that he'd ever say it. He found other ways to punish me."

"He beat you?" Sudhir's voice sounded as if it had been brushed with glass.

She shook her head. "No. He just—ignored me. He was formal with me. Exaggeratedly polite. And distant. Treated me like I was made of porcelain. And—he never touched me again. Never hugged me or consoled me or told me he was proud of me. Even when I got in to Wellesley. And first chance he got, he moved to Florida. Suddenly, I had no home."

The back of her throat hurt, as if a jagged piece of ice were lodged in there. "Even when Mom died. He . . . he just let me grieve. Alone." How raw, how close, the pain felt. It surprised her. She had processed this with her therapist many times, until the memory had lost its sting. Or so she'd believed.

"I wish you'd told me this earlier, Maggie. My God, you're my best friend. I've told you every bloody thing that's happened to me. To think that you would carry this all these years . . ."

"I couldn't. I tried. I wanted to. Sophie always urged me to. But I couldn't."

"Why not?"

Why not? Because it was too confusing, too shameful. Objectively, she had known that she was the wronged party. But always there was the nagging thought that she had made a mountain out of a molehill, that she and Odell—she, in the dumb ignorance of childhood, he, with the angry self-righteousness of youth—had not been sufficiently sympathetic to what Wallace was suffering because his wife had been dying a slow, harrowing death. But then she would imagine if one of her clients confided that her husband was using a ten-year-old child in this way, carrying her to his bed, rubbing against her, and she knew how outraged her response would be. And so, round and round in circles her thoughts would go.

There was also this: Before Wallace had withdrawn behind the wall of silence, of stiff formality, before he'd turned a cold, stony face to her, he had been the most affectionate of fathers. When she was a kid, he had laughed uproariously at her endless repertoire of knock-knock jokes, taught her to ride a bike, enthralled her with stories about his native Jamaica and how he'd come to America as a stowaway on a boatful of bananas, taught her card tricks, held her hand as the four of them walked to the Church of the Open Heart every Saturday evening. While the other men in the neighborhood spent their money on booze and drugs and alligator-skin shoes and stood on street corners tittering at the women who walked by, Wallace Seacole worked two jobs, paid for piano lessons for his daughter, shook his head at the "lazies" who hung around the entrance to their brownstone, eschewed alcohol or cigarettes ("them rich folks' habits," he'd say), cooked lavish Sunday dinners for his family, his soups and stews steaming up the windows of their small kitchen. Until her mother got sick, theirs had been a family envied by all who knew them—and Wallace had been the beating heart of that family.

"Why didn't you tell me until now?" Sudhir was asking again.

Maggie closed her eyes. "I don't know," she said. "I'm just glad I finally told you."

"Me, too." Sudhir let the argument drop.

The next day Maggie saw her first client, Rose, in her new home office. It was a beautiful day in early June, and she and Rose stood near the window and admired the plants blooming in the backyard. Then they got started. Maggie had been the older woman's therapist for several years and figured she knew everything there was to know about her—the passionless but affectionate marriage; the mildly autistic son, Roland, who was now in his thirties and living in Dallas; the daily irritants of working at the public library; the ongoing resentment against a sister-in-law. Sometimes Maggie even wondered why Rose continued seeing her, since the problems seemed so mundane, but she had several clients like this who came for regular tune-up sessions. Maggie was thankful for patients like Rose—they made listening to the harrowing tales more manageable. Besides, she liked Rose and was always happy to see that ruddy face, as plain as the side of a mountain but lit by an ever present smile.

Which was why she wasn't prepared for the story Rose told her that day. It turned out that Roland had a twin sister who'd died in the womb. The doctors couldn't do anything to remove the dead fetus; the risk to the other baby was too great. So Rose carried her other child to term, walking around for three months carrying a dead child. She and her husband had never mentioned his sister's death to Roland. But Rose still woke from a recurring nightmare in which the dead baby called to her, threatened to put its translucent hands around the healthy brother's neck and choke him. "I just can't wash it off," Rose whimpered. "That dirty feeling of carrying death within my body. And the baby in my dreams— it's sinister. So unforgiving. Like something from a cheap horror movie."

Maggie knew Rose was looking at her, to her, to say something, to set things right, but she was stunned. Amazed at her own vapidity, her own cluelessness. How could she have missed something so important in someone she'd counseled for so many years? And yet how could she have known? She was struck by the limitations of therapy, was reminded anew of the opacity of human relations, the inability to truly know someone else. Her mind flashed to the conversation in the car with Sudhir. If her husband couldn't have guessed at her history with her father, how on earth could she have known what guilt poor Rose was harboring all these years?

She cleared her throat. "I'm sorry, Rose. I'm so sorry," she began, hoping that her eyes were conveying the sympathy that she felt for the older woman, more than her words could.

"I know," Rose said. "It's okay."

Maggie had a two-hour break after Rose left and before the next client arrived. She went into the kitchen to make coffee. She reached for the pot and found that her hands were shaking so badly that she had to set the pot on the counter. She stared at her hands, puzzled, and even as she did, she felt the shaking spread through her entire body, so that she pulled up the kitchen chair and sat down. Was she getting ill? Catching a cold? She didn't feel ill. Maybe her sugar was low? Then she felt a sensation in her stomach, and it moved quickly to her chest and then into her throat and escaped from her mouth as a sob. When she heard that sob, followed by its twin, and then by another and another, she was surprised—What the heck are you crying for in the middle of the day? she scolded herself—but unable to stop. She felt grief move within her like a barefoot woman flitting through a dark house.

So much pain. So many secrets. She felt burdened by the weight of other people's secrets, their grief, their trust, their blinking anticipation, their eager faces, the hunger with which they looked at her, expecting answers, expecting cures, expecting miracles. And until this moment, she had always felt capable of meeting their expectations, had believed in her ability to help them part the cornstalks of their confusion, sift through the hard pellets of their grief, and arrive at a new understanding. Until now she had believed in the power of logic, of rational thinking, of cognition, of self-awareness. But not right now. Not as she sat with her head on the kitchen table, hearing herself sob and unable to stop. Right now each human heart felt remote as a coral reef, and every person so mysterious, so unknowable, so incomprehensible, that she wondered how she'd ever do her job again.

Is this what burnout feels like? she asked herself, and before she could answer, an image flashed before her eyes: of her father sitting across from her at dinner and talking to her husband. Sudhir was explaining a mathematical concept, doing his best to explain it in layman's terms, and Wallace was doing his damnedest to follow. They were all doing this for her sake, Maggie knew, but still she was irritated at Sudhir for trying so hard. Just then Wallace's eyes wandered to her face and he gave her the faintest smile, just enough to let her know that he sensed her irritation, that he knew she was as trapped in her seat as he was. No one else caught that exchange, but it flustered her because it told her two paradoxical things: one, that this was all a performance, that Wallace was simply a guest in her house who would soon be on his way; and two, nobody would ever know her as well as her father did. In one look, Wallace conveyed to her both his hold over her and his disinterest in her.

So it's not burnout, Maggie told herself. It was that she was rattled by her father's visit, and telling Sudhir what had happened when she was ten had made her realize that the memory, which she'd assumed was defanged and toothless, still had a bite left in it. That's all. Rose's confession today had just put her over the edge.

In fact, the shaking had stopped a few minutes later, and she saw her other two clients that day without any further problems. But two weeks later, it happened again. Then nothing for a few months, and then the shaking came back. Sometimes the most mundane of confidences could bring it on. When Maggie sheepishly mentioned to Sophie her suspicion that building the home office had somehow knocked down the metaphoric wall between work and home life, Sophie pooh-poohed the idea. Plenty of therapists work from home, she declared. That's superstition.

So Maggie let it go. Accepted the shaking as an occupational hazard. Worked around it. Managed to control it so it wasn't easily apparent to anyone else. Sure enough, she hadn't experienced it in almost six months. Until now. Her encounter with the Indian woman had set it off. She knew what it was, too: Something about how bereft, how existentially lonely, Lakshmi looked had found an echo within her. And when she'd mentioned the bit about her mother being sick . . .

She walked to her office, glad that it was late in the evening and most of her colleagues had gone home. She opened her office door unsteadily and sat down on the desk chair. She sighed. A martini. That's what she needed. A martini and Peter Weiss were just what the doctor had ordered.

5

TODAY IS MONDAY and the husband has day off so he look more relax. He sitting in chair and I feels him staring at me. But when I looks in his face, his eyes shift away from me, as if I a piece of leftover food he sick to look at. Again he ask, "Why you do this wicked thing? I give you everything—food, saris, house. This is how you repay me? By doing the suicide?"

I want to say: This is why I do the suicide—because you have come to see me Friday, Saturday, Sunday, and today and not one time you say my name. Not once you give me the kind touch or say one good word. Not one time you looking at me like I your wife. I seen you look at the butter chicken in the restaurant with more loving than you look at me. I want to say: My family was poor but full of love. My dada prideful of me, my ma call me jewel of her eye. When she young, my sister, Shilpa, follow me like a tail. In my village, everyone say my name. Lakshmi, come do this. Lakshmi, show me how to do that. Lakshmi, you so smart. My teacher always pet my head. Even Menon sahib, our landlord, tell me I am as if his niece. That's why only he puts me in charge of Mithai. He always pinching his son and say, "Munna, see how Lakshmi so good at the maths and accounts. You must learn from her."

I want to say: In my village, the earth is red and soft. When rainy season come, it like a green sari cover my village. The earth smelling so fresh and clean and sweet. I want to say: What this cold, hard place you bring me to? Half year, no leaf living on trees. And ground so bitter and cold, nothing grow. And where the people go? When we driving to the Costco, not one person walking on the street. No melas, no old man selling roasted peanuts, no childrens laughing-playing, no stray dog running round and round, no sweet cow sleeping on pavement, no crow cawing on tree, no nothing. Just long, empty road of silent. You brings me to this upside-down place and you set me in corner like old suitcase. And then you say, "Why you do the suicide?"

But I says nothing. So husband make big breathing sound. "Okay, talk, don't talk. I don't care," he say.

How hard his words is. I feel the tears in my eyes and I open-close eyes fast to make them stop. But he sees and he bends near his chair and pull out tiffin box from cloth bag. "Here," he say. "Rekha sent food for you. Goat biryani and gulab jamun."

Minute he say gulab jamun, my stomach make loud noise, like angry dog. He hear and look so surprise, I begins to laugh. "That Rekha smart." He smile. "She know what you like." He bring out spoon and plate and put biryani on it. "Eat," he say. "Nurse complain to me yesterday you not eating their food."

I makes the face. "Not food," I say. "It is plastic. No chili powder, no cumin. This is dead people food."

He look around. "Be quiet. The white people take insult if they hear you. This their home you are in."

I say nothing. I am eating half with spoon, half with hand. It is first time today I eat. After few minute, I look at husband. "Thank you," I say.

But he shake his head. "Eat slowly-slowly. Otherwise you getting sick and they keep you longer here. Big problem at restaurant, not having you work. When they going to discharge you?"

I don't know meaning of word "this-charge" but I don't want to say. He not even waiting for me to answer. "I had to hire my friend Prithvi's son to be waiter in restaurant," he say. "Stupid fellow, know nothing of being server. All mistakes he is making. Saturday, two customer take off without paying. I need you to come to work quickly."

I feels good, my husband missing me. I feels good with biryani in my stomach. So I feels the courage. "How much you pay Prithvi's son?" I say.

Husband look surprise and then he say, "Minimum wage."

"When I come back, you pay me," I say.

Husband's face look shock. "Did suicide make you crazy? If I pay you, how I pay electric company? How I pay gas bill?" Then he get angry. "Only loose woman speak like this to husband, Lakshmi. I am the one who feed you, clothe you, give you roof over your head. When I come home and find you dead-like on sofa, I call 911 and transfer you to hospital. You know how much this hospital bill going to be? Insurance rate will go up also. Other man would leave wife after this evil business. Such shame you have brought on my family name. Every day customers saying, 'Where your missus?' And what answer I give them? That my missus is doing aram in a hotel room, eating goat biryani and gulab jamun, while I break my back before a stove?"

I feel ashame. "I'm sorry," I say. "I was making a joke, only."

"Joke?" the husband say. "Joke is funny. This is not funny."

I say sorry second time, and when I looks up, I see someone standing inside the room. At first I only sees the white coat because the face is so dark, but then I know who is standing there and my stomach move, like I on a boat. The husband hate the black people and this is same lady who was here before. She standing with one hand in her coat pocket and her head crooked sideways and she frown. She look at back of the husband like he smell bad.

Then she walk into room, and husband hear her and push

back his chair. He open his mouth but she talk first. "Hi. You must be Lakshmi's husband?" she say. "I'm Dr. Margaret Bose. Her therapist."

My husband look like he have heart attack. No one say anything and in that minute, I feels something move inside of me, so I shifts from my husband to her side. I feel bad, but it happen automatic-like—I feel happy watching husband try to think what to say, do, where to look. And she not know how he hate the black people, and I want to protection her, the way I do my Shilpa. But she also stronger than Shilpa, I know, she no needing me to do protection.

"You are Mr. Patil?" she say, and husband look surprise and then say, "Yes."

"Good. I'm glad I caught you. We have a lot to discuss," she say, and then she come to me and put hand on my shoulder. "How are you today, Lakshmi?" she say, and her eyes are so soft and again I think of my Mithai. And of Ma as she lay on the mud floor of our house, the 'rthritis twisting her hand and foots into the crooked shape of the ginger root.

"I am fine," I say loudly and both she and husband look at me surprise.

"Did you have a good weekend?"

"I am fine," I say again, wanting her eyes to stay on me, wanting to build the thread tying her to me, against the husband.

"Good." She smile. "Good."

Husband make uh-uh sound in his throat. "When will she be discharge?" he say. "My business suffering with her absent."

The lady look at him funny. "Well, Mr. Patil, we're hardly at that point. Your wife has just attempted to kill herself. Unfortunately, because of the weekend, I've not been able to work with her much. I realize the pressures on you, but under the circumstances—"

Husband not bother to behave his temper. "Then bring a real doctor to give her treatment. I have a business to run. I cannot leave the business to come every day during visiting hours. Very difficult and very costly."

The black lady's eyebrow go high. "I am a real doctor, Mr. Patil. Now, if your wife has a problem with me, I'd be happy to refer her to a different therapist. But"—her voice get real quiet—"I think you're the one with the problem."

Husband open his mouth, but just then the black lady say, "Now, if you'll excuse us, visiting hours are over. And I need to start my session with Lakshmi."

I feel something prideful in my chest. The husband look like he Pran and he got beat up by Amitabh Bachchan. He don't know whether to go or come, sit or stand. He look at me for help but I look straight at him. What he call this room? A hotel room? If I'm in hotel, he the visitor.

Chup-chap, quiet as a lizard, he gather the tiffin box and take the dirty plate. The gulab jaman, wrapped in foil, he put on the table for me. He look at me again, and then at the black lady, and then he leaf the room.

Soon as he go, I feel like to cry. So alonely I'm feeling without the husband. And wicked, for how I happy when this lady make him defeat. Some jadoo she do, to make me side with her over my husband. I decide I will not speak to her. Let her leaf my room as she make my husband leaf.

She sit down on chair across from me. "I heard you're not eating much here, Lakshmi," she say. "So I'm glad your husband is bringing food from home."

Who tell her I not eating? How she know my husband bringing the food? "Who telling you such lies? Why you care what I eat? You mind your own business."

"It is my business," she say. "Look, my goal is to evaluate you and make sure you're fit to be discharged, okay? So I require your cooperation, Lakshmi."

Such big-big word she using. I don't understand anything she say.

She look at me close. "Are you getting what I'm saying? It's really important that you understand. If you don't, we can get a interpreter, okay?"

"What 'inter-printer' mean?"

"Someone who speaks your language. Hindi? Punjabi? Gujarati? Whatever you speak. And that person can tell you what I'm saying."

"Why you need to speak to me?"

She give out big breath. "Lakshmi. You've just tried to kill yourself. If your husband had not come home early with a headache, God knows what would've happened. Okay? So we can't let you go from here until I'm convinced . . . until I'm sure you won't do this again. Do you understand?"

I nods. "I'm sorry. I am wicked woman for the suicide. I am sorry."

"Sweetie. You're not wicked. You're just in pain. You're hurting. I can see it on your face. And I'm here to help you. But you've gotta let me in."

"You already in," I say, confuse.

She laugh. "In, like, into your heart. Your mind. You have to tell me why you took this step. So that we make sure you don't do it again."

I feel as if I walk into a dark room and turn on the light. I now understands what she is wanting from me. She is wanting my story. Just like when you go to the doctor sahib with cough-cold and he is asking questions—when it started, were you walking in rain, were you eating too many sour mangoes all of once? Then only he knows what medicines to give.

She is wanting my story. In my village, I was champion story-teller. When Ma became sick with the 'rthritis, I would tell Shilpa stories at night so she could go to sleep and not hear Ma's crying. When the bad men hurt Mithai the elephant, I spend night with him and tell him story after story. In school, I always make the other childrens laugh by stories and jokes I was telling.

But I have not told story to anyone in very long time.

"Lakshmi," the lady say. "What happened? What made you do this on Thursday? Did your husband beat you? What brought it on?"

I thinks of Bobby and how he look, standing in that parking lot, holding the statue I gave. I thinks of him getting in his car and how it feeling like my heart remove from my body and get in his car with him. How I know, even then, that Bobby only think of me as waitress in restaurant but I . . . I think of him as . . .

I wants to tell her about Bobby and about his kindness and the California. But then I ascare. What if she tell my husband? What he do if he know I likes Bobby in the bad ways, in the way mar-ried wife must not like other man? He be angry and mean, or he make joke about it. Either way, he hurt me.

I cannot tell her about Bobby, who is beautiful like ice to me. You putting ice in the sunshine, where other people can see, and it melt. Bobby is secret, one of two secret in my life, that I will never tell.

"Lakshmi," she say again, and I know she waiting for me.

"What?" I say. "What you wanting to know?"

She lean toward me. "I want to know," she say, "if your hus-band beat you. Is that why . . . ?"

I shakes my head no. "Never," I say. "Husband, good man. He never doing any beatings."

"So what made you? Take the pills, I mean?"

And suddenly, the pain in my heart so big, it comes out of my eyes and roll down my face. "I's alone," I say. "I have no family relations in this desh. I alone."

The black lady's face is so kind, it making me cry more. "I'm sorry, sweetie," she say. "I understand. It's very hard."

"I used to call my Shilpa sweetie. When I was the teaching her English."

"Who's Shilpa?"

I want to say: Shilpa is reason I'm in this jail of Am'rica. "Shilpa is my sister."

"I see. And she's still in India?"

I am surprise by question. "I thinks so."

"You're not sure?"

I look at the floor. "We not talking anymore. Husband not allow. After marriage, he say I not talking to Dada or Shilpa."

She let out breath. "You have no contact with your family in India?"

"Husband not allow."

She look angry. "Why ever not?"

I look at the floor.

We sit nice quiet for many minute. Then she say, "Tell me about your village. Tell me about where you grew up."

Even Bobby not ask so many question about my life. No one ever take interest. I close my eyes and I smell the earth of my village after the rainy season. And the first thing I am seeing is the well.

6

I T RAINING SIX days nonstop and my father's field is flooding. He sit at home and Ma say he drive her mad with his worry and kitpit. He telling her how to light coal stove properly, how to bake rotis correct way, how to sweep floor. She so irritate, she throw broom at him and say, "You so good, mister, you sweep this mud floor until it become Taj Mahal." Shilpa and I think what Ma say so funny, we laugh and laugh, until Dada make strong eyes at us and raise his hand. But we not afraid of Dada because he never beating us. One time when my report card not good and Ma slap me, it is Dada who cry like a girl, not me.

On six day of rain, Menon sahib come to our house in his blue Ambassador and ask if I can go to his big house for cleaning. His wife in city for few days and Munna and he alone in dirty house. I see Ma is sad that I leaf my schoolwork to help Menon sahib, but she cannot do extra work now. Both her feets having the 'rthritis and it paining her. I am so happy to leaf house and go sit in back-seat of big car with Munna. It is only second time I sits inside a car—first time was taxi that we took from train station one time when we went to city. But the taxi was small and crowding and the smell of the agarbatti that the taxi driver was burning make me sneeze and sneeze. Menon sahib's car is big as my house and Munna is my friend, although he being only five and I am eight.

This is first time I goes to Menon sahib's house without my ma, but I am knowing exact what to do. First I takes the jharu and sweep whole house. I collects the kachra in newspaper and then I get the rag and start to wash floor. I scrubs and scrubs until I am seeing my face in the white tile. Munna sit with me for some time and then he go to other room to play. Menon sahib's house having many rooms. After floor wash, I begin to wash Menon sahib's wife's saris and cholis and bedsheets. My arm feel on fire as I scrub soap on clothes and rub them together. I wish Ma was here doing this jobs, but then I remember how her feets all swollen like a ripe mango, and I feel ashame. I push the hairs out of my eye and scrub harder.

The rain has stop when I finish washing and the sun is coming out. I takes the wet clothes out to dry. Munna is outside also, running around me, making zoom-zoom noise like aeroplane. He try to help me but he too short to hangs the clothes on the line. Even I having problem to reach the top but I managing.

After five-ten minute, Munna quiet. The sun is so hot on my face, it make my skin cry. I hear the mynah bird making song in the trees and I answers back. Woo-hoo, I say, and it listen and then talk back to me.

One minute everything is sweet and peace-like, but then I hear door open and Menon sahib is giving the shout and running toward me. I ascared, thinking I hang his wife's clothes wrongly, but then I see he cover mouth with one hand and pointing with the other. I turns around. Munna has climb on the stone wall of the well in Menon sahib's compound. He now leaning into the well, looking to find his face in the water. As I looking, he move in more, his little feets pushing against the stones.

The mynah bird still making song. The sun still making my face cry. But now there is no sweet in this day. I feel ascare, because in one minute Munna will fall into the well. I kick off my chappals and run. The mud is soft and make shuck-shuck sound from my feet as I move in it. The mud trying to pull me back and so I know running no good. If I to save Munna, I must to fly, fly like the mynah bird in the tree. So I does. I fly. As I get closer to well, I open my hands, like wings of big bird. Just as Munna slipping into well, I close my hands around his legs. He hanging upside down and my knee hit into stone wall and bleeding. But I don't let him go. I hold him tightum-tight until Menon sahib come behind of me and take Munna out of my hands. For one seconds, I ascare Menon sahib has gone mad because he kissing Munna and slapping him at same time. Then he making some noise and moving forward-back, forward-back, and I see he crying. Munna start to crying also, and then Menon sahib kiss his son, all over his face and head. Menon sahib is always so strict, like the schoolteacher. When my dada go to him last day of every month to collect his money, Menon sahib never ever smiling at Dada, just writing numbers in big red book and counting a few rupee notes to give. Dada always feeling poorly when he leave Menon sahib's shop and come home. We never becoming rich, Dada say, because Dada can sell what we grow only to Menon sahib and he never pay enough.

But now Menon sahib is crying more than Munna do, and I feels shy, like I watch something not my business. I begins to walk toward the house, but he put his son down and touch my shoulder to stop. "Lakshmi," he say. "I am in your debts. If I take five more births on this earth, I still be in your debts." And then come part that nobody belief, not even Shilpa: Menon sahib fold his hand to me. Dada say I lying when I tell him. Stupid girl, Dada say. Menon sahib is like a raja. He own our whole village. Why he join hands in front of a eight-year-old girl?

But he do. He say, "Beti, from this day on, you are like my little niece. I will pay your school fees for as long as you go to school."

I so happy, I run all way home to tell Ma and Dada good news. I run through sugarcane fields, and while I run, I seeing myself in my future. I am seeing the Lakshmi that is high school pass. Shilpa and I is now living in Mumbai, in big house next door to Sharukh Khan. I have a big car like Menon sahib and a driver. And I is buying a new sari every week.

But that Lakshmi, high school pass, will never be allow to be born. My naseeb not allow, because my birth star weak. I see that future Lakshmi again, the day I leaving school forever in eight standard. I see her when I am bent over the kerosene stove and when I dipping chapati in dal to feed my ma because the 'rthritis twisting her fingers like root of tree. I see her again when I working with Dada in field, because Ma cannot help him no longer. Every time I see that future Lakshmi, she spit at me, make blood in my eyes.

Menon sahib good, honest man. He pay my fees as he promise. Not his fault that the promise turn out to be short and thin.

Once, only once, I see that future Lakshmi again with happy eyes. It the day my Shilpa become high school pass. You boil, boil, boil milk and what happen? It turn to malai, no? Same way, on day that Shilpa pass school, all my sadness become smaller and smaller and turn into happy.

7

SUDHIR WAS COMING home tonight and she was picking him up at the airport in five hours. Enough time to spend one last evening with Peter, to boil pasta on the stove of his small kitchen, knowing that he was following her every movement with his eyes. To feel the tingling anticipation of when he would put down the glass of wine and rise from the chair, take the few short steps to where she was, and hold her from behind, kissing the nape of her neck. Ever since Friday night, when she'd arrived to pick him up for a late dinner and he had seduced her on the living room couch, they had fallen into a surprisingly easy routine, meeting at Peter's home in Homerville after Maggie got off work. Last night they had planned on going out to pick up some Thai food but ended up in front of the television, eating microwave popcorn for dinner. Peter was fascinated by American TV—that's how he referred to it—because he was on the road so much and seldom had time to watch.

Their bodies, too, had fallen into an easy rhythm. For almost thirty years Sudhir's was the only body Maggie had touched, and she knew it as well as her own—the tight muscles of his back, the dark hair on his chest, the sharp jutting of his hip bone, the callous on his big toe, the dark spot on his shin. Peter's body was a new country to discover and explore, and she felt exactly like a tourist—giddy with anticipation, taking delight in both the familiar and the unfamiliar. In addition, there was the novelty of Peter's

whiteness. Steeped in her parents' quiet but fierce race consciousness, influenced by the books about slavery and Jim Crow that she
read as an undergraduate at Wellesley, she had never been inter-
ested in dating white men. Unlike some of her peers, she didn't
cultivate an active antagonism toward white guys and had never
condemned her black friends who had white boyfriends. She was
simply indifferent to the lures of white skin. When she was a kid,
Wallace had told her enough stories about the humiliations he'd
suffered, working as a houseboy for a British colonial officer, to
turn her stomach. She knew better than to paint all whites with
the same stroke, and God knows she'd had plenty of white friends
in college, but still, when she met Sudhir, she was relieved that,
like her, he was the color of the earth. The joke, of course, was
that in many ways Sudhir acted very much like a stereotypical
white middle-class American male—he spoke proper English,
had bourgeois values, and had grown up in a stable two-parent
home. Wallace had said as much the first time he met his son-in-
law: "Baby girl, you done gon' and married a white man."

Maggie smiled as she felt Peter's mouth brushing lightly against
her shoulders. "Hey," he said softly. "You haven't even left yet, and
already I'm missing you. How is this possible?"

She turned to face him. The thought of not seeing Peter again
made her ache. "I know," she said. How would she face Sudhir at
the airport? Would he take one look at her and know? How would
it feel to sleep in their bed tonight, after having spent four nights
with Peter?

"But I will see you soon, right?" Peter had a curious expression
on his face, as if he'd read her mind.

She sighed. "I don't know. I don't see how. Sudhir . . . When
Sudhir's in town, we're pretty much together in the evenings."

He grinned slowly, a cocky, wicked grin that made the breath
catch in her throat. It was unfair, how handsome Peter was. Sud-

hir was a good-looking man, she knew that. In middle age, he had preserved his runner's body, and although his temples were beginning to gray, he had a head full of dark, thick hair. But Peter was beautiful. The sparkling green eyes, the long, angular face, the curly brown hair, the thin, ironic smile, it all hit Maggie so forcefully at times that she had to look away. The most attractive part about Peter was how carelessly he wore his beauty, like some cheap aftershave. She had the feeling that he would be offended if she ever commented on his looks.

"What?" she said. "Why're you smiling like that?"

"If you have to spend your evenings with Sudhir, then I guess we'll just have to visit during the day."

"And how do we do that? Quit our jobs?"

He grinned again. "My mother always said, where there's a will, there's a way."

But was there the will? Maggie asked herself as she set the two bowls of pasta on the small kitchen table. She was already ashamed of what she'd done during Sudhir's absence. It was so unlike her, this active courting of danger. Peter had a one-year contract at the university; he would be gone to God knows what forsaken country at the end of next semester. Whereas she and Sudhir had a forever contract that tied them to each other. Every strand of her life was woven into Sudhir's. For years, Maggie had marveled at how lucky she was to be married to a man whom she still loved and respected. In her profession, she had seen so many bad marriages, had witnessed how often love corroded into hatred or indifference. She had heard enough stories to know that bad behavior—cruelty, volatility, secrecy, violence, addiction— was rampant in many marriages. The worst thing she could say about Sudhir after all these years was that he was slightly . . . boring. That he was a homebody, not a thrill-seeker the way Peter was. Imagine that. That the worst thing about her husband was that he was predictable in his routines, that he was loyal and steadfast and reliable, and that the highlight of his day was coming home to his wife.

So what was she doing sitting barefoot in Peter Weiss's kitchen? How could she have so easily said goodbye to decades of fidelity, to years of counseling patients about the lasting damage that affairs inflicted on relationships? What did it mean that she had traded in her years with Sudhir for a few days with Peter?

The answer came from deep within her: It meant that, without her knowledge, a drought had existed in her. That she had been parched, thirsty in a way that Sudhir couldn't quench. Unbidden, a picture of her ten-year-old self in bed with Wallace rose in front of Maggie's eyes. And the next instant she knew: The strange, unnamable, ultimately shaming encounters with her father had dried up some part of her, had planted a seed of sexual restraint deep within her personality. No wonder she had picked someone like Sudhir—an Indian male from a conservative Brahmin family who was raised to be courteous to all, to be respectful and protective of women, who was cautious by instinct and precise by training. Sudhir had never seen the drought. Whereas Peter knew, had seen it the very first time they'd met three years ago. Recognized something, with his photographer's eyes, that she herself was oblivious to. In any case, what had happened between them four nights ago was not anything she could explain with her conscious mind. It was not a decision. It was not a desire that she had acted upon. Rather, it was movement. A flow. Like water. Like music. A river does not choose its direction. It just follows the path that has been laid out for it. That was how she had felt, that she had flowed into his body.

"Hey," Peter was saying. "Where did you go? You're hardly eating."

She shook her head. "Sorry."

The green eyes narrowed slightly. "You look so sad."

"I'm not. Really. I just . . ." She swallowed. "It's going to be hard. Saying goodbye."

"So don't," he said promptly. "Hey, I'm not going anywhere." He leaned back in his chair and stretched his arms above his head. "I'm stuck in this job for a whole goddamn year."

Even though Maggie knew better than to take it personally, the comment hurt. "You hate it so much? Living here? Teaching?"

Peter rubbed his eyes. "Ah, God, I don't know, Maggie," he said. "I like it well enough, I guess. It's just that . . . I miss life. You know? Messy, unpredictable life. The adrenaline rush. Visiting new places. I don't do well with routine, I guess." He covered Maggie's hand with his. "Though I'd miss you. And I'm very happy to have reconnected with you."

They smiled shyly at each other as they ate. After a few moments, Peter said, "So how would you like to spend the few hours we have left?" The green eyes sparkled suggestively.

The thought of going directly to the airport from Peter's, which was what she'd planned on doing, suddenly lost its appeal. "I think I'm going to go home for a bit," she said. "Before I go pick up Sudhir. Is that okay?"

Peter opened his mouth as if to argue but then closed it. "Yup," he said simply. "Whatever you need."

Her thoughts were jumbled as she drove swiftly down the darkening streets. She was happy that Sudhir was coming home, she really was. It would be easier to resist Peter once Sudhir was home. She'd be the world's biggest fool to risk her marriage over someone like Peter, she really would. Peter was a birthday party, all candles and cake and balloons. Now the party was over. Sudhir was the rest of the year, the real deal, the place where she'd built her nest. What she and Sudhir had constructed together, someone like Peter could only dream about. If he was even smart enough to realize and envy them what they had, that is. Which she somehow doubted he was.

You don't have to demonize Peter, she scolded herself. You don't have to let your guilt paper over how much fun you had these past few days. Or even over how your body answered his. Maybe everyone is entitled to one harmless fling, to one sexual adventure, and this was yours. A reward for a lifetime of good behavior. Which you will now proceed to implement. Which means you can't do this with Peter ever again.

Promise? she said to herself. Promise?

8

MAGGIE SIGHED. SHE and Lakshmi had sat across from each other in this small, airless room for almost ten minutes, and they were getting nowhere. After days of easy communication, Lakshmi had clamped up again, and Maggie had no idea why. The insurance company was throwing a fit over having to pay her hospital bills, and earlier today, Richard had called Maggie into his office and demanded to know why the Indian woman hadn't been discharged yet.

She decided to try again. "Listen," she said. "Unless you tell me what made you attempt to kill yourself, I can't discharge you. Do you understand? We could resolve this in a few minutes. I know you're as anxious to go home as we are to let you go. Right?"

In response, Lakshmi rose from her bed and wandered over to the window. She gazed out onto the lush green lawn of the hospital for a second and then turned around. "Why this cannot open?" she asked.

"We've been through this before, Lakshmi." Maggie fought to keep the impatience out of her voice. "It's for your own safety."

"In my village, many birds. All different-different color. But crow come and . . ."

"Lakshmi. Not today. Today we need to talk about the reason—" Maggie stopped midsentence, struck by a thought. "Is that why you did it? Because you are homesick? For your village?"

Lakshmi shook her head briefly. "My home here, with my husband. I married woman."

"Then why?"

Again silence. Lakshmi turned back to the window and stared out. Maggie followed her gaze out of the dark room and into the golden June afternoon. Lakshmi had not left this room from the day she'd arrived six days ago. The realization nauseated Maggie. Of course. That was what Lakshmi had been trying to tell her with the stories about the greenness of her village and its many birds.

Maggie got up from her chair. "Come on," she said. "We're going for a walk." The startled smile on Lakshmi's face confirmed the rightness of her call.

Patty, the head nurse, called out to them as they walked past the nurses' station. "Dr. Bose?" she said. "I don't think the patient is allowed to . . ."

Maggie waved her away. "It's okay, Patty," she said. "I'll sign her out."

They rode down the seven floors in silence, but Maggie was aware that Lakshmi was looking at her out of the corner of her eye. For the first time since she'd started working with her, Maggie felt in control. It was a good feeling. Over the years, she'd developed a reputation for being slightly unconventional in her treatments. The hospital staff had looked askance in the beginning, but there was no doubting her ability to work with the difficult cases, and in time, they had learned to trust her judgment. And private practice had taught her the value of flexibility: She had shut the blinds to her office to accommodate a patient who was talking about childhood incest for the first time; she had gone driving on several occasions with a male client who was afraid to drive over bridges; she had kept her eyes closed during an entire session as a patient slowly, hesitantly confessed to having had an affair with her husband's brother; she had allowed a patient to arrive each week with a boom box because Mozart helped her relax. Whatever it took. She did whatever it took to help clients share their secrets with her.

And if that meant walking around the hospital grounds with Lakshmi on a sunny afternoon, that was what they'd do. She already knew that the woman had a hard time maintaining eye contact. This way, Lakshmi didn't have to look at her. And there was something conducive about talking as one walked, the rhythm of the feet allowing the tongue to move also.

"Is it nice to be outside?" Maggie asked. "Get some fresh air?"

"Madam, it so nice. I feels clean, like taking shower in sunshine."

Maggie smiled. "I thought you would like it." She paused for effect and then started walking again, pulling on her lower lip in an exaggerated gesture. "You know, I just thought of something. Most people try suicide in the winter months. Around the holidays, that kind of thing. Unusual to have someone as young as you attempt it at such a lovely time of the year."

As she had anticipated, the younger woman's eyes filled with tears. "I not doing on purpose, madam. I not thinking. I . . . I just feeling so sadly that day. Husband not home, also. I not thinking."

"You mean you hadn't planned it for weeks?"

"No, madam, I swears." Lakshmi pulled at the skin near her Adam's apple for emphasis. "God-swear, madam. That day only, I decide."

Maggie felt something relax within her. So the attempt had been an impulsive gesture. Good. Good. It meant Lakshmi probably would not repeat it.

Still, she frowned as if puzzled. "I don't understand. What happened on that particular day to make you feel so sad? Did you have a fight with your husband?"

"No, no, madam. Not husband fault. I wicked woman. I do wicked thought."

It hit Maggie. Of course. There was someone else. Why hadn't she picked up on it sooner?

They were now about forty yards away from the path that led to the woods behind the hospital, and Maggie decided to walk into the dense grove of trees. Here, on the back lawn, Lakshmi would feel exposed, naked, in the glare of the sunlit afternoon. But the light would be weak in the woods, and if there was one thing that Maggie had learned in her years as a therapist, it was that shame required darkness.

Lakshmi relaxed visibly as soon as they entered the woods. Maggie saw that it was more than the anonymity provided by the shade. For the first time, Lakshmi looked at home, in her element: She plucked a leaf off a tree, crushed it in her hand, inhaled its smell, and then said its name in her language; she got down on her haunches to examine a mushroom growing at the base of a trunk; she turned her radiant face up to gaze at the sliver of sky that showed through the leaves. Despite the awareness that they were wasting time, despite the realization that they didn't have much of a window before her next appointment, Maggie was transfixed. She felt as if these woods were magical, and that they had transformed the sullen, crushed woman into a pixie.

She knew that the pixie would disappear with the next question, but she had no choice. "What was the wicked thought? That made you attempt it, I mean."

Lakshmi, who had been running her hand across the soft spindles of a pine tree, stopped. Slowly, she turned to face Maggie, who held her gaze. Come on, she willed her silently. Tell me, so I can make a judgment about whether it's safe to release you. She saw a cluster of emotions cross Lakshmi's face before it went slack.

"This customer, he came to restaurant every Thursday," she said. "So nice he was, madam. Always saying please-thank-you to me. Always, without fail. He my only friend, madam. And he smell"—Lakshmi looked around them—"he smell like this place. Clean." She plucked a pine needle off the tree and held it to her nose.

Here it was, Maggie thought. She'd slept with this guy and was terrified her husband would find out. After having met the husband, a mountain of a man, Maggie couldn't blame her. He would probably kill her if he knew.

She opened her mouth, but just then, Lakshmi began to sob. The hair on Maggie's arms stood up. In her practice, she'd heard lots of people cry—it was one of those sounds you had to steel yourself to—but she had never heard a sound like this. It's cultural, she told herself, but she knew that wasn't it. She'd attended Sudhir's grandfather's funeral, where his widow had wailed and beaten her chest; she'd seen videos of Middle Eastern women keening during mass funerals; what she was hearing now was unlike anything she'd ever heard. In Lakshmi's crying was the sound you'd make if you were the last person left alive on the entire planet.

A shiver ran through Maggie. For a second her mind played tricks on her—I'll have to describe this to Peter and ask if he's ever heard this sound during his travels, she thought—before she remembered her resolution not to see Peter again. She looked around, not knowing how to interrupt Lakshmi's crying, angry with herself for having brought her to this place. So she was going to coax a cheap little confession out of the poor woman. So what? She would soon be releasing her to the same shitty little life that had made her have the affair in the first place.

She forced herself to speak. "Did he—did this man love you back?" she asked. And knew immediately from Lakshmi's shocked expression that she had made a mistake. At least it had stopped Lakshmi's sobbing.

"No, madam. I told you. I married woman. I's from good family. I never tell Bobby. I just sad because he leaf for the California." The sobbing had ceased, but Lakshmi was looking at her with a wounded expression that made Maggie's toes curl with mortification. What the hell is the matter with you? she scolded herself. Imagining that an immigrant Indian woman would blithely have an affair? Just because you are an adulteress doesn't mean that everyone else is. She caught herself. Adulteress? Where the hell did that archaic word come from? Was that how she saw herself? And why was she projecting her guilt about Peter onto her client? How lame was that?

"He moved to California?" Maggie said. "Forever?"

For a moment she thought the awful sobbing was going to start up again, but Lakshmi merely nodded wordlessly. Above them, the trees rustled and the sun filtered in through the thick leaves.

"And that's why you—? Over a customer?"

Lakshmi nodded again, completely missing the irony. And, Maggie thought, there is no irony, dammit. The fact is that this woman is so completely isolated, so bereft, that the departure of a man she was fond of was enough to make her try to take her own life. A cold wind blew through Maggie at the thought. It was unimaginable, that degree of loneliness, of loss. A protective feeling came over her as she watched the sallow face that was gazing at her with such hunger, ready to accept her condemnation, hoping to gain her understanding.

Maggie was about to suggest that they head back to the hospital when she decided to take a calculated risk. "What did you lov—like—about Bobby?" she asked, knowing that she was pushing open another door that they would walk through, knowing that she was continuing her association with Lakshmi, that their relationship would not end after her discharge.

Lakshmi smiled with her eyes. "He so kind, madam," she said. "He never say I stupid, even when I forgets to bring his Pepsi. He never looks at me with naked eyes, the way the other men customers do." Her voice lowered. "And he look like . . ." She cast her eyes around the spot where they were standing. "His eyes blue like this sky and his hairs color of gold. And his mouth smiling, smiling all the time."

Despite the sadness she felt at Lakshmi's situation, Maggie was amused. So Lakshmi had gone and fallen for a blond, blue-eyed white boy who was moving to California. He was probably a surfer dude. A picture of Peter sitting naked in bed rose in her mind, but she pushed it away. She was not going to compare her affair with Peter to Lakshmi's silent crush on Bobby. Her life was light-years removed from Lakshmi's barren, desolate life. Her marriage to Sudhir couldn't even be compared to Lakshmi's joyless marriage to that horrible man. And yet there it was—that pull, that connection. She had felt it from the moment she had entered Lakshmi's room.

She gently took hold of the younger woman's elbow and steered her in the direction of the hospital. They really needed to turn back. As they walked, she casually asked, "You said Bobby never called you stupid. Does your husband call you that?"

Lakshmi looked at her quickly and then looked away. "Yes, madam," she mumbled. "It his pet name for me."

Maggie felt a rush of anger. "Then you should stop answering to it," she said. "Until he talks to you nice." Lakshmi said something that Maggie didn't hear. "What? I didn't catch what you said."

"I said it not his fault, madam. I am a stupid. Not husband fault he not love me."

What was it about this woman that was affecting her so? She had heard stories from clients a thousand times more horrific than Lakshmi's, and they had not touched her like this. Then again, had she ever had a client who was as vulnerable, as friendless, as the woman who walked next to her, whose fingers were lightly touching each branch and tree trunk they passed, as if she were gathering it all in?

"Do you love him?" The words were out of her mouth before she could stop herself. Maggie kicked herself for asking the question. They were near the hospital, she had to get Lakshmi to her unit, and she didn't have time to explore Lakshmi's answer. "It's okay," she added. "You don't have to answer that."

Lakshmi nodded her assent. They climbed the stone steps that led to the hospital in silence, and then she said, "My ma always say, love come slowly-slowly in the marriage. So I not worry. I do my bed duty with him and I feel nothing. But I no worry. But now it six year past, and I knows the truth—love is not coming for me. I having no feelings for him, madam." A tear rolled down her cheek and she brushed it off roughly.

Maggie was about to respond when she saw Richard Cummings, her boss, walking toward them in the hallway. Cummings cocked an eyebrow as he approached, throwing Maggie a half-approving, half-sardonic look. "Hello," he said. "Enjoying the outdoors a bit?"

Maggie could tell Richard wanted to chat, but she simply nodded and kept walking.

As they waited for the elevator, Lakshmi leaned toward her and whispered, "That man come see me the day I come to here. He say something and something, but it all sound like 'buzbuz-buzbuzbuzbuz' to me. So I says nothing to him."

Lakshmi's body language was relaxed, her tone confiding, and Maggie felt the thrill of a breakthrough as they got in the elevator. "You should've replied to him by saying, 'Buzbuzbuzbuz,' " she said, trying to imitate the sound Lakshmi had made.

The younger woman giggled, a soft, tentative sound. For the first time since they'd met, Lakshmi looked her directly in the eye and held the look. The next minute, they were both laughing. Maggie imagined the quizzical look on Richard's face if he knew they were mocking him, and this made her laugh even more.

"Well, looks like you had a nice walk," Patty said as they walked past her.

Maggie escorted her patient to the room and then lingered for a moment. "Listen," she said. "I'm going to recommend that we let you out of here tomorrow. But you have to continue with outpatient therapy. Do you understand?"

Lakshmi looked confused. "What is the there-py?"

"Therapy. What we've been doing here. You know, talking."

Lakshmi brightened. "Yes, I see. You means, making the friendship?"

"Yes, well, not quite," Maggie stammered, not sure what to say. "Look, what time does your husband visit tomorrow? I'll stop by then. I will have a discharge plan prepared by tomorrow. Okay?"

She let herself out of the room before Lakshmi could reply.

9

Maggie wished the man in front of her would stop pacing. "It's a conditional discharge, Mr. Patil," Maggie said. "Are you with me?"

"This Lakshmi's natak is costing me lots of money," Adit Patil said. "I needing her in the restaurant."

"And you can have her. But she must continue therapy. You understand?"

Adit scowled. "And where from the money comes? How we pay? My insurance not so good. We poor people. Lakshmi make stupid mistake. But now she okay."

Maggie glanced at Lakshmi, who was staring at a spot on the floor, acting for all the world as if this conversation did not involve her. "She's not okay," she said quietly. "She just tried killing herself, do you get that? I'm sorry, but I can't discharge her without follow-up treatment."

"This hospital too far from our house. I will take her to family doctor. For checkup."

"I realize commuting to the hospital is not realistic. And so I'm going to suggest something. I have a private practice out of my home. It's a lot closer to you than this place. Lakshmi can come see me there once a week. Would that work? She can take the bus."

Adit looked at her incomprehensively, shaking his head. "I not following. What is this private practice mean?"

Maggie searched to find the right words. "Like a clinic. A doctor's office. You know? Like your family doctor's office?"

Adit swore softly. In Hindi, he said to Lakshmi, "This woman is a crook. She is trying to put extra money in her own pocket. Now I understand her game."

Maggie noticed the startled look on Lakshmi's face and guessed what Adit had said. "Mr. Patil," she said smoothly. "Before you worry about money, I just want you to know that I will treat your wife gratis—for free. My usual rate is a hundred and thirty dollars an hour." She noticed with satisfaction the stunned look on the man's face. "But since you are, as you say, poor people, I'm happy to work with her without a fee."

She took in the triumphant look that Lakshmi threw at her husband and knew that she'd guessed correctly what he had muttered. He was staring at Maggie openmouthed, and after a second she said, "Well? Do you agree?"

Adit glanced quickly at his wife and then looked at Maggie. "Madam," he said. "I have business to run. I cannot be taxi service for my wife. How I bringing her to you once a week?"

"As I said earlier, Mr. Patil, she can take the bus." Maggie dug into the pocket of her lab coat and pulled out a schedule. "Here. She can take the bus from Chesterfield to downtown Cedarville and then catch a second one to my home. It won't be easy, but it's doable."

Adit frowned. "My wife never take the bus," he said. "Not safe. And she like a child—she will get lost, definitely."

Both women spoke simultaneously. "She's not a child—" Maggie began.

"I can learn," Lakshmi said. "In India, I used to take bus—"

He spun around on his heel and glowered at his wife. "This not India, you stupid woman," he hissed. "What you going to do if you goes in wrong bus? As it is, you having no common sense."

"Mr. Patil," Maggie spoke sharply. "Please don't ever call Lakshmi stupid in my presence. Actually, you shouldn't call her that, period. And like I said, these are the terms of the discharge. Now, if you disagree, we will just keep her here longer."

He opened his mouth to say something, but Maggie forced herself to stare him down. She was glad that none of the nurses were in the room—they might have felt compelled to inform Mr. Patil that Lakshmi couldn't be kept any longer against her will. Maggie was counting on the fact that he didn't know the law and would bend under the pressure of her authority.

Still locking gazes with him, she turned her body ever so slightly toward the crouching Lakshmi. Say something, she willed her. Help me break this impasse.

As if she had read her mind, Lakshmi rose slowly from the bed. "I will learn bus route," she said quietly. "I wanting to go home, ji. I missing my home."

Maggie had no idea if Lakshmi had believed the threat or was playing along. But whatever her reason, it had the desired effect on Patil. "Okay," he mumbled. "Please, you sign the discharge papers. We make arrangement for Lakshmi to come to your clinic."

10

HUSBAND NOT SAYING two words to me, but I keeps looking at his serious face and I tries to keep the laughing inside me. We driving home from the hospital and the fresh air is coming inside the car and is making me so cheerfuls. I am ascare to go home, ascare of what Rekha may say. Husband says he tell all customers that I sick with the flu but that Rekha is knowing the truth. Still, I so happy to going to my own house and store. It funny, house and store never feel belong to me when I live in them, but now I feel they mine. Once we get home, I will eats food when I want, open one, two, three window if I want, go for walk if husband say okay. And nobody wearing white coat. Nobody come in during night to ask me question or give me tablet. I can take shower with my Hamam soap, not little soap they give; I can play my Mukesh and Kishore Kumar music CD when I want, I can drink my own chai and not the hospital tea that taste like bathwater. And at night I will hears my husband snoring and the noise of the cars, not the voice of nurse and wardboy or the screaming of the other patients. Their screaming make me feel like somebody beating me with the stick. In my village, there is madman. He wife die when having baby, and baby die also, and Dada say from that day only, he go mad. At night he sleep under a handcart in market place. And all childrens making the fun of him, they call him Pagal, mad, and they throwing little stones to him. They act like it is a mela, or holiday, when he come. When I little, I feels so bad, I go running to stand in front of him to protection him and my friends get ascare. Move away, Lakshmi, they scream, or Pagal will die you. But he just look at me and touch my head so softly. And then he cry. I feeling so bad, I pick up stones and throw back to my friends. Go away, I shout. They is running away, but at school, they make fun of me for two days. Pagal wants to make you his dead daughter, they teasing me. I not care. My ma always feed Pagal. He sit outside our house, eating food with both hands. When I hear other hospital patient scream at night, I see Pagal hit by little-little stones. But I cannot protection them.

"You take day off today," husband say while he driving. "But tomorrow you start back at restaurant, okay? I'm telling that lazy fellow today is his last day."

First words husband has said to me since we get this-charge from hospital. I know he upset about what madam say to him in my room today. But I think of husband's face when madam say what she say, and it make me feel like laugh. Husband not liking the blacks, and madam both black and woman but she also doctor, so husband has to say yes, yes, yes. Otherwise, he must to pay his friend's son to work in restaurant extra, and husband need me back.

Husband park the car in front of our store, and suddenly I so ashame. In our religion the suicide is a big paap, and I think everyone can look at my face and know I fallen woman. I get out of car and look at the exact same place where I standing with Bobby only one weeks back. But already I not remindering Bobby's face. I know what color his hair and eyes, but is the nose big or small? Is he taller than husband or less? I don't reminder. Most of all, the happy-sad in my chest, whenever I seeing or thinking of Bobby, is gone. Instead, I feels empty.

After locking the car, husband come to my side and look at my face and laugh. "What? One week and you forgot our restaurant? What you looking left-right, left-right, like you stranger?"

"Sorry," I say.

He look me close. "I just making the joke," he say. Then his voice becoming soft. "You happy you home?"

When my husband kind, it make me cry. This irritate to him, because who want a crying wife? Still, I feels the tears in my eyes. "Very happy," I say.

Today, he not irritate. Instead, he put hand on my shoulder. "Good."

We enter store, and I hears sound like fast wind, and Rekha come running and hugging me. "Didi, Didi," she say. "Ae, bhagwan. I so happy you home safe and sound."

Many time I feel the jealousy for Rehka. Always I am watching her watching my husband. Rekha, young, fair, with face that make mens smile. But today I am so enjoy her face, her bootpolish shiny hair, her smile. Today I thank God Rekha work in store with me. With her stories, her joking, her making face behind customers' back, the music she nonstop play, she is good time-pass.

"How are you, little sister?" I say, and see the happy on her face, like I put piece of sweet jalebi in her mouth. I give myself a small pinch. I being mean to Rehka before, always showing off that I am boss's wife. How she must feel?

"Everything is good, Didi, now that you're home."

Rekha's heart pure as ghee. Why I not see before?

Husband puts down on the counter big plastic bag they gave us from hospital. "You take this to apartment and go rest, Lakshmi," he say. "I need to get back to restaurant." He take few steps then turn around. "You take much rest today. Tomorrow is busy day."

I am home. Everything feeling new. And everything feeling same-same.

I feels Rekha's eyes on my back as I takes plastic bag and walks toward back storage room, but I not minding. I knows she wanting to ask me question per question—why I doings such a wicked thing. What they doings to me in the hospital. Do they giving me electric shock, like Rajesh Khanna in *Khamoshi*? I will tell her. But never about Bobby. I only tells madam because . . . I don't know because why. Because she reminding me of Shilpa, and Shilpa is half my voice.

As I climb the stairs to apartment, I puts my hand in pocket and take out the card. Madam has written time of appointment for Monday. At the four-thirty, I must to be there. Restaurant close on Monday, so no problem. Taking the two buses to madam's clinic, big problem. But in front of husband, I is bindaas. In my village, I tell him, I take bus many, many time. I not ascare of being lost.

I walk inside apartment, and first thing I open all the window. As I moving, I reminder everything. How I take water from kitchen tap. How I taking all of husband's tablets. How I drinking husband's daru and how it make me feel close to Shilpa, close to God.

But now I understanding. This wrong way to feel close to God. Only the praying is correct way to see the God.

11

WHEN I WAS in the sixth standard, we have a Talent Show. My job was to say a poetry by Tagore in English. I knows that Ma and Dada not speaking English, but still they be so prideful to see their daughter say a poetry in front of all the rich peoples who giving money for the school. Menon sahib coming also, and because he paying my school fees since I save Munna, I know he wanting to know if he wasting his money or not.

I not understanding what the poetry mean but I learns it by heart. I hearing it in my sleep, and I waking up with it, like Hindi film song from the radio. I says it to Ma. I repeats it to Dada and Shilpa. So why I not remindering it when I must say in front of the teacher? When I stands in front of whole class, my head becoming like the block of ice that the baniya sells in shop. Cold ice, cover in wood dust, so it not melting. I opens my mouth and I sound like a mouse live in there. Chu chu chu, I says. My teacher very nice. She try to courage me. Try, Lakshmi, she say. No need to be ascare. You smart student.

So day before Talent Show, I go for walk in my father's field. It is sunset time and the birds are making chitter-chatter in trees. The sky is orange and peach and grape. The sun red like watermelon. And the wheat in my dada's field so high, it touch my cheeks as I walk. I stop in between the plants so I am in cover. The wind move me just like it moving them. I am no more Lakshmi. I am

tall and green and plant. I growing from this earth that belong to
my dada and his dada.

And then I do some jadoo. I close my eyes and become Shilpa.
I is no longer smart but ugly. I become smart and beautiful. Everyone happy to put their eyes on my face. When they looking
at me, their eye become soft and peaceful. They smile without
knowing they smile.

Lakshmi gone, taken away by the last bird of the evening, who
looking for its tree. Here in Lakshmi's dada's field stand Shilpa,
saying the poetry, not feeling shy, not feeling like she dying when
other peoples looking at her. Shilpa is finishing the poem, "Into
that heaven of freedom, Father, let my country awake."

And when I open my eyes on Talent Show Day, people is clapping for me. Dada looking prideful as a bandmaster and Ma is
wiping her eyes with her sari. Menon sahib show all his teeth and
smile. And when they gives me second prize in Talent Show, same
people clapping again. And when later, I say thank you to Shilpa,
she look surprise because she not knowing how she help me.

And this same way, by leaving Lakshmi in the store and becoming Shilpa, is how I manage to take two buses to Cedarville and
find madam's house.

12

MAGGIE STRAIGHTENED A cushion on the couch, glanced again at the living room clock, and emitted an exasperated sigh. There was no denying that every second that passed without a knock on her door increased her anxiety about Lakshmi's safety and whereabouts.

Finally, in order to shake off visions of Lakshmi on a bus headed in the opposite direction, she threw on her clogs, walked down the driveway, and stood in the front yard, scanning the street for any sign of her client, who, her rational mind told her, was running only a few minutes late. There was no need whatsoever to panic or worry yet. Still, there was no refuting the lift she felt when she saw Lakshmi's distant figure as she slowly but steadily climbed toward the house, located on one of the steepest streets in town. Maggie felt a pang of regret at not having had the decency to pick the poor woman up at the bus stop. Then she caught herself. You can't do this, she thought. You won't be doing either of you any favors if you don't maintain your boundaries. Lakshmi is healthy, young—how old is she, anyway? Maggie tried to remember. Thirty-one? Thirty-two? And the exercise is good for her. Don't make this too easy for her—in fact, you've already made a mistake in not charging her even a nominal fee. A case of your emotions clouding your judgment. Maggie had heard it from other therapists a million times: Clients didn't value what they got for free. It was human nature to devalue what came too cheap or

easy. Lakshmi's husband would've probably taken you more seriously if you'd made them pay something, even if it was a lousy ten
bucks a visit, she told herself.

Lakshmi was close enough now for Maggie to make out that
she was carrying a large bag that was weighing her down. Maggie
felt a flash of irritation. What was it about immigrants that they
always had to carry around half their possessions? No wonder she
was struggling to get up the hill. Maggie moved in the direction
of the other woman. No point in changing two buses to come
for an hour-long session if you were going to be ten minutes late.
Luckily, she didn't have a client coming in after Lakshmi. So they
could go over a bit, she supposed. Still, she was going to have a
frank talk with Lakshmi about the value of her time.

Lakshmi smiled shyly as she came up to Maggie, and seeing
that tentative smile, some of Maggie's anger dissipated. "Hello,
madam," Lakshmi said. "How are you?"

"I'm fine. And you? Any trouble finding the place?"

"No problem, madam." Maggie could hear the younger woman
breathing hard in between her words. She really is out of shape,
she thought. Probably gets no exercise at all. "I give bus stop
name to driver, and he tell me where to get off. Very nice driver,
madam, of your caste."

It took Maggie a second to realize that Lakshmi meant that
the driver was black. She smiled thinly. "Well. Good."

She saw that Lakshmi was looking at the house, taking it all in,
and for a second she saw it through her eyes—how big and osten-
tatious the house must look, with its slate roof, the wraparound
porch, the big front yard with the rosebushes. Lakshmi turned
slightly toward her to say something, but Maggie took her elbow
and steered her up the driveway toward the back porch. "When
you come next week, just come on in from this back entrance.
This is where I see my clients. This door will be unlocked, so just

let yourself in and have a seat. The main house is—well, that's our private residence." She had said the same thing to a dozen other clients, but somehow saying it to Lakshmi embarrassed her. But Lakshmi merely nodded.

Maggie sat in her customary chair, across from Lakshmi. "How was your weekend?" she began, but Lakshmi was digging in the large cloth bag. She pulled out a metal box, which Maggie immediately recognized from her many trips to India. It was a tiffin carrier, the box in which Indians carried hot lunches to the office. What the hell? Did the woman think she was staying for dinner?

"Lakshmi, what are you doing?"

The younger woman beamed. "For you, madam. And your mister. Fresh-fresh food. I prepare this morning, only. Not restaurant rubbish-food, madam. This home foods. I prepare myself. I brings every time."

The lump that formed in Maggie's throat made it hard to speak. Of course. She should've known. Had she ever met an Indian who could accept a favor without needing to repay it immediately? Or who could resist the urge to feed another person? Just a few minutes ago she had worried that Lakshmi would take her therapy sessions for granted, would devalue them simply because they were free. Well, the joke was on her.

Maggie cleared her throat. "Lakshmi," she said. "This is so thoughtful of you. But—I can't. I can't accept this. Do you understand? We have to maintain a professional distance . . ."

Lakshmi was shaking her head. "I no understand. You not liking the Indian food?"

"Are you kidding? I love Indian food. It's just that—I'm your doctor. I can't accept gifts from my patients. We are meeting here instead of the hospital because it's easier for you. But the relationship is . . ."

Lakshmi raised one eyebrow. "In my village, we gives doctor

sahib gift. When Shilpa was born, Dada send to him big bag of rice. Diwali time we give sweets."

Maggie sighed. She suddenly had no idea how to deal with the woman sitting in front of her, who wore a puzzled expression, who, she knew, was seconds away from being offended. She wished Sudhir were home and that she could consult with him. She remembered Dipkabai, the servant who worked for Sudhir's parents in Calcutta, who, out of her meager salary, brought her homemade desserts every day once Maggie had let slip that she had a sweet tooth. And how horrified she'd been at first at the thought of this emaciated-looking, elderly woman spending her hard-earned money on preparing dessert for her, and how she'd refused, and the hurt on Dipkabai's face, until Sudhir had pulled her aside and told her never, ever to refuse the gift of food. It's all the poor have, he'd said. Just say thank you and taste whatever she makes for you. We can always leave her a generous tip when we leave.

But this situation was different, dammit. They were not in India, and Lakshmi was her client, for God's sake. The rules on this were clear.

"Lakshmi," she started again, but the younger woman interrupted her.

"Madam," she said. "You cooking fresh hot-pot Indian food for your husband?"

Maggie smiled ruefully. "I wish. My husband does most of the cooking, I'm afraid."

Lakshmi got a cagey look on her face. "So, madam. Husband not angry that you saying no to homemade Indian food?"

A laugh escaped from Maggie's lips. Damn, this woman was good. Persistent. Not nearly as dead and listless as she'd seemed in the hospital. "Okay," she said, not allowing herself time to process the issue any further. "You win. Thank you. I'm sure we'll enjoy this. But this is the first and last time, Lakshmi. Next week you bring nothing."

She made herself not notice that Lakshmi pretended to look out the window and into the backyard as Maggie spoke. Really, they couldn't afford to spend any more time on this issue. Maggie leaned back in her chair. "So, how was it, going home? How was your weekend?"

"Good, madam. Yesterday very busy in restaurant."

Maggie nodded. "Glad to hear. So, what would you like to talk about today? What's on your mind?"

Lakshmi cocked her head. Then she said, "You liking Hindi films, madam?"

What did Lakshmi think this was? Happy hour? That they were going to spend the time chitchatting? Maggie knew that the very concept of therapy was alien to Lakshmi. Even among Sudhir's educated family members in India, her profession was the butt of many jokes and much eye-rolling, their impressions of therapy formed by 1970s Woody Allen movies and a general belief that Americans were self-indulgent, self-absorbed, and "soft." She was pretty sure that someone from Lakshmi's peasant rural background couldn't fathom the concept of paying a doctor to listen to her problems. A doctor was someone who handed you tablets, gave you an injection, and, in extreme cases, operated on you. She saw the scene from Lakshmi's eyes: two women sitting on a back porch on a gorgeous summer afternoon. Of course the woman wanted to discuss movies. What in Lakshmi's life experience would tell her that this was a medical visit?

Out of the blue, Maggie remembered the bemused look in Wallace's eyes when she told him that she'd switched majors at Wellesley because she intended to become a psychologist. A look that had mocked her, that had wondered how he, a working-class man, had given birth to a daughter who would in all likelihood spend her career listening to middle-class white people talk about their sorrows and phobias. Not that Wallace had said any of this, Maggie remembered. He didn't need to. His face said it all, and she had flinched as if he'd actually insulted her, as if he'd told her that he knew what she was doing—instead of training for a real job, like nurse or school principal or doctor, instead of doing work that would help her people, Maggie was looking to bust out of their rundown Caribbean neighborhood in Brooklyn, to get as far as she could from the winos on the corners, and the young men with their transistor radios and Afros who hung out on the front stoops, and the little storefront church where she'd spent every Saturday of her childhood. Not too many folks from the old neighborhood can afford to see a therapist, baby girl, Wallace may as well have said. That's for the rich folk on the Upper East Side.

Giving her head the slightest shake, Maggie forced herself to focus on the woman sitting before her. "Lakshmi," she said. "Let me ask you something. Do you understand why you're coming here? What we're trying to—"

To Maggie's surprise, Lakshmi bit her lip and dropped her gaze to the floor. "Yes," she murmured. "Rekha explain me. She say you doctor for crazy people. I crazy, so I must come here."

"Oh, but that's absurd. That's just not true." Maggie snapped her fingers. "Lakshmi. Look at me. Look at me. You're not crazy. Okay? Whoever this Rekha is, she's wrong."

"Rekha work in store—"

"Yeah, well. She's wrong. You are here because we're trying to understand why you're unhappy enough to think your own life is worthless. And to figure out how we can make some changes to help you feel better about yourself. But in order to do so, I need you to talk to me. To trust me. Anything you tell me stays here. That means I don't tell your husband or Rekha or anyone else. That's a promise. Do you understand?"

Lakshmi looked at her for the longest time, her eyes wide and wet. Then she nodded. "Understand."

"Good. One more thing. You don't have to call me madam. You can call me Maggie. Think you can do that?"

Lakshmi nodded. "Maggie." She said the name carefully, as if it were a wooden crate filled with breakable things.

"Great. So, I want to know something. You told me once that you have no contact with your family in India. Is that right?"

"Yes, madam."

Maggie let it pass. "Why?"

"Husband not liking my family. He angry at them. Maggie."

"Why? What happened?"

Lakshmi stared at the floor again. After a second, her nose turned red and Maggie saw that she was crying. She waited to see if Lakshmi would speak but, after a minute, knew that she wouldn't. Besides, she could speculate as to the cause—probably a lack of dowry or something like that. It was amazing how many marriages in India got off to a bad start because of greed on the part of the groom.

She took a different track. "Do you miss your sister? Your father?"

Lakshmi seemed puzzled. "I not miss them, madam. Sorry. Maggie. Where they go?" She struck her chest twice. "They living inside here. How I miss them? They always close by."

Maggie smiled. "That's sweet."

But the younger woman looked angry. "Not sweet. Truth. I talks to my Shilpa all the time."

"And what do you say to her?"

"Everything. I tells her everything."

"Did you tell her about Bobby?"

Lakshmi shot Maggie a sharp look and then fell silent. "No," she said eventually. "That I not tell. Nothing to tell," she added fiercely.

"So what do you tell her?"

"Mostly I asks questions. How are you, Shilpa? Did you marries your Dilip? How is his auto repairs business? How you likes living in Rawalpindi? Are you happy? Did you make me an aunt? How is our dada? Like that only I talks to her."

"You don't know if Shilpa is married?"

"No. I leaf for Am'rica before her shadi. But I make my dada give his blessing to her and Dilip. Their love match. Shilpa mad for him. Dilip a good boy but he from Rawalpindi. He not from our village. And he poor. So Dada not happy at first. But I talks to him and then he agree. And I gives Shilpa all my ma's gold jewelry for her wedding. Everything I could do for her before I come, I do. Everything."

Maggie glanced at the clock on the wall behind Shilpa. Ten minutes to the hour. "What is Shilpa like?" she asked, and watched as Lakshmi's face lit up.

"Oh, madam, she was most beautiful baby. I five year age when Shilpa born. Everybody say, 'Lakshmi, you too small, you don't reminder your sister.' But they wrong. I reminder good. Ma make me sit on floor and put baby in my arms. When Shilpa little girl, I get sugarcane from field and give her. She having so little-little tooths but she chew on it. She liking sweet things from the start. And she follow me everywhere. Ma said she give birth to my shadow."

Lakshmi gazed out into the backyard, her eyes cloudy. "She love eating bhindi. You know bhindi? What you call it—okra? And madam, you know Vicks VapoRub? Shilpa like to eat it when she sick. She funny like that. She good student, like me, but she hate doing farmwork. Even when Ma get the 'rthritis bad, Shilpa say no to help our dada. Say her clothes getting dirty. Shilpa love fashion clothes. Dada always to saying to her, 'Beti, you a farmer daughter, not film star.' But Shilpa not loving that life. She like to—"

Lakshmi looked like she could go on for another half hour, and Maggie decided this was a good time to stop. "I'm afraid our time's up," she interrupted gently. "We can pick up again next week." She glanced at the tiffin carrier that sat between them. "If you give me a minute, I'll take the food out and return the boxes to you."

She swung open the door that led from the back porch into the main house and then quickly drew the curtain so that Lakshmi couldn't see in. In the kitchen, she gasped as she saw the amount of food Lakshmi had brought. How did the woman manage to carry this load on two buses? And how many people did she think lived in this house? This food would last Sudhir and Maggie for days.

She heard a sound and nearly jumped out of her skin. Lakshmi was standing behind her, looking around the house. Maggie shuddered, a feeling of violation running through her. In the five years she'd had her home office, no client had ever let himself or herself into the main house. On rare occasions, someone would need to use the bathroom, but that was as far as a client went. And here was Lakshmi standing in her kitchen, unaware that she'd just invaded Maggie's private space.

"What are you doing here? I said I'd be right back," she snapped, not bothering to keep the annoyance out of her voice. But when she saw the look of incomprehension on Lakshmi's face, the anger died down as abruptly as it had flared up.

"I—I not allow here?"

"Well, not usually," Maggie stammered. She pointed toward the porch. "That's my office, you see, and this, this is my home." And in a rush of inspiration, she lied, "My husband doesn't like clients in the house."

Lakshmi's face lit up with understanding. "Like our apartment," she cried. "It above the store. We no allow customer there."

"Yes. Exactly."

There was an embarrassed silence, and then a voice inside

Maggie said, Oh, what the hell. What the hell difference did it make that this poor woman was standing inside her kitchen? Her treatment of Lakshmi was going to be unorthodox, she already knew that, so why make a fuss over this innocent violation of her privacy? The walk that she'd taken around the hospital grounds with Lakshmi, the offer to treat her for free at her private practice rather than hook her up with a therapist in her hometown, the manner in which she'd bluffed Lakshmi's husband into letting her come here, none of it conformed to anything she'd been taught in school. Since the very concept of therapy was unfamiliar to Lakshmi, how could she know what its unspoken rules were?

Maggie emptied the last of the food into her bowls, rinsed out the tiffin carrier, and handed it to Lakshmi. "Many thanks," she said, smiling. "It all looks delicious."

To her surprise, Lakshmi took Maggie's right hand and held it up to her eyes. "Thank you, madam," she said. "For helping me. I know you busy woman. God bless you."

Maggie squeezed Lakshmi's hand. "You're most welcome. Can you come back at the same time next week? And the name's Maggie, not madam."

Lakshmi laughed. "Yes. Sorry. Maggie. Yes, next week. Bye." She headed back to the porch.

She was almost out the door when Maggie caught up with her.

"Wait," Maggie said, jiggling her car keys. "I think I'll run you down to the bus stop. It'll save you a bit of a walk."

As Lakshmi got in the Subaru, Maggie remembered what Lakshmi had said to her in the hospital when she'd tried to explain the concept of therapy. Oh, Lakshmi had said, I thought we were trying to build a friendship. Or words to that effect.

Maggie glanced at the woman riding next to her. Maybe friendship was the best therapy she could offer Lakshmi, she thought.

13

MAGGIE SHOOK WITH laughter as she watched Sudhir take yet another helping of the food Lakshmi had brought. Poor man, she thought, look how deprived he is, stuck with an American wife whose culinary talents don't stretch beyond an occasional pot roast.

"Wow," Sudhir said again. "This is superb. Just superb." He licked the back of his fork before setting it down. "If that girl ever needs a job as a chef, we're hiring her."

This was the second time that Sudhir had referred to Lakshmi as "girl." Maggie knew it was some vestige of the Indian class system, that automatic, unconscious calculation made by middle-class Indians: A peasant woman like Lakshmi, who spoke poor English and worked in an ethnic grocery store, was automatically an inferior, just slightly higher in status than the maids who worked in their homes in India. Even Sudhir, who was so easygoing and indifferent to these matters—at NYU, he had cheerfully interacted with classmates of different races, nationalities, class backgrounds, even majors—was apparently not above referring to the woman whose food he had just enjoyed as "girl."

"What?" said Sudhir, ever attuned to the slightest shift in her mood.

"Nothing. It's just that Lakshmi is in her thirties. She's hardly a girl."

Sudhir eyed her quizzically. "Yah, so?" He began picking up

their dirty dishes. "The more important issue is, did this girl-woman pack us some dessert?"

She pretended to throw a fork at him. "You're hopeless. A pig." She leaned back and patted his belly as he brushed past her on his way to the sink. "You better keep an eye on that little potbelly of yours, honey."

"Rubbish." Sudhir grinned. He set the dishes on the counter and walked up behind Maggie and rubbed her shoulders. "Besides, the great thing about being an old married man is that I no longer have to worry about these things, right?"

Maggie laughed. "You? Not worry about your weight? You're worse than any woman I know." She turned around and pulled him down to give him a quick peck. "Luckily for you, you're married to the world's worst cook. If you'd married someone like Lakshmi, you'd be in deep trouble."

"I married the woman I was meant to marry," Sudhir said, and Maggie felt his words tear at her heart. How could she have risked this to be with Peter? Already, she felt as if she were emerging from some drunken stupor, had come to her senses from an hour of bewitchment. It was the most reckless thing she had ever done, sleeping with Peter Weiss, and thankfully, it was over. She would have the rest of her life to figure out what had made her do it.

"Ae. You still haven't answered me. Did this dream-patient of yours bring us any dessert?"

"Incorrigible, that's what you are," Maggie scolded as she opened the fridge and pulled out a small glass bowl. "Here. I don't know what these are. Looks like the usual Indian enough-milk-and-sugar-to-put-you-in-a-diabetic-coma concoction."

"Sounds yummy. Especially when you word it like that. You want some?"

"I'll pass. I'm gonna finish my wine in the living room."

"Okay. Be right there."

Sudhir followed her into the living room a few minutes later, sat down next to her on the couch, and immediately took possession of the remote. Ignoring Maggie's halfhearted "Hey," he flipped through the channels, finally settling on a rerun of *Rush Hour 2*.

He put his arm around her shoulder and drew her close. "So how was your day?"

She shrugged. "Pretty good. Nothing out of the ordinary. I was so happy not having to go in to the hospital today. You?"

Sudhir ran his fingers through his hair. "Derek came to see me today. He's upset that we took away his graduate assistantship. I told him if he'd focused on his grades last year, we wouldn't be having this conversation now. He didn't like that. Far easier to blame the world than to look at your own self."

Maggie sighed. "Don't I know it. That's what I deal with in half my patients. I just—"

"This country's gone too soft, Mags. Nobody wants to take responsibility for their own behavior anymore. I mean, it's endemic. Everyone's looking for a scapegoat. Just see what's happening in Washington—they blame illegal immigrants, the Chinese, the Afghanis, for everything that's wrong with the country. Same thing with my students—they are ready to blame their grandparents, parents, the neighbor's cat. Anybody but themselves." He tilted his head toward her, a slight smile on his lips. "It's the fault of your profession, of course. Mollycoddling people like that."

"Of course," she said. "Too bad the world isn't run by math professors and physicists. It would be heaven on earth then."

"Oh God. That's a scary thought." Sudhir was quiet for a moment. "Brent stopped by my office today. He wants me to take over as chair of the department next fall. He thinks most of the faculty will go along with that."

"And you waited until now to give me this great news?"

"I'm not sure I want to do it."

"Sudhir. Why not? You're the perfect person for the position. You'd make a wonderful chair."

"I don't know. I'm getting too old and grumpy to put up with people's egos. You know how impatient I get with all the 'I deserve this and I'm worth that'? That touchy-feely stuff is your area of expertise, not mine."

Maggie smiled. She had met Sudhir at a party held at the terrace apartment of a common friend, Jean, during her second week at NYU. Sudhir had already been at NYU for a year by the time of the party. At about ten p.m., another student, Brian, who had been drinking and smoking weed all evening, got teary and melodramatic in that old drunken way. "It's all a goddamn joke, man," he kept saying. "Just a goddamn joke."

"What is?" someone said.

"Life. Just a big, cosmic joke. I'm ready to cash it in, man. Ready to cash it in."

"No. Don't say that," cried Jean, who was pretty loaded herself. And with that, a group of students, many of them psychology majors, like Maggie, began to cajole, beg, and console the drunken man, who kept repeating, "Ready to cash it in."

"Life is too precious," Jean reasoned.

"You can't let them win, man," someone else said.

"You have your whole life ahead of you," urged a young woman with straight blond hair.

Jean flung Maggie a beseeching look, silently asking her to join the intervention, but Maggie felt a slight shudder of apprehension and revulsion. She had grown up in a neighborhood where most of the middle-aged women worked as domestics in the homes of the rich, had watched her father soak his swollen, bunioned feet in Epsom salts after coming home from the night shift of his second job. No way was she going to console some rich, pampered white boy who had smoked too much weed at a party. She edged away from the circle that had formed around Brian.

She went out to the terrace, and after a few minutes, she heard someone clear his throat. She turned around to see a tall, brown-skinned man in a white shirt and jeans smiling at her. "So you're not part of Brian's harem?" he said, and she understood immediately what he meant. The look on his face made her laugh.

"No, I guess not."

The smile got deeper. "If he says he's going to cash it in one more time, I may feel compelled to push him over the ledge myself."

It was a chilly evening, and Maggie pulled her cardigan closer around her. "Can I buy a ticket to watch?"

She caught his start of surprise and then, as he came closer, saw the white of his teeth. "Good one." He offered her his hand. "I'm Sudhir, by the way."

"Soo-dir? Hi. I'm Maggie."

"Not Soo-dir. Sudhir. There's an 'h' after the 'd.' So it's a 'dh' sound."

"Right," she said, mildly annoyed at his persistence.

"Normally, I don't correct people," he said, as if he'd read her mind. "But I don't know—somehow it's important to me that you learn to say my name right."

She turned to look at him, really look, and noticed for the first time how attractive he was. The air between them felt charged, and in order to lighten the intensity, she said, "Hey, are you making a pass at me?"

He smirked. Then the smirk turned into a warm, easy smile, as if they were old friends, as if they'd known each other most of their lives. "Maybe."

They heard Jean yell something, and the next second Brian staggered onto the terrace. "It's a joke, man," he said to no one in particular. "It's all such a friggin' joke."

Sudhir took a few steps toward Brian and put a hand on his shoulder, as if to steady him. "Okay, listen," he said. "You're just drunk, that's all. You're upsetting these women, okay, boss? So how about I either put you in a cab and send you home to sleep off your hangover, or you go into the bedroom and take a nap?"

Brian opened his mouth to protest, but Sudhir squeezed his shoulder. Hard. "Ow, man. Whatcha doing?" Brian squealed.

"Those are the two choices, boss. Which one would you like?"

As the other guests watched, Brian mumbled something only Sudhir could hear. "Great. I'll walk you to Jean's bedroom. And later, I'll drop you off home."

Now Maggie looked at her husband. Apart from the graying of the temples, a few lines on his face, and a slight thickening around the middle, Sudhir looked remarkably unchanged from the practical, no-nonsense guy that night on the terrace. And his tolerance for fools had not increased over the years. She took his hand in hers. "I think you'll make a great chair. You're fair, you don't get rattled easily, people respect you. But it has to be your decision, baby."

He kissed the top of her head. "Thanks. I need to think about it for a few weeks."

Her phone beeped, and she glanced at her watch. Nine-thirty. She hoped it wasn't the hospital. She looked for her phone, remembered she'd left it on the kitchen counter, and got up from the couch with a groan. "Be right back," she said.

It was Peter. "Sorry," the text read. "Need to see you again. Have lunch with me this week?"

Her hands shook as she held the phone. She felt as if Peter were here with them, as if he'd knocked down the front door and entered her and Sudhir's inviolate space. She felt nauseated. She'd made it pretty clear to Peter on the day after Sudhir had returned home that she couldn't see him again. He had seemed to understand. What had happened to make him text her?

"Honey?" Sudhir called. "You coming back?"

"Coming," she answered, shoving the phone in her pocket.

"Who was it?" Sudhir asked as she reentered the room. "It's kinda late."

Her mind froze for a second. "Gloria," she said, mentioning the first name she could think of, their common friend from grad school days who now lived in La Jolla.

"Gloria," Sudhir said affectionately. "How is she? What's she saying?" He patted the couch, asking her to sit back down.

But Maggie continued to stand. "She's fine. Just saying hi." She feigned a yawn. "You know what? You mind if I go upstairs? I have a few emails to send, and then I want to start getting ready for bed. You care?"

He shrugged. "No, go ahead. I'll soon be up myself."

She climbed the carpeted stairs, a sick feeling in her stomach. She couldn't remember the last time she'd lied to Sudhir. What a mistake it had been, getting involved with Peter.

In her study, she studied the text message again. Would it be better to not respond at all? Or to write back and tell him she was busy? What could Peter want with her, anyway? "Need to see you again." What did he mean by that? That he missed her? Or had something happened that he needed to let her know? Had someone seen her entering his house?

She found herself flipping through her phone calendar. She could slip out from the hospital between one and three on Thursday. Surely a quick lunch wouldn't hurt anything. She could even tell Sudhir about it. That might not be a bad thing, actually.

Even as she thought about it, she gave up that idea. Sudhir

hadn't been too impressed by Peter during his first stint at the university. What had he said when they'd visited an exhibit of Peter's war photographs at the university museum? That he found the pictures self-aggrandizing. And Maggie, who had been immediately and intensely attracted to Peter, was in no position to argue, for fear of making Sudhir suspicious, especially since she had a hunch that he was aware of her attraction for Peter. No, she dare not mention Peter's name or the fact that she'd seen him while Sudhir was away at a conference.

She sent Peter a quick text about lunch on Thursday, turned off the ringer, and waited. Sure enough, he texted her back a minute later. "Can't wait to see you," he wrote.

Despite herself, despite the fact that she could hear Sudhir making his way up the stairs, Maggie was aware of the inexplicable, embarassing fact that the thought of seeing Peter again made her heart race.

14

THIS IS THE six week I catch the buses that bringing me to Maggie's house. Both drivers knowing me now but today, I catch earlier bus to downtown. Husband ask why I leaf the house early but I not give proper answer and he not care because restaurant closed today. If I tells him the reason, he only call me stupid. Because before catching second bus, I make a small walk to the downtown park, to go sit at the riverside. My God, this river is so strong and quickly moving, compare to the little river that flow in my home village. Also, water so clean here and you can see little-little stones at the bottom. I wanting to take off my shoes and walk in the water as I do with Shilpa at home, but this is Am'rican river, and I not know if public allowed to walk in it. In this country, there is big signs saying to not walk on grass. In my home village, everyone walk on grass— cows, buffalo, old people, childrens, chicken, dogs. I think they not allow walking in this water.

But it so peaceful to sit here. First time since I come to Am'rica, I not with husband or Rehka or in restaurant or store or car or apartment. I's all alone and I loves it. First time I feel everything not borrow. What I mean by that? When I with the husband, I seeing everything through his eyes—moon, sun, sky, tree, parking lot, store, everything. If he feeling sun too hot, I feeling upset. If he cursing the cold, I angry with snow. My brains not thinking my own thoughts. But just now I feeling cool breeze on my skin.

The sun feel so nice on my body. The trees singing soft song that
I am hearing. And my eyes, always burning from the hot oil and
spice and onion chop in the kitchen, is sipping the green of the
grass like I's sipping a cold orange Fanta.

Two bench on the right, young man and woman playing music,
singing Am'rican song on the guitar. It sound so beautiful, like
church bell near our store. Other people in park claps when they
finishing their song, and although I feels very shy, I claps, too.
"Come on, Lakshmi," I courage myself. "No one knowing you
here. You in Am'rica now. You can claps, too."

What I wants to know, what is this hot dog? Everyone in
Am'rica eating it. At first I think it dog meat but now I know it
make of beef. One time I ask the husband how it taste, and he
make dirty face and say, "Chee-chee. In India, we not feed even
stray animal such bad food." But Rekha say it is number one foods
in Am'rica, so I thinking husband not know.

In our religion, we not allow to eat beef, so I gets the shock
when Maggie say her husband eat all meats. Maybe he convert
to beef when he marry her? Sometime Maggie say something so
fast, I confuse, but I ashame to ask her because then she think
I stupid.

Because I give Bobby the statue of Lakshmi, he send me a
present also. Bobby send me Maggie, I knows for sure. If I not
tries the suicide, how I meet Maggie? Her husband not even
shopping at our store, going to that cheater in Cedarville who
always charging extra. So how else we could meet? Even though
I not always understand Maggie, she so kind and patient with me.
Always she courage me—Lakshmi, you not stupid, Lakshmi you
not ugly, Lakshmi you great cook, Lakshmi you can go to night
school to learn the proper English, Lakshmi in Am'rica you can
do anything. And she show favor in my life. She ask many-many

question about Shilpa and Dada and Ma and the husband. She
even know about my Mithai, who I loves next to best after my
sister and father. Nobody in my life ever want to hear my stories
but her. Maggie is the important doctor but she never give tablet
or injection. I ask her last time and she laugh and say she is story
doctor. I laugh also but not understand the joke.

I knows it is time to walk to bus stop but I feeling so happy sitting at riverside. Dada always say the river is flowing in my body,
I so loving water.

I open the schedule, check time of next bus. I can sit here for
maybe five-ten more minutes. Stop is close by, only. A bee goes
goos-goos-goos around my head and it sound like it praying. I
feels sad thinking I must say good-bye to river soon, but then
I have brand-new thought: I can make repeat here next week.
Take early bus again and walk to this park. I am so excite by this
thought, I feel a-choke, like I cannot breathing properly. Then I
relax. I have learned to take two buses. I have not got lost once,
even. My husband not knowing his wife enjoying scene-scenery
in downtown, like a real Am'rican. I can do this again. I can come
here every week.

Anytime I am prideful, God find way to punish me good-proper.
So what you think? I miss second bus to Maggie's house by two
minute. So I has to wait for next one, and now I's fifteen minute
late. My heart sound thum-thum-thum like a tabla as I climbing
hill of Maggie street. Other time I love to look at the big houses,
the pretty flowerpots, the tall trees on Maggie street. But today I
look not left or right, just straight and half-walking, half-running
on pavement. I get to the driveway, turn left in it, my face cover
with sweat, breathing sounding like bad brake on old truck, and—
dhoom!—I runs straight into a tree or wall or building. It happen

so soon I not able to look what I run in, because next thing, I is sleeping on my back, looking up at the sky. But then sky view is blocked, because man's face looking at me, speaking something, his forehead pinch with worry. The man face brown like mine, and brown look so pretty over blue-sky background that I smiling.

"Can you hear me?" man saying. "Are you okay?" I starts to shake head yes, but then his face turn and he calls, "Maggie? Can you come out? There's been an accident."

Now my breath moving again in my body and allow me to speak. "I okay," I says. I tries to get up but man put hand on my shoulder.

"Just a minute. Maybe we should make sure nothing's broken before you attempt to get up?"

Now I's laughing. I put both hand behind me and lift up, so I sitting on the grass near driveway. "I okay," I repeats. "When I young, my sister and I use to bet who can jump from taller tree. I always winning." The Indian man smiling and this courage me to talk more. "My ma always say, 'Beti, you fast as cheetah and strong as Mithai.' "

"Mithai?" He look puzzle.

I laugh. "Not mithai. Mithai. My elephant. In my home village. He my friend."

"You jumped off trees and you had an elephant as a friend?" The man raise his eyebrow. "Some childhood, you had."

Suddenly, I feel ascare. Does this man think I show-off? Or liar? Or loose woman, talking to mens on street? I straight my blouse and stand up. My backside paining but I don't say anything.

"So, are you really fine?" he ask, and his caring remind me of Maggie. And next minute he say, "By the way, I'm Sudhir. Maggie's husband."

He give me hand for shake, but the husband angry if I touch stranger man's hand. So I folds my hands, like proper Indian wife. "Namaste," I says.

He looks surprise but then nodding. "Namaste. And you must be Lakshmi."

"How you are knowing my name?"

He acting like I ask stupid question. "What? Should I not know the name of the woman who brings me wonderful food cach week?"

I look at my empty hand. First time only, I bring no food this week. Husband get angry last evening. Say I giving away too much food to Maggie. Say I must to stop. Like fool woman, I listen.

I fold my hands again. "I so sorry, sir. I forgetting your food at home this week. But next week I bringing you tops food."

"No, no, no. I don't expect you to. Not every week." Sudhir shake his head left to right.

"Lakshmi?" Maggie come down driveway. Her face going from smile to frown. "You're really late. I was getting worried." She turn to her husband. "What're you still doing here?"

Sudhir point me with his chin. "We had an accident," he say. "I knocked poor Lakshmi down to the ground. She seems to be all right, though."

Maggie give Sudhir exact look Ma use to give Dada when he do stupid mistake. "What, were you texting while walking? Really, Sudhir. You can't even be trusted to make your way to the car without knocking people down."

Sudhir make funny face and wink me. He looking like old film star Shashi Kapoor, I thinking. So handsome.

Maggie give him quick kiss and say, "Bye. I'll see you tonight. Call if you're gonna be late." She give him small push. "Now, go. Lakshmi's already late for her session."

"Next week I promise I brings you best food," I say.

"And I promise to knock you down again," he answer. Then he smile, wave, and walks to where his car park on street.

Maggie take my hand as we go toward back porch. "What happened? Why are you so late?"

I about to tells her about the river and the grass and how I feels without body when I sits there, but I don't. I not know why I keep secret. But river is mine. I not wanting to share. Not even to Maggie. "I miss second bus," I says, and she satisfy.

"Okay, so what's on your mind this week?" Maggie ask, just like every week.

As if I have ghee in my mouth, the answer slip out. "Money," I says.

"Okay," Maggie say. She give couraging smile. "Go on."

But I myself not knowing what I mean. Since I having no money of my own, why for it on my mind?

Then I looks down and see my empty hands. Hands that not carry a tiffin box today for Sudhir sahib. How ashame I feel when he thanks me for cooking. I's poorer than beggar in my home village, I think. Even the low-caste Dalit farmers have some moneys of own. But I poor wife of rich businessman. The husband spend forty-fifty dollar every week on whiskey bottle. He treating his cardplayer friends to free food. He sending moneys to his sister in India every month. The husband only poor when he next to me. I works like a dog in his restaurant, in grocery store, but no salary. Even Menon sahib, who do so much favor to my family, who pay for my schooling, even he pay me little bit when I do accounts for his shop. But the husband is maha kanjoos. He see me as lime from which he squeeze last drop.

"Lakshmi?" Maggie foot move, as she doing when she inpatient. "Talk to me."

I swallow knot that come into my throat. One hot tear fall on my hand. I staring at it, because it looking like jewel. This is the only jewelry you ever have, Lakshmi, I think, and then more jewels landing on my hand.

"Sweetie? There's some Kleenex on the table if you need it. Why don't you tell me what's wrong?"

"My husband not giving me any pocket money," I say. "How you Am'ricans say? Allowance. I works and works in his business but I having no money of my own. Anythings I wants, I must to check with him first."

"Why don't you just take it?"

"Take how? From where?"

"I don't know. Where does he keep his money? His wallet?"

Sometime Maggie so stupid, I get irritate with her. "How I can touch his wallet?" I ask. I know my voice loud but I can't help. "He say he know if even ten cents missing."

Maggie sit back in her chair. "As his wife, you have a legal right to half of what he owns, Lakshmi. You know that, right?"

I so angry, I cannot sit properly. Plus, my backside is paining. "What I wanting half of his stupid restaurant for? Or half of grocery store? What I do with them? Wear them on my head?" I pulls on skin between my thumb and finger. "I just wants to have some extra money. Like twenty or thirty dollars a week. Bas. Why he can't give me that?"

"What would you do with that money, Lakshmi?"

But I not wanting to answer spending question. I wanting to answer earning question. I look at Maggie's big backyard. So many-many flowers and trees. At the end of yard is view of whole town below. I saw last week when we took walk around the yard. "Maggie," I says. "How you get to be rich in Am'rica? How you buying big house like this?"

Maggie look embarrass. "This is about you, Lakshmi," she say,

"So tell me, how do you think you can earn some money each month?"

I feel like if schoolteacher asking me question and I not knowing answer. "I don't knows," I say.

"Well, let's make a list of what you're good at. You know, what skills you have."

I hear the husband voice come through my mouth. "I's no good at anything. I big stupid."

Maggie look angry. "Hey. We decided two weeks ago you wouldn't talk about yourself like this. Remember?" She look at me quiet for minute and then she say, "You're a very smart woman, Lakshmi. Now tell me, what are you good at?"

I wanting to tell Maggie but Ma always telling not to be show-off. But inside myself I think, I good at maths. Menon sahib say he make more money after I do accounting books for him. And I's only fourteen years old then. And I takes good care of peoples. Shilpa, Dada, Ma. Last year Ma living, I doing everything for her because her fingers so twist. Shilpa at school all day, Dada working on our kheti. Ma and I's alone at home. I combing her hair, giving bath, feeding her, brush teeth, moving her in bed. Best part, Ma never sad. I telling her joke per joke, giving her news of village, singing Kishore Kumar songs, telling dialogue from *Amar, Akbar, Anthony* movie, her favorite.

Maggie make noise in her throat, like water boil. She waiting for me to talk.

"I good at cleaning," I say. "Sweeping, washing, making bed. Also, I likes to cook." I looks out the window. "And I loving to do planting. On balcony of our apartment, I grow tomatoes, cilantro, everything. All in pots."

"Well, those are great skills. You could get work cleaning people's homes. You could do landscaping for folks. Maybe do catering for parties? You have so much to offer, Lakshmi."

I laughs but it sound like I chokes. "The husband not allow me to go to other people's house to clean their dirt. Who he then going to get to help at store and restaurant? And we already do party catering. But he do all the cooking for that."

Maggie look at me. Her lips get tight, like thin piece of string. After some time, I feels hot. Why she look at me and not saying anything? Maggie my only friend in Am'rica but still I not knowing her well. What she think?

She open her mouth. Her eyes look liquid, like ink. She lean forward in chair. "Lakshmi," she say. "Every time I suggest something, you tell me why you can't do it. It's always 'My husband don't allow this and my husband won't allow that.' You never even try. You never ask him. You just assume things. You—"

"Please? What you mean by 'assume'? I not understand word."

"Assume. You know, believe. Take it as truth."

"Ah. I understand."

"Yes, well, here's what I want to say: When I look at you, do you know what I see? I see a young woman who is smart, bright, full of life. A woman who is not happy with her life, who wants to make some changes. Who wants to be independent. But she's scared. She isn't willing to take any risks. But here's the thing, Lakshmi. In order to grow, we have to take a chance. Even if it's scary. Especially if it's scary. Otherwise, nothing changes."

I having so many feeling, I don't know what to say. First I shy because Maggie say I smart, bright, and fool of life. I feeling prideful also. But then I's angry because Maggie not understand my life. Her husband who look like Shashi Kapoor, allow her to joke him, kiss him in driveway. My husband look at me same way he look if small, hard piece of bone stick in his teeth when he eat goat curry. Like something bad happen to him. My husband not allow me to drive, to call my sister, to make friends, to watch TV if he sleeping. One time when we first marry, I begs him to take me to lakeside to see lake. You know what he did? He fill water in bathtub and say, You want to see water? Look. Lake is just like big bathtub.

But among many things I feel by Maggie's words, I also feel something I not know name of. Something shiver, like what I use to feel when I sleep in bed and think of Bobby. Not dirty thought but something light. Like something good may happen. Like what if Maggie correct and I can change in my life?

"Lakshmi. Look at me. What're you thinking?"

I not sure how to tell Maggie twenty thought going zoom-zoom like race car in my head. So I say wrong thing, I say what I not belief. "I thinking that it is good if human being not get what he is praying for. Only God know what we need, not human being."

Maggie shake her head. "Come on, Lakshmi. You don't really believe that, do you? How does anything change if we don't work toward our goals?"

I quiet. I know Maggie correct, but I also know what I say is little true. Human being ask and ask for things. When Ma was so sick the last week, and in so much pain, still I was begging the God to not take my ma away. Day and night I pray, even when she screaming, even when she taking so much medicine, she doing soo-soo in bed. And when she dead, I so tired with God. But still I praying, please let me see my ma again, one time only. God listen until He fed up with me. Then He teach me the lesson.

"I wants to tell you story," I says to Maggie. "About dream I have."

Maggie look like she going to say no. Then she give out long breath and sit back in chair. "Okay," she say. "If you like."

15

AFTER MY MA die, I have a dream one night. I dream I meets with God and He asking me to make one wish. So I thinks and then I says, Make it so that for one day out of whole year, everybody get to meet their love ones who dead. People from heaven come to earth and spend whole day with living family. They can have party, picnic, festival, watch the TV together, go for the drive, I don't cares. Whatever living ones want them to do, they do.

So then God says to me, Who decide which day of year you can visit dead love ones? Everybody have different-different day or same day?

Now I gets ascare that God giving me my wish, so I say, You decide, please. You God.

So God think for minute and then He smile and say, August 15. That the day every person on earth get to spend with their dead love one.

As soon as He say date, I know why He pick it—August 15, India Independence Day. Ma was always telling me, God make whole world and all the peoples, but he love India tops. Before I use to argue, Ma, if God love India best of all, why He make it so poor? And Ma explain that just like a mother love her sickly child the best, God love India because it weak and need most protection. Before, I not sure if Ma making up story or not. Now I know Ma telling hundred percent truth.

So then I thinking, This is January, only. I trying to count how many days left until August 15 and I hurrying, hurrying, in my dream, count fast. All the time I ascare that August 15 so far away, but still I making plans for how to make Ma welcome when she come to visit. I think what foods to cook for her, what sweets to buy, whether to buy Coca-Cola or Fanta for her. Then I remindering that Ma won't come alonely; she bring her dead brother, maybe, because he having no alive family, and her dead parents, surely. Maybe some other friends who I don't know come with her? Our hut too small for such big party. Maybe Menon sahib letting us have party in his house? But then I remindering that Menon sahib having to have the party for his dead relations, also, and then I really ascare. Maybe whole world not big enough for all the dead love ones to come back. Where we going to put them all?

Now I understanding that I not really wanting to see all the dead love ones. I only wants to see my ma. So I turn to God with new request. But He is gone. I screaming and screaming for Him to come back so I can say him that I change my mind. I is crying now, looking for Him everywhere. And then God really angry with me 'cause he shake and shaking me, and I open my eyes, but instead of God, it my dada looking at me. "Lakshmi, Lakshmi, wake up," he say. "Why you crying in your sleep, my child?"

When I sees the kind in my dada's gray eyes, I feeling so happy, I get straight up from floor and put my head on his shoulder. He touch my hair. "You had a bad sapana, eh, child?" he say. "Don't be ascare."

I am feeling so happy to leaf God and be back with my dada. But then I feeling so sad because I know I not seeing my ma on August 15. In my dream, Ma seem so nearby, and now she so, so far again. My dada kind, but not having power like God. God having power, but not kind like Dada. But between Dada and God, my dada win.

My ma always say, God make world perfect, Lakshmi. He not put extra leaf on tree or one extra hair on your head. He make everything exact-exact. Our job to be happy with what he give. In famine time, he give us not one grain less than we needs. In good time, he give us not one grain more than we needs. I use to argue with Ma. Why for I still then hungry, Ma? Why my stomach still growling like a dog? And Ma smile and say, So when you sees a stray dog, you will knows to feed it. And then Ma take scoop of rice from her plate and put it on mine. Eat, she say. I not hungry today.

At that time, I eats everything Ma put on my plate. I not notice how thin she become. The need of my stomach was bigger than the need of my eyes, you see. But today, Maggie, I understands everything. How she took the food out of her mouth and put it in ours. Today, each time I eat a mango from our grocery store, I reminder how Ma never ate mango fruit. She only suck the big seed. The soft, sweet fruit part, she gave us. The best part of my ma, we got. What was left for her was the 'rthritis and the pain and the hungriness. And this made her happy. Because that what it meaning to be a mother.

Today I know: If I could choose between meeting my ma again or meeting God, I choose her. Each time I choose her.

Maggie be quiet after I finish my story. I knows she not understand why I telling this dream or what my story mean. After a minute, she look at clock on wall and say, "Well, it's time to stop for today."

I feel bad. Telling about my ma has make her come into the room with us, and I feeling again the sad I feels when she die. I fourteen year old then, but I become grown woman when my ma die.

Maggie stand up and I also. I about to say, "Okay, bye," but I see Maggie face red. Her eyes crying. I so surprise.

"It's hard, isn't it?" she say. "Losing your mom. God knows I
still miss mine. After all these years."

Something magic happen. I fly. Fly out of this room in Cedarville, over mountain, over river, fly like bird or like Air India, until
I standing in front of my dada's house. Inside, house is full of old
women. Shilpa and I is standing barefoot, holding hands. The old
womens crying, make caw-caw sound, like crows in early morning. But I's not crying. I's using my sleeve to wipe Shilpa's tears.
I telling her not to be sad, Ma is happy now, that I her ma now,
and I will look after her perfect-perfect. I promises her nobody
will make her to stop school. I will work two-three times more to
make the money. I tell her Ma is with the God now, and her body
is not paining. I saying everything other people saying to me. But
inside, my heart sour and rough as a guava fruit. Inside, someone
clean me empty like a pumpkin.

And I never cries. Not when they puts Ma's body on the pyre.
Not when priest make fire and Ma turn into smoke and ash. Not
when I hears Shilpa crying at night. Not while helping Dada in the
kheti. Not when doing accounting for Menon sahib, writing in the
big red cloth ledger. Not when Ramu, the stray dog Ma give milk
to every evening, sit outside our house and cry whoo-whoo-whoo
for one straight week. Dada finally make Ramu go away with stick,
because he say Ramu know his heart better than God do.

I tell you truth: I wicked woman. I never cries for my ma's
death.

But now I catch Air India plane back to Maggie's porch. I see
the tears in Maggie's eyes. They looking like stars in night sky. For
first time since I meeting Maggie, I feeling useful.

"You know why you missing your ma?" I says. "It because dead
peoples needs to know we still remindering them. Otherwise
they feeling alonely, thinking we forgets them. That is why only
God gives us missing feeling in heart. To keep them company."

Maggie take my hand and squeeze. "You're wonderful. But I'm supposed to help you, not the other way around."

"Why you alone to help? We friends, no?"

She look to saying something but then she stop. "Sure," she say. "Sure."

16

MAGGIE EYED THE boxes of frozen hors d'oeuvres that Sudhir was tossing into their cart. "Honey," she gasped. "I thought this was a small dinner for your chair and a few other faculty members. Who do you think's gonna eat all this food?"

Sudhir stopped in the middle of Costco, a sheepish look on his face. They stood under the fluorescent lights, facing each other, vulnerable to the mad frenzy of the other shoppers, who maneuvered oversize carts around the couple. "Ah, yes, I've been meaning to tell you. I sort of changed my mind. I mean, I'm thinking if we're throwing a party, why not invite the entire department?"

Despite her dismay, Maggie laughed. "You're incorrigible. Remember you promised me last time we weren't doing any more big parties?"

"I know. But really, I was going to invite at least two other couples along with Brent and his wife, anyway. So I figured, what's fifteen more people?"

"You don't know the difference between six or fifteen? And you're the math professor?" Maggie reached out for a bottle of olive oil as they began to wheel the cart again. "At least promise me you won't invite any grad students."

"Well," Sudhir began. "That's hard, you know."

Maggie shook her head. I don't know why you're surprised, she told herself. When she'd first met him, Sudhir was sharing an apartment in the Village with three other students. Located above a bakery at the corner of West Third and MacDougal, it was the gathering place for all their friends. Sudhir and his roommates, two other Indian students, and a guy from Brazil cooked steaming pots of food every weekend—aloo gobi, rice pilaf, fish curry, Chinese spring rolls, Manchurian chicken—and the apartment filled with students wandering in and out, eating off of paper plates. Someone would bring a bottle of rum to make piña coladas; someone else would carry in a blender and a bag of ice. There would be killer games of gin rummy in one room, teams playing Scrabble in another. The apartment was like an all-night salon or speakeasy. There was just one sacrosanct rule—no one was allowed to touch Sudhir's stereo system. It was a cheap Panasonic three-in-one affair, but it was the first real purchase Sudhir had made in the U.S. out of his graduate assistantship money, and he loved that stereo. The others groaned and mocked the music he played as hopelessly outdated—in the late 1970s, Sudhir was still listening to the Beatles, Bob Dylan, the Bee Gees, and Simon & Garfunkel. Maggie, raised on the R&B records Wallace used to play, tried introducing him to Sly and the Family Stone, James Brown, Jimmy Cliff. But of all these performers, Sudhir really loved only Bob Marley—a fact that Maggie grew to regret when, in the late fall of 1980, he went through a three-month period of repeatedly playing "Redemption Song" back to back with Dylan's "Hurricane" until he drove them all crazy.

But Sudhir's hospitality, the casual ease with which he opened up his home to his friends and their friends, his generosity in feeding whoever wandered in, the commune-like atmosphere that he created, spoke powerfully to Maggie. She had not known how lonely she was until she met Sudhir and his brand of Indian hospitality. By this time, her mother was long dead, Wallace had moved to Florida with his new wife, Odell had settled in Paris, and Maggie was commuting to NYU from Brooklyn, where Mrs.

Tabot, their old neighbor, was still renting her a room. The four years at Wellesley had been fruitful but isolating, hers being one of a handful of black faces on a campus that felt wintry-white. She was popular, or at least well liked, and her roommates and professors were too liberal and sophisticated for her to experience any overt racism. And for a city girl, there was an ever present awe and gratitude for Wellesley's tranquil, pastoral beauty, for its sheltering embrace. The rude awakening, the bruising delivered by the real world, came each time she and her friends drove into Boston. The first time she tried buying apples at Haymarket, she looked into the ruddy, hostile face of the Irish vendor, who yelled at her for touching the fruit, and she shuddered. She walked on, telling herself to not take it personally, that she had just encountered the legendary Boston rudeness, when she heard him mutter, "Dirty little black bitch." She spun around, her eyes already filling with tears, but he was smiling at another customer, using a paper towel to wipe down the apple.

But such incidents were rare. Wellesley's brick buildings, its lush, woodsy campus, its air of erudition, its intellectualism, protected her. What it didn't, couldn't, protect her from was the knowledge that for all practical purposes, she was totally alone. Odell often told her to move to Paris after graduation, that he would support her while she continued her education, but she knew better than to take him up on the offer. Her brother was in a new marriage, a baby on the way. There was no way she was going to show up at his doorstep.

And so Sudhir's apartment, with its strange odors, its outdated music, its open front door, its all-night conversations and card sessions, its Indian guys who walked around barefoot on the green-carpeted floor, became her refuge.

Maggie had grown up in a home where her parents had only occasionally had guests over for dinner and then just another couple and their kids. Their main source of socializing were the Saturday gatherings held at the Church of the Open Heart, which the family had attended faithfully until Maggie's mother, Hilda, took ill. Packed into the tiny storefront church with its two oscillating wall fans, the Elder Lawrence Jemmont beaming at his parishioners, they sweated, prayed, and clapped as they sang, gave praise to the Lord, and finally, feasted on whatever food people had brought— jerk chicken, goat curry, fried plantains, currant rolls. The atmosphere in the MacDougal apartment revived her dim memories of those long-past Saturday socials. But the thought of inviting all these people into her home and then cooking for them, as Sudhir did each weekend, was alien to her.

Until she went with him to India the first time after they were married. Then it all made sense, and she realized that the hospitality he displayed to all guests was larger than he was—it was cultural, hereditary, something coded into his DNA. Their time in India was an endless procession of relatives visiting them at Sudhir's parents' home, and going to visit relatives at their homes. Every visit, no matter how short, involved food. They were invited, begged, forced, emotionally blackmailed, arm-twisted into eating a meal at every home they visited. There were hurt feelings if they refused; inter-family rivalries were provoked if they let slip that they'd eaten at the last home they'd visited. They were cajoled into staying for dinner, and if not that, having dessert or a fruit juice, or come, come, at the very least some sweetmeats, baba, and if not even that, please, you cannot leave without taking a cup of tea. As infuriating as it was to be browbeaten into eating, Maggie learned something important about her husband during that visit. She realized that Sudhir had simply, perhaps unconsciously, duplicated his Bengali upbringing in his apartment in New York, and she learned that he had done more than provide her with a sense of home, of family, of belonging—he had done the same for himself. One of the things she'd always admired and feared about Sudhir was how self-sufficient and self-contained he seemed, and now she saw how deep that instinct was in him. What he didn't have, he built.

I guess it isn't surprising that we are apparently hosting a party for more than fifteen people, a bemused Maggie thought, half-watching as Sudhir put three cartons of eggs into the cart. She was about to stop him when she heard a voice call her name.

She knew who it was before she turned around, heard the thick accent and recognized it as Lakshmi's. Her heart sank a bit as she saw that Lakshmi's husband was also walking toward them. Instinctively, she leaned in to Sudhir.

"Hello, Maggie. Hello, sir." Lakshmi's voice was breathless, as if she'd been running. "From far away, I see you. I says to my husband, that's Maggie madam, for sure."

"Hello, Lakshmi," Sudhir said quietly, and the other man looked startled. Before he could speak, Lakshmi said, "This is Sir, Madam's husband. Sir, this is my mister."

Adit Patil looked uncomfortable, but Sudhir smiled pleasantly. "Hi, how are you?" he said. "I think I was in your store years ago. Business is good, I hope?"

The man shrugged. "Chalta hai," he said. "Economy is so bad." A look of cunning came over his face. "If we can get business from more top clients like you, sir, we will do better. I can offer five percent discount on many items."

Lakshmi looked mortified. "Sorry," she said to Maggie, shaking her head. "Husband always thinking of business, only."

But Adit didn't look remotely chastised. "That what business-man do." He waved his hand in the direction of his cart. "That's why we here to do the weekly shopping. For restaurant. Work is our life." He eyed their cart, which was brimming with frozen foods. "You also opening restaurant, sir?" He grinned, and Maggie thought it made him look fifteen years younger.

Sudhir laughed dutifully. "No. Just stuff for a work party we're having next weekend."

Adit turned an accusatory eye on Maggie, and she thought she knew exactly what the man was thinking—what kind of wife doesn't cook for her husband's party? She flushed and heard Adit say, "You should give us catering order, sir, for future party. We provide napkin, plates, food, hot plate, everything. We can do serving also. You just sit and enjoy."

The man was really shameless, canvassing for business in the middle of Costco. Unable to look at Lakshmi, Maggie turned toward Sudhir. "Okay, sweetie," she said. "We should go."

Sudhir was looking at Adit with a peculiar expression. "Why wait for the next party? I'm happy to give you the order for this one." He waited for a second and then lowered his voice. "But here's the deal, boss. My guests are tired of the usual Indian restaurant fare—you know, butter chicken, saag paneer, and all that. I want to serve something special."

"We will make fresh, special food, sir—"

"No. You don't understand. I want something totally different. Like the homemade food your wife brings for us every week." Sudhir rubbed his chin in an exaggerated way that only Maggie recognized as deliberate. He snapped his fingers as if something had just occurred to him. "In fact, I'd like her to cater the party. And we will pay her, of course. What do you say?"

Even as she understood what Sudhir was doing, Maggie was surprised. It was so unusual for him to interfere like this. But then she remembered: A few days ago, she had shared with him what Lakshmi had told her about wanting to earn her own money. Sudhir had been fiddling with the stereo, and she had thought he was only half-listening to what she was saying. Obviously, her husband had heard every word—and heard the frustration in her voice as she had recounted Lakshmi's plight. She felt a surge of love and gratitude toward Sudhir.

But she was also concerned. No matter how loosey-goosey their arrangement, Lakshmi was still technically her client. It was a violation of every ethical rule to hire her to work for them. Sudhir knew better. Now she would have to be the bad guy and squelch the idea before—

"My wife no good cook, sir," Adit was saying. "She not know how to do catering-fatering. But I can—"

"Excuse me, Mr. Patil. Your wife is a fantastic cook. We have proof of that." The words were out of her mouth, sharper than she'd intended, and the man was glaring at her with open hostility. What the hell was she saying? And why?

Sudhir smiled the bland, inoffensive smile that she had come to know so well. "Arre, why are we discussing this? It seems like we ought to ask Lakshmi's opinion, no, since she's the person who would have to do all the hard work?" He turned toward Lakshmi. "I have fifteen-twenty guests coming next Saturday. Do you think you can manage such a large order?"

Lakshmi turned mutely toward her husband, who appeared to be doing some mental calculations. Before either one could speak, Sudhir added, "I don't want to spend more than five or six hundred dollars on food. Can you manage on that budget?"

Adit looked at his wife, blinked twice, and Maggie saw Lakshmi relax; for the first time, she looked directly at Sudhir. "I can manage," she said. Then, with a quick glance at her husband, "But I do all cooking in your kitchen, sir. That way, food remain hot and fresh. I can do serving to guest also."

Her husband looked like he was about to protest, but Sudhir said, "Done." And before any of them could say anything, Sudhir put his arm around Maggie and said, "Okay, honey. We need to move. I'm sure you can call Lakshmi during the week and work out the details."

"We talk tomorrow, yes, Maggie? When I comes to sees you?"

A hundred ethical concerns were once again raising themselves in Maggie's head. She forced herself to smile. "Okay," she said. She nodded at Adit. "Nice to see you."

"Thank you, madam," he replied, not a trace of the earlier hostility in his voice.

She waited until they were out of earshot before turning toward Sudhir. "Hey," she said in a soft voice. "What was that about? Lakshmi's my client. This is really blurring the lines, you know."

"I know." Sudhir paused in front of a large box of ginger cookies before deciding against them and wheeling the cart forward. "Look," he said at last. "You haven't told me much about Lakshmi's situation, but you did mention she came to you from the hospital. So . . . I can use my imagination a little bit, okay? And the other day you mentioned the money thing." He threw a quick glance at Maggie. "I know a thing or two about immigrant women like her, okay? Poor, uneducated, isolated . . ."

"Lakshmi has an eighth-grade education."

"Yah. Probably in some decrepit, government-run school. That's why she speaks the awful English that she does."

"Your point is?"

"My point is, Maggie, you can do years of therapy with her. And with all due respect, it won't change one damn thing in her life. Because what Lakshmi needs is not analysis. What she needs is a job. Independence. Money of her own."

Maggie looked at her husband with begrudging admiration. There it was, evidence of Sudhir's scientific, pragmatic mind. Without having spent an hour with Lakshmi, he had sized her up accurately. The funny part was, Maggie had believed that she was helping Lakshmi by listening to her stories about life in her village, her relationship with her parents and sister, even stories about the damn elephant. She had tried to figure out the symbolism of the elephant, what Lakshmi meant when she talked about him, why he loomed so large in her stories. But sometimes, she now chastised herself, an elephant is just an elephant. She imagined taking the case of Lakshmi and her beloved elephant to the next meeting of the American Psychological Association, what a field day her colleagues would have trying to understand the sexual, cultural, linguistic significance of the animal. She suppressed the giggle that formed in her throat.

"What're you thinking?"

She put an arm around Sudhir's waist. "I'm thinking how lucky I am to be married to you rather than some dewy-eyed humanities professor."

"Don't you ever forget it." Sudhir grinned.

She smiled back. And pushed aside the picture of Peter that flashed across her mind.

17

W HEN MAGGIE WALK inside our grocery store, I feel like it Diwali, when we all go to see the firecrackers lighted from Menon sahib's veranda and every house in the village burning at least a small oil lamp. So bright, so happy, everything seem. I knows she coming to pick me up but still I feeling so excite when she walk inside. She remove the sunglasses and push to her head, just like film star, and then smile when she see me.

"Hey," she say. "You ready?"

"Just few more minutes," I say. "Need to pack few more items." Out of side of my eye, I see husband, counting and writing down everything I take from store—two packets of gram flour, big bag basmati rice, two large packet of cashew nuts, packet of tapioca. Now he stick pen behind his ear—why he do this? he look just like the fat baniya who sit in Menon sahib's warehouse—and come to Maggie.

"Lakshmi pack half of store," he say to her, pointing to the five cardboard box waiting by the counter. "Enough food for two parties."

Maggie look surprise at amount of food. She open her mouth to say something but I move quickly toward back of store where freezer is. I takes out three packets of frozen parathas and puts them in cloth bag before husband can see. All morning he watching me like a lizard, telling that I going to broke him with amount of food I taking. Truly, he is having no shame—Maggie giving me the there-py free of charge all this time, but he not feeling his debt.

I comes back to where they are. Husband giving her tour of store, as if it is White House. I feels angry to him but also understand. What else poor man having? This store his life. The husband tell me his story: how he come to the New York seventeen year ago. He work in friend's restaurant daytime and drive taxi at night. Only sleep on Sunday. No go to movie, temple, nothing, just work and work. Live in apartment with four other mens. And slowly, slowly, he save the money. First he build his parents the house in their village. He get his sister marry and pay big dowry. Then he hear about this business in Chesterfield from another friend. The owner is selling because his wife die in upstair apartment—my apartment—and he so sad he wanting to move back to India. So the husband come from the New York, take look, and next day he make the offer. Get whole business cheap, apartment come with furniture. He even keep bed other lady die in. After Rekha tell me story of other lady die in bed, I say no to sleeping in it. For one week, I sleeps on sofa. Then husband curse me and call me stupid but he buy new bed.

Maggie see me and nods. Husband still talking but Maggie ready to go. I look at the clock on the wall. I wants to go before Rekha come. "Hello, ji," I say to the husband. "Can you help carry boxes out to car?"

He angry with me for stopping his story, but he pick up boxes.

Maggie's car have no roof and I so excite. Always I wanting to sit in such car. After we put grocery in truck, I gets in. Husband still giving me instruction—make sure oil not too hot or it burn, dessert should be out of fridge for half hour before serving—as if this his recipes, not mine.

Maggie get in, thank him, and start car. "What time you be home?" husband call. "Remember, tomorrow morning . . ."

"Oh, it will be late before we can drop Lakshmi off," Maggie say. "I will need her to clean up after the party. So please don't worry."

Maggie take charge in such way, husband don't know what to say. He just stand there shaking head as we drive off.

In my village, there is railway track. The trains that pass by so crowded that many men passengers riding on the roofs. When I small, I begs Dada to let me ride train roof, but he say it dangerful, every month many accident. But it look so free and happy to me to ride on top of train.

Maggie's car give me same free feeling. The breeze make my hair dance and my heart feel the music. I's so lucky, I think. In last few month, I walk in woods with Maggie, I sits by the river alone, and now I ride in this car. I turns to look at Maggie. Ma used to say: When the God enter into your house, he not enter looking like the God. He enter looking like human being. God enter my life looking like Maggie.

"Holy cow," Maggie say, laughing. "I don't think I've ever seen you look this happy. What're you grinning about?"

"Grinning?"

"Smiling. Like this." She make face to show me.

"Ah." How's to make Maggie understand? I don't know why I so happy. "I is happy because . . . for so many reasons."

Maggie pat my knee. "Good." She look serious. "I want you to remember this feeling. How you feel right now. This is what we're working toward. Do you understand?"

I nods. But I not understand. How you work toward happy? Happy is by chance, like whether enough rains come for crops one year or not. Like whether you beautiful like Shilpa or ugly

like me. Happy is same feeling as running barefoot through the
fields. Then one day your ma get sick and you stop running.

First time I enters Maggie house through kitchen instead of back
porch. As we walks in, I hear the voice I hearing all my life. It is
Dada's best singer, Hemant Kumar, singing Dada's most best song.
It say, *Tum pukar lo, tumhara intezaar hai, tum pukar lo.* Dada use
to sing song to Ma all the time. It mean, You call for me. I is waiting for you. It not sound beautiful when I says it in the English. In
Hindi, it open hole in your heart. And after Ma die, Dada play this
song all the time on tape player he keep near his bed. Every time
I hears this song, my body hair get raise. Hemant Kumar voice is
soft like butter melt in pan. When he sing, it is like touching small
piece of sky, or your mother's hand cold on your face when you
having the fever. It is beautiful love song, but it make you feel sad
and empty and slow. Even the husband love this song. When it play
on CD, he get look on face that make me cry.

    "Hi," Sudhir sir say as he come to us to take boxes out of
our hand. He put them on kitchen platform. He wearing white
kurta-pajama and I feels so happy. Even in this Am'rican house
I have India.

    "You like this song?" I ask Sudhir sir and he shake head yes.

    "Very much," he say.

    "You see movie?"

    "*Khamoshi?* Yes, I believe so. But many years ago. I don't re-
ally remember it."

    "Dharmendra sing this song, not Rajesh Khanna," I says. "Wa-
heeda Rehman in love with him. But he not loving her."

    "I see." He smile, like I say something joke. He turn to Maggie
and say, "You see? Bollywood songs. The great equalizer."

    I not understanding what he meaning. Maggie taking out the

Ziploc bags of onions from the fridge. "We chopped them last night," she say. "In the food processor. A little less work for you."

I a little ascare to cook in this kitchen. Everything look so new and rich, and what if something to break? But I remembers what Rekha tell me yesterday. "You great cook, Didi," she say. "You will cook so tasty food, these peoples will forget even their grandma's name."

"You show me where everything is," I say. "After that, both you go relax. I does everything."

"No way," Sudhir sir say. "I want to learn the recipes. I'm gonna stick around, okay?"

What I can say? His kitchen, he pay. He the boss. "Okay, sir," I tell to him.

Both mister and missus talk at same time. "Lakshmi, if you're not comfortable having Sudhir help you, just say so . . ." "What's this 'sir' business? Just call me Sudhir . . ."

They both so loving to me. Even at Menon sahib's house, I never made so welcome. "Many thanks," I say. "Good if Sudhir babu stay with me in kitchen. Job will go by quickly."

Sudhir rub his hand. "Great. So put me to work. What do you need done first?"

Before I reply, Maggie say, "I'm going upstairs for a couple of hours, okay? I have an article to finish." She smile at me. "I picked up some stuff for sandwiches earlier today. I'll make lunch for us in a couple of hours."

Sudhir babu give Maggie small kiss and then turn to me. "Okay, what do you need?"

I give him bag of garlic. "Please to chop these in little-little piece. I will start to fry onion."

In the restaurant, the husband like to cook alone. At home, he not enter our kitchen. It is nice to have the company while cooking. And Sudhir babu so nice. He put on more Hindi songs and often he sing along. Sometime he ask me what film this or that song from, but when he see I need to think, he being quiet. He help me understand the oven buttons and how to use food processor. When kitchen begin to get hot from cooking, he get me big glass of ice water and put slice of lime in it. He taste my gravy with his finger and say it is the best, better than his mother's food, even. In his own house, in his own kitchen, he treat me like I am mistress and he taking order from me.

18

THE PARTY WAS a success. Everyone had a great time, and the last guest didn't leave until after eleven-thirty. The wine flowed freely, the conversation easily, and Lakshmi's cooking was a hit. People went back for second and third helpings; even Brent Wolfstein, the patrician, silver-headed chair of Sudhir's department, cleaned his plate with his fingers, while Lakshmi beamed and urged him to eat more. Lakshmi herself was a revelation—an hour before the first guest arrived, she slipped into a red and gold outfit, and later, she waited on the guests as if she were the hostess of the party. She explained the ingredients of individual dishes, regaled small clusters of guests with stories about her mother's cooking, advised people on what spices to stock their kitchen with. Maggie marveled at the transformation—there was not a trace of the sullen, depressed woman from a few months ago. She had the feeling that she was witnessing the real Lakshmi: the Lakshmi who had existed in India, before her unfortunate marriage to a man who didn't care about her, before her exile to a strange and foreign country.

Now they were driving her back home, and Maggie was worried. Lakshmi had insisted on staying to clean up after the party and it was well past midnight and they had at least a ten-minute drive ahead of them. Maggie had a feeling that Lakshmi's husband would not be happy about his wife returning home at this late hour, and she dreaded facing his hostile, glowering face. She had enough on her mind—the fact that she was meeting Peter while Sudhir was in town, the fact that she had a conference paper due next week, and . . .

And. What was nagging at her? This slightly dyspeptic, deflated feeling was more than the normal letdown that she experienced after a festivity. So what was it? What explained this melancholy as she sat in the backseat, listening to Sudhir and Lakshmi talking quietly in the front? She remembered feeling happy when Brent had whispered, "I'm sure Sudhir has told you that I'm urging him to apply for my position. I think he'd be a shoo-in, Maggie. Make sure he applies." She remembered the almost maternal pride that had surged through her when she'd overheard Nasreen Chopra, whose husband taught in the physics department, ask Lakshmi whether she was available to cater a party for her next month. And her growing delight as two other guests had asked Lakshmi for her phone number.

In a flash, Maggie remembered: Lakshmi bending at the waist, holding a tray of lamb kebabs before a seated Gina Adams. Gina had popped one in her mouth, her eyes widening with delight. "Gosh, these are incredible," she'd said to Lakshmi. "We've been to India several times, but I've never tasted food like this." A smiling Maggie had walked up behind Lakshmi, and Gina turned toward her. "This woman is a find," she said. "How on earth did you get this lucky? How did you get her to cook this delicious food for you?"

Before Maggie could respond, Lakshmi had shrugged and said, "Why not I cook for her? Maggie my best friend."

Gina had nodded and smiled uncertainly, as had several of the other women within earshot. Perhaps it was the uncertainty in Gina's smile, the older woman's confusion at Lakshmi's easy blurring of class lines, that made Maggie say, "Well, we're not really . . . That is, we're just trying to help her."

Lakshmi had half-turned, gazed at her for a moment, and then hurried away into the kitchen. Maggie lingered in the living room, chitchatting with her guests, willing Lakshmi to come back out with fresh hors d'oeuvres. After a few minutes, she excused herself and strolled into the kitchen. Lakshmi was sitting on a stool, sipping a glass of water, and staring out the window. "Hey," Maggie said gently. "Are you resting? You must be so tired."

Lakshmi shook her head curtly, staring at the table. "I okay."

"Listen," Maggie said. "What happened—"

Lakshmi rose. "I goes now, Maggie," she said. "I will take the bus back. Everything is ready. You just please to put out to serve guests."

Maggie felt a rising desperation. "Lakshmi," she said. "You can't leave in the middle of the party." She put her hand lightly on the younger woman's wrist. "I'm sorry. I said something stupid . . . I know I hurt your feelings. I know you . . ." She shook her head and started again. "I'm a doctor. Do you understand? I'm not supposed to be friends with my patients. Not for my sake but for yours," even as she asked herself, Is that really the reason why? "But you know what? You were right. You are my friend. And I'm sorry that I denied it."

Lakshmi looked at her, and Maggie saw that her nose was bright red. "I not angry with you, Maggie," she said. "I have eyes. I see. I know your friends have important job, go to the college. I know I's nothing . . ."

"Don't say that. Please."

" . . . that I can't be friends with people like you."

"Listen," Maggie said fervently. "My mother had a high school education. My father didn't finish sixth grade. And yet they were two of the smartest people I knew. Okay? So don't tell me—"

"Honey?" Sudhir came into the kitchen, a Heineken in his hand. "What are you doing? Aren't there any more appetizers coming?" He looked from one woman to the other, suddenly aware of the tense atmosphere. "Is everything all right?"

There was a second's silence, and then Lakshmi smiled. "Everything fine, Sudhir babu," she said. "You go. I bring food out in ten second." She hurried toward the oven and pulled out a tray.

Sudhir threw Maggie a quizzical look before leaving the kitchen. She waited until he was out of earshot and then walked toward Lakshmi. "Thank you," she said.

"Mention not." Lakshmi gave her a slight push. "You go out, also, na, Maggie. I take care of everything."

Maggie had left, not knowing how much Lakshmi understood or whether she was still insulted. She had hoped to have a chance to resume the conversation after their guests left, but Lakshmi had rushed around, anxious to clean up the kitchen and go home. Maggie had been much too tired to force the issue, and the moment had passed.

Now, in the car, she could only hope that Lakshmi had forgotten the earlier rudeness. Maggie closed her eyes and heard the steady murmur of Sudhir and Lakshmi's voices. Sudhir was laughing softly at something Lakshmi was saying, and the sound of it filled Maggie with pleasure. She knew enough from her visits to Calcutta that in India, Sudhir would not talk to someone from Lakshmi's station in life as easily as he was doing right now. So much would divide them in India: language, region, class, caste, education. Here in America, all the differences paled under the imperative of their brown skin. And the tenuous links they shared—a love for Hindi film music, a passion for Indian cooking—carried so much more weight here than they would back home.

Stop it, Maggie scolded herself. You're overthinking things. And what's with this sudden color consciousness? (A snapshot of Peter's white, strangely vulnerable-looking bare back flashed before her eyes, but she blinked and the image disappeared.) Sudhir likes Lakshmi. It's as simple as that. He is amused by her. He recognizes her goodness, her innocence. Also, he feels sorry for her. That's it. In any case, I'm glad that my husband likes my friend.

Friend. How easy it was to think of Lakshmi as a friend. But claiming her as one in front of her guests, why, that had proved to be a different matter, hadn't it? Both of her parents would've disapproved of the way she'd rebuffed Lakshmi a few hours ago. Though her mother had been light-skinned enough to pass, the very idea was anathema to her. Instead, she had married Wallace Seacole, the darkest-skinned man she knew. For years, Hilda worked at a small paper factory where she was active in the union and her coworkers were blacks and other dark-skinned immigrants. Hilda felt a natural affinity between herself and them, even when the new immigrants initially saw her as nothing but a small, invisible black woman. Once they got to know her, they recognized her formidable intelligence, her energetic, relentless devotion to the union, her scathing humor, her matter-of-fact compassion and generosity, and they loved her. At home, Hilda never said a bad word about whites as a race—although she had a lot to say about individual bosses and policemen and grocers—but her loyalties were clear. She threw in her lot with the darker races, not because they were morally better or smarter or kinder than whites, but simply because they were oppressed. In sports, in politics, in war, her loyalty was always with the underdogs—the Red Sox over the Yankees, the Vietnamese over the Americans, even African dictators over their colonial masters. She remained silent only on the question of the Israelis versus the Palestinians; she would shake her head at the absurdity of two oppressed peoples fighting each other.

This was how they'd been raised, she and Odell, though, of course, Mama had died while still young. Maggie hardly remembered the years when Mama lay wasting away in bed. Now, if she ever dared to allow herself to think of those awful years, all she could conjure up was a figure in bed that started out as a woman and ended up as a ghost. Of a frail voice that would call "Hello, darlin'" when she came home from school. Of a bony hand that would reach out to stroke her hair, of curious gray eyes that would search her face like a searchlight, looking, looking, for something, until it would seem to Maggie that the most important thing in the world was that her mother find whatever she was hunting for in her daughter's face, that what she saw reflected there should please her. And then the dry lips would thin into something that Maggie presumed was a smile. If a ghost could smile.

In the car, Maggie blinked back the tears that formed in her eyes. She leaned forward in the seat and lightly tapped Lakshmi on the left shoulder. She turned around immediately. "Hah, Maggie?" she said, her voice eager and strong despite the long day and the late hour.

Lakshmi's voice was so devoid of malice, so trusting, that the tears returned to Maggie's eyes. She had obviously been forgiven for the earlier slight, and it surprised her, how relieved she felt. "Listen," she said. "I've been thinking. You had all these people asking you to cater for them. I bet some of them will also need a housecleaner. You should . . ."

"You think so, Maggie?" Lakshmi's voice had a breathless tone that made Maggie laugh. She's so young, she thought. She often forgot that Lakshmi was only in her early thirties. With a whole life ahead of her.

"I do. But here's what I'm thinking. You're gonna need to learn to drive, Lakshmi. It will make your life so much easier if you can drive."

There was an abrupt silence. She noticed that Sudhir was looking at her in the rearview mirror, but it was too dark to see the expression on his face. Then Lakshmi said, "I's ascare to do the driving."

"Nonsense. Sudhir can teach you. He's a great driver."

Both of them spoke at once: "My husband, he not allow gents to teach me driving." "Ahem. Ah, Maggie, I don't think that's a good idea for me to teach Lakshmi. If someone were to see us . . ."

Good God, Maggie thought. I'm not asking you guys to have sex with each other. What's the big deal, for heaven's sake? However, she knew better than to say that aloud. She knew she was testing Adit Patil's patience by whisking away his wife like this. She had to respect that Lakshmi knew her own circumstances better than Maggie ever could. "Okay," she said, sighing. "It was just an idea."

She began turning her head to look out the window again when she heard Lakshmi say, "But Maggie, you can teach me to do the driving. We can do the there-py in the car instead of the house, no?"

She was about to refuse when Hilda Seacole spoke to her: This solidarity business I used to talk about ain't just—what do you youngsters call it?—theoretical. It means putting your body, your physical self, on the line, baby girl. Even when—especially when—it ain't convenient.

But Mama . . . Maggie started to argue, but Hilda had vanished. What was left was a vibration in the air, a certain expectation, as if Hilda were scanning her baby girl's face, waiting to see what kind of a human being she and Wally had raised. Maggie looked around for a way out, tried to think of something that would let her out of the hole she'd dug for herself. But Hilda Sea-cole had pulled up the rope after her.

"Yeah, okay," she said reluctantly. "I guess we can give it a try."

She lifted her head to see Sudhir looking at her in the rearview mirror. This time there was no mistaking what he was thinking. He was laughing at her.

19

L AKSHMI CLIMBED INTO the driver's seat of the parked car and then swung her feet so they were hanging out the door. Bending slightly, she removed first one shoe, then the other, pivoted, and threw them in the backseat. She put her bare foot against the gas pedal, so that the car emitted a low growl. Maggie felt like growling herself. "What're you doing?" she asked.

"My uncle is truck driver," Lakshmi said. "He always say wearing the shoes not good for driving. Maybe this is reason why I is not driving good."

No, the reason you are not driving good is because you're an absolute imbecile when it comes to things mechanical. The uncharitable thought crossed Maggie's mind before she suppressed it. Stop, she chided herself. Everybody sucks when they learn to drive. Remember how bad you were when you first started? Thank God Odell had the patience of a saint.

She forced herself to remember how easily Lakshmi had passed the written exam to get her temporary license. Her reading comprehension was much better than her spoken English. Maggie had driven her to the DMV and had sat nervously in the waiting room while Lakshmi took her test. Maggie had not expected her to pass her first time, let alone do as well as she had done. Lakshmi, however, didn't seem surprised at all. So be supportive, Maggie told herself. There's nothing stupid about this woman.

But the next second, the car made an awful scraping noise and Maggie's good intentions went out the window. She jerked around to see that Lakshmi was turning the ignition even though the car was already running. "Stop that," she yelled, smacking Lakshmi's hand to knock it away.

The noise stopped abruptly as Lakshmi's hand fell into her lap. It was replaced by a stunned silence as a startled Lakshmi stared at Maggie. Already, her nose was turning red.

"Oh, shit," Maggie said. "I'm sorry. I just reacted to the sound of the car. . . . You don't turn the key when the car is already on. It can damage it. You understand?"

Lakshmi gulped hard and nodded. These driving lessons are no more fun for her than they are for you, Maggie reminded herself. She sighed. She was distracted today. She had begun seeing Peter again, despite repeatedly telling him that their affair couldn't continue. Each time he'd nod and say that he understood. And then, two days later, there would be a text or an email from him asking to see her. And being a weak, contemptible idiot, she would find herself driving to his house, practicing her speech of how this was the final time they would be meeting, how she really meant it, how much she loved her husband. Peter would be waiting for her and she would recite her practiced speech and he would nod solemnly and he would kiss her and . . .

God. Was it her, or was it hot in this car? Maggie's hand involuntarily went toward the air conditioner knob, but Lakshmi said in a pleading voice, "Please, Maggie, I's cold."

Maggie gritted her teeth. She should've insisted that Sudhir give Lakshmi driving lessons. He was so much more patient than she was. What Lakshmi and Sudhir had said about Lakshmi's husband being upset if she was riding around with a strange man—well, they were lying to him anyway, right? Instead of being at therapy, this was what she and Lakshmi had done the last three weeks. What was the damn difference who taught her to drive?

"Maggie? What you need me to do?" Lakshmi's voice was tentative, shaky, and hearing it, Maggie felt a pang of guilt.

"Let's just drive around the parking lot a few times," she said gruffly. "I want you to focus on keeping the steering wheel steady." As always, the car took off like a shot. "Easy," Maggie said, trying to keep her voice even. "Don't step on the gas so hard."

"Sorry, sorry."

"It's okay. Now concentrate." She reached over and steadied the wheel. "Why are you jerking the wheel? You want to keep it straight, like so. Nice and easy."

They circled the lot a few times, Lakshmi gripping the wheel tight, her entire body stiff and scared. "Relax your shoulders," Maggie murmured. "No need to take the corners that hard. The car should glide into a turn."

Lakshmi appeared to be heading straight for the lamppost. Maggie tried to gauge the distance from the car to the post, forced down the tension she was feeling, wanting to trust Lakshmi, not wanting to point out the obvious but unsure whether she would have to replace her front fender. At the last second, just as a yell was forming in her throat, Lakshmi threw the car to the right, yanking the steering wheel dramatically, as if enacting a car chase from a movie. Then she slammed on the brakes.

Maggie bit down on her lip to suppress the rage she was feeling. She was aware of Lakshmi staring at her, expecting to be chastised, but she looked away, waiting for her heart to slow down and her anger to recede. When neither happened, she said in a clipped voice, "Are you daydreaming? Or did you not happen to notice the twelve-foot pole in front of you?"

"I sorry, sorry. I not wanting to learn the driving. It not happen for me. My husband telling truth—I am maharani of stupid." Lakshmi banged her head forcefully against the steering wheel.

"Lakshmi. Stop that." Maggie was shocked at the violence with which the woman had struck her head. To lighten the mood, she added, "You'll crack the steering wheel with that hard head of yours." Lakshmi did not so much as pretend to get the joke. Maggie put her hand on the younger woman's head and stroked her hair. "Come on, now. Everybody finds it hard at first. It's like anything else, you know? You gotta stick with it." Even as she said the words, Maggie began to believe them, and for the first time this afternoon, she felt hopeful that Lakshmi could learn to drive. She felt her own bad mood lift, buoyed by that hope.

Lakshmi raised her head. "I having something to tell you," she said. "A secret."

Maggie sighed to herself. All she wanted was for this lesson to be over so she could go home and lie on her couch. With a nice cold rag on her head. "Okay," she said.

"I try to learn the driving before. The husband teach me first year I come to Am'rica."

Maggie raised her eyebrow. "Really? How come you didn't—"

"Because I embarrass to tell you," Lakshmi said in a rush. "I failing, you see. The husband doing so much shouting-shouting, I get ascare. He not kindly like you, Maggie. After few time, he give up. Say I too stupid to learn."

Maggie was surprised—and flattered—to hear that Lakshmi thought she was being kind. Goes to show how low the bar is, she thought. "Well, you can't give up now," she said. "Just imagine how much freedom this is going to give you. Look how far you've already come. You want to build a catering and housecleaning business, yes? Think how much time you'll save not having to take the bus."

"I knows. I knows. That's why only I was so excite to learn."

"And you will," Maggie said firmly. "Listen, in Calcutta, all those auto rickshaw drivers and taxi drivers, you think they have the schooling you do? No, they are total duffers." She was aware that she was slipping into a kind of Indian English, trying to talk to Lakshmi in a way she would understand. "And they all drive, no? If they can learn, why can't you?"

Lakshmi looked surprised. "You sits in rickshaw, Maggie?"

"Yes, of course." She didn't want the conversation to veer off topic. She knew how tired and frustrated both of them were, how easy it would be for them to drift onto some other, comfortable subject, like her visits to Calcutta. Maybe go get an iced coffee somewhere, she thought dreamily. She forced herself to sit up in the seat. "Come on," she said. "A few more rounds. Next week you'll be ready to drive on the road."

Lakshmi squealed in horror. "No, Maggie. I too ascare. No driving on roadside. Not after last week."

"You are scared? What about me?"

The two women eyed each other and then emitted nervous giggles. Last week Maggie had urged Lakshmi to venture out of the school parking lot and onto the residential side street. Lakshmi had sat at the edge of the parking lot, screwing up her nerve, and then shot out into the street—into the left lane. "Jesus, Lakshmi. Stop," Maggie had screamed, even though there had been no oncoming traffic. "You're in the wrong lane. This isn't India. We drive on the right side here. You know that. Now, pull into this driveway and turn around. Jesus." Lakshmi had been so flustered that she'd been unable to put the car in reverse and back out of the driveway, and Maggie had taken over.

Now, remembering, Maggie said, "I think I lost five years of my life last week."

"That's why only I don't want to drive on the roadside, Maggie."

"Okay, then. You just go everywhere driving from one parking lot to another. Maybe you can drive all the way to India someday in that way."

Lakshmi giggled. "You big joke-master, Maggie."

"Okay. Enough dilly-dallying. Drive."

"Dilly-dawllying?"

"Dilly-dallying. It means wasting time. Like you're doing right now."

"Dilly-dallying. Dilly-dallying." Lakshmi repeated the words out loud as if they were a mantra. And maybe they focused her mind, because Maggie noticed she was driving better.

20

SATURDAY. MAGGIE'S FAVORITE day of the week. And here they were, ushering in the weekend with her favorite activity. She and Sudhir had been coming for open swim to the campus pool every Saturday for at least the past six years. As she closed her eyes and floated on her back, Maggie felt the sun on her face, filtered through the large skylight, and the tight muscles in her aching neck sang and blessed her as they released. Around her, she heard the muffled sounds of the Carpenters' "For All We Know," the distant screams of the kids splashing in the shallow end, felt the disturbance in the water that the other swimmers created. None of it bothered her or even registered. This was her time. The intrusions of the world, its clatter and chatter, would have to wait. The lapping water, the cathedral ceiling, the sun pouring in through the skylights: Maggie felt as if she had waited all week for this moment, that she'd earned it. For one merciful hour, she could silence her thoughts, as if switching off an alarm clock. What took their place was a blissful, precious calm.

She had floated to the side of the pool when Sudhir caught up with her. "Hey," he said, shaking the water out of his hair.

She noticed his skin glistening in the water and felt a proprietary pleasure at the sight. "Hi, honey," she said. "You headed for the hot tub?"

"Not yet. I'll swim a few more laps, I think. But I was wondering—you wanna go to that Chinese place for lunch?"

"And regain whatever few calories I've burned? You know how long I've been trying to lose the last ten pounds?"

Sudhir's eyes darkened as they took in the long neck, the muscular arms. "You look pretty damn good to me."

She grinned. "Well said, honey. I've trained you well."

He began to smile back at her, but a second later, his eyes narrowed as they focused on something—or someone—past her. "Oh, great," he muttered, and Maggie turned her head to look. The sun was in her eyes, but the next minute, her stomach lurched as she recognized the swimmer. It was Peter. Of all the dumb coincidences . . . But then she knew. Peter's being here was no coincidence.

"Why, hello," Peter said in a voice that sounded dangerously insincere to Maggie's ears. "Wow. What are you guys doing here?"

"Hello," Sudhir said stiffly. "I didn't realize you were back in town."

"Oh yes. They gave me a visiting position for the year. How are you . . . It's Sudhir, right?"

"Right. And this is my wife, Maggie. I'm sure you remember her." Maggie heard some inflection in Sudhir's voice but couldn't place it. Was he mocking Peter? Or her?

"Yes, I do." Peter grinned broadly.

There was a strained silence, and after a second, Sudhir said, "So it's been how long since—"

"Three years."

"Ah, yes. I see your photo byline occasionally. In *National Geographic* mostly, right?" Sudhir smiled politely, but Maggie could tell it was a strain. He really dislikes Peter, she thought with wonder. It was so rare for Sudhir not to like someone.

"Yup. In fact, a couple of years ago I was in India for them. Did a photo shoot on the extinction of the Bengal tiger," Peter said. "I lived with the tribals for over two months." He fingered the thick black cord he wore around his neck. "You see this?" he said, lifting the yellowed pendant. "That's a tooth from a man-eating tiger that the villagers killed while I was there. They gifted it to me."

Sudhir shivered. From distaste, Maggie thought. But he only said, "I'm cold." He turned to Maggie. "I'm going to swim a few laps. And then I'll see you in the hot tub?" His eyes searched her face, and she realized that it wasn't a statement but a question. Sudhir wanted some kind of reassurance from her. She felt her face flush.

"Just let me know when you're ready," she mumbled.

He nodded and swam away. Maggie waited until he was out of earshot and then turned toward Peter. "Why are you here?" she hissed. "I told you—"

"I know. I know. But I can't. I need to see you again."

She wanted to finish this conversation before Sudhir finished his lap and headed toward them again. "Peter," she said. "Don't do this. I love my husband. Do you get that? I'm not going to do anything that—"

He leaned toward her and said something so intimate, it took her breath away. Her cheeks burned, and she looked at him sternly, but he held her gaze and she was the first to turn away. Because what he'd said was true. She loved Sudhir, but it was Peter's body that she craved. "Go away now," she said as she moved away from him.

"Will you come see me?"

"Yes, okay. Now go."

"When?"

"I don't know. Tuesday, maybe."

"Call me, babe."

She didn't bother to reply. She'd never known that it was possible for a heart to pound with fear and croon with joy at the same time.

Forty minutes later, Sudhir and Maggie walked toward the car
in silence. As he pulled out of the parking lot, she touched his
arm lightly. "What happened to your mood?"

He shrugged. "I don't know." After a few minutes he said,
"There's something about that man I can't stand. Pompous asshole."

She forced her face and voice to remain neutral. "Who?"

Sudhir took his eyes off the road to glance at her. "You know
who. That Peter guy."

She attempted a careless laugh. "Oh, honey. You hardly know
him. Why're you letting him upset you?"

Sudhir brushed the hair off his forehead. "I know. It's crazy.
But there's something so . . . predatory about him. Ethnocentric
bastard."

Sudhir's characterization of Peter was so contrary to Maggie's
opinion of him that the words escaped her mouth before she
had time to think. "How so? I mean, he seems entirely comfortable working in foreign places. I've never detected anything,
you know, ethnocentric about him . . . about his photography, I
mean . . ." Her voice trailed off, and she was suddenly nervous.
Was she defending Peter too vigorously?

"Oh, come on, Maggie. Usually, you're the one who notices
these things. Haven't you seen the stuff he photographs? Bare-
breasted women in third-world villages, impoverished African
children with their arms outstretched, asking some white relief
worker for aid. Why the hell doesn't he do a photo shoot in Idaho?
Or in New York? Isn't there poverty there that needs to be"—
Sudhir took his hands off the wheel to make quotation marks
in the air—"'documented'?" He made a dismissive sound. "Nah,
he's a user. He gets off on other people's troubles."

She was about to protest the unfairness of that statement when it occurred to her: Sudhir couldn't be objective about Peter. Because he was jealous. And he wasn't even conscious of it. But seeing Peter again had aroused some primal male instinct, had ignited a barely recollected memory-feeling from when they'd met him three years ago and Maggie had been drawn to him.

"I mean, what kind of man wears a freakin' tiger's tooth around his neck, for God's sake?" Sudhir continued. He glanced sideways at her for confirmation.

She nodded. "I agree." What she was remembering was the first time she'd slept with Peter. Afterward, she had lain with her head resting on his chest, listening to his racing heart. He had murmured something, and as she had raised her head to listen, the edge of the tiger's tooth had grazed her below the ear and she'd let out a startled yelp. Peter had massaged the spot tenderly and, from then on, remembered to remove his necklace before they made love. For an irrational moment, she wanted to tell Sudhir this, to prove to him that Peter was more than a "user," that behind the brusque photographer lay a kind and thoughtful man. She kept silent.

"Anyway. Let's not spend any more of this beautiful day talking about that guy," Sudhir said. "Okay?"

She was only too happy to comply. "Okay," she said.

"You still feel like going out for lunch?" he asked in a tone that suggested he was no longer keen on the idea.

"Only if you do."

"We have so many leftovers at home. Maybe we should . . ."

"Whatever you want. I don't care."

They rode half a mile in a stiff silence, and then Sudhir said, "Did you know? That he was back in town, I mean?"

She tensed. "How would I know?" She forced herself to look at Sudhir.

He shrugged. "I don't know." He paused and then said in a rush, "I guess because you seemed so enamored by him—by his work—the last time."

"Sudhir," she said very quietly. "Are you trying to pick a fight with me?"

He puffed his cheeks and exhaled loudly. "No. I don't mean to. It's just . . . ah, forget it."

"I think that's a very good idea."

By the time they reached home, the tension had ebbed enough that Sudhir had his arm around her shoulder as they walked in the house. "How about I fix us a sandwich?" he asked, and she nodded, although she felt faintly nauseated.

She sat at the table and watched him stack the sandwich in his usual neat, methodical way. He seemed to have gotten over his bad mood, but Maggie was queasy. Her neck muscles tensed as she kept reliving their conversation in the car.

Sudhir knew. The only thing working in her favor was that he didn't know that he knew.

BOOK
TWO

21

NOBODY IN MY village is knowing how Mithai the elephant come to us. We go to sleep one night and we are having dogs and cats and mice and chickens and goats and cows in village. But no elephant. But next morning, Kissan the doodhwala is going to Menon sahib's big house to deliver the milk and what he see there make him almost faint. Because standing in the yard in front of Menon sahib's house is Mithai. He is a baby, only three or four months old, but Kissan said he had such a big shocks, he spilling some of milk on the brick path. And what you know? Mithai take two-three big step to where Kissan is standing all shaking, and he licking the milk up. Then Mithai take his trunk and touching his forehead, like he saying salaam to Kissan for the milk. Then Kissan ascare no more. He know this is elephant from a good family, not one of those mean animal who sometimes go mad and killing everything in forest.

So Kissan ring doorbell and Menon sahib's wife come out and she scream and go wake up her husband. And Kissan say Menon sahib come to the door all sleepy and irritate with his wife but then he see Mithai and he rubbing his eyes. Kissan feeling proudly then, because he find the elephant. And then, Kissan tell us, what you think happen next? The baby elephant sit on back legs and touch trunk to his forehead, like he salute Menon sahib. Kissan say, Menon sahib get tears in his eyes. He look at elephant, look at wife, but he not able to speaking. Then he go outside house and stand in front of Mithai. And Menon sahib, our landlord, ruler of our village, richest man in whole district, a man who bow his head only in temple, take his hand and do salute to the elephant.

Stop, stop, stop, Dada say, laughing, when Kissan tell this part. You adding liquor to your milk these days, Kissan? Menon sahib serious man. He not do salute even to government official. And he salaaming an elephant? Take your drunk stories to someone who may belief you. Jao, go on.

Belief, don't belief, what I care? Kissan say. All I know is, whole village gathering at three today in the marketplace to see our guest. You and your family only ones not there. And Kissan say goodbye to Ma, smile at me, and go.

Dada laugh again after he leaf. "That rascal telling big fat lie." He look at me. "Chalo, enough time waste. Lots of work in field today. You ready?"

I goes with Dada, and even though sun is hot today and my body melting like a candle, I work. When Dada stop for lunch, I keep working. "Enough, re." He frown. "You wanting to kill yourself? Here, eat a chapati, at least."

"No, Dada. I's not hungry." Instead, I go to tiffin box and take three of the pedas Ma pack for me for dessert. I put them in the pocket of my kameez to eat later.

I works until it is two-forty. Then I say, "Dada, I want to go to marketplace. To see the elephant. I go for half hour only."

Dada smile. "So my daughter breaking her back working to go see the elephant that come out of Kissan's daru bottle." He look up at the sky for a minute and then again at me. The blue of sky drop into his smiling eyes. "Okay. Go. But I'm telling you, Kissan is big bluffmaster."

I runs through the field that I know as well as the inside of our little house. I go home first to pick up Shilpa, who I know back from school. Ma ask me question but I just change into my slipper, grab Shilpa hand, and we running down mud road toward the market. On the way, I am telling Shilpa about the elephant and she as excite as me. As we get to the market, noise of the crowd tell us where to go.

In front of Menon sahib's shop, big crowd gathering. I still holding Shilpa's hand and we pushes through crowd of people. Shilpa, Lakshmi, they scold us, but they moving for us. When we get to front, we see him. The elephant. I take one look, and I loving him. He so small. He look just like a baby. His eyes so tiny and his body fat, like Menon sahib's wife. He is having two tails, a big one, like a water pipe between his eyes, and a thin one, like hairs from a broom, on the backside. I try to reminder what name the front tail is call and then I knows: trunk.

Shilpa is jumping up and down as if we at the mela. Everyone in crowd acting like they at the mela. Only Menon sahib is serious. He standing next to the elephant and touching him softly-softly. Then he take a dried coconut from a basket and call to Munna, who is now eight years old. He give Munna the coconut and lead his son's hand toward the elephant. I knows Munna ascare. Everyone stop breathing. The elephant take coconut in his trunk, go to put it in mouth, and then stop. He hold it above his head and then he throwing it on the ground. Then he crushes on it with his left foot. I hears the coconut break open, and when he lift his foot, I see the white inside of the coconut. So do the elephant. He pick up the white pieces and puts inside his mouth. This is clever elephant, everyone say. Everyone so excite, they start to whistle and clapping. Now Menon sahib smile, as if elephant is Munna getting good marks at school.

"Brothers and sisters," Menon sahib say. "We are not knowing how this guest showing up in our village. I will send word to nearby villages to see if a circus has lost an elephant. If so, we must return him. I will also file a police report. But if nobody comes for him in a few weeks, we will know that this is the god Ganesh come to bless our village. He will live among us as our honor guest."

Vithal chacha, our next neighbor, take step to near Menon sahib. He bow his head. "Beg pardon, lord," he say. "This animal not staying baby for long. We have all seen elephants at the cinema. They big animal. Who responsible for his feeding?"

Menon sahib close his eyes as he thinking. "I will," he say after one minute. "I taking care of this whole village, correct? Can I not feed some grass and sugarcane and coconuts to our god Ganesh?" He look at the crowd. "Of course, all of you must be helping. If this animal remain with us, I will take one percent from your crops for his upkeep."

"Fas gaye," Vithal chacha say softly next to me. "We trapped." And everyone else agree with him, but softly, so as not to make angry Menon sahib. Nobody want to give cut from their money to pay for elephant. All of sudden, the happy of meeting the elephant turn into angry, and I get ascare. I knows some people will throw stone and stick at the elephant when Menon sahib not protection.

The thoughts that someone hurting this baby make me cry and I leaf Shilpa's hand to wipe my eyes. The elephant watching me and now it coming toward me. I feels a little ascare but I forcing myself to be steady. It come and stand in front of me and look at me from its eye, small like a keyhole. It take its trunk and touch my hair, then my face. Shilpa scream and move away but I stand fix, like full stop. It trunk feel like blindman Vikram's hand on my face when he trying to see how much I grow. Menon sahib come near me but he looking at the elephant with a puzzle. And then the elephant put his trunk in my pocket and take out the pedas.

Before I can stop him, he open his mouth and put them in. "Ae," I yell. "You a thief."

Everybody laughing now. Elephant, too. He look at me like a naughty child who teacher catch cheating. Then he walk away, like he dancing. The crowd whistle and cheer. So what you think? He come back and check my second pocket. Nothing in there. But I putting my hand out and petting his trunk. It rough like tree branch. I never touch or even seeing an elephant until today. But when I touching him, it is exact same as holding a friend's hand. Like meeting someone you always know but forgetting to meet until now.

"This not our Lord Ganesh," Vithal chacha yell. "This elephant is a bada bluffmaster."

Everybody laugh. "That his name. Bluffmaster," someone say. "He's a chor. Thief. We call him Chor."

"No, no. His name Peda," Munna yell.

But Menon sahib come to me and his face look same-same as three years back, when Munna almost falling in well. "What do you say, Lakshmi?" he say. "What should we call him?"

I no need to think. "Mithai," I say. "His name is Mithai. He sweet like mithai."

As soon as I say his name, Mithai make a loud sound, like a train coming to a station or a hundred water buffalos making noise. Everyone take one step back. Everyone but Mithai, who come forward to me. And with his trunk, he put little-little kiss on my face. It feels funny-pinching and I laugh.

Menon sahib stand straight. "Mithai is good name. I will build tent for him behind our house. You people are welcome to come do his darshan whenever you like. He will bring our village good luck." He smile. "Of course, remember to bring pedas whenever you come. And now namaskar to all of you. Mithai needs to rest."

The crowd say namaste to Mithai and slowly walk away. But I am not wanting to leaf Mithai. I wanting to stay near him. I take Shilpa with me and runs. "Munna," I says. "You needing help in maths homework?"

He make tall face. "I always needs help in maths homework."

"I can come tomorrow," I says. "After work."

Menon sahib puts his hand on my shoulder. "Girl," he says. "You not tired after working all day in the kheti?"

"No. I comes. To help Munna. And I helps with Mithai also. Maybe to give him bath?"

Menon sahib smile. "I see. I see. Okay. Ask your dada. If he willing, I pay you to help with Mithai."

"Pay me? I comes for free," I start to say, but Shilpa squeeze my hand and loudly sing "Jana Gana Mana," the national anthem. Anytime I say something stupid, Shilpa sing "Jana Gana Mana," so peoples cannot hear me. She younger than me but smart.

It start to rain as Shilpa and me go home. But we skipping all the ways, our feets making glup-glup noise in the mud. Shilpa thinking I's happy because of money Menon sahib is offering. But it is not that. It is because I am now having a brother. Mithai all alone in this world. Why his dada or ma leaf him, I not knowing, because he is not a bad son. But that okay. I will take care of him. I will give him bath. I will take him pedas when I go. Every day I will feed him one of my rotis and some dal. I will making sure he never alonely for his family. I his family now.

22

I NOT TELLING STORY of Mithai khali-pilli, for no use. I telling to—as Maggie say—to make the point. I telling to say: Maggie right, husband wrong—I is not stupid. Because of Mithai, I gets the job at Menon sahib's store, doing the accounts. From my moneys I pays for the medicine for my ma the last year she living. Medicine not save Ma's life but it give her some pain-free time.

I don't know what I going to do with moneys I saving from my jobs now. Half I gives the husband but halfs I keep in different bank than him. Sudhir babu help me open account. Maggie say I's a businesswoman now. Every week I cleaning four house, counting Maggie house. At least four-five time a month I get catering order. Sometime I prepares foods in our restaurant kitchen. But sometime, if Maggie is knowing the family, I goes there to prepare in their kitchen. Christmas and New Year time, we so busy. Husband have his catering; I have mine. One or two time, he steal some of my recipe.

How I get to my jobs? I will tell. I drive. It snowing now and I ascare—this area have so many hills—but I drive. You know why? Because I more ascare not to. I more ascare to sit at home, to work at husband store and restaurant, to be dead from inside like I was for six years. Husband not happy with my new life but he happy with free moneys I give him. I still help Rekha arrange items on shelves every morning. At eleven o'clock, I leaf for my jobs. Husband hire friend's son to serve in restaurant. I lose six kilos just from all work I do. Husband say people will think he starve his wife, but I feels good. I have so much energy. How Maggie say? I fool of life.

Last Sunday, husband do something very sweet to me. We at Costco and he tell me to go buy the oils, eggs, milk. He say he coming straightaway, and when he come back, he holding a box. It is the GPS. He buy it as present for me, to help me with my cleaning jobs. It is first present he ever buy me, and there and there, in the middle of the Costco, my eyes heavy with tears. He look like he embarrass by me but I can tell that inside he feel prideful. When we get home we eat dinner and he show me how to make work the GPS. He so happy playing with it, he looking like little boy, and I go to him and kiss his head. He look up surprise and now it his eyes who wet. Seeing him look so surprise, I feel ashame. I know my husband as alonely in this marriage as I. It is I who keep him from marry the woman he love. Nothing to do about that now. But after a long time I again think, Maybe husband learn to love me? Maybe he can be train to look at me way Sudhir babu look at Maggie? Or Bettina look at her cat?

Bettina Bennett is a senior citizen woman who live alone in big house two miles from Maggie. Her husband use to work with Sudhir babu but he dead. First time I see Bettina house, I so upset. Not because I ascare to clean such big house. But because Bettina living there by herself. "What if some bad mens come in the middle of night to thief you?" I ask Bettina, but she only laugh. Nothing happen to her, she say. "I'm strong as an ox."

"Ox?"

Bettina shake her head. "It's just an expression. It means I'm really strong."

And she is. All white hair but she swim and go jog, which means to run for no reason. Do yoga. If Bettina born in my village, she would be bend over and thin and old and staying at home all the time. Her daughter-in-law making her chapatis and tea. Instead, Bettina go out with friends to the movies, drink wine with dinner every night. She even offer to teach me the English but I say no. I having my own business—where I'm having the time? Beside, my English better just from working in Am'rican homes. The other day, I say "Oh, shit" for first time. Maggie laugh and laugh.

Bettina waiting at the door as I get out of the car—my husband loan me his 2006 Honda Civic to take to jobs—and walks up to her house. She not look happy. "Late again, Lakshmi," she say. "Second time in two weeks."

I feel my face burning, like I standing in front of gas stove. "I sorry," I say. How to explain I ascare driving up the hilly street during snow? So I drives very slowly and other drivers blow horn at me and give me their fingers.

Bettina in bad mood today. "That's it? No explanation?"

I swallow the shame I feel. Bettina still standing near the door, and I say first thing come inside my head: "Lots of traffic today. Sorry." Where I get this lie? Last night I watching Am'rican TV show. The police officer say this line to his girlfriend.

Bettina open her mouth to say more but I goes to broom closet and pull out her vacuum cleaner. She look at me for one more minute and then go into the living room. As soon as I start cleaner, I reminder something—Ma in last few months before she die. Anytime Shilpa or I late coming home, she start the fight with us. Where you been? Why you late? You bad girls. Complain, complain. Shilpa use to get angry but I understand—Ma is sad to be by herself. She needing the company. Same thing with Bettina. Old people in my village use to say, Being alone in old age is biggest curse of all. They's right. Bettina shout at me because she missing me.

I turn off vacuum, open my purse, and takes out the packet of sweet fennel seeds. We sell these at our store and Bettina love these. I go into the living room and offer packet to her. "Please. For you," I say.

Bettina eyes get big and she smile. Like small child, I think. "Thank you, Lakshmi," she say. "How much do I owe you for these?"

Every week we say same dialogue. "No mention," I say. "Present for you."

"That's very kind of you." Bettina put down the book she reading. "Will you join me for a cup of tea?"

"Yes, please," I say. "Shall I make?"

"No, no," Bettina say. "You carry on. I'll call when tea's ready."

So I goes back to vacuuming. First few weeks, I feels bad to let Bettina serve me tea. Now, I knows. Am'rican women don't like having the servant. In India, women proud to have servants. It mean you's rich. Here, it meaning same thing. But Am'rican women not feel good being show-off. It make Bettina feel like we same if she make the tea. So I lets her.

As we drinks, sitting side-beside on her couch, I thinks of all the years I spend working for Menon sahib. Each time I enter his house, I was remindered again that I's from lower caste. Once, only once, Menon sahib let me sharing the food with his family, using their plate and glass. His wife take objection, say he pollution the house, but Menon sahib so happy that day, he shout at her to listen to him. Only once.

If I tells Bettina what Menon sahib treat me, she will laugh. Or get angry. I tell you truth—I still miss my India. I missing the smell of fruit trees, the rich, dark mud of our farm, I missing how nobody having enough to eat but people always help with a little rice or ten-rupee note. Peoples poking nose in each other business, but they also making my business their business. Still, Am'rica is the tops country. Here, I can sit side-beside with Bettina and drink tea. No separate glass or cup kept for me. Here I can drive car and no mens make dirty eyes watching the woman driving.

"We have landlord in my country," I hears my voice say. "He good to my family, but he from different caste. He die of shock if I sit on his couch like this."

Bettina frown. "Ah, yes, the caste system. Was he a Brahmin?"

I surprise. "You know about Brahmin caste?"

"Yes, of course." Bettina pause and then say, "Were you an Untouchable?"

"Excuse, please? Untouchable? I not knowing that word."

"You know, the people who were like the outcasts?" Bettina close her eyes and try to think. "Gandhi tried to help them? I think they're like the folks who clean the latrines and stuff?"

I stare at Bettina. Is she thinking I's a Harijan? A Dalit? The lowest of the castes? Does I look like a Dalit? Would my husband, who own store and restaurant, marry a Dalit? "No, madam," I say loudly. "I's from higher caste. Just not Brahmin."

Bettina nod, like it all same to her. "I see," she say.

But I feeling angry-confuse. I wants Bettina to understand who I come from, how I may be housekeeper in Am'rica, but in my country, my father own land. And I does the bookkeeping for biggest landlord in our village. Who one day allow me to eat at his table.

"Bettina," I say. "I tells you story of how Menon sahib, our landlord allow me to eat in his house."

She finish her tea and looks around the room. "Shouldn't you get on with cleaning the house, dear?"

"I will. But first I tells you about Mithai," I say.

23

A RRE, BAAP. ARRE, baap, arre, baap.
Mithai only a baby but he eating like guest at a wedding feast. When Shilpa was baby, she drink milk only, bas, nothing else. Mithai want to eat everything.

Menon sahib come stand next to me. "There is the saying in our community," he say, pointing to Mithai. "It is said, 'If you wanting to destroy your enemy, gift him an elephant.' I am wondering if I am having an enemy who hate me. This animal will eat me out of my house."

I not knowing if Menon sahib serious. Can Mithai eat Menon sahib's big house? I take out chapati and vegetable I bring for Mithai. "I will feed him," I say. "No worry. Every day I will bring him food."

Menon sahib put back his head and laugh. "Oh, you, Lakshmi," he say. "You little . . ." All of sudden, he kiss the top of my head. I get the shock. Menon sahib is Brahmin. He never enter our home, not even take glass of water from us. When he pay Dada each month, he putting money on the table so he not to touch his hand. And now my chapati make him kiss me? Menon sahib also seem to get the shock. He scratch his nose and then he say, "You like my niece. My Munna living because of you. You don't worry. I will take the care of Mithai. I am giving you my promise."

That evening I gives Mithai bath. I taking tub of water and cleaning him. He love it. He close his eyes and make sweet-sweet sound and his ears move like a hand fan. But Mithai so naughty. He put his trunk in the tub, pick up water, and then spray me. I feeling shy because I am big girl now and my body show through my wet cloth. No, Mithai, I say, and next time his trunk go to water, he spray on himself. When Shilpa was little, she hate taking the bath. But Mithai love it.

Taking care of Mithai make my heart happy. I takes care of Ma also, but she so much in pain, she has lost her happy. No matter how much I doing for Ma, I can't help her. But Mithai make me full. I can see him grow, become less ascare, like his home with us now. Mithai teach me big lesson—it easier to love someone if you can make them happy.

Arre baap, arre baap, arre baap.

What jadoogar do spell on my Mithai? He evil now. He raise his trunk and make horrible noise. When Bhutan, his mali, go up to him, he try to crush him with his foot. He not touch his food. This elephant make my hair turn white, Menon sahib say. My family getting no sleep last night, he make so much commotion.

"Maybe he sick," I say.

Menon sahib turn to me. "Maybe. But what I can do? Hardly any people-doctor in this area. Where I going to find doctor for an elephant?"

"Seth," Bhutan say. "This elephant gone mad, I telling you. He dangerful. We need to kill him."

I get red when I hears those words. "Shut up, you stupid," I yell. "Mithai need our help."

And now, Bettina, funny thing happen. Mithai hear my voice and the horrible noise stop. He walk to the end of his gate, sit on his back legs, and look at me. I looks into his eyes. Usually, Mithai's eyes full of masti, fun. Today they looking so serious. So sad. Then Mithai make loud, long noise, and both Menon sahib and that stupid Bhutan take two step back. I stay. I know Mithai speaking only to me. He saying, "Help me." Just like when Ma need to do soo-soo in middle of night and need help. She no saying the words or waking me up. I automatic get up and go give her bedpan. Mithai asking me for help.

I open the gate to go in. Both Menon sahib and Bhutan yelling. "Stop, Lakshmi," my landlord say. "He could hurt you."

"Nothing more dangerful than mad elephant," Bhutan yell. "Get out of there."

I cannot hear them. All I hear is my Mithai's voice. I not even reminder to be ascare. Mithai not mad. He just in pain. But why?

I reach my hand and touch Mithai trunk. What you think? He turn his head toward me and put trunk around my shoulder, like he my best friend and we walking home from school together. I wants to tell Menon sahib to leaf, to take Bhutan with him and leaf me alone with Mithai. But I cannot. Menon sahib is the boss.

"Mithai," I say soft. "Lie down. Come on, jan." Mithai love when I calls him jan. It mean life, love.

He drop to mud floor so hard, whole tent shake for one second. I can hear his breath—hummf, hummf—and I know my Mithai is sick. All of suddens, I feel young. I only fourteen-year girl. What I know of treating sick elephant? My ma I can help because she talk. But Mithai cannot tell me how he sick.

But my hands must be older than fourteen. Because on their own, they examine Mithai's body. I begins with his trunk. I looks inside his big nose. I touch the inside pink part and Mithai sneeze, shaking his head. I pulls my hand back quick-quick. All time I keep looking at Mithai's eye. His eye will tell if I near trouble spot.

When I look inside his big fan ear, Mithai whine and bang his left leg on the hay. For one minute I think Mithai have earache but then I reminder—he feel the tickle near ears. Always. I keep

moving my hand. When I touch Mithai right leg, he stiff his leg
and pull away. Oh, I think, he have leg fracture. But then I angry
with myself—I just learn "fracture" word from Shilpa last week,
so it playing in my head. No need to think Mithai have fracture.

Then why he pulling leg and moan? "Mithai," I whisper. "What
is wrong?"

Mithai let me touch his leg again but I know he ascare. Just
then that Bhutan jump to his feet. "Seth," he say to Menon sahib.
"That elephant will crush that foolish girl. I not responsible for
her death. As Mithai's mali, I say to please stop her. What she
know? I already do full inspection of the animal."

Hearing his voice, Mithai let out huge roar. His whole body get
tight and then shake. I feel my hand move, like I touch electricity.
"Tell him to leaf," I say to Menon sahib. "Tell Bhutan to go out.
Mithai ascare of him."

Menon sahib think for minute and then turn to Bhutan. "Out,"
he say.

Bhutan look at me with such hateful. He spit on the ground.
"Idiot chokri," he say. Then he goes.

I continues to touch Mithai leg. I press, massage, press. He not
in pain there. Then I gets near his feet and he raise his head and
start making moan sound. He look me straightum-straight in the
eye. For first time, I's a little scare of Mithai. And I knows I near
the problem. I moves toward his feet. And even though there is
no light except from the opening of the tent, I sees it right away.
And I begins to cry right there and then.

"Lakshmi? What is it, beta? You come out if you scare," Menon
sahib say.

But I not hear or see him. I only see the hate. The meanness.
In my life, I hear so many evil story from Dada. About how, two
village from us, the Brahmin landlord kill whole family of Dalits
to death because they ask for more pay for their crop. About how

mother-in-law burn new bride for not bringing enough dowry. About how, during British raj, the goras use to make villagers trap poor tiger in cage and then the white mens go shoot the jailed tiger. But until now, age fourteen, I never having my own evil story.

Three nails. Someone put three nails into Mithai's foot. Mithai big animal but his foot pad soft, like sponge. One nail maybe accident, but three? Not possible. Someone—who?—do this to hurt Mithai. Who? But even as I try to let Mithai know I will help him, I know who did this evil.

"Menon seth," I yell. "Please to go catch that badmash Bhutan."

"What? What is it, girl?"

"He allow someone put three nails in Mithai's foot," I yell.

Menon sahib's face go dark. He hurry out of tent.

"Mithai," I say. "You safe now. We will help you. Nobody hurt you again. This my promise to you."

He just look at me out of those tiny eyes. Even though he still in great pain, he look relax. He trusting me.

"So what happened?" Bettina ask. "Did you find that scoundrel? Was it the caretaker who did this? Why?"

I smile. Bettina no longer alonely. My story take her out of Cedarville and puts her in the tent with me and Mithai. For first time, I fully understanding what is Maggie's job, what she say about why telling story is important.

"It was Bhutan. See, Menon sahib is good man but he making one mistake. He asking all villagers to give one percent of their crop every month to Mithai's upkeep. People in my home village is poor people, Bettina. They watching elephant eat more than their own children. So they jealous. Then they angry. They offers Bhutan three hundred rupees if he fixes Mithai good and proper. So Bhutan do his wicked thing. Then he tell Menon sahib Mithai mad. Best to shoot him."

Bettina give big shiver. "Horrible man. I hope he lost his job."

"Oh, Menon sahib give him good-proper thrashing. And when he find out why Bhutan acting so mean, he ask me what he is to do. Can you imagine, Bettina? I fourteen-year-old girl and richest man in village asking me decision. So I tell him truth—people hungry. They cannot give cut to feed Mithai."

I don't say anything more. After few minutes Bettina say, "So he stopped taxing them, I hope?"

I quiet but Bettina looking at me for the answer. "Well?"

"He not listen to me," I say softly. "He still charging them."

"Terrible, greedy man."

But I remindering how Menon sahib beg Mithai's forgiveness. How he pay for doctor to come to take out nails from Mithai's foot. And I never forget how he take me to his house and ask his missus to put extra plate at the table. She looking like heart attack. I sit in hall with Munna while they fighting in kitchen. She say feeding low-caste girl like me will pollution the whole house. That God will give Menon sahib leprosy or TB and bring hundred years of drought if he allow me to eat at their table. He say he tired of all God talk. He say Munna living because of me, Munna smart in school because of me, and now Mithai pain-free because of me. She is a deserving child, he tell his missus. Feeding guest in our home, that is also Hindu religion, he saying. From outside, I feeling all embarrass but from inside I grinning. I imagine Dada's face when I tell him the story. He will not belief me.

"I don't know that what he did was so great," Bettina say. Then she smile and put her thin hand on mine. Her skin look wrinkle, like used aluminum foil. "I'm so glad you're living here, Lakshmi. Away from such ridiculousness."

Is Bettina correct? I not know. Same-same problem everywhere, I think. When I see Maggie next, I discuss with her.

24

T HIS IS WHAT I don't get," Sylvia said. "Why are you doing this? What are you getting out of it?"

Maggie shook her head. "That's just it. I know it's madness, but I just don't seem to be able to cut it off."

"Are you in love with him?"

"Oh, God, no." Maggie was surprised at how emphatically the words slipped out of her mouth. "I love Sudhir."

"Well, he's obviously fulfilling something that's missing in your marriage. So the question is . . ."

Maggie shook her head again, impatiently this time. For the first time in the years she'd been seeing Sylvia, she was a little irritated with the older therapist. This line of questioning was too predictable, too easy. She fought the urge to jump to her feet and pace the small room. She knew Sylvia would look askance if she asked for them to go for a walk, as she had done so often with Lakshmi and some of her other patients. For a second, she was proud of her own skills as a therapist, was glad that she didn't feel constrained by the techniques she'd learned in school.

"Come on, Maggie. Try. You're so close to something, I can feel it. What is it that Peter gives you that—"

"Sylvia. It's not like that. This has nothing to do with my marriage. Sudhir and I are happy. It's just that with Peter . . . I have this connection with him. Can't explain it. It's been there from the first time we set our eyes on each other three years ago. I fought against it successfully back then, but now I—"

"So it's strong enough to risk the breakup of your marriage?" Sylvia asked sharply, and Maggie's head jerked back involuntarily, as if she'd been slapped. Her eyes filled with tears.

"No. Of course not. That's the whole reason why I keep talking about this sordid story. I guess I'm just looking for the strength to break it off—and then have it stay broken off."

"What would it feel like, not seeing him again?"

Sylvia asked the question gently enough, but Maggie felt such a heavy emptiness in her chest that it took her breath away. A feeling of incredible loneliness, of being adrift in the world, overcame her. She closed her eyes briefly and saw herself on a raft on an ocean that grew wider and wider as the raft grew smaller and more distant. The figure on the raft was not moving. Rather, she was lying in a position that was instantly familiar: the pose of the model in Andrew Wyeth's *Christina's World*. She opened her eyes quickly to escape the desolation of that image, but she had her answer. Because she had recognized the blue dress she was wearing in the image: It was a dress she'd had when she was eleven years old. And the desolation of being alone in the world— she had worn that feeling as often as she had worn the dress. It had been her second skin in the years after Odell had confronted their father about his peculiar nighttime overtures and Wallace had responded by ignoring her completely. Mama was alive then, but if she'd noticed that Wallace was no longer playful with his adored baby girl, she had never mentioned it. She was probably in too much pain to care. She had died two days after Maggie's birthday, spending her last two months in a morphine-induced stupor. Until Maggie had her first boyfriend at sixteen, nobody touched her in love or kindness except some of the old ladies in their neighborhood, who would pat her head and exclaim how much she looked like her dear departed mother. Wallace's dismissal of her was total. He would come home from his first job at four, fall asleep on the couch for an hour, wake up, make dinner, and be out of the house to his second job by seven. The half hour when they ate supper was their only time together. At first, after Mama's death, they continued eating at the kitchen table, as they'd always done. But after a few months, Wallace began to carry his plate to the TV, and pretty soon she joined him there. He would return from the convenience store at one a.m., and often Maggie would force herself to lie awake until she heard the key turn. Those hours alone in the apartment were some of the loneliest in her life. It left a permanent mark on her, this loneliness, abating only after she and Sudhir became a couple.

"Maggie," Sylvia was saying. "What is it, my dear?"

Hearing the concern in Sylvia's voice made Maggie realize she was crying. She looked at her, unable to speak. "I . . . can't . . ." She felt cold; felt her body shaking. She reached for the Kleenex on the table beside the couch. "Sorry." She sniffed. "Something you said . . ."

"What?"

". . . about not seeing Peter again . . ." She roughly brushed away the tears on her cheek. "It just brought back this memory."

"What's the memory?"

"The way my dad neglected me after my brother confronted him. About, y'know, that stuff."

"Does Peter remind you of—"

"No. Nothing like that. Just that I think I'll feel empty if I stop seeing Peter. That same kind of horrible emptiness."

"You're no longer that helpless little girl, Maggie."

"I know."

"And you have Sudhir."

"And I have Sudhir. Who loves me more than I deserve." The tears fell again, but for a different reason. The second round of tears was being shed by a woman who felt a profound sense of gratitude for having found a man whose love for her was steady as a flame. For her stupidity at doing anything to risk that love. She had won. With Sudhir, she had won. Wallace's cruel neglect had not crushed her, had not left her damaged. Rather, she had recognized Sudhir's purity, his decency, immediately.

Maggie exhaled loudly. "I think you've helped me realize something, Sylvia," she said. "I just need to process it a bit more on my own."

Sylvia smiled. "Glad to be of help."

They talked for another ten minutes, and then her time was up. "See you in two weeks?" Sylvia asked. "Same time?"

"Yes. Sure." She handed Sylvia a check and rose to leave, but the older woman stopped her by leaning over and touching her arm. "Maggie. I just want to say—I know this is hard. Calling it off with Peter, I mean. And that . . . I recognize your struggle." Sylvia paused. "That's all."

Maggie nodded. "Thanks. See you next time."

It was an uncharacteristically warm winter's day, and Maggie lingered on the street for a second before entering her car. In the distance, the snow on the mountains glittered in the afternoon sun. Maggie looked up to a perfectly blue sky and then frowned when she heard the chirping of a bird. It's a false alarm, birdie, she thought. It's not close to being spring, even though it feels like it. Don't get your hopes up.

She got into the car, turned on the engine, and realized she couldn't drive. Couldn't move. The loneliness that she'd felt a few minutes ago lingered. Even though she felt ridiculous, even though there was a chance that Sylvia might look out her front window and catch her sitting in the car in front of her house,

Maggie leaned her head on the steering wheel. The warm plastic dug into her forehead. What was the matter with her? What about Sylvia's innocent question had triggered in her the bleakness, the utter solitariness of those dark days of childhood, when she'd felt she was losing not one but both parents? Even at Wellesley, she had felt that deep existential solitariness, walking alone around the lake at dusk, her hands thrust deep into her jeans pockets, barely glancing at the posse of girls she passed on the path, because their ruddy complexions, their well-scrubbed faces, only accentuated the difference she felt. It wasn't about being black, although that was part of it. It was the feeling of being a castaway, someone who had been thrown away by her own father.

But hadn't she successfully dispelled that desolation over the years? She had never been lonely, not like that, since she'd met Sudhir. Her years with Sudhir had been—were—rich beyond any fantasy she could've had, filled with warmth and kindness and travel and friends and parties and a large extended family in India who had taken her to its bosom once they saw that she loved their Sudhir as much as they did. Sudhir's sister, Reshma, was like the sister she'd never had; just last week Reshma's youngest daughter, Deepa, had called Maggie, called her, not Sudhir, to discuss some boy problem that she was having.

Homecoming. She'd had a sense of homecoming from the first time she'd met Sudhir. From their first meeting on that rooftop terrace, he got her. Understood her jokes, her moods, her silences. Included her in all his gatherings, invited her to all his parties, opened up his home to her. There was the inconvenient fact that he did this with everyone he met. At times, when she'd catch him looking at her in an unguarded moment, she'd suspect there was something special, an understanding, that flowed between the two of them. But in the next second, Sudhir would smile at someone else, welcome another visitor into his home, slap someone else on the back, insist that everybody try the new dish he'd just cooked.

It had gone on like this for over a year. In that year, Maggie tried dating other men, but to them she had to explain her jokes, make excuses for her silences, translate her words. After a while, she stopped trying. Sudhir didn't seem to notice one way or the other. Occasionally, he'd inquire about a past boyfriend, and when she'd shrug, he'd nod and say, "He was a nice guy. I liked him."

"Do you ever not like someone?" she teased.

He thought for a moment. "My third-grade teacher. She was a bitch."

She'd decided that they were to be only friends. That Sudhir was gay or asexual or that she was simply not his type. That she would remain in his life but on the periphery, and that it was time to start dating again. So when he told her, in his casual way, that a bunch of his friends were going to hear Bruce Springsteen and they had an extra ticket and would she like to come, she almost said no. When she saw the beer-guzzling crowd, the massive amplifiers, the line of policemen, the general mayhem, she was sorry to be there. But it turned out to be a magical concert, on a cold, crisp fall evening. The trees around them were bare, but as the sun went down, a full moon ascended in the sky. Springsteen reminded her of a white James Brown, playing like the devil, on fire with youth and passion. But the true revelation was Sudhir himself. She had never seen him like this: tousled hair, eyes closed, head tilted skyward, mouthing the words to most of the songs, glancing at her now and then and smiling a deep, warm smile. He had never looked so beautiful, so young, so . . . free. So completely, purely himself. And as the night went on, it became impossible to remain in their seats. Here it was, a crowd on its feet, unable, unwilling, to sit down, the music entering their bodies, moving their feet, shaking their heads, singing, singing, singing along with the sprite on the stage who inflamed them, seduced them, aroused them with his incessant beat.

And then it happened. Halfway through the show, a count-in, a jaunty piano intro, and then: "Got a wife and kids in Baltimore, Jack." Maggie remembered it as if it were yesterday: The crowd screams in recognition, hands rising in the air, the thrilling sound of thousands of voices singing together. And Sudhir turns toward her, slowly, eyes still closed, and then he opens them and looks at her, looks at her, and she is about to say something funny or ironic, but then stops because all of a sudden she can't breathe, she has just read something in those brown eyes, and she knows how long and how desperately she's needed to see that message in Sudhir's eyes, how unsure she has been this last year and how certain she is now, and she opens her mouth to confess something but suddenly her chin is resting on his shoulder because they are slow-dancing, just shuffling their feet in time together, really, in that tiny space, but dancing all the same, Sudhir's arm tight and strong around her waist, his other hand holding hers in place over his heart. *Everybody has a hungry heart.* She sure did, didn't she? She sure did and didn't even know it, didn't know it until this moment, but already that hunger is receding, replaced by something she has no name for. Happiness? Contentment? No. Belonging. That's it. Coming home.

She decides to sneak a peek at Sudhir's face, turns her head slightly, and he moves, too. They stare at each other for a second and their lips meet unplanned. The kiss is the most natural thing Maggie has ever experienced. "Hi," he whispers to her, and she replies, "Hello."

That was it, Maggie now thinks. They held each other for the first time at that concert and had never let go. If she'd once been unsure whether Sudhir loved her, she had never been unsure since. All these years he had been by her side, steady, consistent, reliable. They'd had their challenges—the commuter marriage, when she stayed at NYU to finish her Ph.D. while Sudhir graduated and took his first teaching job in the Midwest; the three miscarriages and the cold, growing realization that they would remain childless while most of their college friends had babies; the inevitable culture clashes as they learned to become a couple. But by the time they moved to Cedarville seventeen years ago, they had built a life together. Sudhir knew about Wallace's abandonment of her, even if he didn't know the reason for it, and he was determined to compensate for every wound, every slight, his wife had suffered. Everything that Wallace had not been, Sudhir was. Everything that Wallace was, Sudhir wasn't. Everything that Wallace had stolen from her, Sudhir had replaced.

Maggie lifted her head slowly from where it rested on the steering wheel, blinking as a shaft of afternoon sunlight assailed her eyes. What was she doing? How could she risk hurting a man who had spent the last thirty years shielding her from the world, who had loved her with a steadfastness that still astounded her? She knew how Sudhir flinched if she so much as raised her voice at him, how sensitive he was. How long did she think her fling with Peter would remain a secret? How long before someone in this goddamn village—Cedarville called itself a city, but Lord, coming from New York, she knew better—saw her driving to Peter's house and let something slip? Or Sudhir picked up her phone by accident and saw a text from Peter? She tried to carry it with her at all times when she was home, but what if she slipped just once? Even if she didn't get caught, surely it was unfair to Sudhir regardless, this clandestine sneaking around, this hypervigilance, the secrecy and lies?

Maggie frowned. Oh God. Oh dear God. She was behaving just like her father. This was what Wallace had done, sneaked around behind his dying wife's back, crept into her room in the dark, lied and made her lie. Maggie shook with anger, although she was unsure of the target of her anger—herself, her father, or something larger and more amorphous than that: genetics, destiny, the curse of childhood abuse. Damn. She had tried so very hard not to be like Wallace. She had been so responsible in her adult relationships. Even her choice of profession was predicated on a desire to help people, to heal, rooted in a belief that people could choose happiness, could choose health, could choose to live an honorable life with integrity.

Integrity. Maybe she should give up that word for at least a few years. Until she had made things right with her unsuspecting husband, who came home from a day of teaching or a week at a conference, not knowing that his wife had spent the afternoon or evening walking around naked in a cottage on the outskirts of town, or had reached home an hour before he had and had gone directly into the shower, scrubbing her skin until she was rid of the smell and the touch of Peter Weiss. Until she could look at herself in the mirror again without flinching. Until the self-loathing, which sat like a small island in her stomach, floated away.

Maggie looked in the direction of Sylvia's house, fighting a strong urge to crawl back inside, to process with her the revelation she'd had about mimicking Wallace's shabby behavior.

And then she thought: You don't need Sylvia. You know exactly what you need to do. Even if it hurts like hell. Even if it means experiencing the old childhood feeling of abandonment. Because you're an adult now. A grown woman, in a good marriage.

She took her cell phone out of her purse and sat holding it, staring out the windshield. It was two p.m. on a Tuesday. Peter would be at school. She could leave a long message on his home machine. That way, she would avoid the complicated fusion of shame and exhilaration she felt each time she tried to break up with him and he talked her out of it. Not this time. Not this time.

She dialed Peter's number and waited for the answering machine. Listened to his whimsical greeting and smiled involuntarily. Took a deep breath. And then spoke into the machine. She went on for so long that it cut her off and she had to call a second time. Her voice was firmer now; she could hear it herself. She ended by saying she'd loved every moment she'd spent with him, but she knew it was time to end things, now, before anyone got hurt. And that she would not respond if he tried calling her again, which she hoped he respected her enough not to do.

She hung up and threw the phone on the seat. She knew Peter well enough to know how prickly he could be, how easily his ego could be bruised. Peter, she suspected, didn't pursue women past a certain point. Also, he would know that she had deliberately chosen to call when he'd be away from home, and that, perhaps more than her words, would keep him away.

So. It was done. She had done it, proved to herself that she was different from her father, that Wallace had not corrupted her down to the core. Peter would be leaving the university at the end of the semester anyway. She had simply expedited their inevitable parting. Now she could focus on the rest of her life with Sudhir. And if she occasionally felt that something was missing, that Peter had brought out a side of her—a sexually alive, unpredictable, exuberant side—that she'd never know again, if she ever found herself comparing her husband unfavorably against Peter's ambition and worldliness, she would tell herself that it was the less flamboyant qualities of trust, reliability, dependability that made for a good marriage.

Maggie gathered up her hungry heart and drove home.

25

I's TIRED TONIGHT. When I finish cleaning MaryJo's house today, her friend Gina stop by with request: She having the party tomorrow and her maid is calling sick. Could I please to clean her house next? She pay extra.

I wanting to say no but I not knowing how. I also remindering what MaryJo tell me recently—Gina find out she has special type of the 'rthritis called rummytoy 'rthritis. Gina's hands not twisting like Ma's, but still, how to say no to someone who sick? So I say yes. I calls husband to say please to eat something for dinner, as I coming home late. He do his usual fuss on the phone but I just listen and then say bye.

Later, husband look up when I walks into the apartment. My feets hurting so hard, I walking like—how you say in English? I don't know the wording—like langdi.

In the husband's face, there is no kindness. "This is result of your greed," he say, pointing to my feets. "Bas, one-two jobs you get and you've become money-greedy. Now you thank your Maggie for this."

My temper chili-hot these days. "Why for khali-pili you drag Maggie into this? What Maggie ever steal from you? Has she eaten even one grain of salt that belong to you? If anything, you is in her debt."

"I in her debt?" Husband voice loud as mine. "I? What that

darkie do for me? She filling my wife's head with big-fancy thought. She trying to break my—"

The pain from my feets now enter my head. This man give me headache. "Don't call her darkie. That—that insult. Your own skin more dark than Maggie. Her name—call her proper. 'African-American' is proper way."

Husband look at me with his mouth open. "Wah, wah, Lakshmi," he say. "You think because you have some few house-cleaning job, because you driving car and listening to those stupid tapes to learn the proper English, you now Am'rican membsahib? Who can now teach her husband how to talk?"

I so tired, I only wants to sit on sofa and listen to my Manna Dey CD. Why this man chose this time to start fight with me? I remember what Sudhir babu say to me other day. He say since I am U.S. citizen, I have exact same rights as everyone, even the president. I am same as everyone, even white people, Sudhir babu say. I wants to tell the husband this, but I not a fighter-cock like him. So I keeps shut.

Thanks God, he shut up also. He go back to watching his Bollywood TV channel, and after few minute, I go and sit next to him on sofa. It is old Raj Kapoor movie and we watch quiet for few minute. I put one feets on the sofa and massage it. One time when I cleaning Maggie's house, I go into her living room and she lying down on couch and Sudhir babu massage her feets. I feels so many things then—embarrass, as if I watching them naked, but also the sweet pain in my heart, like when Raj Kapoor never get to marry the heroine. I think, Why my husband never show kindness for me?

"You see this movie when you young boy?" I ask, and husband nod yes.

"Of course. It was top hit. Play in the cinema in my village for more than one year, solid."

I smile. Talking about Hindi films, husband's favorite subject. He know all songs, who star in what picture. Because I thirteen years younger than husband, I not knowing all same movie he knowing.

"So what happen in the end?" I ask.

Husband laugh and tap my hand two times. "Woman," he say. "You so impatient you cannot wait until end?"

"I have to get up to warm up food for me. I's starving. So I will miss ending."

Something happen then. Husband give big sigh and get up from couch. "You sit," he say. "I go heat your dinner. I seen this movie hazaar times." My mouth become so open, the husband laughing. "Close your mouth," he say, "before the fly get in."

I hear the ting-tong of stainless steel pots as husband takes out food on a plate to heat. I look around this room for the angel who is hiding here. What other reason why husband preparing my plate? Maybe he wanting the sex tonight? But for that, he not needing to heat my food.

And then I listen: The voice of Mukesh is singing one of Raj Kapoor's most top-hit song. So sad, so beautiful, the song sound, like the first drop of rain after the earth is old from waiting. I remembers one night when Shilpa still a baby and she cry and cry because she hungry. Shilpa born during year of worst drought, and we having so little to eat that Ma get weak and not able to make enough milk for baby. So she always hungry and Dada go mad because crying baby and starving wife make him feel so bad. The night that Shilpa cry till one o'clock, he get up and turn radio loud, so he not hear baby crying, and this same Mukesh song play on radio. And what you think? Little Shilpa get all chup. And two minute later, she falling to sleep.

Angel name Mukesh is in my house right now. Music is how

angel talk. Everybody know that. It is Mukesh that turn my husband's heart soft. Music make people want to be good. It make him bring hot-hot plate of food to me, while I sits on the couch like a maharani.

Husband put the food on coffee table. "Eat," he say, but I wait, embarrass to eat while he standing in front of me. His face frown when he see my feets. They is swolled from standing all day. He say something under his breath and then says again, "Eat. Food getting cold."

When he leaf the room, I begin to eat but I also feels alonely. Why he leaf? Does my feets look so ugly it make him sick? I hears water running in the kitchen. Is he washing the dishes? If so, Mukesh not only angel, he saint. I knows I should helping him but it first time all day I's eating and the food is hot and tasty. Why I say no when MaryJo offer me the sandwich earlier today?

I finish eating and puts the plate on table. I fighting with my eyes, because I wants them to stay open to watch ending of film and they wanting to be shut. For one minute, I let them win, and bas, I am sleeping sitting on sofa.

"Lakshmi." Husband voice sound angry. "Wake up."

"I's awake," I say, rubbing my eyes, swallow my yawn. And then my eyes really open big.

Husband has put a towel on floor near me. On the towel is the pink plastic basin. Inside basin is steamy hot water. And also on towel is box of Epsom salts. "Here," he say. "Put the feets inside this. It take down the swelling."

But now it is my eyes who is swolled. With tears. "You make this for me?"

He give a short smile. "Who else?" he say, like he irritate, but I hears the pride in his voice.

Maybe angel not in this room. Maybe I dead and I in heaven. "Many thanks."

"Mention not. Now, woman, you going to sit there and let water get cold?"

"No," I say, slowly putting one feets in and then the next one. Within one-two minute, I feel the tired leaving my body.

Husband come sit next to me. "How it feel?" he ask.

"Like Taj Mahal and Las Vegas combo," I say. "Tops."

He look surprise and then he laugh. Pranab, one of his card-player friend, saying this every time he get good cards. "Lakshmi," he say when he stop laughing. "You getting smart in your old age."

The words slips from my mouth, as easy as a letter slip into a postbox. "Maybe if I get smart, you begin to love me."

Hard to say who more shock, him or me. The words come out of my mouth but they not dead. They fly around in the room like pigeons and we too embarrass to look at them. "I just—" I begins, but he break in my words.

"Who say I don't love you?" he say in joking voice. "Woman, why you being stupid again?"

I know he trying to free me, to make me not feel embarrass. But now I wants to talk, to break this hard coconut shell we have lived inside for six years. I remembers how Maggie hold Sudhir babu's hand when he come home from work, and before I can stops myself, I pick up the husband's hand. But once I holding it, I not knowing what to do next. Keep it on his leg? Move it to mine? Hold it in air? He help me by putting both our hand on his knee. "Ji, I wants to say something," I says. "I wants to say, I so sorry for what happened before. I knows you not loving me. It's okay. I knows you are a good man. You kind and honest. You deserve good wife. I sorry for how I destroy your life. If I return to earth in ten lives, I still not deserve your forgiveness. I's sorry."

Six years these words living inside me, moving from my heart to my mouth, back into my heart. Why I not say them before? Maybe because I ascare, like I is right now. Without turning my head, I look at the husband. He not looking at me. One minute, two minute pass. I hears tick-tick of clock on the wall. Then he say, "No sense talking about past, Lakshmi. It was our destiny, bas. God's decision."

We both looking at Raj Kapoor film still, but so many tears in my eyes, Raj Kapoor look like I seeing him from my windshield on a rainy day. What the right word? Blurty? Blurry. After a minute, husband get up from the sofa. "I need to tally day's receipts on the computer," he say, but I know he making excuse to go leaf me. What I say upset him also.

I stay on sofa after he go into bedroom. Slowly, the water in the basin get cold, just like the cold that entering my heart.

26

M AGGIE LOOKED AT Lakshmi curiously, wondering if she'd ever seen the younger woman this upset or agitated. Lakshmi had called early this morning and asked whether she could come. "It is a Urgency," she'd said. "If you have one hour, please to fit me in."

Today was Maggie's day off from the hospital. She had planned on running errands this morning, before her first patient came in at two, but that would obviously have to wait. Unlike some of her patients, Lakshmi would not have called unless it was truly a crisis. "Yes, of course," Maggie said. "Can you be here by ten?"

A brief pause and then Lakshmi said, "Yes. I suppose to help Rekha today, but she can manage alone."

Now that Lakshmi was sitting on the leather chair in front of Maggie, she was strangely tongue-tied. She would start a sentence, stop, let it fade away. Begin again and then shake her head furiously, as if to deny the tears that kept filling her eyes.

"What is it?" Maggie asked again. "What's wrong? You said it was an emergency."

"I . . . It is, Maggie. But not like that. What I saying is . . . It from before. Last night . . ."

"I don't under—"

"Maggie. I have to tell. A secret. Something bad I do."

"Whatever it is—"

"But I cannot tell. Like this. I feeling your eyes on me. Please, can we go for short walk? Please."

It was the end of February. There was no snow on the ground but it was still only thirty-eight degrees. Maggie's knee gave an involuntary stab at the thought of walking in the cold. But Lakshmi looked like she was going to collapse in the office if Maggie refused. "Okay," she said shortly. "Let me go get my coat."

At least the wind was low and the sun was out. Maggie crossed to the sunny side of the street, Lakshmi following closely. "Okay," Maggie said. "You want to tell me what's going on?"

Tomato, the orange tabby from a few houses down, came down the driveway to rub against them, and Lakshmi bent to stroke him. When she got up, Maggie saw that her nose was red, but she couldn't tell if it was from the cold or if Lakshmi was crying. She decided to wait.

"Maggie. If I tell you a secret, do you promise not to bump me?"

"Bump you? What do you mean?"

Lakshmi looked impatient. "You know, bump me. Stop being my friend."

Maggie bit down on her lip to suppress her laughter. "Oh. You mean dump you. Not bump."

"Okay. But you promise?"

"What a ridiculous question, Lakshmi. Of course I won't stop being your friend. Or your therapist," she added.

Lakshmi turned her head and stared at Maggie as they walked, looked at her for a long time as if gauging her, trying to decide something. Suppressing a sigh, Maggie put her hand on Lakshmi's shoulder. "My dear, whatever it is, you'll feel better after you tell me. Now, what is it?"

For the first time that morning, Lakshmi smiled. "Shilpa and

I use to walk like this, with her hand on my shoulder. Ravi chac-
cha, who is oldest man in our village, use to bless us when we
walk past his house. 'May you two sisters always be this close,
not only in this janam but the next life also.' And Maggie, I always use to think, Of course we be this close forever. We sisters,
no? I never think day can come when I don't know if my Shilpa
is dead or alive."

"Is this—secret—about Shilpa?" Maggie asked softly.

"Yes. No. Yes. Maggie. Belief me when I say everything is about
Shilpa. Even when I makes this big sin, it about Shilpa." The tears
rolled down Lakshmi's face. "Although to save my Shilpa, I kill
someone else."

They had arrived at the park at the bottom of the street, and
Maggie gestured toward the lagoon. Apart from six or seven Can-
ada geese, there was no one else there. "Want to walk around the
lake?" she asked.

Lakshmi nodded. Because of the cold, they walked briskly,
and by the time Lakshmi was done with her story, they were both
a little out of breath.

27

IT WAS THE third and final day of the mela, and Lakshmi, Shilpa, and three of their friends were eating their second plate of pyali, the spicy concoction of chickpeas, onion, and boiled potatoes that all the girls loved. Flush with the monthly wages she'd just received from her bookkeeping job, Lakshmi was treating the other four. "Didi," Shilpa gasped. "Can we have some sugarcane juice next? This is burning my mouth."

"Arre, peanut." Lakshmi laughed. "At least finish one thing before asking for something else." She laughed again because it was a beautiful warm night, because the rain had held off, because there were three hours before the annual fair closed for the season, because she was here with her sister and her friends, and because she had money in her pocket. She tossed her head back at the inky night sky, whose stars had been overshadowed by the lights of the mela, but then her laugh caught in her throat and she frowned. Standing less than ten feet away from the group of girls was a man, a tall, dark-skinned, middle-aged man with scanty hair that he had combed forward onto his forehead. Even a quick glance told Lakshmi that there was something different about this man, something foreign, the cut of his blue shirt a little more stylish than that of the other men milling around, the cut of his hair a little less severe than the local people's. A foreigner in their midst. What made the laugh die in her throat was the intensity with which he was staring at them. Lakshmi turned her head involuntarily, to follow his line of vision, and realized with a start of outrage that he was staring at Shilpa, her baby sister, who was totally oblivious to his gaze, who was licking the last of the chickpeas off her lips in a manner that Lakshmi knew was innocent but also, she could see, could be mistaken for seductive. She felt a flash of anger toward the stranger, who was, she knew for sure, misreading her sister's innocent gesture, and who was staring at her with a boldness she found shocking. She moved her body a few inches, positioning herself between Shilpa and the man, blocking his view of her, and was rewarded by a glare. She glared back and the man looked startled, as if he'd just re- alized that she had caught him looking. He turned away hastily, and Lakshmi was about to turn away herself when she saw him talking to a man whom Lakshmi vaguely recognized.

She'd had enough. "Come on," she said roughly, tugging at the sleeve of Shilpa's kurta. "Put that empty bowl down."

"But Didi—"

"Didn't you hear? Let's go."

Ignoring the complaints of their other friends, she hurried Shilpa along. "Where are we going? What's the rush?" Shilpa grumbled, but as always, she allowed herself to be led by her older sister.

"You said you wanted ganna juice, correct?" Lakshmi said, and knew she'd said the right thing when she heard Shilpa's squeal: "Yes."

But when they got to the sugarcane juice stall, the man and his friend were there. Lakshmi felt a pinprick of apprehension. Did the man know them? Why was he following them? Why was he looking at them so boldly? What gave him the right? She wished her dada were here, but after accompanying them to the mela on the opening day, Dada had refused to go with them the next two nights. "You foolish girls, go," he said. "I see everything there is to see first day only. Why for I want to go again?"

They had looked at their father in puzzlement, unable to explain the obvious—they wanted to go again and again because they'd had a great time on the first day and wanted to relive their pleasure: to eat more bhelpuri and other snacks, to ride on the Giant Wheel until it made them dizzy, to watch the actors in their makeup and costumes reenact parts of the Mahabharata, even though by the second day, they knew most of the dialogue by heart. It was the annual mela! It came only once a year. And it took them out of the sleepiness and hardship of their daily lives and jolted them awake with fun, music, games, excitement, lights, color, made them hear the buzzing of their youth, awakened their Bollywood dreams and made them seem possible. It connected them to the wider world because people from the surrounding villages also attended the mela, so in three days, they saw more people than they did in the rest of the year. Of course they would go back to the mela, squeezing from it every drop of color and excitement, so that their normal black-and-white lives came alive in reds and blues and greens for those three days.

Now Lakshmi felt her father's absence. Because the girls were almost done with their drinks, but the men lingered. She was amazed that none of the other four seemed to have noticed. The shameless man's eyes were almost sticking out of his head as he dirtied her beautiful sister with his looking. Again she situated herself between the two of them, feeling his eyes drilling holes into her walled back.

When she turned around again, they were gone. Lakshmi looked left and right, unable to believe her luck, but couldn't see them. Wait, now she spotted them, walking briskly away, the tall man in the blue shirt stooping slightly to hear what his friend was saying. "Go, go," she said silently to herself. "Take your dirty rubbish somewhere else."

"Ae, Didi, kya hua? What for you looking like you drinking sour milk? This juice is sweet, no?"

The other girls giggled, and Lakshmi allowed herself to be pulled out of her outrage. The man was a foreigner, obviously a city fellow. Lakshmi had heard that city people did not have good manners. Nobody had taught the stranger that men from good families did not stare at unknown women as if they wanted to . . . Lakshmi blushed and shook away the picture forming in her head.

"Let's go look at the stall where they selling bangles and all," Shilpa said, and Lakshmi readily agreed.

By the time the fair ended that night, she had forgotten about the stranger and his rude foreign manners.

Her stomach lurched when she saw him again. Sitting next to Dada on the rope bed in front of the house. The late-afternoon sun glinting off the big gold watch that he wore. Lakshmi, who had come home after spending the day tending to Menon sahib's accounts, suppressed a shudder when she saw the thick wrist upon which the watch sat, and below it, the fat short fingers.

"Arre, beti, come," Dada said. "Come, we have some good news to share."

The man rose from the bed and folded his hands. "Namaste ji," he said, a slight smirk playing on his lips, as if they were sharing a joke that excluded Dada.

Lakshmi gazed at Dada, who looked happier and less burdened than he had in years. Was this stranger a jadoogar, that he could make her father look ten years younger? She raised her eyebrow in silent inquiry at her father.

"Beti, come sit," Dada said, patting the bed, but Lakshmi

continued standing. After a moment, Dada continued, "Achcha, stand then. But—"

"You said you had good news," she interrupted. "What is it?"

Dada laughed. "We have a proposal," he said. When she looked at him blankly, he added, "A marriage proposal, I say. For our Shilpa."

"Who from?" Lakshmi asked, wondering whether Dilip had found the nerve to ask Dada. But why hadn't he told her first?

"Arre, wah. What kind of question is that, beta?" Dada glanced at the man who sat beside him. "From this young man, of course. His name is Adit Patil, of Annavati district. And he come to us all the way from Am'rica."

The man folded his hands and said namaste once again, but Lakshmi ignored him. Did Dada have cataracts, she wondered, that he thought this mountain sitting beside him was young? "He almost your age, Dada," she said. "How he can marry our little Shilpa?"

Patil shot her a venomous look. "I only thirty-nine years old," he said.

She ignored him. "Plus, what our Shilpa wanting with the Am'rica?" she continued. She lowered her voice. "They say all people there eating beef."

"'Scue me," the man interrupted. "I owning famous restaurant in Am'rica. And we never serving the beef." He smirked again, as if he had trumped Lakshmi, and she stared back, not afraid to let her distaste show on her face.

"See, Lakshmi?" Dada said eagerly. There was an appeasing quality in his voice that embarrassed her. "This is a good man. He come highly recommended by Vithal, from our village."

She felt a flash of irritation at her father and, in order to hide it, asked, "Where's Shilpa?"

"She go over to Jyoti's house to study for tomorrow's exam."

Dada turned to face the stranger. "My little daughter very smart. She working as stenographer but now taking computer course. Both my daughters smart. Both my daughters go to the school." He pointed at Lakshmi with his chin. "But this one had to stop after her mother get sick."

The man barely raised his eyes to look at Lakshmi, who felt her face burn. Why for Dada had to tell about her life to this stranger? She opened her mouth, but the man beat her to it. "Your Shilpa can go to the college in Am'rica," he said expansively. "I myself will pay for the fees."

Dada beamed. "My daughter going to college? I wish my Shilpa's mother was alive to witness this day, beta."

The man shot Lakshmi a triumphant look. "And as I mentioned earlier, uncle," he said in a loud voice that Lakshmi was sure was for her benefit, "I will not be requiring a dowry. In Am'rica, we don't believe in dowry-fowry."

That explained the look of relief on Dada's face. What father wouldn't be relieved at a suitor not wanting lakhs of rupees or a car or at least a refrigerator and a stove for the favor of taking his young unmarried daughter off his hands? For a moment Lakshmi softened. Perhaps she had misjudged this man. But the next second, she remembered Dilip, and her heart sank. Shilpa would never agree to this proposal. And what then? Would Dada actually force her, marry her off against her wishes?

"Beti, are you going to stand around like a statue, or will you go inside and make us some tea?" Dada's voice was teasing, but his eyes were serious. Her rude behavior was not going unnoticed.

She nodded and ducked her head low to enter the house. She fired up the old kerosene stove, pulled out the dented pan, measured two cups of water, and added the tea leaves. As she waited for the water to boil, she could hear the two men outside, heard their laughter and the murmur of their voices rise and fall. "I's sorry, beta," she heard her father say. "My Lakshmi raise her sister after their mother's death. She like a tigress when . . ." She couldn't hear the rest of her father's words as the man spoke over them. Lakshmi could make out only "my elder sister" and "women are like that."

She lingered in the kitchen a moment longer than necessary, reluctant to join the two men, but at the last minute, some ancient propriety made her grab a small plate and place six Glucose biscuits on it, to serve with the tea. Balancing the two cups and the plate, she went back out, and when the man saw her, he jumped to his feet and took one of the cups out of her hand. His fingers grazed hers as he removed the cup, and she jumped back, spilling a few drops from her father's cup. She hoped the man had not noticed, but he had, and he raised his right eyebrow slowly, as if puzzled by her obvious dislike of him. "Thank you," he said in English. "Good tea."

In response, she turned to her father for guidance. They had never received a marriage proposal, and she had no idea whether to participate or leave the negotiations to the two men. But apparently, they were done talking, because after a few more sips, the man set down his cup on the ground below the rope bed and said, "Well, I've taken up enough of your time. I am leaving for Mumbai tomorrow for a few days, but my oldest sister get in touch. She will bring you the horoscope and anything else that you need. My only request is that if you accept my proposal, we plan for the shaadi in two weeks, ji. I needing to get back to my restaurant, you see."

Dada looked startled. "Two weeks to plan a shaadi? Beta, how to plan so quickly-quickly? Beside, I have to see about my Lakshmi. How it look if younger daughter get marry before older one?"

The man's eyes flickered dismissively over Lakshmi's face.

"Times different now," he said to Dada. "If good proposal come first for younger daughter, what can you do?" He leaned toward the older man. "Not too many mens not wanting dowry, uncle. Even my own family angry with me. Saying I come back from Am'rica with modern ideas. But with money you save, you can give this one a big dowry." Lakshmi flushed, hearing what the man insinuated but didn't say—that with her plain looks, she would need it.

Dada nodded slowly. "You are talking sense, beta." He blinked a few times. "I just wasn't ready to losing my Shilpa so soon. Ever since their mother died—"

"Uncle. If you like, even after marriage, she can stay with you. Of course, custom is that after wedding day, the girl moves to live with her husband's relations." He sighed heavily. "But you a widower. I understands. So she can stay here. Getting her visa for Am'rica will take a few months, no? That time, she can spend here."

Despite herself, Lakshmi found herself admiring the man's tenacity. He had an answer for everything, this one. How else he could have big, famous restaurant in the Am'rica?

The man rose to take his leave. "My sister drop off the horoscope tomorrow. We will wait for your reply then."

Shilpa wasn't studying at her friend's house, as Dada believed. Lakshmi knew exactly where she was—at the cinema hall two towns over, with Dilip. For the last year, any chance she got, Shilpa spent with that young man. Lakshmi missed spending time with her baby sister, but she understood. She liked Dilip. The owner of a small auto repair shop that he had opened two years ago, Dilip was hardworking, honest, and best of all, always quick with a laugh. When they were together, he and Shilpa acted more like brother and sister, always laughing, joking, pinching, teasing. Dilip had just one black mark against him: He was poor. On his mechanic's income, he supported his parents and three younger siblings. Lakshmi knew what that meant—Dilip's parents would look to marry off their only son to a woman who came with a big dowry. Dada could maybe afford a good dowry for one of them. But both? Even if he mortgaged the house, there was not that much money. Not that either one of his daughters would allow him to do so; just a few months ago, when Lakshmi had urged Shilpa to tell Dada about Dilip, Shilpa had insinuated as much. "I know Dada can't afford dowry for both of us, Didi," she'd said. "Dilip and I, we young. We not hurrying to get married. We wait." What Shilpa left unsaid was obvious: We wait until someone proposes marriage to you. We wait until we know how much of a dowry they'll demand to marry a twenty-six-year-old woman with a face as brown and plain as a chapati. And then we'll know how much money is left over for me.

Now there was this complication. Or was it an opportunity? It was almost unheard of—a man owning a famous restaurant in Am'rica, proposing marriage to a woman without even checking to see if the horoscopes were compatible, and as if that were not enough, refusing a dowry. All because he had lost his heart to her at a mela. It seemed like a miracle, something that would happen in a Hindi film. Except the man doing the proposing was no Sharukh Khan or Abhishek Bachchan. He was a bulky, serious-looking man with thin hair, wanting to run away with her young, beautiful sister. She could never imagine Shilpa punching this man playfully on the arm as she did Dilip, couldn't imagine him laughing at Shilpa's silly jokes the way Dilip did, couldn't picture the two of them singing out loud as they rode on a scooter.

Lakshmi's head jerked up at the thought of Dilip's scooter. She knew the spot where Dilip usually dropped Shilpa off on the far side of the field, so she could pretend she was returning from Jyoti's house. Her father looked up as she rose from her cot, turning his gaze from the old TV that Menon sahib had given them. "You going somewhere, beti?"

"Thought I'd walk the little one home from Jyoti's. You know how she is about walking home alone."

Dada nodded. "Go get her, beti. She always was afraid of darkness."

Even though it was dusk, she walked across the familiar land swiftly, her feet knowing each rut and ridge in her father's field. She had just reached the small side road when she heard the sound of Dilip's scooter. "Didi," Shilpa said breathlessly, her brown eyes worried as she slipped off the scooter, "What is it? Is Dada . . . ?"

"He fine. Everyone fine. I just wanting to take evening walk."

Dilip leaned over, his usual smile a little broader today. "We have some good news for you, Didi." He rumbled the engine of his scooter. "Shilpa will tell you," he said. "Achcha, chalta hu. Bye."

They waited until they couldn't see Dilip's silhouette, and then they linked their arms around each other's shoulders the way they always did and began the walk toward home.

"So what's the good news?" Lakshmi asked.

"Yes, yes, Didi, wait, na, I was just going to tell." Shilpa stopped walking and turned so the two women were facing each other. "You know Roshan? He working in Dilip's garage? Well, Didi, he tell Dilip that he like you. But he ascare of you, since you work in Menon sahib's shop and all. He think you a big shot."

Lakshmi felt her face flushing. Roshan had been in school with her. Even as a boy, he had been polite and soft-spoken. And nice-looking. To cover up her embarrassment she asked sternly, "Why for Dilip talking about me to strange men?"

"He didn't, Didi. Roshan only came to him. For the advice."

A flock of birds flew overhead, making their way home in the dying light of the day. Lakshmi traced their frenzied flight, and as she looked skyward, her eyes filled with tears. Ae bhagwan, she thought. Why you playing such tricks on your Lakshmi? She had always admired Roshan but had never imagined that he had so much as noticed her. But he had, enough to talk to Dilip about her. Even the fact that she was long past marriageable age had not stopped Roshan from liking her.

But what use? she told herself fiercely. If she were to even consider marriage, where was money going to come for Shilpa's wedding to Dilip? And as long as she, the oldest, remained un-married, how could Shilpa marry?

"Didi? Are you happy that—"

"I have news, too," she interrupted. "Somebody came to the house today. With marriage proposal. For you."

"Big joker, you are, Didi." Shilpa began to giggle but stopped abruptly because of what she saw on Lakshmi's face. "Didi?"

"No joke," Lakshmi said, shaking her head. "No joke. He from Annavati district," she continued. "He seeing you at the mela and making inquiries. He came and talk to Dada today. Say he wanting to marry you in two week, tops. Then he return to Am'rica, where he stays, and make the visa for you. You goes few months later."

Even in the gathering dark, Lakshmi could see the fear on Shilpa's face. "And what did Dada say?"

She shrugged. "What can Dada say? We will make inquiries also, to see what kind of khandan he come from. Husband family more important than husband, Dada saying. Tomorrow he send-ing his horoscope to match with yours."

Shilpa's voice was quiet, but there was a quality to it that scared Lakshmi. "And you, Didi? What did you say?"

The heat rose in Lakshmi's face. Why did Shilpa sound like she was accusing her of something? "What can I say? I's a woman. Who ask me? This between the menfolks, Shilpa."

"I love Dilip. You know that, Didi. Still you didn't say any-thing?"

They were close enough to the house that they could see the blue glow of the television through the window. Still, Lakshmi didn't bother to keep her voice down. "Yesterday you begging me not to tell Dada about Dilip. Today you angry that I keeping my mouth shut. What you want from me, Shilpa? What you want?"

In reply, Shilpa quickened her pace. "Wait," Lakshmi called. "Listen to me." But the younger woman only walked faster.

Their father greeted them at the door. "Did you give our munni the good news?" he asked.

"Dada," Shilpa said. "I don't want to marry the man from Am'rica. I am happy here in our little village."

The old man shook his head. "Arre, Munni, beti, you just ascare. We will make inquires, but if horoscopes match and if what we hear about his family is good, then why wait, beti? We poor people. How many good offers we going to get? I want to see my daughters settle in life before I die."

"Then marry Lakshmi first. She's older."

A look of embarrassment came over Dada's face. "What to do, beti? The offer is for you. And with not having to pay dowry for you, maybe I can find good match for Lakshmi."

Shilpa looked sharply at Lakshmi and then back at her father. "What you mean, no dowry? He not wanting dowry?"

Dada looked incredulous. "You not tell her that? Best part you not tell her?"

"No chance I'm having to say anything. She just—"

"So I am the bakri here? The goat who has to be killed so Lakshmi has money for dowry?"

Lakshmi shut her eyes, afraid that the hurt would leak out of them. In all her days, she had never heard Shilpa talk like this. She shook her head, trying to focus on what Shilpa was saying.

"Dada, listen. I am going with someone. I didn't want to say until. But his name is Dilip. And we having feelings for each other. We wanting to marry, Dada."

The old man looked confused, then stricken. "Dada, come sit," Lakshmi said, steering him to the cot. She ignored his accusatory "You were knowing?" and hurried into the kitchen to fetch him a glass of water.

"Now you telling me this?" Dada was saying when she returned. "After I invite that poor man into our house and welcome his proposal? Do your father's name and izzat mean nothing to you, beti?"

Shilpa was crying now. "I knows, Dada. I am sorry. Dilip was wanting to save some money before coming to you. His car repair business new, Dada. He supporting his whole family. We just trying to—"

"Wah, wah. So we spit on offer from rich businessman from Am'rica to wait on some fool mechanic to save money," Dada said viciously. "One time God sending good luck to our house, and we telling God to please get out. Shabash, beti. Well done."

"Dada. I loves Dilip. We wants to marry." Shilpa shot an angry look at Lakshmi. "Didi. Why you not saying anything?"

Lakshmi felt slow, dim-witted, could feel the gears of her brain creaking and grinding to a halt. The girl who had flown in order to rescue a small boy from drowning in a well, the girl who had won a prize for reciting a poem, the young woman who had looked an elephant in the eye and seen the source of his pain, the woman whom the richest man in the village treated like a favored niece—that Lakshmi had disappeared, had been chased out by the man appearing like a nightmare earlier today. This Lakshmi, who sat mute as the two people she loved most dearly in the world talked over each other, couldn't figure out whose side to take, who had the better argument. Her heart ached for her baby sister, whom she had never been able to deny anything until now. But pitted against their father's claim, Shilpa's mewing, her declaration of her love for Dilip, felt childish. Dada was right—ignorant of his daughter's involvement with Dilip, he had given his word that he would take the other man's offer of marriage seriously. His reputation, his name, was at stake. Even if they could ignore that, it was impossible to ignore the compelling financial argument. Nothing changed the fact that a marriage proposal without dowry was the kind of blessing for which most families would give thanks forever. Blinded by his desire for Shilpa, the man had made this preposterous offer. Blinded by her love for Dilip, Shilpa was rejecting it without considering it.

There was yet another side. Her side. Was it her fault that she was born without much of the natural beauty that Shilpa possessed? That she was born to a poor father who couldn't afford two dowries? That her parents were cursed with no male offspring, which meant they had no way to offset the cost of marrying two daughters? Just finding out that Roshan had made inquiries about her had opened up a whole new vista. If Shilpa were to say yes, and if Roshan could look past the stigma of having her younger sister marrying first, there would be money for her to marry.

"No," she said to herself, but the startled expressions on the other two faces told her she'd said it out loud. No. She would not put her desires ahead of her sister's. She was tin; Shilpa was gold. Shilpa was born beautiful; she was born ordinary. It had always been so, and she had never resented or challenged this hierarchy. She was happy to be the mule so that Shilpa could be the racehorse. She had dropped out of school, taken care of their mother, worked like a man beside her father in the fields, ingratiated herself into Menon sahib's life, all so Shilpa could finish school, not be burdened with the care of their mother, not have to toil in the fields. Even though she was only five years older, she felt as if she had given birth to Shilpa, felt that parental obligation to bear any burden, put up with any humiliation to ease Shilpa's way. And it had worked. It had worked. Shilpa was one of the few women in their village who had finished high school. She now had a good secretarial job in town and was also taking a computer science class. She was in love with a kind, cheerful fellow with dancing eyes. Her hands were soft and unbroken, a constant source of pride to Lakshmi.

"No," she said out loud. "Dada, Shilpa already find someone to marry. Dilip is a good boy. She will be happy with him. Give her your blessings."

"And what about you, beti?"

She managed a laugh. "What about me? I stay here, Dada. Same as always. Who going to take care of you in old age if I also leaf?"

Dada looked at her with his wise gray eyes as he pulled on his mustache. "You not give enough yet to this family, Lakshmi?" he said quietly. "You still wanting to give more?" He shook his head with a disgusted look. "Best student in the whole school, you were. That you give up to take care of your poor mother. It kill me, but nothing to do. Then you do the man's work in my fields so that this little one can go to school. Still I say nothing. Now your back is becoming crooked from bending over accounting books for a man who call you his niece but won't let you enter his house since his fat wife do puja to purify it after he force you to eat there." Dada's eyes were red. "Enough. No more sacrifice. I will not allow it." He turned to face his younger daughter. "Munni. It your turn. Your Didi has given enough. I's a poor man. I don't have luxury of let you make the love marriage. This is a good proposal. If your horoscope match, I getting you married in two weeks."

"Dada, no," Shilpa and Lakshmi said simultaneously, but Dada turned his head sharply away.

"Enough," he said. "No more talking. I's your father. It my job to think about both my children. This is my decision."

"But Dada," Shilpa said.

Finally, their father raised his voice. "Munni, stop. Stop. Now go, both of you. I needs to rest. Tomorrow is busy day."

As they walked out of the room, Shilpa turned toward Lakshmi. "This is your fault," she hissed.

"But—"

"I'm telling you right now, Didi. I will kill myself before I marries anyone but Dilip."

"Shilpa. Don't speak rubbish."

"You see. You just see."

"Think of Dada. Think of—"

Shilpa turned on her. "Why?" she said. There was a wildness in her voice that Lakshmi had never heard before. "Why I think of Dada? You saw how little he think of me."

"He just wanting us to be happy . . ."

"Liar. He wanting you to be happy. He make sacrifice out of me to make sure you happy and settle in life."

Lakshmi looked away to hide the horror and sadness on her face. This was the first real fight she'd ever had with Shilpa. Please don't let their horoscopes match, she thought. Or let Dada find out that Adit Patil is a drunkard. Or that he doesn't come from a respectable family. Please. This is our only chance.

The reports on Adit were good. No smoking. No excessive drinking. Sent money from Am'rica each month for family support.

Older sister was respectably married but still looked after their elderly father. And the horoscopes matched.

The gifts began to arrive as soon as the wedding day was fixed. The wedding would be held in the groom's village, about fifteen kilometers from their own. They could invite some of their guests, of course, but since the groom was paying all expenses, please to kindly keep the numbers down—and oh, because of the groom's tight schedule, they would skip the usual pre-wedding rituals, like the mendi ceremony.

First came the red and gold sari that Shilpa was to wear on her wedding day. Then a plainer green sari for the elder sister and a white kurta-pajama set for Dada. Next, Adit's sister dropped off a set of two gold bangles, a gold necklace, and gold earrings to be worn on the wedding day. Oh, and what size shoes did the new bride wear? No, no, they would provide the shoes. Her younger brother was a businessman in Am'rica, he could afford a pair of wedding shoes. Along with the shoes arrived three pairs of shalwar-kameez suits and two pairs of Kolhapuri slippers. Oh, and a bottle of perfume that he had carried all the way from Am'rica. It was said that all of Am'rica smelled as sweet as this perfume.

My brother, he has more money than sense, the sister giggled during one of her visits. He's too generous for his own good. As if to prove her point, one week before the wedding, there arrived another gift: two lean, muscular goats, meant to be slaughtered and fed to those residents of the village who would not be invited to the wedding. Everybody knew what the gift meant: One goat would've been enough to feed the village, a generous enough gesture. Two was extravagance—a way of showing that this was not some ordinary marriage, and the groom was not some ordinary man from the village, like, say, a farmer's son or a cobbler or a schoolteacher. Or an ordinary car mechanic. This groom was a successful businessman from Am'rica. Even Menon sahib was impressed by the gesture. Went around shaking his head in disbelief the rest of the day. The second goat was sheer carelessness, which itself was a luxury only the rich could afford. It was a way of saying, Kill the second one also, or keep it as a pet for milk, it's up to you, makes no difference to us. That shrug of the shoulder which only the rich can afford.

With each gift, Shilpa got more subdued, as if cowering under the weight of the gold, vanishing under the spread of the red and gold sari, rendered mute by the scarlet blood that would soon flow in the dark fields after the Muslim butcher had expertly slit the goats' throats. Her objections to the upcoming nuptials became less vociferous, her insistence that Dada cancel the wedding less adamant. Lakshmi felt relief. The gifts proved how much Adit loved Shilpa. Maybe she was beginning to feel his love also? Shilpa was about to turn twenty-two, and it would be years before she could marry Dilip. Maybe she wanted to escape her older sister's fate? Despite her regret that her baby sister would be moving so far away, despite her shame that she was not earning enough money to allow Shilpa to marry the man she loved, Lakshmi felt a creeping sense of excitement as the day of the wedding drew near. There was so much to do. She had hired an air-conditioned taxi to drive them to Adit's village. Jyoti was to come over early that morning to do Shilpa's hair and to apply the mendi to her hands. Lakshmi herself had stitched the blouse that Shilpa would wear under her sari. She had packed a small suitcase for Shilpa's overnight honeymoon. In another break with tradition, Adit had insisted that they spend their wedding night not in his father's house but at a hotel that had sprung up on the outskirts of town. The next day, after taking lunch at her new in-laws' house, he would drive her back to Dada's house, where she would stay until her visa arrived.

Jyoti came to their house the afternoon before the wedding. Lakshmi opened the door and joked, "You's forgetting the date? Wedding not till tomorrow."

The girl smiled. "I knows, Didi. But some of us friends wanting to take Shilpa out. We having surprise for her."

Lakshmi nodded approvingly. "Good idea. I go tell her you here."

She stood in the doorway, watching as the two younger women walked toward the main road, leaning in to each other, giggling as they whispered to each other. Despite her happiness at seeing Shilpa laugh for the first time in days, Lakshmi felt a twinge of sadness. She once was like this with her school friends, but that was so long ago. Years of responsibility had beaten the care freeness out of her; lack of contact with those her own age had left her friendless. She had no close friends—the bearer of her whispered hopes and apprehensions happened to be an elephant. Once Shilpa flew to Am'rica, the last link with her own youth would be severed.

She turned away from the door, surprised at her uncharacteristic envy of Shilpa. And yet so much had been different between them these past two weeks, the lifelong closeness between them evaporating, as Shilpa spent more time with Jyoti and Lakshmi busied herself with wedding preparations.

It was to be a small wedding by the village's standards—only seventy guests, including the eight invited by Lakshmi's family—another of Adit's gestures toward modernity. But the distribution of goat meat, along with the sweets that Lakshmi had made, had gone a long way toward appeasing the bruised feelings of those not invited.

She had fed Dada his dinner an hour ago, but Shilpa was not yet home, and Lakshmi felt annoyed. Why didn't Jyoti say if their surprise included taking Shilpa out for dinner? With a sigh, she served herself some vegetables on Dada's used plate and took out a chapati from the bread tin. She would've preferred not to eat dinner alone on the last day her sister would be in this house as an unmarried woman. On the other hand, how could she begrudge Shilpa time with her friends?

She looked up, startled, when she heard the knock on the door a half hour later. Why was Shilpa knocking instead of walking in? When she answered, it was Jyoti, her eyes wide, her face drenched in sweat. "Kya hua? Where's my sister?"

In reply, Jyoti shoved a piece of paper into her hand. "Note for you, Didi," she said. "It explain."

"What?" she started, but Jyoti was already hurrying down the road, taking the same path that she and Shilpa had languidly walked down a few hours ago. Except this time the girl was almost trotting.

Lakshmi glanced at the piece of paper, read the first line, and felt her stomach drop with fear. "Wait," she called after Jyoti, but when the girl didn't stop, she raced out of the house after her. Within a few seconds, she caught up with the younger woman and spun her around. "What? What is this? This note says . . . You foolish girl, what you done?"

Jyoti's eyes shone in the dark. "What I done is helping my best friend marry the man she love. Which none of her family relations do to help her." She glared accusingly at Lakshmi.

Lakshmi felt her cheeks flush. "You. What you. Think. That I?"

"Shilpa say you and your dada sell her body so you can be married next."

A wail started from deep within Lakshmi. "No, no, no. This all wrong. I fights Dada. I's on Shilpa's side." She stopped

abruptly at the sight of a passing bicycle, and she used that time
to pull herself together. "Tell me," she said urgently. "Where my
Shilpa now?"

"With Dilip."

Lakshmi blanched. "Where?" she whispered.

"They gone away. Hiding somewhere until the wedding canceled."

Lakshmi looked up at the night sky, as if expecting it to land
on her head. This was the end of them, of Dada, of their family
name. A young woman spending the night before her wedding
with another man. Word would get out. Strangers from five villages away would hear about this beautiful, impulsive girl who
had thrown her life away, who had given them permission to spit
in her face, who had gone from being a high school graduate to a
prostitute in one heedless moment. This kheti, this unforgiving
patch of land out of which her father had coaxed things to grow;
this earth that he had battled and loved until he was a bent old
man, older than his years; this house that her parents had built
out of years of hard labor, their thin limbs the beams that held it
up, their blood and sweat mixed into the cement that made up
its walls; this family name that they had nurtured and fed like
a prized pet, this family name that belonged not to them but to
their ancestors, this izzat, this honor, that they valued more than
anything else, that compensated for the daily humiliations and
trials of their lives—the tense silence with which they waited
each harvest season while Menon sahib weighed their produce
and decreed how much it was worth; the lecture they had mutely
listened to when the local moneylender, who charged thirty percent interest, told them that having a pucca house was an in-
dulgence they couldn't afford; the terrible fear that grew each
day the rains stayed away—this stupid careless girl had tram-
pled upon their family honor, had risked all their lives with one

thoughtless gesture. Lakshmi swallowed the bile that rose in her mouth.

She stood staring at Jyoti, noticed the righteous set of her mouth, and wondered what to say, what words to use to convince the younger woman that what she believed was so right—two young lovers reunited by her, Jyoti—was in fact horribly wrong. That everything depended on finding Shilpa right away, on bringing her to her senses and then bringing her home. For a second she hated Jyoti and, by extension, Shilpa, all these young, stupid, childish girls who liked shiny objects, who believed in love rather than responsibility, whose heads were turned by the Bollywood snake charmers ShahrukhBobbyRanbirImran, who forgot that they were the daughters of farmers and laborers, who lived in their decrepit homes and impoverished villages without noticing the squalor because their dreams were of marbled houses along Juhu Beach in Mumbai. In the second that they stared at each other, Lakshmi felt she was old enough to be Jyoti's mother, old enough to be her grandmother, felt like the oldest woman in the world. How clearly she could see the fate that awaited Shilpa. Nothing would matter—not her beauty nor her high school diploma—nothing would be enough to protect her against the scorn of their neighbors. And the irony was that eventually Dilip would leave her, for what man would willingly marry a prostitute? Lakshmi could see it so clearly, the arc of her sister's destiny, that it shocked her that Shilpa hadn't.

"Jyoti," she said, trying to fight off her panic. "You please listen to me. You take me to where they are hiding. I promises you. She will not have to marry Aditji. I am giving you my promise."

"You cancel the wedding first." Jyoti's words were tough, but her voice was shaky, and Lakshmi grabbed on to that shakiness.

"Does you understand what will happen to Shilpa if someone finds out she alone with Dilip at night? They . . . they spits on her, calls her a . . ." Lakshmi forced herself to say the ugly word and was gratified when she saw Jyoti flinch. "Jyoti. You like my younger sister. You knows how much I loves my Shilpa. You knows what I done for her. If, if anything happen to her, if anybody say something wicked of her, I . . ." The tears fell, hot and furious, dripping down her face. "I will sacrifice anything for Shilpa. Anything. Including my dada's heart."

The two women stared at each other, shocked. Lakshmi opened her mouth to explain, but just then Jyoti reached over and touched her lightly on the shoulder. "Didi. Say no more. I understands. And I will take you to Shilpa."

Lakshmi ran back into the house to put on her slippers and to tell Dada she was going out to do some last-minute shopping. The old man started to protest, but she was already out of the house. "Where they are?" she gasped as they walked.

They were in an apartment in town owned by one of Dilip's customers who was a long-distance truck driver. When Lakshmi walked in without knocking, they were sitting on the sofa watching television. Dilip sprang to his feet, while Shilpa remained on the couch, her mouth open.

"Come," Lakshmi said without preamble, reaching for Shilpa's thin wrist. "We talk later. First you come home."

"I not leaving." Shilpa held on to the sofa.

"Not leaving? You wants to spend night here with the man you not even engage to?" Lakshmi pointed to the door. "You know what happen when you walking out of here? The world spit on you. Say you are loose woman. Do you think Dilip's mother allow her son to marry a loose woman? Think of your future, Shilpa."

"I's thinking of my future, only. That's why I here. I don't want to marry that ugly man. His sister shown me his photo."

"It's okay. Wedding is cancel. You not marrying that man. But for now—"

"You lying, Didi. You trap me. You . . ."

Lakshmi felt Dilip tense beside her. Out of the corner of her eye, she saw him shake his head disapprovingly at Shilpa. Jyoti was at the far end of the room, as if hoping to be swallowed up by the walls.

"Listen, girl. I see you the day you was born. I feeds you, change you, take care of you my whole life. When I ever tell you the lie? When?" Lakshmi narrowed her eyes. "Munni. It is good that you loves Dilip. He a good boy. But because you loving someone new, not give you permission to stop loving peoples you love your whole life."

"Cent percent correct." They all jumped at the sound of Dilip's voice. It sounded more firm than Lakshmi had ever heard it. "Didi is correct." He walked over to crouch before Shilpa. "You won. And you too stupid to know. Didi say you not marrying that ugly giant. Bas, Didi's promise enough for me. Should be enough for you, too, Shilpa." Turning toward Lakshmi, Dilip folded his hands. "Maaf karo, Didi. Please to forgive. We make huge mistake. What to do, Shilpa say she going to swallow rat poison. I got scared, so I bring her here."

"Rat poison? Shilpa, have you gone mad? Is your Didi dead that you act this way?" Her eyes glittering with tears, she pulled Shilpa up to her feet, embracing her as she did. The younger woman held back for a second and then flung her arms around Lakshmi, sobbing.

Shilpa fell asleep soon after they got home, and listening to her soft breathing, Lakshmi marveled at the callousness of youth. Shilpa seemed to think that, having extracted the promise from Lakshmi, the worst was over. Despite the fact that they had not awakened Dada to break the news when they reached home. Despite the fact that she knew Adit's family had spent lakhs of rupees on the wedding and that the blot of shame of a canceled wedding would spread and cover not just their family but his also. Shilpa's breath was as quiet and steady as a baby's, and she was not tossing and turning in bed, as Lakshmi was. It was the wrong sister who was lying in bed drenched in sweat, staring up at the ceiling. It was the wrong sister who tried to think of a way to save face, to spare both families the humiliation that was undoubtedly coming their way tomorrow. It was the wrong sister who sat up in bed, her heart pounding, as an idea came to her. Because it was the wrong sister who was about to marry Adit Patil.

And so it was:

Adit's father and sister wait at the entrance of the open-air reception hall for Dada and the bride to emerge out of the air-conditioned taxi. They inquire about Dada's oldest daughter and are informed that she is home with the stomach flu. Adit's sister is about to ask more questions, but they are distracted by the appearance of the groom, who looks resplendent in a gold-embroidered jacket and a saffron-colored head scarf. As per local custom, the bride's face is covered by her sari, so that Dada has to steer her toward where the wedding mandap has been set up. Someone puts two heavy rose and jasmine garlands around the necks of the bride and the groom. They smell cloyingly sweet, heavy as a premonition. For a second, the scent of the flowers, the heat under the veil, the sheer duplicity of what she's about to do, it all gets to her, and she thinks she is about to faint. But just then strong arms steady her—she's not sure whose—and she feels herself maneuvered to sit in front of the sacred fire that's burning in an urn set on the mandap. She fights a moment of panic. It is all happening too soon. Even though she knows Adit insisted on a simple ceremony—he arrived at the reception hall in a car instead of on a white horse, for instance—she had not expected things to move this fast. She had thought there would be more time. Even through her sari, she feels the heat of the fire around which they sit cross-legged. She hears the sonorous chanting of the priests. It is happening. She is getting married. In another moment, she feels him taking her hand in his. She tenses, wondering if he will notice anything, but as the seconds pass, there is only the chanting by the priests. When directed, they feed rice into the fire, still holding hands. She feels blind, being led into a new life by a force stronger than her will, and finds that she doesn't mind the feeling. Next they walk around the fire seven times. They are now husband and wife. As proof of their life together, one end of the groom's head scarf is tied to the bride's sari. They take seven steps into their new life together. Each step symbolizes something meaningful—strength, prosperity, happiness, harmony, and the like. As the priest explains the meaning of each step, the sob in the bride's throat grows larger.

It is time for the bride and groom to feed each other a sweet, a symbol of the sweetness of married life. She breaks off a piece of ladoo and places it delicately into his mouth. It is his turn. Before he can feed his beloved new bride, he has to lift the veil. His hands shake slightly from the anticipation of seeing that beautiful face, a face he has told his sister he has been unable to forget from the first time he set his eyes on it. He raises the veil and sees a different face peering at him. Already, there are tears in the eyes gazing at him, and beyond the tears, a deep, dark fear. But he barely registers all this. The shock, the disappointment, the confusion is too great.

A moment passes. Then another. Then someone screams. Maybe it's the groom. Maybe his sister. In any case, it seems to the bride as if this scream will never stop. As if it will reverberate through time, through history, through the dark, dingy tunnel called her future, so that she will hear it every day, every minute of every day, for the rest of her life.

28

LAKSHMI HAD FINISHED her story, but they did not speak. As they walked around the lagoon, it was as if they were both hearing it, the scream that Lakshmi had described. Maggie knew she should say something, that Lakshmi was expecting her to, but she couldn't. None of it made any sense to her—the deceit, the betrayal, the sheer chutzpah of it. Like something from a movie. Who in real life acted this way? But then she remembered this had happened in India, and India was not real life. The most heartbreaking, most desperate, most bizarre stories she had ever heard all came from India. It wasn't just the poverty. Even among Sudhir's middle-class relatives, such stories were legion. Every story was epic; every emotion was exaggerated; every action was melodramatic. Desperate love, mad obsessions, outbursts of rage, bizarre self-sacrifice, self-immolation. Young women eating rat poison, jumping off buildings, or burning themselves alive. Young men throwing themselves onto railroad tracks in the path of on-coming trains. It was as if they didn't value their bodies at all. And all this self-destruction over issues that in the West would be solved by a simple elopement or estrangement from one's parents or a move to a different city.

Knowing that her distaste was showing on her face, knowing that Lakshmi was watching her carefully, Maggie forced her mind away from these thoughts. After all, there were more urgent matters at hand. Lakshmi had come to her with this confession because she needed absolution. Maggie could scarcely imagine the guilt that the woman had been living with. Well, yes, she could, but this was about Lakshmi, not her. She knew she should say something kind and reassuring to her client, but what? The honest fact was that her sympathies had changed. For almost a year, she'd seen Lakshmi as a victim, a semiliterate immigrant woman trapped in an inhospitable marriage. Lakshmi had just rewritten the narrative so that the villain now seemed like the hero. Well, not quite the hero, but at least a sympathetic character. It made Maggie question all the counsel that she had given Lakshmi, question the very foundation of her therapy. She couldn't imagine staying married to someone who had pulled such a huge fraud. Why had Adit?

"Why didn't he just leave?" she asked. "I mean, he obviously sent for you, applied for your visa and everything. Once he learned the truth, why didn't he just, you know, divorce you?"

"That what I thinking will happen, surely. I marries him to spare gossip about Shilpa. This way, she can tell that unmarried older sister lie and cheat to be first to marry. Also, that way, divorce is my fault. Not the husband's. That my thinking. But Maggie, what you know? So much commotion and upset at the wedding ceremony. And my husband shouting, shouting at my poor dada. Calling him a badmash, a chor—you know, a crook and thief. Finally, I say to him, any name you wanting to call, you calls me. Not my dada. So he call me a wicked name, but his old father go up to him and hold his arm. 'Chup, beta, chup,' the old man say. 'You don't talk to my new daughter-in-law in this manner.' "

Lakshmi shook her head as if she could hear the old man's voice. "Everyone become very hush, then. Husband's father look to me and say, 'Come, beti, come touch my feet and take my blessing.' 'Baba, you not following,' my husband say. 'This is not the woman I plan to marrying.'

" 'No, this is woman God planning for you to marry,' my father-in-law say. 'In our family in a thousand years, no man ever leaf his wedded wife. Now you want to leaf this girl? What will happen to her if you do? All these people will bite at her flesh like wild dogs. I will not allow it.'

" 'But Baba—'

"The old man bang his walking stick. 'You call me father but still you arguing with me? Is this your training in Am'rica? This is your kismet, beta. You cannot run from your kismet.'

"And what you think, Maggie? Husband look down at his feet and say, 'Yes, Baba. You correct.' "

Again, Maggie felt that distaste. Was Lakshmi valorizing a crazy old fool who had sold his son's happiness because of some antiquated notion of family honor? She had never felt as distant from Lakshmi as she did right now. "So that was it? Adit listened to his father?"

"Yes. Of course, his sister still angry at us. Go up to Dada and asking back for everything they give us. I say to her she can have the gold jewelry right now, at the wedding, only. But for sari I'm wearing, she has to wait until tomorrow."

"What happened after the reception?"

"Husband and I goes to hotel for honeymoon. He leaf me alone in hotel room and say he going to bar. Until then, I never stay alone even one day. He not return to room until three in the morning. He come in the room and go to sleep on the sofa." Lakshmi stopped walking. "That was my honeymoon. Next day, he drive me to Dada's house. Drop me near the house only. I wanting so much to explain, to say sorry, but it like talking to stone building. I's so ascare, I say nothing."

"Well, you can't blame him, I suppose." The words slip out of Maggie's mouth. "I mean, I can't imagine his reaction . . ."

Lakshmi looked at Maggie closely. "That only I'm trying to

tell you, Maggie. That our marriage not his fault. I know you not liking my husband. And I explaining to you, he not a bad man. We has a paper marriage. Not real ones, like you and Sudhir baba. My husband love my sister, not me."

Maggie blinked, ashamed of her reaction, of the understanding she saw in Lakshmi's eyes. It was a gamble Lakshmi took, she realized, telling her this sordid story. She had risked losing the only friend she had in America, so that Maggie would stop judging her husband harshly. This is another sacrifice in a long line of sacrifices. When will this woman ever learn to live for herself?

"I . . . I don't know what to say, Lakshmi," Maggie said. "That is, I feel sorry for both of you. You know?"

Lakshmi turned her head slightly to face Maggie and smiled. "I knows, Maggie. That's why only I wanted to tell you." She continued to look at Maggie in a curious manner, as if bracing herself for rejection but hoping for something different, some assurance, some gesture to show that nothing had altered between them. Maggie knew this but was frozen, unable to provide the absolution that Lakshmi wanted. She felt as if Lakshmi had told her a story from medieval times, something so primitive and ridiculous that she could not wrap her mind around it. She had heard scores of lurid stories from her in-laws, but she had never known any of the characters involved. Until now.

Desperate to get away, she looked around the lagoon, hoping to run into somebody she knew. She longed to glance at her watch, wanted more than anything to be able to say, "I'm afraid our time is up for today," but knew that would seem too obvious. As they walked, Maggie became aware that she was angry. She was slipping. Usually, this was the kind of information she would've coaxed out of her client by the third or fourth session. Had her distaste for Lakshmi's husband blinded her to the situation?

"Why are you telling me this now?" she asked. She could hear the cold, raw quality in her own voice. "I mean, why now, after all this time?"

Lakshmi was quiet for so long that Maggie started to repeat the question. Then the younger woman spoke. "Yesterday, when I gets home, my feets is very tired. They paining me. The husband goes and gets the warm water for me to soaks them."

Maggie felt as if Lakshmi had presented her a riddle and expected her to solve it. So the guy gave her a warm soak. So what? "So?" she said cautiously. "What about that made you decide to tell me?"

Lakshmi took Maggie's hand in hers, an unconscious gesture that warmed Maggie's heart despite the coldness she felt. "I is sorry, Maggie," she said. "I know I should have told you sooner. But what to do? I was so ashame to tell. Also, I's ascare that you would bump me if you knows."

This was the opening to reassure Lakshmi that she intended to do no such thing, that their relationship would survive this revelation, that she understood the social and economic pressures that had driven her to such a drastic solution. In fact, this could be a teaching moment—she could say something about patriarchal societies such as India (though she wouldn't use the term "patriarchy"); could point out that it was Lakshmi's lowly status as a woman that had led her to this end; could discuss the unfairness of a dowry system that penalized a woman for being born a woman, punished a father for having a daughter instead of a son.

But she didn't. Couldn't. She opened her mouth, and no words of consolation, or solidarity, or empathy emerged. The moment passed. The silence between them stretched. In that silence, Maggie pulsed with awareness of their differences rather than their similarities. At their first meeting, she had been struck by how much they had in common: their marriages to Indian men, the early death of their mothers. Now she was aware of how superficial those similarities were. And how vast the chasm that separated them—education, language, nationality, race. It was laughable to think they could ever be friends. It was Lakshmi who had willed their friendship into being. As for Maggie, she had mistaken sympathy, affection, and pity for friendship.

Lakshmi was looking at her expectantly, but this made Maggie even more unwilling to respond. Enough. She had done enough for this woman walking beside her. She had bent the rules of their professional relationship to such a degree that the rules scarcely existed; she had taught her to drive; she had permitted her into her home and allowed her to mingle with her friends; she had helped her earn a steady income. All this because she had seen Lakshmi as a victim, as a helpless immigrant woman trapped in a loveless marriage to a dour, domineering man. Now she understood that it was Adit Patil who was the true victim, that it was he who was trapped in a marriage to a woman he was not attracted to, all because of his father's twisted sense of honor. And now Lakshmi was seeking absolution, as if it were Maggie's forgiveness to grant, as if she could dispense grace as easily as a Catholic priest.

No. In the church where she had spent her childhood, grace was neither cheap nor free. It had to be earned, and the earning was not easy. She came from a hardy, stoic, marginalized people to whom nothing was given for free, not even forgiveness. Although Maggie seldom thought of that little storefront church where she had spent so much of her childhood, she thought of it now. She had been much too lenient with Lakshmi. She had allowed the younger woman to blithely break down the professional barriers between them; had allowed her to set the ground rules; had gone along with her strange requests. And in the process, Lakshmi had taken her for a ride over an entire year.

She was dimly aware that her reaction was a little extreme, that it had deeper echoes than her conscious brain was registering. That beneath her outrage at Lakshmi, there hid another outrage—at her own betrayal of her husband's blind faith in her. Perhaps, buried even deeper, was an older, more potent emotion—the helpless, un-expressed outrage of a little girl, too young to articulate or under-stand her father's violation of her trust.

She was too comfortable in her anger to process this. It felt good, this clean, undiffused anger, so much easier than the heavy combination of sympathy and responsibility that had colored all her interactions with Lakshmi. She had spent so much of her pro-fessional and personal life trying to understand people, to make excuses for bad behavior, her life governed by what Sudhir termed her "on-the-other-hand-ism." It was freeing to step out of the gray and into the black and white.

"What you thinking, Maggie?" Lakshmi asked. There was a trembling quality in her voice, and it pulled Maggie out of the vortex of anger she was slipping into.

"I was thinking . . ." she began, but then her left hand invol-untarily raised itself, and she glanced openly at her watch. ". . . that it's time to get home. I can't be late for my other clients," she added unnecessarily.

"Yes. Of course. Sorry."

They walked in silence up the trail that led them away from the lagoon. Seven more minutes and we will be home, Maggie thought. Thank God I have some time to myself before the next appointment.

Beside her, Lakshmi spoke so softly that Maggie didn't hear what she said. "Excuse me?" she said. She glanced at Lakshmi, and despite herself, her heart pinched at the sorrow she saw on the brown face.

"I saying that the worse part of all this is, it take my Shilpa away from me," she repeated.

"You mean because you left for the U.S.?"

Lakshmi shook her head. "No. I means even before that. When I was still living in my dada's house, waiting for the visa to come."

Maggie hated herself for asking but she did. "Why? Where did Shilpa go?"

"Nowheres. Her body is still staying with us. But her heart was gone." Lakshmi slowed her pace and turned to face Maggie. "She angry with me, Maggie. One day she is saying I making fools of our family by making fake marriage. Next day she saying I is wanting to be first to marry, being oldest daughter. That's why I plan this paper marriage. Nothing I say to her—that I do it to save both our family's izzat and save Mister's face—mean anything to her." Lakshmi's voice was as raw as crushed glass. "Bas. From that day only, I lose my sister. Who I loves from the minute she born."

There it was again—the familiar combination of pity and obligation that she always felt toward Lakshmi. Maggie tried to recall the sense of betrayal she had felt a few minutes earlier, but it had vanished, dissipated, like hunger after a meal. "We can't be responsible for other people's reactions to us, Lakshmi," she said. "We can only make sure that our intentions are good." But her words felt hollow to her, empty lines out of a textbook, devoid of the daily bruisings suffered by the human heart.

Surely Lakshmi heard that rote quality in her voice, because she flung Maggie a curious look and resumed walking. Maggie's heart sank as she realized that she had failed a test, that she had not given her best to her client. It was one of the most salient rules of psychotherapy—to remain objective, to accept without judgment a client's revelations. And God, she had heard so much worse over the years, had sat nodding as clients revealed extramarital affairs, abortions that were kept secret from partners, tales of domestic abuse. None of those confessions had rattled her the way Lakshmi's story had.

This is different, Maggie argued with herself. Lakshmi is not just a client. She's a friend.

There it was. The inevitable result of blurring the lines. She had blithely flouted all the rules of her profession, and this was the consequence—her inability to provide Lakshmi with the basic support she needed.

Out of the blue, the trembling started. She had not suffered from an episode in so long that it took her a moment to recognize what was happening. She glanced sidelong at Lakshmi to see if she'd noticed, but the woman was staring at the ground as she walked. Maggie placed her hands in the pockets of her jeans to steady their shaking. She forced herself to take a few deep breaths. Focus, she said to herself. Focus. This is still Lakshmi's hour.

She swallowed a few times to wet her mouth and then she spoke. "So what you said to me before—that you hadn't written to Shilpa because your husband forbade it—is that not true?"

Lakshmi's forehead knitted in confusion. "Pardon? What is 'forbade' mean?"

"Forbade . . . he told you not to. Stopped you from writing."

"Ah, yes." Lakshmi nodded vigorously to show her comprehension. "No, no, I not lying to you, Maggie. Husband so angry with my family. He say we cheaters. He tell me not to contact them again."

The gust of anger that ran through Maggie was sudden and forceful. "And you just listened?" she asked, hearing the unintended harshness in her voice.

The younger woman shrugged. "What to do, Maggie? I eating my husband's salt, spending his moneys. Plus, I making this sin against him."

"But you're not. Not now, I mean. You have your own income." She was shaking hard, but it was impossible to say whether it was

from anger or that other thing. In any case, they were not too far
away from the house now.

Lakshmi's eyes narrowed. "Maggie. What wrong? Why your
body doing this?"

"I don't know. I think I'm cold," she lied.

"You sick. I come in and make you some hot-pot soup."

"No." The word came out louder, more emphatic than she'd
intended. "No," she said again, softly. "I told you. I have a client
coming in after you."

"But—"

"Lakshmi. I'm okay. Just let it go. I want to ask you, what's
stopping you from writing to your father and sister now? After all
these years?"

"I's ascare, Maggie. What if they not writing back? What if
Shilpa still angry with me?"

Maggie was a little out of breath as they climbed up the steep
incline that led to her house. "When you came to my house the
very first time, were you scared?" she asked.

"Arre, baap." Lakshmi swatted her forehead. "Yes, of course."

"When you came to America in a big plane, were you scared?"

"I thinking I fainting, I so ascare."

"When you drove for the first time, were you scared?"

Lakshmi grinned. "Okay, okay. I understands."

They had reached the house and stood facing each other in
the driveway. "Think of how far you've come," Maggie said softly,
trying to keep the breathlessness out of her voice. "And then ask
yourself how much farther you wish to go."

Lakshmi's eyes were wide, and Maggie noticed how young she
looked, her dark hair lit orange by the midmorning light. "Yes,
Maggie."

"Okay. I have to go in and prepare for the next client. I'll see
you at the same time next week?"

"I can make the vegetable soup for you in a half hour—"

"Lakshmi. I'm okay. Just cold. Don't worry. Now go."

"Okay."

"Bye." She turned to make her way up the driveway.

"Maggie?" Lakshmi called after her. "Many thanks."

"You're welcome."

She was aware that Lakshmi stood at the bottom of the drive-way and watched until she was in the house and the wooden screen door had banged behind her.

29

I DRINKS WATER FROM the bottle I keeps in my car but the burning, burning in my stomach not getting quiet. I lower the window, then put it back up, but still the shame sit in my stomach and refuse to leaf. I fix my mind to focus on the road—baap re, the roads near Maggie's house so twisty-turny—but my thought keep going back to fifteen minute ago, when I give up my darkest shame to Maggie, and instead of blowing it out like a candle, she blow it up like a balloon and give it back to me. And now it is sitting in my stomach, getting more bigger.

I angry with myself. I angry with Maggie. Then I angry with myself for being angry with Maggie. Then I angry with Maggie for making me angry with myself. Bas, I angry.

Why I tells Maggie true story of my marriage? What I want from her? Maggie kind but she is Am'rican woman. How she understand our village life? Her eyes getting so big when I tells her how we receive the two goats as present. Who in Am'rica giving the goat? Here, they giving the gift card. Just other day, the husband asking Rekha whether we should start printing the gift card for restaurant also.

Someone pull in my lane ahead of me and my foot hit the brake hard. And then my hand hit the horn. In Am'rica nobody hit the horn khali-pilli, for no reason, like they does in India, but today I's so angry with how Maggie judge me, I keeps my hand on the horn. Everything so neat and quiet in Cedarville, but I crack the quiet with my horn. It sound so loud and sudden, a group of birds fly out of a tree and go straight up into the sky.

It my mistake. For telling. On TV last Sunday, the Christian priest say, "The truth shall set you free." Maybe that what I think? That telling Maggie what sin I do will make me free? That I make her understand the big joke of my life—I marries my husband so he can save his honor when he divorce me. Instead, his old baba interfere and force him to stay marry. What I think will be one-hour marriage now turn into a six-year punishment.

Maggie not feeling sorry for me. She feeling sorry for the husband. Which I understand. I feeling sorry for him also. Every day for six years. So why I not liking it when Maggie do same as me?

Oof. I's being stupid. What I expects from her? Maggie so good to me; why I want what she cannot give? Ma use to say: Bee give the honey, bee also give the sting. Up to us, whether we want the sting or the honey. Maggie give me so much honey. Why I go tell her my old story until I feel her sting?

For first time today, I looks out of car window and notice how green everything look. It still February, but winter is soft this year and the snow little. I stops at traffic light and lean my head out of the window. I sees the grass on people's lawn. Will husband and me ever have our own house? Or will we always live in smelly apartment where the dead woman live and die? What he collecting all his money for? In first month after I come here, husband make very clear he not wanting children by me. I not blame him—who want to make children with cheat woman?—but it hurt me so deep, in place where my breath come from. Always, I thinks I will have many childrens. So many childrens I take care of—Shilpa, Munna, Mithai—and it is nothing I learn in school. It come from inside me, knowing how to care for anything that is small and hungry and need me. So when husband say he not wanting the children, steel door close in my heart.

But I cheer up when I think of Shilpa making children with Dilip. I will be auntie to all her children, I thinks. But then husband say rule number two: I is to forget my family. They all cheater.

The sun hit the redbrick on the buildings in downtown Cedarville and I wishes I could make the painting of it. One thing I never understanding—how the world be so beautiful and still holding so many sad people. When I was small child, I use to think that I could cheer up anybody who sad by showing them the love. Now I knowing the truth: Between love and beauty, beauty winning. I could learn to love my husband, but he still hunger for Shilpa's beauty, even though he never get it for even one full day, even though it never his, even though it only make him depress to not have it.

A thought enter my head and it is so correct, so big, so truth, that I almost runs down the man crossing street in front of me. I stops to let him pass and then I speeds up all the way home. I carry the thought as I gets out of the car, carry it careful, like I balance a pot of water on my head and not suppose to spill a drop. I walk into the store and see the husband kneeling near the can foods. A woman customer I don't know standing next to him.

"Ji," I say. "I needs to talk to you. Now, only."

He pick up the mango tin for the lady and stand up. "I am busy," he say. "Helping customer. Can't you see?"

"I knows. I can see." I smile at lady. "Anything else you need, madam, Rekha can help." I take husband hand and pull it. His mouth open with surprise. It first time I touch him in public.

"What—?"

"Please. I needs to talk."

He give sorry smile to lady customer and then follow me. I take him up the stairs going from store to apartment. I hear his breathing, huff-huff, as he climb. He gaining too much weight eating his own oily foods. "What is it, Lakshmi?" he say when we standing in kitchen. "You know how bad it look—"

"I know," I say. "I know everything." I feeling giddy. It is time to set the water pot down. Time to tell him the truth thought that roll into my head. "You know how you always call me stupid?" I start.

He make irritate noise. "Woman, if you want to start the fight—"

"No. No fight. I just want to say, you wrong. I's not stupid."

He turn around to go downstairs. "Okay."

"No, I's not stupid," I say quickly. "You's stupid."

He come back into the room. "What you call me?"

I laugh. "You. You's stupid. Not me. You know why? Because you choosing beauty over love. You choosing ghost woman over real wife. You choosing Shilpa, who never loves you, over a wife who cook for you, clean for you, worry for you, who even give you her money from her business."

"Stop it," he say.

"No. No. Today you listen. You want to know why I marry you? Not to takes your money. Not to come to this dead country. Not to steal your business. I marry you to save your family name. To make up for my sister's insult. How I knowing your baba force you to not leaf me? Or that you listen to him? If you wanting to blame someone, blame him. Curse him."

"You say one bad word about my father and I—"

"No. I never say one bad thing about your baba. But I do curse you. Not for ruining my life. But for ruining your."

"What you mean?"

"I mean you stupid. Chasing after a face you saw for ten minutes at the mela. While here you having your own wife who you treats like she a garbage. But who know your habits? Is it Shilpa? Who hears you snoring at night? Who knows what soap you use? Who knows what favorite dish you're liking? Who knows what

whiskey you drinking? It is I. I's your wife. Not Shilpa. She nothing but paper. Remember what you telling me when I come to
this house six year ago? 'Forget your family,' you say. But all this
time, you the one who remembering Shilpa. You the one making
her yours when she not belong to you. Even her one fingernail not
belong to you."

I close my eyes, wait for the slap on face that will come. Husband never hit me before but I also never insult him before. So
I close my eyes and wait. My face burning, like his hand already
slap me. But no pain. When I open my eyes, he still standing.
His lips move but he not say anything. His eyes is red with tears.
He pull out his handkerchief and blow the nose. But still he not
speaking. Or hitting.

Looking at him, my heart hurt. "Sorry," I say. "Maaf karo. I not
meaning to—"

He put his finger to his lip to shut up me. "Enough," he say.
"Bas, enough."

And then he turn and go into bedroom and shut the door. Quietly. I stand in the kitchen like beggar woman outside the jewelry
store, with my hand out. But it is not his gold coin that I begging
for. It is not even his love. I just wants that when my husband look
at me, it is me he see. Not Shilpa, not dream woman. Just me. Just
me. Just ugly, broken, motherless me.

30

SUDHIR WAS MARCHING in the commencement ceremony for the first time in six years. Usually, he shunned graduation day events. This year he'd made an exception because of Susan Grossman, a disabled student who had finally earned her master's degree and who had requested Sudhir to personally hand her the degree. He had agreed immediately.

Now, sitting in the bleachers and watching her husband walk past her in his robes, sensing rather than seeing his bemusement at the scene before them, Maggie tried to catch his eye. But Sudhir was walking languidly in the procession headed toward the stage, stopping occasionally to wave to a student who called out his name, pointing something out to Larry Andrews, who was in line ahead of him. Whatever Sudhir had commented on was apparently funny, because Maggie saw Larry let out a guffaw.

She felt a small movement as the people in the row behind her shuffled to accommodate a latecomer. A second later, she heard a familiar voice whisper, "Hey."

Her head shot back and she turned slightly, even though she already knew it was Peter. Her stomach collapsed. She had not seen Peter in months. What was he doing here?

As she debated whether to respond, she felt his breath on her ear. "I'm leaving. In a couple of weeks. I thought maybe we could get coffee. Before, you know, I took off."

A bolt of disappointment ran through her at the thought of

Peter's departure from campus. But there was no question—she could not trust herself to see him again. "I can't," she murmured, hoping he could hear her over the din of the crowd. "But I wish you the best."

"Listen," he hissed in her ear. "I'm going back. To Afghanistan. I need to see you before I leave."

The thought of Peter being in Afghanistan, in harm's way, made her tremble. How terrible it would be to be married to someone like Peter, she thought, and was thankful for Sudhir's stable, nondramatic choice of profession.

She realized that Peter was leaning forward, waiting for her to answer. How soon before the processional reached the stage and Sudhir took his seat and stared into the crowd, searching for her? "I'm going to ask you for a favor," she said. "Please find a seat elsewhere. Please. I'm requesting you."

For a sickening moment, she thought he was going to refuse, but then she sensed him exhale. "Okay. Whatever."

She forced herself to stare resolutely ahead when she felt the rustle in the row behind her as Peter left. After what seemed like a safe amount of time, she turned her head casually and scanned the crowd. Almost immediately, she spotted Peter sitting six rows behind and to her right. He was staring directly at her, and when their eyes met, he smiled that knowing, sardonic Peter smile. I know you were looking for me, the smile said. I know you can't keep your eyes off of me.

She looked away, her cheeks burning. Arrogant bastard. That's what Peter was, a cocky, arrogant bastard. The next second, her anger was extinguished by a thick grief. It was one thing to stay away from Peter while he lived nearby. It was quite another to think of him on the other side of the earth, courting danger, breathing the dust of a faraway land, focusing his camera on unspeakable violence and ugliness. To know that she may never see him again. Never. Something twisted in her stomach, an extra organ that grief had bubbled into existence, and she winced in pain. Still, she would not let herself turn around again.

Instead, she focused on the stage, following Sudhir with her eyes as he took his seat in a row of chairs behind the podium. She knew what it meant to Sudhir to have Susan graduate, the pride he took in her accomplishment, and she had offered to come to the commencement before he asked. This is why you're here, she now reminded herself. To support Sudhir. And Susan. The fact that Peter is sitting behind you, staring at you so intently that you can feel his eyes boring into your back, is beside the point. He is the past. Peter is the past. Sudhir is your present. And your future. Remember this. Don't lose sight of it for even a moment. Be strong, she said to herself, be strong.

As soon as she thought those words, she felt better, felt her stomach unclench. She leaned forward, resting her elbows on her knee, and concentrated on the exuberant faces of the students on the stage. Thirty minutes later, when Susan Grossman walked onto that stage on her double crutches, and Sudhir rose, beaming with pride as he waited for her with her diploma in his hands, a feeling of intense love for her husband tore through Maggie. In the excruciating moments that it took for Susan to reach the podium, Maggie remembered it all—how timid and shy Susan had been when she entered the program, how Sudhir had personally fought with the administration to make every possible accommodation for his student, how he had invited her for supper on the day Susan had been so discouraged that she'd thought of quitting, how, after dinner, Sudhir had in his usual methodical, thoughtful way, presented the reasons why dropping out would be a mistake, and Susan had turned to both of them, her face shiny with a tenuous new hope. Susan was only twenty-six years old but had already known a lifetime's worth of obstacles. She'd had one lucky break, and that was having as her adviser the man who was presenting her a degree, who briefly looked astonished as Susan leaned in to him for a hug, whose hands fluttered uncertainly for a second before he returned Susan's embrace. Through her own tears, Maggie saw the look on Sudhir's face and knew that he was as caught up in this moment as his student was, but then she was distracted by the cheering coming from the bleachers on the left side of the gym. Maggie craned her neck and saw two middle-aged people rising to their feet as they clapped and hooted—Susan's parents, she presumed—and then there were whoops from the front seats as all the graduating seniors from the math department began to cheer Susan. The whole scene probably lasted only a few seconds, but Maggie had the unreal sense that it was something she would remember for a long time to come. This was where she belonged, with the man who flung a shy smile at his cheering students before he returned to his seat. See that? she wanted to say to Peter. This is who my husband is—unassuming, decent, non-flashy, but the reason someone like Susan Grossman will have a job someday. He's the reason they're all cheering her today. He is not running away to some dangerous, exciting place like Afghanistan. He will not get his name in the newspapers. No, he will stay here and put his shoulder to the wheel and continue doing what he does so well—teaching generations of young students, inspiring them, picking them up when they fall. It may not count for much with you, Peter, but it does matter, what Sudhir does. That's why I'm here today. That's why I came. To say that it matters.

Even while she argued, she could see the unfairness of accusing Peter of a position that he had never taken. Peter had never said a mocking or disparaging word about Sudhir. It was her own mind that had betrayed her, in the early throes of passion.

When the benediction was over, the audience waited until the professors in their colorful robes left the stage and walked down the aisle toward the exit doors. As he passed her, Sudhir mouthed, "I'll meet you outside. Near the tent." She nodded and blew him a kiss, wanting Peter to notice the gesture. Sudhir gave her a startled smile, and then he was past her.

As she moved toward the doors, Peter fell in step with her. "Hey," he said. "You're making me grovel. I'm not used to that." Although there was a teasing note in his voice, Maggie could hear the undercurrent of frustration.

She stopped and turned to face him. "What do you want from me, Peter?" she said, aware that at any moment she could be overheard or spotted by one of Sudhir's students or colleagues. "My husband is waiting for me outside. Don't you know when something is over?"

She had never taken this tone with him, and Peter raised his right eyebrow. He watched her in silence for a full second before he said, "Boy, you're cold." He spun around and strode away from her.

She resisted the reflexive urge to ask him to stop and to apologize. This was not how she'd wanted it to end with Peter. But she was paralyzed. Something about Peter's accusation of coldness, coupled with his own cool rejection, the aloof way he had gazed at her before walking away, as if the warmth and sweetness between them had never happened, echoed Wallace's abrupt abandonment so many years earlier. Maggie stood alone, shivering slightly, a pinpoint of stillness in a crowd of shouting, moving, laughing people. In a flash, her attraction to Peter became crystal-clear—they were the same kind of men, Peter and Wallace, charismatic, enigmatic, capable of great warmth and great detachment.

Stunned by the insight, Maggie allowed herself to be moved forward by the cheerful crowd, hardly aware of being propelled toward the doors. Was she really so obtuse that she'd never recognized the similarities between Peter and her father? If so, she should turn in her license and take down her shingle.

She walked out of the gym and into the lobby and heard a soft "Hi." It was Sudhir. "I thought we were going to meet outside near the tent," she said, thankful that she'd sent Peter on his way, her heart lurching at the thought of the close call.

Sudhir shrugged. "Once we got outside, I realized I could just wait for you here." He took her hand in his, and she hoped he wouldn't notice how sweaty her palm was.

"But what if I'd come out of another door? What if I'd gone down a different aisle?" She realized that she was prattling, waiting for her heart to regain its normal rhythm, wanting to distract Sudhir from noticing that anything was amiss.

He shrugged again. "Based on where you were sitting, the probability of which door you'd exit from was over eighty percent."

She burst out laughing. The answer was so Sudhir. She squeezed his hand. "I'm glad you waited for me, honey."

Maggie stood under the giant white tent, a glass of wine in her hand. Sudhir was talking to the parents of a graduating student. Marianne Johnson, who taught in the psychology department, came up to her. "Hey, Maggie. Long time, no see. How have you been?"

As they chatted, Maggie looked out of the corner of her eye to see Peter standing outside the tent, his head bent a little as he listened intently to a young woman in a white dress with tanned arms. The sun caught in Peter's hair when he threw back his head to laugh at something the woman had said, and Maggie felt her throat tighten. She forced her attention back to what Marianne was saying.

"It should be illegal to be that handsome, yes?" Marianne

said, and with a start, Maggie realized that Marianne had caught her looking at Peter. She blushed, struggled for a lighthearted response, but her mind froze. "Yup," she said, nodding, wishing away the gruffness in her voice.

She kept her eyes focused on Marianne and, as soon as she could, excused herself and headed toward Sudhir. "Oh, hi," Sudhir said as she approached. "Let me introduce you to a few people. This is my wife, Maggie."

She saw the usual mix of surprise and calculation in their eyes as they came to grips with the fact that Professor Bose, whom they'd heard so much about from their children, was married to a black woman. Usually, it amused her, their reaction, but today it barely registered. She took his arm and squeezed, their usual signal, and sure enough, after a few more minutes of chitchatting, he pulled her aside and asked, "What's up?"

"Do you want to stay much longer?" she asked. "I have a headache."

He grinned. "I was ready to leave a half hour ago. You know me and these affairs. Let's go."

They stepped into the bright sunshine, passing within a couple of feet of Peter; if Sudhir noticed him, he didn't say. Peter seemed totally engrossed in his conversation with the woman he had been talking to earlier. Maggie realized with a pang that he didn't so much as look up as they walked by.

And that's a good thing, she told herself as they walked toward the parking garage. Peter will be gone in a few weeks. And then it will be time to start living the rest of your life with Sudhir. The rest of your life.

BOOK
THREE

31

He WAS LEAVING town. Forever. The movers had picked up his furniture yesterday. He had loaded his car last night, eager to head out of town first thing in the morning. He was driving cross-country, headed toward his sister's house in Washington, D.C., giving himself a week to make the leisurely drive. The plan was to stop at a few national parks along the way.

He walked out of the cottage where he'd spent the past year without so much as a backward glance and got into his car. He hoped to beat the rush-hour traffic on his way out of town.

R.E.M.'s "Bad Day" blared from his stereo as he got onto the freeway. He sang along. There was a heavy feeling in his heart but he ignored it.

He was almost past the Cedarville exit when he found himself yanking the steering wheel to the right and getting off at the exit ramp. It was an impulsive, almost unconscious decision and it took him a second before he understood that he was heading toward downtown Cedarville. When he got there, he realized that it was too early, so he headed to Dolby's for breakfast. He sat at a corner table, hunched over his blueberry and granola pancakes, arguing with himself, commanding himself to stick to the plan, to head down to Orchard Road and get back on the freeway. Not to do what he wanted to do. It would be better this way, he knew, cleaner. That way, there would be no mess for someone else to clean up. He knew this.

He lingered over breakfast. His throat was so dry that he ordered an OJ, flagged down a waitress who was walking by. She was the chatty type, smiling suggestively at him as she set his glass down, and normally, he would've enjoyed the mild flirtation. He had spent so much time in places where women were kept behind locked doors, walled-off in their homes, or covered in their chadors, that he considered it one of the perks of returning home to America, the easy flirtations, the light conversations, the simple pleasure of seeing women on the streets, in restaurants, in the movie theaters. Normally, he would've smiled back at the waitress, tried to guess where she was from by her accent, maybe lightly touched her hand as he paid the bill. Not today. Not now, not for the last year, because all his senses had been engaged by a single woman. Who was not single at all but married.

He smiled grimly at the joke. He paid the bill and left the restaurant. It was still only nine a.m. Too early. Too risky. Besides, there was no hurry. It was Tuesday, and he knew she didn't go in until two p.m. on Tuesday; she used the mornings to catch up on her paperwork. He would wait.

He wandered around downtown, window-shopping to kill the time. He thought that he might buy her something, but he was too agitated, too restless, to walk into a store and deal with a salesperson. No, he needed to be alone, so he made his way to the little park with the wooden benches and the trees that grew tall around the riverbank. He sat on one of the benches and stared at the water. He had seen so many rivers in his line of work. Rivers so dry that they looked more like the suggestion of one, a fingernail scratch on parched land. Rivers lush and clean and swift-flowing like this one, surrounded by abundant earth. Rivers dark and oily with human blood. Rivers bearing the carcasses of dead animals while children splashed and played at their edges. Rivers humming with fish and rivers sinister with crocodiles and alligators.

This river was nice. He knew that if he plunged his hand into it, it would be cold and the water would taste sweet. There would be no foul taste, no chalky or dusty flavor, no odor. No suspicious-looking object would be lying in its bed. In fact, from where he sat, he could see clear to its green bottom. He knew the taste of such rivers. They tasted like home. Like America—reliable, tidy, organized, safe.

You're nuts, he thought in disgust. She's made you loopy. Better watch yourself. He had seen it many times, among soldiers and war correspondents. Love made you loopy. Dreamy. Tricked you into thinking that the world was a nice place. Made you forget the dangers. And that was all it took—a moment's forgetfulness. A second's sloppiness—getting into the wrong car, trusting the wrong person, not checking out of a hotel in time, stopping to help a stranded traveler, not being on guard for an IED, not being suspicious of the young man wearing a bulky jacket on a hot summer's day. You closed your eyes for a second to imagine a loved one's face, took your eyes off an unknown object to glance instead at a photograph or finger the medallion you wore around your neck, and the next minute, all that was left of you was that finger. He had seen it so many times, and he wasn't going to end up like that, no siree, he wasn't.

And yet he had to see her. One final time. He couldn't leave town, not like this, not after how he had misbehaved at commencement. He'd had no right to accuse her of coldness when all she was doing was protecting herself. But that was the very fact that had stung him so—that she felt she needed protection against him.

He rose from the bench. The late-May sun blazed in the sky. He would simply drive by her house, and if the husband's car was not there, he would knock on the door to say a quick goodbye. He wouldn't even enter the house—he didn't want to know its layout, didn't want to have to imagine her in its rooms. And yes, he would apologize. He hadn't meant to act like a bastard, he really hadn't. That's all he wanted to do. Tell her that he hadn't meant what he said. Yup, that was what he would do, all he wanted to do, and then he would get the hell out of this sodden town and not stop until he was over the state line.

It was ten a.m. and she was still in her sweats. She had woken up at six this morning, taken a quick shower, made herself coffee, and then hit the stack of papers on her desk. She had worked steadily for three hours, and now her back was stiff.

She rose from her chair, rubbing her back with her left hand. Maybe if she left for work a little early, she could squeeze in a quick walk around the lake. She had meetings starting at three, which meant more sitting. She felt a twinge of pain at the thought.

The silence in the house was as thick as carpet. It felt good to have the house to herself, although Sudhir was returning home this evening, and she'd be happy to see him when she got back late tonight. A low humming began somewhere outside her window, the indistinguishable sounds of late spring. She stretched and decided to make herself another cup of coffee.

She had just taken her first sip when she heard a knock on the door.

This is wrong, this is wrong, everything about this is wrong except for the part that is so right, and what is right is so right, might makes right, white is right, right is right, wrong is right, wrong, he said he was wrong, what he'd said to me was wrong, he stood at my doorstep looking so forlorn, little boy blue, so lost and confused, blue, so blue, those baby blue eyes looking at me, searching my face, but wait, his eyes are not blue at all, they're green, but blue, he's blue, he's my little blue man, my blue lover, his white skin blue as ice, his breath against my hot skin like blue vapor, my body lost in space, in ether, which is blue.

I am cold, ice-cold, and he covers me with his naked body; I am hot and he cools me with his naked body. I am lonely and he befriends me with his naked body. I am hungry and he feeds me with his naked body. His autumn hair falls across his forehead and brushes my face; his honey saliva coats my tongue, my open mouth. His face is so near mine, it is my face. When he blinks, his eyelashes tickle me. When he exhales, I inhale his breath. I give up my breasts to the wisdom of his hands.

There is no church that is like this. There is no temple, no mosque, no synagogue that is like this. There is no holy that is like this. There is no evil that is like this. There is no deceit that is like this. Oh, but there is no holy that is like this. This is what religion was invented for—to keep this holy in check. Under control. Because unleashed, it can look like this, it can burn like this fire that is capable of burning down this bed, this house, this life. Because unleashed, it can roar like this, like the sound of the oceans roaring in unison, like the sound of the four winds howling.

And then we are at rest. And then we are spent. Then we are lying on clean sheets in a bed in a house in the twenty-first century. Then our bodies begin to assume their everyday shapes again. Then our breaths come to nest in their own bodies. Then everything falls back into place. Then our tongues reenter their own caves. Then breasts become the business of their bearers. Then the oceans are once again separated by continents and the four winds quit their howling and we become two people again. Then I lie panting, my ear on his chest, listening to the sound of his racing heartbeat calming itself down.

It is in this silence, in its own way as holy as the jumbled noise that went before it, that I hear the bedroom door open.

32

You ASK ME why I do what I do and I tell you I don't know. Gods swear, I telling the truth. Since Tuesday, I asking myself the exact question hundred times, why I do what I do, but I telling you, I not knowing.

One answer is, I's in shock. This is what happen: I not suppose to go to Maggie house on Tuesday. I suppose to clean for Joseanne madam that morning, but when I gets to her house and begins to clean, her vacuum machine is died. She is all worry because they having party on Friday and need to have the clean house. So I thinks, Maggie not mind if I run in and borrows her cleaning machine. Maggie so generous like that and she introduce me to Joseanne in first place. I think Maggie may be home because sometimes she do her writing work on Tuesday morning. And even if she not home, no problem, I have key and I just go in and take the machine.

Maggie car not in the driveway. I rings doorbell, then I remindering it not working. I knocks the front door two times, and when no answer, I uses my key to go inside. I say, "Hello? Maggie?" but no answer so I thinks she not home. The cleaning machine kept in closet in guest bedroom, I knows. So I goes upstairs to get it.

I opens the door and what I sees, I cannot forget. I cannot forget but I also cannot say. It is so shock that I feel like I going to vomit and faint and laugh and scream all in one breath. Maggie in the guest bed with a guest. A whiteman who is not Sudhir babu. I feel like I have enter the wrong cinema hall and am watching the wrong film. So I just standing there and then my eyes meeting with Maggie's and for one minute I thinks she is to cry but then her face get mean and she yell, "Get out." And then I am shutting the bedroom door and running down the steps and into the living room. My hand is on the front door handle when I hears Maggie's voice saying my name. "Lakshmi," she call. "Wait. Jesus God. Please wait."

So I stand like a statue with my hand on the door, waiting for her. My head going buzz-buzz from the inside, like an insect stuck in it. My whole body cover in sweat and again I feels like I will fainting, but I stand. Maybe Maggie say something that take this crooked picture and make it straight again. Maybe she tell me something that make me see I make the mistake.

She come down the stairs barefeet, wearing a white robe, and I see her hair all messy and her face swelling. She look like homeless woman. I feels bad for her but then I see the picture I don't want to see in my head, and I feels my heart become small and hard.

"Lakshmi," she say. "I just want to . . . oh my God. I don't know what to say. Can you just . . ." Suddenly, her voice become angry. "Jesus, Lakshmi. How about knocking before letting yourself in? Or ringing the doorbell for—"

"I knock two times," I say in loud voice. "Your doorbell not working. I told you last week, only. And I call—"

"Why are you here, anyway? It's not your day for cleaning or therapy."

Before I can explain, a tall man in blue shirt come down the stairs. He buttoning his shirt while coming down and I turn my eyes away from such shamelessness. I looks at Maggie but she is staring at the floor. Something in her jaw move, like she eating chewing gum.

The man stand in front of us and Maggie say to me, "So what do you need, Lakshmi?" Her voice change, as if I am stranger on a bus.

"I come to loan vacuum machine," I say quickly, not looking at the man. "Joseanne madam's machine is broke. I thinking you not home," I adds loudly. "I knocks and call you." I wants the man to hear I not entering people's home without knocking.

"Okay." Maggie's voice soft now. Something broken in her eyes. "Why don't you just go up and get it? Go ahead."

I not wanting to enter the room of Maggie's badness but I not having a choice. They both looking at me. And so I goes up the stairs. The bedroom door is open. He has put the bedspread over the dirty sheets, and seeing how clean the bed now look, I want to vomit again. But I keeps my eyes on the closet. Just then, I sees it on the floor. A neck chain with a pendant. But this not a regular gold-silver pendant. This looking like a tooth. Some big animal tooth. This badmash man kills some poor animal to take away his tooth. I think of what those ugly men in my village had done to my poor Mithai and I feel poison. Maggie allow this man to touch her body. Maggie, who having happy marriage to Sudhir babu.

My heart crack like the chicken bone when I thinks of Sudhir babu. I see him chopping garlic to help me in kitchen. Or his head bending over the important books he read at his desk. Or giving Maggie a kiss each time he leaf for work. Maggie, who cheat on him with this ugly man. Maggie, who so judging me when I tell her about my paper marriage to my husband. Instead of understanding why I doing fake marriage, Maggie siding with my husband. Who she to judge me? My husband cent percent correct—all blacks cheater and liar.

The neck chain in my hand. I knows I should give it to the badmash man. Instead, I take out vacuum machine, and before I goes down the stairs, I enters the main bedroom. I knows

Sudhir babu's side of bed. Quickly, I opens the drawer of his bed stand. Many months ago, Sudhir babu had shown me a copy of the *Gitanjali* that he read every night before going to bed. He love that poetry book, he tell me. I now put the neck chain on top of the book.

From downstairs, I hear them talking softly, like two thief. Liar and cheater. Liar and cheater. I know they waiting for me to leaf to start their dirty business again. I climb down the stairs one step at time because of heaviness of the machine. Not one of them come to help me.

In living room, I not look Maggie in the eye. "Good day, madam," I say, and Maggie get look on her face like I hit her. Then only I realize I call her madam instead of Maggie. But she not saying anything, and I open the door and walk out of the house.

Only when I'm two blocks away safe, I start to cry. I park my car on side of road, put my head on steering wheel. I not knowing what I cry for. Maybe I cry for Sudhir babu, who is trustful as a new baby? Maybe I cry for Maggie, how she look when I call her madam? But then I knows the truth—I crying for myself. For what I losing in one minute. Because I can never go back to that house. That I am sure of. Which mean I not seeing my Maggie again. And then something get hard in my heart. How is she your Maggie? I says to myself. How you belief anything she say after the wickedness she do? I reminder again how shock Maggie look when I tell her how I trick my husband on my wedding day. The burning I feel in my stomach on that day enter my body again. But this time I not feeling ashame. This time I feels angry. Why Maggie trick Sudhir babu with that white badmash? Why she trick me?

Randi. The ugly word come to my head and I shock. In my whole life, I never think that word about a woman. Why now, and that also about Maggie? But what else to think? Only loose women do what Maggie do. And that too with the whiteman who button his shirt in front of me, as if he master of Sudhir babu's house.

All of sudden I thinks of Bobby. How I use to dream of him as my husband snore next to me. How he make me feel especial, how he so kind to me. Maybe this whiteman make Maggie feel same way? But then I shake my head, no, no, no. My love for Bobby pure. I never touches him, never kiss him. Also, Bobby so sweet. He never wear animal tooth on his neck the way this man do.

That reminder me. Of what I do. Sudhir babu out of town, I know. But he coming home this evening. What he do when he find the neck chain? How he know what it meaning? Maybe Maggie say she buy it as the gift? He will belief her, even if he think it stupid gift. My heart slow down. It not my meaning to hurt Sudhir babu. Let him think his wife buy him the stupid gift.

I starts to drive toward Joseanne's house, but I knows I cannot go inside. Joseanne home today and all worry about her party and she wanting to talk and talk about menu and if she need to order more food and what time I come with food on Friday. I know she waiting for me to come back with vacuum machine, but I needs to be alone, needs to get the picture of Maggie in her guest room out of my mind. I takes out my cell phone—it is my cell phone, I buy from my own money—and dial Joseanne number. She yell and scream, say she going to cancel Friday order, but I don't care. Let her try and find caterer who can put up with her worry nature. I come tomorrow and finish cleaning house, I tell her, and close the phone.

It is two o'clock when I gets home. Husband is busy in kitchen so I go straight up to apartment. Rekha want to talk but I tell her I not well and need to sleep. Two hour later husband come up. "What wrong?" he say. "Rekha say you sick?"

Is he being kind? Or is he upset because I not working in

store? But then I see the lines on his forehead and I know he worry about me. "I's okay," I say. "I coming downstairs soonly." But as soon as I say this, I begins to cry, and now he look confuse.

"Lakshmi," he say as he sit on side of bed. "What wrong? You having the fever?"

In a flash, I seeing the look on Maggie face as she sleeping with her head on the whiteman's chest. She look peaceful. She smiling like she just finish a plate of jalebis. I reminder this and then I feel like I is having the fever. My head feel heavy with the evil thoughts they carry. Maggie rich. She having big house, beautiful garden, topless car. Most important, she having happy husband who love her, not a husband who in love with a girl he seen for ten minutes at a mela. How she can trick Sudhir babu? If Maggie not happy in her life, what chance for me?

"Ya, baba," husband say. "You looks like you mad with fever."

"I's not sick," I say. "I—I just . . ." He bend his head to side, waiting for me. "I . . . you correct. About what you say about the blacks. They all liar and cheater. Maggie, too. She, most of all." And now I crying so hard, husband put his arm around me. First time ever he do this outside of the sex. But then, first time ever I cries like this in front of him.

"Chokri, chokri, what's wrong?" he says. "What Maggie do to you?" And despite my sadness, my heart jump. Husband call me girl. Not old woman. Not stupid. Girl.

What Maggie do to me? Nothing. Everything. She trick me. She confuse me. She go from being my teacher to becoming plain woman like me. I trick my husband into marriage with me. She trick her husband during marriage with her. She turn out same as me. Ordinary. Maggie mean so many things to me. But never ordinary.

"Chokri," the husband says. "What are you crying for?" His arms are tight around me, and in the middle of my tears, I feels a tickle. Down there. I never feels this way about my husband before. I shift position in the bed slightly. But it enough for him to notice. His eyes become big and he stare at me. He lick his lips, his eyes never leaf my face.

He say something I cannot hear and then he bury his face between my breasts.

I caters Joseanne's party on Friday. As usual, guests go latoo-fatoo over my cooking. Mostly, this makes me feel good. Today I not notice. I am looking to the front door every two minutes, waiting for Maggie and Sudhir babu to enter. How I will meet Maggie's eyes if she come to talk to me? What I will say if she ask me why I create mischief by putting the neck chain in Sudhir babu's drawer? What I answer if Sudhir babu ask why I leaf the vacuum machine in the garage instead of coming inside the house? I looks at the door every two minutes, wanting them to enter and not wanting them to enter.

By nine o'clock I know one of my prayers come true. They not coming. Why? That I not know. Maybe one of them tired or sick? Maybe they forget party invitation? Maybe Maggie not wanting to see me? Then my anger come back. I also not wanting to see her.

But today, Saturday, I get my answer. My cell phone ring while I am waiting on customer at the store and I pick up without checking caller name. For one second the line is quiet, and then Maggie say, "Lakshmi? It's Maggie." Her voice stiff like cardboard.

"Hi," I say, although my chest feel like it held by rubber bands. Why Maggie calling me? To tell she calling police? To curse at me the way old women in my village do? To ask me to forgive for filling my mind with picture I don't want to see?

I waits. Quietly. Customer trying to ask me question but I walk away from him. Then Maggie says, "I just wanted to let you know that, under the circumstances, I obviously can't continue treating you."

My mouth is like famine, empty of word. Maggie sounding so far away, like she calling from Pakistan. She saying she not never wanting to see me again, which is what I want also, so why I feel sadly?

"Are you still there?" Maggie voice sharp.

"I's here." My own voice sound like squeaking of mouse.

Even though we both quiet, I can feel Maggie anger, like faraway thunder. But still I cannot speak, and after few minute, she say, "Okay. Well, that's it, then." I know she about to hang the phone, but then she say, "One more thing. I can understand your anger at me. But why you had to hurt Sudhir, I don't know. I guess I'll never understand that. After all, we've—he's—been nothing but kind to you."

What can I say? She correct. But why she not lie to Sudhir babu and tell him necklace is a gift? I wants to say sorry. I wants to say: It was a serpent of wickedness deep inside my stomach that make me hurt you and Sudhir babu. But I say nothing.

Maggie let out sharp breath. "Okay. I can see there's nothing to be gained from this. Guess I was hoping for an explanation or something. Silly me."

I opens my mouth to say, No, wait, please, let me say something. But Maggie has put down the phone.

I walk down the aisle of our store, where the customer is complaining about my rudeness to Rekha, who say something to me. I don't hear what she say. Air. I needs air. I opens the door and goes outside. I walk a few steps away from the store window, so Rekha cannot see me. Then I walks some more.

One other time I run out of store like this was on Bobby's last day at restaurant. Later that same day, I had tried the suicide. And because of this, I meet Maggie. Who is now gone away also.

Almost one full year gone since that day. But nothing has change. My hands were empty on that day. They empty today. My heart was alonely then. And it still.

But then I think, Lakshmi, you wrong. Everything has change. You have change. You will never try the suicide again. Maggie has show you the value of your life. Maggie burn your old life and make you a new one. Now you having your own business, cell phone, car. Even husband treating me more good than before. Something change inside him after I call him a stupid for loving Shilpa more than he love his real wife. For few days after, he look at me different, as if some jaali covering his eyes is gone. One time in the store I make mistake and not charge customer for biscuit packet. He open his mouth to call me stupid, like always. But then he stop and say, "Simple mistake. Anyone can make."

And last Tuesday, when I come home from Maggie's house and my husband come upstair to check on me? We make the love then in middle of afternoon. First time my husband not pulling for me in the dark. First time he looking into my eyes and first time he smiling, like he not angry at what he seeing. When we are finish, he stay with me for long time, and when he get up to go back downstair, he act like he sorry to go.

A plastic bag blows from the parking lot and dancing in front of my feet. I bends down and pick it up. Maggie say people in Am'rica littering so much that there is a country of plastic bottles and bags growing inside the sea near the California. The litter blow across the whole country to go swimming inside the California sea. Maggie get upset when she talk about it, but in my mind it make such a pretty picture—blue and pink bags flying like birds over the whole country. I wish I free like that, to go where the breeze taking you.

I knows it is time to go back inside store to help poor Rekha.

Saturday our busy day. I knows this is my life, with Rekha and husband and store and restaurant. For one year, my life became a big house because Maggie enter it. She give it color and new shape. But Maggie now gone. And I have no idea whether the new house can stand or it fall down.

33

MAGGIE WAS GRATEFUL that Sudhir had offered her a ride to the campus pool. For the past two Saturdays, he had made some excuse for driving separately, and even though he was sullen and silent during the drive there today, hope flared in her heart. But then she looked at him out of the corner of her eye, took in the stiffness of his posture, the set of his mouth, and her heart sank again. The rigidity that had taken over Sudhir ever since he'd discovered Peter's neck chain, that frozen quality, as if his body were encapsulated in a slab of ice that nothing could melt—not apology, not entreaties, not offers to enter couples counseling—was very much present. And yet this was the first time they'd been in the car together in several weeks. The proximity enforced an intimacy that their large house, with its many rooms to escape to, didn't. And surely Sudhir had known that it would when he offered her a ride.

For the past two weeks, Sudhir had studiously avoided her at the pool, chatting instead with the other regulars and looking away if his eye accidentally caught hers. Once or twice she'd swum up to him, made some observation or comment, and he'd paused and heard her out, nodded, and then swum away from her.

Remembering this now, as Sudhir parked the car in the open lot, Maggie felt a spurt of anger. It was this coldness, this precision, this control over his emotions, that had driven her toward Peter in the first place. How unfair it was that, because she was the one who had the affair, Sudhir could forever be the aggrieved party. How unfair it was that he would never have to take a cold, hard look at his own behavior, his culpability. If their friends ever learned about her affair—and Maggie had no idea whether Sudhir was talking to anyone—she would always be the cheating spouse, and Sudhir would forever be the martyr.

But by the time she changed out of her street clothes and emerged into the pool area, Maggie's anger was spent and replaced by sharp regret. She remembered again how uncomfortable Peter had been after Lakshmi had fled the house, how eager to get out of the house himself. There had not been a trace of the warmth, the neediness, with which he had looked at her as he stood at her front door a few hours earlier; it was the hunger in Peter's eyes that had made her invite him in, secure as she was in the knowledge that he was leaving town. They had stood wordlessly in her living room as Lakshmi gathered the vacuum cleaner and left, their earlier passion already a distant memory. Even as the enormity of what had just happened, what Lakshmi had just seen, dawned on Maggie, Peter offered nary a consoling word. He was already eyeing the door that Lakshmi had recently exited, looking at it and the open road that lay beyond, with the same hunger he'd looked at her. Distraught as she had been, Maggie had marveled at Peter's talent for self-preservation and realized it was this quality that allowed him to do what he did. Peter was, above all, a survivor. He had a degree of self-absorption, of single-mindedness, that probably only one percent of the world's population shared. He was in elite company, along with the professional athletes and actors and politicians and sociopaths. Peter would always sweep aside anyone who came between him and his work. Domestic drama—angry husbands, distraught wives, jilted girlfriends—was anathema to him. Maggie had realized all this in a flash. Or rather, she had always known it; it was part of Peter's attraction for her, how light, how unbound and ungoverned, his life had seemed. There was none of the earth-binding heaviness of mortgage payments and car loans and work schedules and family obligations. Peter, and men like him, were the last nomads, the bird-men, the world a series of open doors that they could slip in and out of. In the last few seconds that she gazed at him before he kissed her lightly on the cheek and left, Maggie saw how she'd romanticized his life. Peter had always seemed so rugged to her, so manly, in contrast to Sudhir. But the Peter who stood shuffling his feet had the face of an immature youth, someone who had never been tempered by domestic routine, by duty, by the weight of being responsible for another's happiness.

She had looked away, afraid that he would see the contempt in her eyes. And as she did, a long, silent wail started somewhere deep within her. How wrong she had been. How poor her judgment. What a lousy trade, risking her marriage to Sudhir for the sake of someone like Peter. She had gotten it right the first time with Sudhir, had hit the luckiest of jackpots—a good marriage—and she had screwed it up. Over what? Over a man who stood shifting from one foot to another, emptily saying that everything would be okay, leaving her to clean up the mess they both had made.

We are earthbound creatures, Maggie had thought. No matter how tempting the sky. No matter how beautiful the stars. No matter how deep the dream of flight. We are creatures of the earth. Born with legs, not wings, legs that root us to the earth, and hands that allow us to build our homes, hands that bind us to our loved ones within those homes. The glamor, the adrenaline rush, the true adventure, is here, within these homes. The wars, the détente, the coups, the peace treaties, the celebrations, the mournings, the hunger, the sating, all here. And this is something Peter, for all his travel, for all his worldly sophistication, will never know. He will eat at the finest restaurants in Paris but will never know the bliss of having your spouse make a pot of chicken noodle soup on a damp Saturday evening.

She had been genuinely happy when Sudhir came home that evening, felt truly free, as if she had kicked a drug addiction and now could be the person she was meant to be, could fully be the spouse Sudhir deserved. Despite having gotten home just an hour before she did, Sudhir had already prepared dinner, and her heart tore with gratitude at this kindness. This is marriage, she told herself, these small, precious gestures of responsibility and love. I will never do anything to jeopardize this again, so help me God.

Her world was still whole, unsundered, when she offered to do the dishes and clean up while Sudhir went upstairs to prepare for bed. She turned on the kitchen radio, unaware of how her life was unraveling, unaware that after getting into his pajamas, her husband had opened the drawer of his bedside table, reaching for the book of poems that he read nightly before bed, his hand touching an unfamiliar object. She didn't know that while she listened to NPR, Sudhir was turning the necklace in his hand, recognizing the tiger's tooth immediately, but unable to make sense of the inexplicable, to shape a narrative that would explain why Peter Weiss's ridiculous necklace would land in his bedside table. And then a germ of suspicion attacked his mind. He shook his head to shake it off, but it took further root, bringing with it unwelcome pictures—the breathless quality in Maggie's voice when they'd met Peter at the campus museum during his first stint here, the shameless way in which he'd openly flirted with Maggie, the way the tiger's tooth had sat flush against Peter's pink skin in the pool a few months ago, the sour, dyspeptic feeling in Sudhir's stomach when he'd seen the bare-chested Peter talking to his wife in the water. By the time he walked back into the kitchen, where Maggie was drying the last of the dishes, the necklace dangling from his index finger, Sudhir had solved most of the puzzle. The only missing piece was what Maggie was trying to tell him by placing it in his nightstand.

Maggie watched terror-stricken as Sudhir stood in front of her, resisting the urge to scream. Sudhir was speaking to her, his lips were moving, but the thumping of her heart, the roar of her blood, drowned out all other sound. No easy lie sprang to her lips. There was too much going on—the mesmerizing effect of Sudhir dangling the chain in front of her, the seething anger in his eyes as he asked for an explanation, her initial outrage that Peter would stoop this low, that he would deliberately break up her marriage even as he left town. "Why was this man in my house?" Sudhir kept asking, and even as she struggled to answer in a way that would allay his suspicions, she knew it was too late. This is it, she said to herself, the chickens come home to roost. As soon as she thought this, she knew with certainty that it wasn't Peter who had betrayed her but the last person on earth whom she would've suspected of betrayal. And then she mocked herself for her naïveté, remembering Lakshmi's story of how she had tricked her husband. If anyone is capable of betrayal, she told herself, it's Lakshmi.

Sudhir had left the house that night. Gotten into the same clothes he'd shed earlier and left without taking even his toothbrush. He came home the next morning and silently got ready for work. She hadn't had the guts to ask him where he'd spent the night. After he drove off, she dialed the hospital and called in sick.

She had spent the day driving around town, alternating between disbelief and bone-piercing grief. How could she have screwed up this badly? How could she have hurt Sudhir? But toward evening, as she drove home, she felt a strange peace. She and Sudhir had been together through thick and thin. It would be a long, hard journey, but they would make their way back. They had to. They had to.

She found Sudhir on the back porch with the lights turned off. "Hi," she whispered. "Can I sit with you for a few minutes?"

She heard the faint rustle of his kurta and knew that he had shrugged his assent. She lowered herself on the love seat next to him. They sat in tense silence for a few minutes, and then Maggie reached over and took Sudhir's hand in hers. She forced herself not to notice how cold and lifeless it felt. "I want to tell you something," she said. "Something I realized today. Can you listen?"

"Yup," Sudhir said.

She was unnerved by the flatness of his tone, by the dead-weight of his hand in hers. She sighed. Sudhir was not making this easy, and really, who could blame him? But she knew she had to try.

"I've been thinking of how humans are basically earthbound creatures," she started. "You know? How our concerns are rooted to this earth, to family life."

This was not what she wanted to say at all. Already she could feel Sudhir's impatience with her.

"Listen," she said urgently. "What I'm trying to say is, I realized today that you are a hundred times the man Peter will ever be. He . . . he means nothing to me, Sudhir. My life is here with you. I know this now. And I'm sorry for . . ."

Sudhir shook his hand out of hers and rose slowly to his feet. He stood over her for a moment, and now that her eyes had adjusted to the dark, she saw that he was shaking his head. "If it took you this long to know that I'm a hundred times the man that Peter is, Maggie, then all I can say is I'm sorry. You're far more stupid than I ever imagined. Frankly, I'm insulted to even be compared to that pompous asshole."

She sat in shock, staring into the dark, after Sudhir left the room. In all their years together, he had never talked to her in this way. She knew that she had blundered, that her inarticulate words had actually made things worse between them; that what had felt like a revelation to her was an obvious fact to Sudhir. And not because Sudhir was a vain man—he was in fact the most self-effacing of men—but because he was wise. He didn't need to have an affair to learn the value of what they'd built together.

Maggie had hated herself then, and she carried that self-hatred into the pool with her this morning. But the warm blue water felt like forgiveness. With each lap she swam, the self-loathing dislodged itself a tiny bit. A welcome blankness fell over her mind, a respite from the anguished thoughts that fired like shards of coal in her brain. After a few more laps, she floated on her back, listening to the Mozart playing on the overhead speakers, looking up at the glass ceiling, recalling a hundred other Saturdays when she and Sudhir had been in this pool together, feeling a sense of connection even when they were at opposite ends, Sudhir flashing a grin or mouthing her a quick kiss whenever their eyes found the other.

Madeline White, a professor in the history department, entered the pool, spotted Maggie, and swam up to her. Maggie inquired about Madeline's recent hip surgery, asked how her husband, Phil, was doing, and then excused herself. Small talk in the pool was beyond her today. She was aware of Madeline's start of surprise as she turned abruptly and swam toward the far end of the pool.

Ravel's *Boléro* was playing overhead, and Maggie swam a few more laps. Feeling a tiny cramp in her calf, she decided to stop, holding on to the pool wall as she stretched out her leg. After a few minutes, Sudhir swam up to her. "Everything okay?" he said, shaking the water from his body.

She looked at him, took in the dark hair slicked down on his forehead, the slender shoulders, the flawless skin the color of tea, and thought he'd never looked more beautiful. She smiled at him. "Yes. Thanks for checking." This was what she'd felt the other day but had been unable to say: It was this shorthand, this history, this knowing of each other, these daily acts of kindness, that she'd come to value, that she'd never again take for granted.

She opened her mouth to say something, but Sudhir spoke first. "I just wanted to tell you. I'm leaving next Saturday."

"Leaving for where?" Sudhir usually gave her his travel schedule as soon as he knew it.

He looked away, staring at a spot beyond her shoulder. "Leaving . . . moving out. I got my own apartment."

She felt something within her collapse so dramatically that she was glad the buoyancy of the water was holding her up. On land, she would've fallen, her legs unable to sustain her, she was sure. She felt as if her very soul, her spirit, had escaped from her, so that her body was an empty shell, the facade of a tall building, with no rooms, no hallways, on the inside. A cold, icy fear entered her. Her eyes stung with tears.

Her lips moved. She said nothing.

His eyes flickered over her face and then moved away, as if distressed by what they saw there. "I'm sorry," he said. "There's no other way. We can decide what to do about the house later. You can stay there forever, I don't care. I'm not going to fight you over anything. You can have anything you want. I just . . . I want a quick divorce, that's all."

Divorce? Had Sudhir really just said that word? That nasty, unimaginable, not-applicable-to-us word? But why was she so surprised? People got divorced all the time. Hell, she'd be out of business if half of her clients weren't divorced or contemplating it. But what did those people have to do with her and Sudhir? Her

Sudhir. She had known him practically her whole adult life. He
was her partner. Her life mate. Her deepest, closest friend. Her
family. He was her family. One didn't divorce family, did one? But
one didn't cheat on family, either, did one? Betray them, wound
them? Well, yes, people did. One did. And they had to take you
back. Family had to take you back. That was the whole point of
family. The way you took Wallace back, you mean? Well, no, that's
different. He was never really sorry, he never really apologized.
Whereas me, I'm repentant. I'm a penitent. I will walk on hot
coals to express how sorry I am. I will climb a mountain made of
broken glass on bended knee in apology. I will atone. But please,
God, not this. Nothing with Peter, not the sweetest, maddest moment of lovemaking, is worth this, this destruction, this cleaving.
Because that's what it will be—a cleaving, one half of me gone,
since Sudhir is the other half of me. The better half. God, he always was the better half. How could I have not known it?

    She heard *Boléro* build up to its rousing climax and thought,
I will remember this moment forever, the rest of my life. I will
never again be able to listen to this piece of music without remembering this moment when my soul left my body and I was
still alive. But the next second, a fury blew through her, blasting
away the icy numbness of a second ago, and she thought, Fight,
fight, fight, do not give up without a fight, you idiot, this is your
life, your love, you are fighting for. Make him change his mind,
make him see the stupidity of his actions, make him stay, just
make him stay, today and the next day and the next, until some
normalcy seeps back into your lives, until the scab begins to form,
until healing happens. We will do couples counseling, we will
make changes, we are sentient, intelligent, caring people, we love
each other, we have the advantages of education and culture and
wealth, we have a great support system, we can afford the best
therapists money can buy, we can do this, we can make it work, we

will succeed, because if we fail, with all our advantages and privileges, what hope for the millions of others who don't have half the things that we do? Say something, say something, something perfect, something wise and loving and accurate, get through to him, this is Sudhir, this is no stranger, this is your Sudhir whom you've known since he was twenty-three years old, Sudhir who courted you with his soft manner and easy smile, Sudhir whom you married at city hall in a simple ceremony attended by only your grad school friends, Sudhir who took you to Niagara Falls for a honeymoon even though both of you were flat broke, Sudhir whose first car in the U.S. you helped pick out, a secondhand Chevy, Sudhir who took you to Calcutta for the first time a month after he got his citizenship, Sudhir for whom you, born and raised in Brooklyn, moved to this lily-white college town, something you've never quite made your peace with, this is Sudhir, I tell you, look past the opaque eyes, the mouth that is already arranging itself in lines that you don't quite recognize, this is your Sudhir still, even if he's receding in front of your disbelieving eyes, claim him, fight for him, claim him before it's too late. Or is it too late?

"Honey," she said. "Can we talk about this? I— This is not the place for this serious a conversation."

He shook his head impatiently. "Sure. We can talk. But my mind's made up. I've already signed the lease. And the movers are coming Saturday."

Her chin wobbled. "I don't understand. How you can. After all these years. Just like that."

She saw something flash in his eyes before they turned cloudy again. But she knew what he was too much of a gentleman to say: He didn't understand how she could, either. After all these years. Just like that.

Sudhir was talking, and she forced herself to listen. "The apartment's not that far. It's on Garden Street. Just three miles away. I will still come and mow the lawn every week. And if you ever need anything . . ." Sudhir looked uncomfortable. "I will, you know, help in any way I can. With money or whatever else."

Despite herself, she smiled. Of course. He had it all worked out. Down to the mowing of the lawn. He would not shirk his responsibilities. She had his parents to thank for that, she knew. The elderly Bengali couple—whom, she realized, she would never see again—had instilled in their son a lifelong sense of duty and obligation. Funny to think that, just a few months ago, she had found his sense of propriety stifling. Had wished he were more carefree, more lighthearted, like Peter. Now she knew: Peter was built out of shifting sand, transient as a child's sand castle. Sudhir was a rock.

"You're serious about this," she whispered in a half-question.

Another swimmer brushed past them, and Sudhir leaned toward her. "There's no other way. I can't be in that house anymore. Every time I look at you, I see . . ." He blinked hard. "I'm sorry."

They stared at each other, a shocked expression on both their faces. Then Sudhir raised his hand in a half-salute, half-wave, a gesture as familiar to Maggie as her own skin. "Achcha," he said. "I'll go swim a few more laps. And then I'll be ready to leave whenever you are."

She stood at the edge of the pool, watching his dark head bobbing in the water, watching the rustled water he left in his wake. After a few minutes, she floated on her back, staring up at the ceiling, wishing there were a way to drown in the pool without anyone noticing, feeling as if the water holding her up were her enemy, feeling herself lying in a watery coffin. She wondered if the part of her that had escaped out of her body upon hearing Sudhir's chilling words would remain lost to her the rest of her life.

BOOK
FOUR

34

MAGGIE STOOD IN front of the little cottage with the gray siding. Behind her, she could hear the sound of the waves, background music to the frenzied chorus of seagulls. A slight breeze carried the taste of salt water to her lips. It also shook the stalks of the lavender bush in the right corner of the small front yard.

"So? What do you think?" Gloria asked.

"It's beautiful. No, it's more than beautiful. It's perfect."

"Wait'll you see the inside. It's an adorable little place."

Slow down, Maggie said to herself as Gloria unlocked the front door. Gloria has a vested interest in this, don't forget. Then she chided herself for being suspicious. She had known Gloria since her first semester at NYU, where they had taken a statistics class together. They had remained friends through the years—Gloria had been one of the witnesses to her city hall wedding to Sudhir; years later, Maggie had flown in for a week after David, Gloria's first husband, had died from cancer at the age of thirty-four. She had also been present at the birth of Gloria's son from her second marriage and, a few years later, had helped her pack when she and her new husband, Martin, had moved out to California.

So when Gloria had heard that Maggie and Sudhir had split, her first reaction had been to laugh. In disbelief. After Maggie had convinced her that it was true, that Sudhir had indeed moved out, Gloria's second reaction was to insist that she call to straighten him out. Swallowing her pride, Maggie had given Gloria Sudhir's new phone number. Gloria was now a top-selling Realtor who sold multimillion-dollar homes in Southern California. Her powers of persuasion were legendary.

A subdued Gloria had called back a half hour later. "I'm sorry, honey," she said. "He would hardly talk to me. I've never known Sudhir to act like this. He— His mind's made up, honey. I'm so sorry."

"I know. He's changed."

"You want to come out here for a few weeks, hon? You know, just to get away?"

Maggie hadn't been able to go just then. She was working like a fiend, staying late at the hospital, taking on new patients at home. For one thing, she needed the extra income now that Sudhir was gone, and for another, time was her enemy. If she didn't stay busy, the smoke of regret blew into her mind, clouding it, threatening to destroy her carefully planned days. So she stayed busy, forgetting to eat lunch or dinner, unaware of the dark circles under her eyes, ignoring the loss of weight and the startled looks she received from clients who had not seen her in a few months. She tried meditation but found that she couldn't sit still long enough, so she took up running, racing up and down the steep streets of her neighborhood every evening. If she ran long enough, her fevered mind stopped replaying the familiar loop of the fateful day when Lakshmi had walked into the bedroom and destroyed her life. At the end of each day, she collapsed on her king-size bed, acutely aware of the loss of Sudhir's body next to hers, willing him to return. A few times, unable to sleep, she had called Odell in France, waking him up in the wee hours of the morning, sobbing her regrets to him. As always, Odell listened carefully, quietly. But once they hung up, it was still only Maggie in the silent bedroom.

By October it was apparent that Sudhir was not coming back. It did not escape her notice that instead of stopping by to check on the house every Saturday, he was going longer between visits. Their conversations were brief, perfunctory. It was a new kind of loneliness, this, not as pungent a pain as she'd experienced when he first left, but more hollowed out, chronic. It made her feel old before her time. She had always struggled with melancholy at this time of year, affected by the shift in light, by the translucent leaves, whose extravagant beauty hid their imminent death. But for the past three decades, she'd had Sudhir's love to protect her against the coming chill. Now she felt stripped of that protection, vulnerable.

So when Gloria called again and invited her out for ten days to celebrate her mother's eightieth birthday, Maggie said yes immediately. Gloria and Martin had a big house in La Jolla, and she needed to be around other people. Besides, she wanted to see Gloria's mother, Felice, again. The old lady had always been good to her during those long-ago days at NYU, when she had missed her own mother so much.

And now here they stood, in front of the little cottage in Encinitas where Felice had lived until they'd moved her to assisted living six months ago. "The housekeeper has been away on vacation," Gloria was saying as they crossed the painted front porch. "So it may be a little dusty."

Maggie barely heard. She was looking at the scruffy hardwood floors of the sunny, airy living room, the overhead wooden beams, the lace curtains on the many windows, the beautiful woodwork around the tiled fireplace, and trying to keep her heart still. This is it, a voice in her head said over and over again. This is home. She had always disliked the large modern house in Cedarville. This house fit her like a glove. And she hadn't even seen the kitchen yet.

The next second they were in the kitchen, with wallpaper that hadn't been changed since the 1970s and a beautiful old stove that reminded Maggie of the one in the apartment in Brooklyn. Her eyes filled with tears. "This is—perfect. This house has such character, such spirit."

Gloria beamed. "I knew it. I bet Martin last night that you'd love it. Wait'll you see the upstairs. I mean, it needs work, but . . ."

"Of course, it's nothing I can afford. And it's not like I can just up and move."

Gloria eyed her quietly before nodding. "Let's go see the up-stairs."

There were three bedrooms, one slightly larger than the other two. All had views of the ocean. Maggie thought of her enormous master bedroom with its vaulted ceilings and attached bathroom and shuddered. How lonely she had been in that room night af-ter night. In contrast, she felt so safe in this snug, human-scaled room, with its old but cheerful wallpaper and roughed-up floor.

"Well? What do you think?"

"It's lovely."

"And it can be yours."

Maggie laughed. "Gloria. Don't give me your sales pitch. I'm not one of your millionaire clients. There's no way I could afford anything like this."

Gloria shrugged. "Don't be too sure you can't. Values have fallen around here something fierce. Besides, I spoke to Martin. I'm sure we can work something out."

Maggie felt a spurt of excitement. Move? To California? Start anew in a place with no memories, no regrets? She shook her head. She had a steady job at the hospital. Her private practice was doing well. Her life, such as it was, was in Cedarville. Hell, she was fifty-five years old. Far too old to move to a new place where she had no friends except Gloria.

"It's not like you'll be alone," Gloria said as if she'd read her mind. "We'll be nearby. I would love to keep Mom's home in the family, so to speak."

Maggie leaned over and kissed Gloria's cheek. "Thanks. But really, even if I took out every last penny out of my savings, I can't afford California real estate."

Gloria shrugged, headed down the stairs with Maggie following, walked into the kitchen, and put the kettle on for tea. They settled at the table, sipping their tea, before Gloria spoke. "You could sell the house and ask Sudhir for your share. You can rent this one here for the first year or however long yours stays on the market. And I'll sell it at a very reasonable price."

"But G. Why would you do this? This is a beautiful house. Someone will pay you top dollar."

"No, they won't. As you can see, it needs work. The housing market is bad. And I told you, if you're nearby, I don't have to worry about you. Have you looked at yourself in the mirror lately?"

"Don't make me cry, G."

"Hey, goofball. In case you haven't noticed, I'm tryin' to cheer you up."

Maggie shook her head. "It's too soon. I need to stay put for now. I need my job." She forced into her voice a merriment she didn't feel. "I'll tell you what. If, by some miracle, it's on the market a year from now, we'll talk."

"He's not coming back, Maggie," Gloria said softly.

Maggie looked away. "I know," she mumbled. "I know."

She went home five days later, convinced that she'd made the sensible choice. California was seduction, with its surf and sand and ocean and sun, all gleaming white teeth and linen shirts and sandals. No more seductions for her. She took a cab home from the airport, thinking how strange it was that Sudhir was not there to pick her up. It was nine-thirty when she turned the key and walked into her kitchen. The first thing she noticed was the note from Sudhir on the granite countertop. "Hi," it read. "Hope you had a good time with Gloria. I spoke to the lawyer. The divorce will be finalized on Nov. 13. We have to go sign some papers on that day. Hope you're free."

She swallowed the bile that rose in her throat. She went to the fridge and found a weeks-old bottle of white wine. She took a swig directly from the bottle and then went around the dark house turning on the lights. By the time she reached her cavernous bedroom, she'd made up her mind.

She reached Gloria's answering machine. "Hey," she said. "I'm home. Listen, if it's not too late, I've changed my mind. I want to buy your mom's house. I may have to rent, you know, for a year or more. But I want to move. I'm ready."

35

Now that I no more going to see Maggie on Mondays, I goes on outings with my husband. Restaurant and store close on Mondays so it become our especial day. The first time I not go to Maggie's house on a Monday, he take me to the Chinese restaurant. He knowing I loves the Chinese food. Week after that, husband find out that there is Bharatnatayam dance concert on the college campus, so we go there. I know Sudhir babu teach on this campus but I never goes there before. On the way, we pass by the hospital in Burnham where I first meet Maggie, but not husband or I saying anything. I reminder everything that Maggie say and do, how she make me feel comfortable and safe. How she take me for that walk out of the lockup and show me I human being and not the animal. My heart break like a glass bangle when I thinks of Maggie. And husband can tell I sad, because what you think? He take his hand and put it on top of mine.

After that first time, we go to campus for functions often. I like seeing young student laughing, talking, joking. It remind me of how Shilpa and I use to run to school when we little children. In my next life, I wanting to come back as the college student in Am'rica. It is best life I can think.

Today we leaf after seeing a Hindi film arrange by the India Student Association. It is a comedy film, and as we walk to our car, the husband is making the face and saying funny dialogue from the film. He comic man, my husband. I know I never tell you before. I myself not knowing until recent.

It is cold today, even though it is almost end of March. My nose is red, my eyes like water tap, and I pulls the scarf to my face as we walk down the hill toward car park. The wind blowing so loudly that at first I think I hearing mistake when someone say, "Hi, Lakshmi." But the man in the black coat has stop in front of me and my stomach do a spin because it is Sudhir babu. First time I see him since almost ten months, and he look hundred percent different. His hair is long, his face thin, and he having light beard. He look sick, like man who been in hospital.

Husband take my hand in his. He stop in middle of laugh and I sees shock on his face also.

"Hello," I say. "How you?"

Sudhir babu smile like it hurt his face. "Good. I'm good. And you?"

"Good," I say, because what else to say? What I's really wants to say is I wish this hill crack open and cover me inside it. Because I am reason Sudhir babu look like he do. Joseanne madam has told me that Maggie and Sudhir divorce. Where Maggie now living, I not knowing, but the day when I find out about divorce, I drive by their house and see the for-sale sign.

Husband make uh-uh noise in his throat and Sudhir babu smile his new smile. "Business okay?" he ask.

"Yes, sir," my husband say. "Thanks God."

Sudhir babu nod. He quiet and then say, "Well, I should get going. Nice to see you both."

And he put his hands in his coat pockets and walk away. I turn around to look at him, wanting to say so much, to touch his feet and begs him to please forgive me, but he go around building and then he gone, like a bhoot. "Come on, Lakshmi," husband say, still holding my hand, and I follow him.

In the car, I feel my whole body dead. My nose, ears, hands dead from the cold. And my heart dead from how Sudhir babu look. I reminder the look on Maggie's face when I last see her and I wants to cry. Husband driving quietly, not saying anything, all our joking-foking about the film now stop. At red traffic light, he turn to me and say, "I's sorry for you."

For ten months, my husband tell me he proud that I expose Maggie's wickedness to Sudhir babu. You do correct thing by leaving the neck chain for him, Lakshmi, he say. So many time I thinking that my new happy with my husband build on Maggie's grave. But today he seeing the truth—I not just punishing Maggie. I punishing Sudhir babu also. Today my husband understanding truth of what sin I do. And still he say he feel sorry for me.

At that moment, in the car, I begins to love my husband. "I loves you," I tells him and then, because my face burn with the shame, I look out the window. Maybe he not hear me.

But he do. He take my hand and hold it to his heart. With his other hand, he drive.

Late that night, husband wake me up. He turn on bedroom light and sit on the bed, smiling. "What, ji?" I say. "Tummy upset?"

He laugh. "No. No tummy upset." And I see he holding his cell phone.

Still I confuse. "Who calling so late?"

"Nobody." He put phone in my hand. "It nine o'clock in the morning in India. Call your dada."

I looks at him as if he gone mad. "Dada not having phone," I say.

"Tuch," he make sound. "Chokri, use your akkal. Call the shop of that landlord of yours. You still having his phone number, na? Tell them to call for your dada. Then you call back in half hour."

I shakes my head. "But you said . . ."

He bite his lip. "I said many things. I's sorry. My baba always told me it was a maha paap, what I doing. Not allowing you to talk to your people." He touch my shoulder. "Go wash your face. And then call. Go."

Dada sound exact like six year ago. He not even surprise that I call. Menon sahib more surprise to hear my voice than Dada. It is as if Dada always know that his Lakshmi never forget him. He talking about the kheti and new cow he buy and how my rascal Mithai chase Menon sahib's fat wife around the yard last week when she be mean to Munna's wife. But then he give me the biggest news. Shilpa have a son. He three years old. She and Dilip doing well. I am auntie. His name is Jeevan. It mean life.

When I hang up, I having phone number for Shilpa. I also having the new life. Jeevan.

36

Husband laughing at me. Look at her, he say to Rekha. She still have two-inch space in the box, so she looking for something to pack in it. I pays him no attention. I mailing gift package for Jeevan in prepay postal box. I looks around store for something that he enjoy. "Ae, Lakshmi," husband say. "This Indian grocery store, no? What you going to find here that they not getting in India?"

I already talk to Shilpa six time. She sound like old Shilpa, not the angry sister I live with until my husband send for me to Am'rica. I ask her question per question about Jeevan, what his taste, what he like to eat, drink, wear, size number. I already been to Walmart and Target for toys and clothes. I buy chocolate, sweets, stuffed bear from drugstore. But a little space left in box. I want to pack it so full, when Jeevan open it, things fall out, like shower.

"Here," husband tease. "Put in a fresh hot samosa. It will be nice and stale by the time he get parcel." My husband is big comic these days.

I go behind the counter. There are three silver statues of goddess Lakshmi for sale, and I pick up the biggest one. I wrap it in the brown paper and push it into the box. "Hey, hey." Husband not joking now. "This costing seventy-five dollars, Lakshmi. You know how post office in India is. Postman will open the parcel and steal everything. Why you wasting money?"

I take two steps to face my husband and look into his eyes. "This is for my nephew," I say quiet. "I wants him to know my name. So I sending him statue name after me. You having objections?"

Husband look away first. "Okay, waste money if you want." But he not force me to put it back on shelf.

I nods and go back to wrapping my parcel. This is love—not what we say to each other but what we not say. Sometime it just one look exchange. Sometime one word. But underlining everything we say or not say, something else. Something heavy and deep, like when we in bed and looking into each other's eyes. For six years, everything between husband and me was on top, like skin. Now it hidden, like bone and muscle. I not explaining this good. But I feels the difference. He care for me now. He finally see me. And he like what he see.

Ma wrong about one thing. When I was girl, she only talk about love in the marriage. In Hindi movies, same thing. All love, love, love. Singing and dancing in the snow in Kashmir or in Shimla. Nobody tell me what make real marriage—respect. Ever since day I call husband the stupid for loving a ghost, he begins to respect me. And once I see he no longer loving a ghost, I respect him.

Now I says to him, "Listen, ji. When you go out today, can you post this parcel for me?"

He make long face, wink at Rekha, but I know he just acting. He will take it and soon my nephew, Jeevan, will be knowing he have a second mother in Am'rica who love him as much as his first mother do. Jeevan cut from my Shilpa's body. My blood flow in his vein. He now as real in my life as moon in the sky.

In the afternoon, after closing restaurant at three, husband leaf to go errand running. Rekha having bad stomach cramp today, so I tell her to go to storage room and lie down. I feels bad not offering her my bed when apartment is so close by, but home and business two different place. She puts flat cardboard on the floor and lies down. I tell her to put Zandu balm on her stomach but she say no. Her wish.

It is quiet today. One Am'rican lady come in wanting to buy curry. I say to her, What you need? Curry leafs? Chicken curry in frozen section? But she wanting curry powder. No Indian customer buying readymade mix—everyone making their own. But I happy to sell to her. Then she ask me what she do with it and I gives her recipe for making the curry.

After she go, I pulls up stool and begins to look at the accounts book. Usually, I doing this upstairs in the evening because Rekha don't need to know our profit business. But today Rekha sleeping, so, as husband like to say, the coat is clear (what that mean?). The company that send us goat meat every Wednesday increase price last month, so I doing new maths. Maybe I find new supplier close by.

The front door bell ring as someone come in. The sun come in strong, so I cannot see his face, but it is male customer. I say hello and go back to my book. The store is long-shaped, and usually, customer shop first before coming up to the counter.

But when I look up, the man standing in front of me. My shock so great, the pen fall from my hand and roll under the counter. My hand go to cover my mouth. It is Sudhir babu. Looking more thin and sick than when I see him on campus week and half ago. He still not shave and his hair dirty. He stand in front of me, long and thin, like a candle whose flame put out. When he smile, it is cold as snow.

"Hello, Lakshmi," he say and I knows—he come to kill me. In open daylight he going to shoot me, like those mens who walk into the school with the gun. Why today only I sent my husband to post office? Why Rekha sleeping in stockroom today? Sudhir babu come to shoot me for what I do to his marriage.

"Forgive me," I say. Something roll down my cheek and then I knows that I is crying. "I not trying to cause mischief in your life, Sudhir babu. I myself not knowing why I doing what I do."

"What are you talking about?"

"I in so much shock," I say. "I only come to borrow vacuum machine. But I poking my nose in your business and I so sorry."

He shake his head. "No, no. That's not why I came. Oh I see. You thought . . ." He quiet for a minute. "No need to apologize," he say. "You did me a favor. If you hadn't . . . done what you did, I'd still be in the dark. Living a lie." His body shiver, like he cold.

So why he here if he not angry with me? Maybe he here to shop for grocery? But Maggie say they shop with that baniya who cheat customer left and right. I see again how thin he is and I ask, "You hungry, Sudhir babu? I gets you some food from restaurant?"

This time his smile warm like gulab jamun, not cold like kulfi. "Lakshmi. Always wanting to feed people."

"I go make you plate."

He put his hand on the counter. "No. Really. I . . . I don't have much of an appetite these days. Which reminds me of why I came by." He stop because the door open and a customer walk in. It is Mrs. Purohit, regular customer. I knows she will not disturb us until she finish shopping and ready to pay.

"Yes?" I say, to courage him to go on.

"Well, I have a new place now. A two-bedroom apartment. And I need someone to clean for me. I tried one of those maid services, and they were awful. And so I wondered, you know, if you're not too busy, if you'd fit me in."

"Yes," I say before he finish. "Of course. When you wanting me to start?" Everything I have, every dollar in my purse, is because of this man and his wife.

He look surprise and happy both. "Really? Wow. That's great." He rub his chin with his thumb. "One other thing. I was wondering if, maybe every two weeks or so, I could purchase some cooked food from you? You know, stuff I could freeze and reheat."

Sudhir babu not knowing how his words knife my heart. What has happen to this man that he so delicate and weak? But I don't show him the sad I feel. Instead I say, "Sure. I brings you fresh food every time I come to clean. How often you want cleaning?"

He look embarrass. "You know, I don't even know how much you charge," he say. "Magg—my ex-wife used to handle all that."

He cannot even say her name but her fingerprint all over Sudhir babu. "Don't worry about charge-farge," I tell him. "We discuss this later. First let me come clean."

"Okay," he say. He look at me and his eyes big and empty, like eyes of ten-year-old orphan boy. "I'll write my new address for you." He take out one of his card and write behind it. "Can you come on Monday afternoon?"

Monday I cleans for regular customer but I not saying no to Sudhir babu. "Sure," I say. "I will be there."

"Thanks, Lakshmi," he say. "It will be nice to see you again."

After Sudhir babu leaf, I ask myself why for he not hire cleaning lady close to his house? But I know the answer: Like myself, he also value the time Maggie, he, and I work in the kitchen together. Like myself, he miss her. He and I remind each other of her.

He let me into his apartment on Monday and the smell almost let me out again. It is so strong, it like a person pushing me out. Anyone else, I would leaf straightaway, but this Sudhir babu, so I stay. When he show me around, he so embarrass. "Sorry it's such a mess," he say. "I've been so busy with work."

"Your class finish soon?"

"Ah, um, actually, I'm on sabbatical this semester."

"Excuse? What is the sabb . . . ?"

"Ah, sorry. It's a leave. You know? A leave of absence."

"You not going to the job?"

"Correct."

"But your boss not angry with you?"

"No, no. Absolutely not. It's just like—ah, like a vacation, you know?"

But I not know. There not be one day of my life that I not working. How Sudhir babu not go mad with so much extra time?

Now he notice the tiffin carrier I carry. "Goodness. This looks like way too much food." But I see how quickly-quickly he take it from my hand.

"You can freeze it," I say. "Until next time."

"Thanks." He walk into the small kitchen and set the food on the counter. Then he give me a showing of the apartment. It so small and tight, more like my apartment than like his old house. How he fit his things here? Before I find out, he say, "So, I have to run out for a while. Can you manage?"

"Yes."

I starts with the kitchen. First I empty the tiffin into plastic bowls and put away in the fridge. Then I washes all the dirty plate in sink and put in dishwasher. Clean the counter, stove, microwave. Takes out the three bags of trash sitting near trash can. Sudhir babu use to be so neat and clean. How he can live like this?

Next I cleans the bathroom. Shower not be clean in weeks. Sink have soap mark stuck to it. Wastepaper basket full. By time I gets to living room, I tired. Still, I pick up newspaper pile. Arrange magazine on table. Dust and polish furniture there.

Three hours I is cleaning but Sudhir babu not back. I open door to his office but it so full of books and paper, I ascare to go in. Books on floor, books on desk. How I know what to move? I shuts the door.

Only bedroom left to clean. If he not home by time I finish, I will just leaf. I go in and what is first thing I see? The bedstand from old house. Before I think, I opens the drawer. What do you think? He has his copy of *Gitanjali*. And on top of it is the neck chain. I sees it and I wants to vomit. Why he keep it here? He and Maggie divorce, he living on his own, but still he chain himself like this. Because of this he not shave or eat and live in apartment smelling like something dead living in it. And something dead is living in it—him. The neck chain is rope around his neck. Why he not cut the rope?

I close the drawer and begins to vacuum. Now I wants to be out of this apartment before Sudhir babu come home. I work quickly, something moving in my blood. After few minute, I know what it is—the anger. I's so angry at Sudhir babu. No, I's angry at all the mens. These mens. Why they so weak? Six years my husband waste being in the love with a ghost. Six years waste over what he saw for ten minute at the fair. And now Sudhir babu. Choking himself with another man's neck chain. What is point of divorce from Maggie if he still living with her every day?

I stop the vacuum. If Sudhir babu come home now, I will say something not good to him. Better if I leaf now. Next week I do good-proper cleaning of full apartment.

When I go to front door to leaf, I see he put envelope on it with my name. It carry hundred-dollar bill—more than my usual charge. I wants to leave the change for him but then I remembers the tiffin carrier of food I bring him. Husband not happy I working for Sudhir babu in first place. Giving free food make him more mad.

I takes the lift downstairs and walk quickly to my car. I not wanting to see Sudhir babu again today because I feel confuse about him. Seeing that neck chain in his bedstand turn my sad into angry. I think of Dada after Ma die. My husband missing

Shilpa for so many years. Now Sudhir babu keeping reminder of what he lost. All these mens crying over women. All wanting what they cannot have. What I am suppose to do to help them?

Lakshmi, you going mad or what? I tells myself. What Sudhir babu got to do with Dada? Or husband? Why khali-pili you taking out your gussa on him? But I know the answer—I's the cause of his sad. I the one who break up his marriage. For this paap I has to answer God one day. Maggie and Sudhir babu take the snake into their home. They good to snake, they give it friendship, they find it job, they teach it to drive car. And one day Maggie look away for one minute and the snake bite and release the poison into their life. That snake, me.

But here is the thing: Until I release my poison, I not knowing I carrying it in my heart. What make the poison? If I can talk to Maggie, she make me understand my own heart. But Maggie one person I can never talk to again. I not even knowing where in Cedarville she live. I too ascare to find out.

My own life good now. I have my own phone, job, and car. Every day husband and I getting more close. Even night relations between us like normal husband-wife. Few days back, I joke with him to shave his mustache and next morning he do. It make him look like young boy.

Everything in my life good. But like a radio song, a voice play in my head. And it say to me: You build your temple of happy on someone else's grave.

37

HARD TO IMAGINE that almost a year had gone by since she'd moved into the cottage. Maggie sat on her front porch, cradling the cup of herbal tea, gazing out at the ocean. The days were shorter now, and the evenings carried a nip in the air. Still, what a welcome change the weather was from the frigid temperatures back home.

Back home. She had never thought of Cedarville as home. Until now. California was wonderful. Each day the sun felt like a hand conferring its personal blessing on her. She couldn't believe that she lived in a house on the beach. Going into the grocery store and hearing the multitude of languages still gave her a thrill. She was renting office space in a building owned by a friend of Gloria's and was steadily building a new practice. Everything in her life was good. Everything in her life would be wonderful if not for the fact that her heart was a thousand miles east of where her body was.

She seldom thought of Peter these days. If she did, it was with befuddlement. What on earth had made him shine the way he had? Why had she found his tinsel so attractive? What had possessed her during those few final hours of weakness? If she had said goodbye to him at the door, if she had spent a few minutes of idle chitchat and then walked him to his car, he would've been on his way and Sudhir would still be by her side. She had been so resolute when she'd finally broken up with Peter. So sure it was the right thing to do, so relieved after it was done. Yes, she had grieved at the thought of never seeing Peter again. But that would've passed. It did pass. She'd refused to engage with him at commencement, hadn't she? Hadn't she? She'd been tempted, she'd been put to the test, and she had passed. So why did he have to show up on her doorstep, looking more desperate and forlorn than she'd ever seen him? Why had she said, "You want a Coke or something for the road?" and then let him enter her house? Why, when she had she turned from the fridge, Coke in hand, and realized that he was standing inches away from her, hadn't she moved away?

He had never even touched the bloody can. She had put it back in the fridge later, after Lakshmi had left, after he was gone. And then she'd walked back to the kitchen, fished it out of the fridge, and thrown it in the trash can.

Yes, California was as beautiful as the storybooks said. If Sudhir had moved here with her, it would be paradise. Their life in Cedarville had been pretty much paradise, but not because of the granite countertops or the second-floor balcony from which they could see the lights of the valley. It had been paradise because she'd lived there with her love. Her true love. Who had been given to her in a moment when the universe was feeling benevolent. What were the odds? What were the odds that a rootless girl from Brooklyn, homeless for all practical purposes by eighteen, would find a boy from Calcutta, whose family had raised him to be so secure in their love for him that he in turn bequeathed that same stability and security to her? No wonder Sudhir was as devastated as he was. Nothing in his life could've prepared him for her betrayal.

Had Lakshmi also been unable to fathom her behavior, unable to cope with what she'd witnessed? Is that why she did the dastardly thing that she did? Then Maggie remembered Lakshmi's story of how she'd wed her husband, and she shook her head. Anyone who could've trapped a man into marriage the way Lakshmi had, knew a thing or two about betrayal. If anyone should've cut Maggie a little slack, it was her.

She wasn't letting herself off the hook. She knew that, ultimately, it wasn't Lakshmi who had broken apart her marriage. She knew that. But Lord, to think that it was her last tryst with Peter that had caused all this trouble. That it had changed the trajectory of her life with Sudhir forever. So that she was sitting on a porch facing the Pacific, feeling as lonely as the setting sun.

She drained the last of her lemon tea and got up. There was something she'd wanted to do for several weeks, something she'd been putting off—writing a letter to her in-laws. To her ex-in-laws. As hard as parting from Sudhir had been, it was harder to accept that she'd never hear Sudhir's parents' lilting voices on the phone again. She had spoken to his sister once, but Reshma had sounded so devastated and confused by the divorce that Maggie had known they would not stay in touch.

Now she went indoors to her tiny study and pulled out a sheet of writing paper. She wrote:

Dear Papaji and Mummy—

Both of you have been on my mind for so many months. I miss you and am hoping that this note finds you in good health.

She stopped. How much had Sudhir told them? She had called him last week, to get his permission to contact his parents, and although he'd said yes, he'd sounded so vague, so distant. "I can't tell you what to do," he'd said in that new feeble voice of his, as if he'd been smoking pot. "It's a free country."

"Does that mean you don't want me to?"

"No, it means you do what you want to."

"Do they k-know? About why, I mean?" she'd asked, hating the stutter in her voice.

"About how you cheated on me, you mean?"

"Look, Sudhir. I don't want to fight with you. I . . . We'll talk some other time." She had hung up as soon as she could. And regretted it as soon as she had.

Maggie set her pen down. She would finish the letter tomorrow, maybe. There was so much she wanted to say to the elderly Bengali couple who had welcomed her into their home as a daughter. It didn't feel fair to lose Sudhir's entire family along with Sudhir himself. Such a loss was too great, out of proportion to her crime.

Exile. The word popped into her head as Maggie turned on the light to her bedroom. She was in exile in California. Banished from her known life, from all the people she loved most in this world.

How easy it was to hate Lakshmi for the havoc she'd wreaked. If only that were where it ended, if only Lakshmi could remain the sole object of her hatred. But it was the teary face staring back at her in the bathroom mirror that was the true object of her scorn and recriminations. Maggie stared at that face for an extra moment and then switched off the light. The welcoming darkness threw its arms around her.

38

Today is December 21 and my catering business so busy
for Christmastime parties, I hire Rekha's older sister, Smita,
to help me in the kitchen. Sometimes, when restaurant close after
lunch, husband help me for a few hours also. But today I have to
drive to Cedarville to clean Sudhir babu apartment because he
coming back from India tomorrow. He being gone for three weeks
and apartment not been clean since before he leaf. He gives me
key with request that it be fresh before he come back. So I tells
Smita what I need done in kitchen and go.

First time I entering Sudhir babu apartment without him
there. As I turn the key, I reminding of the day I enters Maggie
house and find her in the bed with the whiteman, whose name is
Peter, Sudhir babu tell me. But this apartment is empty, I knows,
so no problem. I come in, shut the front door, and then I scream
when I hear a voice say from other room, "Hey. Who's there?"
And before I can make sound, door to Sudhir babu's office open
and he come out. He look like a madman. His hair not comb for
days, his eyes red like devil. He not shave or shower. And in his
hand, there is cigarette. Sudhir babu not a smoker.

In the dark passageway, we look at each other. "Ah, Lakshmi,"
he finally say. "You scared me. What're you doing here?"

I points to my bucket. "I come to clean. You say to clean before
you return from India tomorrow."

He look confuse as he comb his hair with his fingers. "Oh.

I see. Well, I didn't go. As you can see. Last-minute change of plans."

Sudhir babu have chance to go seeing family in India and not go? "What wrong? You sick?"

"No, no. Not sick. Just . . . couldn't deal with it all, y'know? Too many questions, too much drama. Maybe I'll go in the summer." He take smoke off his cigarette and then say, "Please. Come in," as if I am guest at his party. Then he turn around and go into his office.

I goes into the kitchen and begins my work but my heart feeling sick. I finds empty beer bottles in the trash can and I feels even worse. Who is these people? God giving them everything to be happy and still Maggie go cheat on Sudhir babu. And him? He have health, good job, money, everything, but still he sick for Maggie. If he love her so much, why he giving her divorce? If he hate her so much, why he giving her attention? I thinks of what Shilpa say on the phone last night: "Dilip work very hard, Didi, but business only so-so. But we not complain. We satisfy together." If my sister can be happy in India, how Sudhir babu, who live and work in this rich country, not happy? Even cows in Am'rica fat, like they have money. That's why only they call them cash cow. But Sudhir baba, he looking worse than the beggar in India.

It take me long time to clean kitchen. Next I goes into his office. He sitting at the computer, holding his head. He look up when I standing at the doorway. "Sorry. I clean other room and then clean here last."

"No, it's okay. Come in."

I not feel like disturb him with vacuum so I begins to do the dusting. After a minute he say, as if talking to himself, "Do you know how long I've been alive? Over twenty thousand days. There's a website that calculates it for you. You just put in your birth date. Can you imagine? The pounds and pounds of rice and sugar and meat I've consumed, the amount of water I've ingested, the gallons of gas I've burned? All that consumption just to stay alive. And the worst part is, nothing to show for it. Not even a child of my own."

I stop the dusting. "Why you not have children?" I ask.

"Because Magg—she couldn't. She had three miscarriages, you know."

I surprise to hear Maggie not be able to have children, because she so like mother to me. And I also angry that he still won't speak her name.

"What? Why're you staring at me like that?"

I looks at Sudhir babu for long time. Then I does something I never do before. I sits down on the chair in front of him. "I make a big mistake," I says. "I leave the neck chain for you to find because I angry with Maggie. I once tell her a secret. Of something wrong I do. And she not fully understand me. She—she judge me. And so when I get chance, I do this bad thing. To hurt her. But I not think of what it do to you."

"Forget it. I told you before, I'm grateful that . . ."

I shake my head. "I not think of what it do to you, Sudhir babu, because I thinks you are strong man. Smart man. I not knowing you as weak as you are." His body jerk at the insult, but I not stopping. "I not knowing you as stupid as me. If I know you same as me, I not do such an evil thing. But I's poor village girl. You are professor. So I thinks you more smart than me. I's wrong."

Now his whole face is red, like his eyes. "Have you gone mad, Lakshmi? What the hell are you talking about?"

"How long you knowing Maggie, Sudhir babu?"

"None of your business."

"Since long time. She told me. Accha, tell me, how many times she hurt you?" He not say anything, so I answer, "Once. With one man. And for that, you treats her like the stray dog. For that, you not able to say her name? She make one mistake, Sudhir babu. Who you know not making one mistake in their life?"

I wants to tell him so much: about how I trick my husband into marriage, about how he hate me also, about how, in past year, we slowly leaf the past behind. But Sudhir babu getting up from his chair and he angry. I get up, pick up my dust cloth, and as I leaf the room I say, "I no better than you, Sudhir babu. Maggie my best friend. She ask nothing from me, just give and give and give. But because of one time she judge me, I do this wicked thing. Maggie better than both of us."

Sudhir babu's face drop like he going to cry. "Stop," he say in soft voice. "Just go. Please."

I not prideful for what I doing to him but I also not ashame. He so much older than me, but right now he feels like my young brother. "I's sorry, Sudhir babu," I say. "I not mean to hurt you. But please, think of what I say. Maggie make one mistake. Please to forgive her." I point to cigarette pack he keep on his desk. "You dying without her. Go bring her home. She love you."

He laugh. But it sound like he spit something bitter. "Bring her home? My dear Lakshmi, don't tell me you don't know? Maggie's moved. All the way to California. She couldn't wait to get as far away from me as possible."

Something in my heart die. Maggie move to the California? Why I not know? Why nobody tell me? Why Sudhir babu not mention? All these months, I look for her every time I go to Costco, ascare to see her, hope to see her. Always I thinking, at some time I run into her. Now I knows I never see her again. Just like Bobby. What is this California that steal everybody who I loves?

"Hey. What's wrong? Lakshmi. Are you okay? Here, sit. Let me get you a drink."

He run to the kitchen and get me ice water. I take one, two sips and put it down. Now I feels shy, stupid. Who I to give Sudhir babu the advice? So much I not knowing. Why I interfere to his life? He not my relation. When I can speak again, I say, "When she leaf?"

He look as sad as I feel. "Almost a year ago. Soon after the divorce."

I nods. Nothing more for me to say. I gets up. "I's sorry for how I speak to you. I forget my place for a minute." I looks at the floor, not wanting him to see the tears in my eyes. "I finish cleaning today, Sudhir babu. But best if you finds some other cleaning lady for next time."

I feels him looking at me but he say nothing. I pick up my water glass and take it to kitchen. Then I go to living room and begin vacuum. I start with the furniture. There is food crumb everywhere. What has happen to my old Sudhir babu? And how is Maggie? She so far away. Who make her eat? Who look after her if she sick? Is she smoke cigarette like he do? Does she talk to Sudhir babu? Is she still love him? So many questions I wants to ask. But no need to. I create enough trouble for both of them.

After apartment clean, I pack my things and quietly open the front door to leaf. I not wanting to see Sudhir babu again. My heart hurt too much to see his pain. I not wanting to take his money after the insult I give him. My work here is finish.

39

S HE WAS ALREADY half an hour late leaving for Gloria's house when the phone rang. It was Odell and Juliette calling from Paris to wish her a merry Christmas. Odell wanted to make sure she wasn't planning to spend the day alone and was relieved when she told him she had been invited to Gloria's. He asked if she'd received the check he'd sent her for Christmas, how the house was, if she was making new friends. She could tell he was worried. "Odell. I'm okay," she finally said. "Now will you stop acting like my older brother?"

"I am your older brother." She heard the smile in his voice. Also the protectiveness. "Here, talk to your sister-in-law. She's dying to speak to you."

"Maggie?" Juliette's voice had the breathy quality it always did. "How are you, dear? I wish you'd listened to your brother and come spent Christmas with us."

"Oh, me too. Maybe sometime in the summer. And I'm fine. Honest. Stop worrying about me. So how many people did you guys have for dinner last night?" she asked, trying to change the subject.

They talked for a few minutes before Juliette handed the phone back to her husband.

"Have you talked to Dad today?" Odell asked.

"No, not yet."

"You gonna?" Even from this distance, Maggie could hear the

anxiety that poor Odell always felt about running interference between their father and her.

"I guess so."

"Boy, that sure sounded enthusiastic, Mags." They laughed, but then Odell grew serious and said, "Look. I don't blame you. But . . . he's getting old, Mags. And believe it or not, he's worried sick about you. He's, like, called me a dozen times to ask how you're doing."

"Instead of calling me, you mean?" Her words came out sharper than she'd intended.

"Mags. I'm not gonna argue with you. Just . . . call him, would you?"

"Okay. Okay. I said I would."

"Good. I love you, baby girl."

"Don't call me that. Christ. I'm fifty-six years old."

"But you're still my baby sister. So deal with it."

They laughed again. After a few seconds, Maggie said, "I should hang up. I'm already late for Gloria's." She paused. "Love you, Odell. Give Juliette and Justin hugs from me."

"Will do. And you give Sudh— Oops. Sorry. Slip of the tongue."

Her heart caught, but she managed a laugh. "No problem. Merry Christmas."

She hung up and was about to dial Wallace's number when her phone rang again. Odell must've forgotten to tell her something. "Yesss?" she said in an exaggerated deep voice.

There was a silence and then she heard Sudhir say, "Maggie?"

Her hand began to shake involuntarily. "Oh, hi. Sorry. I thought you were Odell. I was just . . ."

"How is he? And Juliette and Justin?"

"He . . . He's fine. They are all fine." And then she half-lied, "He sent his love to you."

"Huh." What was that she'd heard in his voice? Skepticism?

Surprise? Why was he calling her, anyway? And on Christmas Day?

"Merry Christmas," she said.

"What? Yeah, you too." He sounded preoccupied but also sharp, not half-drugged, as he had the last time they'd spoken.

She waited for him to explain why he was calling, steadying one hand with the other, but he was silent. "Sudhir," she said gently. "Is everything okay?"

"Yeah. Sure. Everything's fine." But she heard the crack in his voice.

"What—?"

"Lakshmi was here," he said quickly. "She's been cleaning for me."

Her throat tightened at the sound of Lakshmi's name. And at the news that Sudhir had let back into his life the woman who had destroyed both their lives. They had always shared a bond, those two. Hell, it was Sudhir who had launched her catering career. Maggie felt a renewed spurt of anger at Lakshmi's treachery.

"I see." She forced her voice to stay neutral. Why was he telling her this? To rub salt in her wounds?

"And—and she said a few things. About us. At first I was angry. She was way over the line, you know. But then I had a few days to think about it. And she was right. You know?"

Was he drunk? What the hell was he talking about? Maggie glanced at her watch. She was a full hour late to Gloria's, and God knew what the traffic would be like. "Sudhir—" she began.

"No, wait. Basically, she called me an idiot. Said I was weak. That is, an idiot for letting you go. And weak for pining away for you."

The tears that came into Maggie's eyes made the room go blurry. Hope fluttered like a trapped butterfly within her. Her brain felt sluggish, heavy, no help in trying to parse Sudhir's words. Was Sudhir saying he was an idiot for losing her? Or was he merely relaying what Lakshmi had said? Was there a difference? And did she really believe that Lakshmi would talk to Sudhir in that manner? Was he making this whole thing up? She wanted to scream with frustration. "I'm not following what you're saying."

"That's because I'm not saying it well." He fell silent for a moment. Then, "If I ask you something, will you answer honestly?"

A dullness spread through her, extinguishing the hope that had flared. "I don't know," she said woodenly. "What is it?"

"Did you love Peter?"

She didn't want to do this. She didn't want to rehash the past with Sudhir. That was the whole point of divorce: that you didn't have to process things. Divorce was a cleaver—with one swift motion, it separated the past from the present, two people from each other. She opened her mouth to refuse his question, and then she thought, Why the hell not? It was a reasonable enough question. Surely Sudhir had earned the right to know the answer. He should've asked her when he first found out. But he hadn't, and perhaps he couldn't have at the time. He was too hurt, too wounded. Too afraid to know the answer.

"No," she said. "Never. I was always clear that my life was with you. That I love—loved—you."

"Then why?"

Here she could draw the line. The why was something she hadn't fully answered for herself. Even if she had, the why was something she would keep for herself, guard it even from Sudhir. The why went too deep, too far back, into the very shaping of her. It had something to do with her mother's death and Wallace's abuse and the damage done. It had to do with needing shelter and stability and Sudhir at one point in her life, and then, in her fifties, briefly needing something larger, wilder, more exciting. It had to do with containing multitudes, with being a complicated, contradictory, complex human being. The why was like God or the meaning of life—unanswerable. Unknowable. And she was okay with that.

"Sudhir," she said as gently as she could. "What's the point?"

He cleared his throat. "Okay. Fair enough." Abruptly, he asked, "What are you doing today?"

"Going to Gloria's. I'm already an hour late."

"Oh. Sorry. You should go."

"Sudhir? What is it?" She could sense his agitation.

"Nothing. Just that . . . Lakshmi also said that you'd made one mistake in all these years. One mistake. And for that, I threw you away."

Something opened up inside her, a yawning hole of regret, grief, sadness. All of a sudden, she understood what he was trying to say—it had all been futile. A waste. They had both acted rashly, and for this, they had paid a huge price. It was one thing to divorce a spouse you didn't love. But their love still bled, which meant it was fresh and alive. No wonder they both hurt so.

"And what did you say?" Her voice was husky, unrecognizable to her.

"Nothing. I said nothing."

There was a long silence. "Well, then. I guess there's nothing to say."

"Well . . ."

The disappointment she felt at knowing that this was where things ended, that Sudhir was unprepared or unable to take things any further, turned into impatience. An image of Peter, intense, passionate, demanding, flashed before her eyes. How doggedly Peter had pursued her each time she'd tried breaking up with him. This was what Sudhir lacked—that fierceness, that go-getterness. It was this quality that had made Peter attractive to her.

"My cell phone's ringing," she lied. "It's probably Gloria, wondering where I am."

Though she could sense his reluctance to let her go, he said, "Yes, you better get going."

"What are you doing today?"

"Me?" He sounded surprised, as if having plans on Christmas were preposterous. "Oh, I don't know. Several people have invited me for dinner. But I think I'll just go to a movie."

It hurt to think of Sudhir alone in a movie theater. It's not your problem, Maggie reminded herself. "Maybe you should go to dinner. Be with people."

"Maybe." There was a short silence and then he said, "Achcha. Bye."

"Bye. Merry Christmas."

She hung up and wandered listlessly to the front porch. She debated whether to call Gloria and beg off from dinner, her mood ruined by the strange call from Sudhir, but decided to follow her own advice. She looked out at the ocean, hazy in the early-afternoon sunlight. It looked as lonely and restless as she felt. She replayed the desultory conversation with Sudhir in her head, trying to make heads or tails out of it. Had Lakshmi really spoken to him in that manner? Why? Why had Sudhir allowed her into his home in the first place? And what did Lakshmi think she was doing by playing Dear Abby? Appeasing her conscience?

Maggie fumed about Lakshmi for a few minutes but then ran out of gas. The fact of the matter was, she couldn't hate Lakshmi. She'd tried for the past year, but she couldn't. Instead, what she felt when she thought about her was mortification. That Lakshmi had seen her naked—in more senses than the obvious one. That she had seen Peter naked. That she'd had her illusions destroyed. Maggie knew that Lakshmi had looked up to her. She was sorry to have turned out to be such a lousy role model. She was sorry that their friendship had reached such an abrupt, ignoble end. Lakshmi had brought a lot of vitality and wonder to her life. She missed that.

Maggie sighed. She knew she should call Wallace but couldn't muster up the psychic energy that it would take. I'll call him from the car, she decided. As I get closer to Gloria's.

She picked up her house keys and grabbed her purse. As she locked the front door, she made a resolution. She would not accept any more phone calls from Sudhir. It was much too unsettling. She had cheated on him. He had found out. They had divorced. Those were facts. That was the reality of their lives. They both had to live with that.

40

AFTER CHRISTMAS I thinks the parties stop but Janice and Dick Russo wanting me to cater their New Year Eve party. Forty-five peoples they invite, and I having to feed them all. All day today husband, Rekha, Smita, and I cook. For first time, I asking Rekha to come with me tonight to help serve. I's too tired to do this alone.

I sitting on toilet pot in Janice's bathroom since last five minute, rubbing my feets. Someone knock on the door but I not answer and they goes away. Janice having such a big house, I's sure there many other bathrooms. Few month ago she ask me to do weekly cleaning but I says no. Such big house take eight hours or more to clean. I tell her my schedule is pack. Of course, if Janice find out I quit Sudhir babu's house, she may ask again. But Sudhir babu become like a sadhu—he not seeing anyone, I thinks, so how she going to know?

Rekha alone with serving the food, so I know I needs to get up and help. But still I sits, rubbing my feets. Tomorrow I ask husband to give me the massage. Thanks God restaurant and store both close tomorrow.

It only eleven o'clock yet. Janice say that in one hours they will all watch the TV to see silver ball drop from the sky. She also wanting me to serve the guests the champagne wine at that time. For this reason I cannot go home. She also buy funny hats for her guests and some paper horn to blow. Janice not inviting any childrens to the party but then she buy her guests toys that make them act like childrens. If I living to be hundred years old, I not understanding Am'rican peoples.

Someone knock on bathroom door again and I gets up from pot. I opens the door and gets biggest shock—it is Sudhir babu who knock on door. He look as surprise to see me. "Oh, hi," he say. "I . . . I didn't know . . ." His face get bright. "Did you cater? Tonight?"

What he think? That Janice invite me because we best friend? But one thing about Sudhir babu, I can't be angry to him. Also, he not looking like crazy man anymore. He look like Shashi Kapoor again. His hair still long but the beard gone and he wearing clean white shirt and blue jean. "Yes," I say. "Plenty food left. You go eat."

He smile. "Lakshmi. You were born to feed people. Thanks. I'll use the bathroom and then eat. I'm starving."

I goes into the kitchen to make plate for Sudhir babu. Janice come up, wanting something, but I tells her to ask Rekha. One good thing—my food so especial, they all a little ascare of me, in case I say no to cater their party. So what I wants, they do. Janice go to find Rekha and I make plate for Sudhir babu. By the time he come up to me, the food nice and warm. I watch while he eats. "What about you?" he ask. "Did you eat yet?"

Minute he say this, my stomach growl. He laugh so hard little foods come out of his mouth. "Guess that's a no," he say, and before I can reply, he cut small piece of lamb and holding fork up to my mouth. I so shock I turns my head. I never had strange man feed me before. Even the husband not to do this. "You eat, Sudhir babu," I say. "I fix my plate later."

He begin to eat and I can know he's not eating all day today. After a few minute he speak with his mouth full. "Okay," he say. "I have a confession to make. I lied. Actually, I knew you were going to be at the party tonight. I ran into Janice a few days ago and she told me. You are the reason why I came." He swallow his food and then he face me. "I called her. Maggie. A few days after you were over. I thought about what you said and I called her."

My mouth suddenly so dry. "So what she say?" I not even knowing he know how to reach Maggie. Maybe he come to tell me they going to marry again? My heart light at the thought. This is only way God will forgive me for what I do. Otherwise I will have to do hundred rebirths as punishment.

But he make a tall face. His eyes look tired, confuse. "I don't know what happened, Lakshmi. Everything was so clear in my head when I picked up the phone. Then it all got jumbled and nothing came out right. She finally hung up. And I've called three or four times since then, but she hasn't called me back, so I guess it's over." Then he laugh, but it sound like two piece of coal rub together. "Who am I kidding? It's been over for more than a year. Right?"

I shake my head yes but I confuse. What is so hard about saying sorry? What so hard about telling Maggie he make mistake? Why these educated people make everything so puzzle? Then I has an idea. "You go to the California, Sudhir babu. You go and bring Maggie home."

He get a look on his face I never see before. He look like Mithai when I am making him do something he not wanting to do. Except Sudhir babu not kicking dust and stamping his foot the way Mithai do. Instead, his eyes turn hard. "I think I've humiliated myself enough," he say. "Anyway. It's better this way. You know what they say—you can't go home again."

This is truth. Look at me. Seven years in Am'rica and I not go home one time. But Sudhir babu not having the husband who not allow him to go. And Maggie not so far away as Dada and Shilpa. Then I knows what stopping Sudhir babu. It something bigger than husband or plane ticket. It is gamand. He being prideful. Every year when I stands first in my class, Ma gives me the advice: Daughter, she say, never be gamandi. What you have, given to you by God. You just a basket into which God puts the flowers. Flowers not belong to you. They belongs to God. Same way, your clever belong to God.

But I cannot tell Sudhir babu to not be prideful. He is a man. He my elder. So I get up and start putting dirty bowls in the dishwasher. He sit in the kitchen, quietly eating. But then Janice come into the kitchen and ask me to bring out the bottles of the champagne wine. I open the fridge and take out the bottles. "Come on, Sudhir," she say. "It's almost time for the ball to drop." He smile at Janice, put down his plate, and walk toward me. "I'll help you," he say, and smile again. He take a few of the bottles and I carries the others to the dining room. I looks for Rekha, but so many people, I not sees her.

Some of the mens go out on back porch and open the bottles. They sound pop-pop as they opens. Then they fills plastic glasses. The champagne look like soap bubble. Sudhir babu picks up a glass. "Will you have some?" he ask me, but I shake my head. I am remindering the first time I tastes the daru when I tries the suicide.

"Lakshmi, what's wrong?" Sudhir babu say.

"It hot here, no? So many peoples. I think I go to kitchen."

"But—"

I goes. I hopes he not following me, but so many people there happy to see him, he having no chance.

In the kitchen, I pull up stool and sit. I look at all the dirty dishes and I knows I cannot wash them tonight. Maybe I ask Rekha to stay and clean. I can pay her extra. I think of going home to bed and I yawns as if I already there. In a few minutes, I hear them in the other room. They are all saying, "Ten, nine, eight . . ." as if they childrens in school learning to count. Then I hears them cheer and say "Happy New Year" again and again. I wish Rekha would come in the kitchen now so I have someone to say "Happy New Year." It already New Year in India and I think of Shilpa and pray for her and little Jeevan to be happy. And Maggie also. I know that in the California there is lots of sunshine, and I know we get mangoes from there that we sell in our store. And so I prays that Maggie always have life of sunshine and mangoes.

Everybody in next room talking, laughing, cheering. I alone in this kitchen, and even though I knows husband waiting for me at home, I feels as if I am only person in this world. The people in the next room have their good English, they clever, they knows how to make the jokes, they live in big house like this one, they having good job, good marriage. They knowing what their nephew look like, they visit their sister and old father when they feels like. They not live in small apartment on top of store which smell of onions and garlic from restaurant below. I not living in the same country as them.

And then I thinks, Only one other person here who as alonely as me. Only one person who also lose something and he also missing it. Only Sudhir babu share my pain. And I's the person who build that pain for him.

When I looks up, he is standing at the door to kitchen. He smile and his eyes is so kind. "Happy New Year, Lakshmi," he say.

"Happy New Year, Sudhir babu."

He take a sip from his glass, touch two fingers to his head, and go back into Janice's living room. He only one who take the time to give me the greetings. Even Rekha not come.

It is as Sudhir babu turn to leaf the kitchen to go back to the party that the idea come to me.

41

TIMBER LAKE IS only ten-minute walk from my apartment. I not knowing this until two month ago. Since I find out, I walking here every morning. I leaf my house at seven and walk for hour. So far, the snow not come this year but the ground is hard, like it prepare for snow. All the trees shivering in cold, like I does. Today I walks fast, to leaf behind the ugly words husband say to me yesterday. They flying loose in my mind, like kites during the Makar Sankranti festival.

By the time I reach the bridge, I's sweaty and I stops. This wood bridge my favorite stopping point. I lean on the railing and looks at the blue lake. The sun make it shine like a wedding. Far away, I can see the snow on the head of the mountain. The water look so peaceful, it take away the fever in my mind. I wants to be like this lake, I thinks. Peaceful. Quiet. Keeping its fishes and ducks and plants alive without complain. Without asking anything for itself. Like a mother.

I walk from left side of the bridge to right. Here, Timber Lake become someone else. It jump over big rocks and become the waterfall. It run fast, loud, angry, like a goonda who wants to fight. This side make my heart beat fast, like loud music. This side like the teenager daughter. As the water falls below, it makes the splash which wet my face. The cold feel like someone slapping my face, asking me to wake up. I lean over the railing to feel more of the waterfall. Each slap remove the dead skin from my thoughts.

The sound it make so loud, it cover up my husband's words that I carries with me on my walk today.

As Sudhir babu leaf the kitchen on New Year's Eve, I gets an idea: I will go to the California. I will brings Maggie a letter from him telling that she must come back home. He will not go to her, so I must. I will also beg Maggie's forgiveness for what I do. I will tell her, If you not forgiving me, Maggie, and return home, my soul be force to take endless rebirth in this ugly world. I have done the sin against you. Only you can pardon me. I not leaf the California until she come with me.

The idea seem very good that night as I driving home. It also seeming very good when I wakes up next day. But when I mentions it to the husband while we taking our breakfast chai, he look shock.

"You want to do what? You fly in plane only one time before, and you wants to fly to the California? And poke your nose in their business again?"

"It become my business. I's the reason they divorce. And Sudhir babu—"

He slap the table so hard, the teacup jump. "Enough. Bas. No more nonsense talk. From now on, I forbid you to talk to that Sudhir babu. Or his randi wife."

I feels like he slap me when he calls Maggie that word. I feels so much angry, my eyes fill with tears. "Next time you use that word, I cut your tongue," I say. "It's okay for the mens to make big-big eyes at young women. But us women—we not allow. Maggie not loose woman. She good woman."

Then husband do something evil. He laugh. "If you make threat to me, Lakshmi, I takes you back to that madhouse hospital. And this time I leaf you there. Forever."

Something drop from my heart to my stomach. Is he telling the truths? Can he put me in the lockup again? Forever?

Husband finish the rest of his tea. Now that he win, he make his voice soft again. "Chalo," he say. "Enough of this crazy talk. Your place here, Lakshmi, with me. Now, come on. Lots of work to do downstairs today."

I looks at the waterfall, and for one minute, I wishes I could get up on this railing and jump. I thinks of landing on the water, floating down the rocks until I drowns. No more worries, no more tensions. But then I stand straight. Lakshmi, I thinks, you has to chose. Who you? Who you wanting to be? Calm and steady lake or angry, tough waterfall? You wants to shelter and protect everybody like the lake, or you wanting to follow your own path, like waterfall? Lake will stand in one place, always. Waterfall go different places, always.

For one minute, I is all alone on the bridge. I see other peoples out for early-morning walk but they far away. I stands in the middle. I close my eyes. I try to listen. The lake is quiet as death. The waterfall is noiseful like life.

In one minute, I thinks of everything. How I save Munna from drowning. How I save Mithai from those wicked mens. How I save Shilpa. Ma I cannot save but I help. I have try to be the good person. But now it is time to save myself.

I walk toward the waterfall. It sing as it jump down the rocks. I chose the life.

I gets in the car and I phones Sudhir babu. He still sleeping but he answer the phone.

"Sudhir babu? It Lakshmi."

"Huh? Wow. What time is it?"

"It early. I needing something from you."

He awake now. "Sure. What? Are you okay?"

"I's fine. I going to the California. To meet Maggie. So I needs her address."

"What?"

I repeat what I say.

"I . . . I don't think that's a good idea, Lakshmi. She's—you know, angry. At you. In any case . . ."

I shake my head. These mens. Why they's always telling us what to do? "I's going," I shout. "To ask for her to forgive me. Also, to carry letter from you asking her to come home. To Cedarville."

He laugh. "What? Are you nuts? You don't know Maggie. She'd . . ."

I looks at my watch. Husband angry if I not home soon to help in store. Then I think: Husband angry once I tell him what I decide. So little angry, big angry, what difference it make? "Sudhir babu. Listen. I coming to your house in half hour. I pick up letter from you then. Also, address. Okay?"

"Okay? No. Not okay. Look, this is—"

He say more. But I cannot say what. Because I hangs up the phone.

I look at the time. It is eight-fifteen. Rekha leaf her house soon. I call her next. Ask her to go on the online and find out how much ticket to the California cost. Where in California? Rekha ask, but I not know. Stupid, I tell myself. I will tell you later, I say. In meantime, I in your debt if you not mention to my husband. If Rekha surprise, she not say. Instead she say, No problem.

Then Rekha say, "Didi? You okay? You sounding funny."

"Funny, how?"

"I'm not sure. Different."

I smile. "I okay."

Rekha hear the waterfall in my voice.

42

For one whole week, husband and I fighting nonstop. He say absolute no-never to me going to find Maggie. But I keeps thinking of the waterfall and I stay powerful. He make threat, he tell me I can no more call Shilpa, he say he will lie to doctor that I try the suicide again. Then new doctor will put me in lockup. But something happen when husband say this. He look ashame. His eyes move a little bit, his hand shake. I take notice and then, like the waterfall, I keeps moving. First I ask Sudhir babu to find out from Maggie's friend if she in town this month. He tell her he wanting to send Maggie important parcel, so he need to know. Next Sudhir babu make me hotel reservation. I tell Rekha for which airport to find me ticket. Ticket is very costly. Rekha say to wait two week; she say cost come down then. But I having Sudhir babu's letter in my purse. I having guilty feeling in my heart. So I gives Rekha eight hundred dollar from money I save from my business. And she buy ticket with her credit card. Then I pays Rekha sister to work in store while I gone. It January, so no catering orders this week, thanks God.

Two day before I am to leaf, husband come to me. "You really going?" he say. "Who taking you to airport?"

I surprise myself. "You is."

He give me bad look. "Don't act smart," he say. Then, "And

who pick you up other side? How you getting to Maggie house?"

He asking question I not know answer to. "I take the bus."

Now he make fun of me. "Take bus? Girl, you crazy. You think this is India, where buses go everywhere? California is rich people's state. They don't have buses. Know why? They don't want peoples like you showing up to their expensive house."

I look away from him, not wanting him to see tears in my eyes. I do so much for this man; I takes care of his house and his business. Why he cannot help me? Why he acting like this? All his new love for me gone, like water that boil away from the pan. Why he have such hate against Maggie? She not doing anything bad to him. Instead she help him, by helping me.

"I will manage." I begins to walk away from him.

"Listen," he call, and I stop. "I already make the arrangement for you. My friend Ashok is cabdriver there. We use to drive cab for same firm in New York. Now, he having his own company. He will come pick you up."

This time I not ashame to let him see my tears. "This is true?" I take his hand and hold it up to my eyes. "Bless you."

"Okay, okay," he say, embarrass. "No fuss."

Two days later, I gets out of the plane in San Diego airport. First thing I do is call husband. He stay on phone with me until I reaches the baggage claim area. There, I sees a man carry a cardboard with my name. "Namaste, ji," I say.

"Namaste, auntie."

"How you can drive the taxi with my husband? You is so young."

"Oh, that wasn't me, auntie." He laugh. "That was my dad. He's busy, so he sent me. I'm Kishore."

As soon as we leaf the airport building, I knows I am in a different country. California is in Am'rica, but the air, the sunlight, the trees, all different than my state. It look more like India, except it having less dust, noise, and peoples. I wearing my heavy winter coat, but all the other passengers here look like birds— free and light, wearing slippers and short pant. We not even in Kishore's car yet and already I feels new.

Kishore put my suitcase in his car. He say we first go to hotel to drop the luggage. "Maybe you'd like some lunch?" he ask. "You must be starving."

I so hungry. But I also wanting to see Maggie. "I not wanting to waste more of your time, beta."

He laugh again. "Don't be silly, auntie. Dad said I have the whole day with you. I'm at your service."

I have a thought that make my heart jump. If I have a son, maybe he be like Kishore. A boy full of smiles and laughing. I look at his beautiful face. "Okay, then. Maybe we eat some lunch first."

Hotel seem long distance from the airport. Kishore say nothing is nearby in the California. But I enjoying this car ride. I lower window to feel the breeze on my face. It feel like freedom. I close my eyes for a few minute and then open again. From far away, I see a long blue ribbon. "What is that?" I say.

"What, auntie?"

"That." I point. "That blue thing."

He turn to look at me. "Why, auntie. That's the Pacific."

"Excuse?"

"The Pacific. You know, the ocean?"

I not understand. This ocean look as blue as heaven. But the ocean I see one time in Mumbai was gray in color. How this one so blue? I thinks about this for a minute. "Ocean is like birds," I say. "All different-different color."

Kishore laugh. "I don't know, auntie. This is the only one I've ever seen."

He make a turn and get on different road and then my eyes see such beauty that it almost make me blind. The ocean is light blue and it stretch more far than I can see. The sun play in the water like it is a child taking a bath. The sand is so gold, it shine like jewelry. The air smell salty and my whole body feel relax, as if the California is giving me a massage. "Kishore," I say. "Beta. This . . . is this the place where God live?"

The boy laugh. "Everybody who comes here for the first time has the same reaction," he say. "But yours is the most priceless, auntie." His voice get soft. "But it is beautiful, isn't it?"

The hotel is beautiful also. The bed is beautiful. The man who bring my luggage to the room is beautiful (Kishore say he wait downstair to give me time to relax and get change in my room—what he mean?). The tile in bathroom beautiful. But you want to know the most magic part of the California? It make me feel beautiful.

I washes my face and then go into my room to get fresh clothes from the suitcase. I sits on the edge of the bed and it feel so soft and comfortable. The pillow so white and fat, it make me sleepy. I think, I will rest my head for five minute only. Kishore tell me he in no rush. I close my eyes and first thing I see is the ocean. How the white wave look, like a thousand childrens doing flips in the water. How the air smell like salt. How it tickle my face, like Mithai use to do with his trunk.

A loud sound in the room wake me up. I wake with a jatka, my heart going dhoom-dhoom. Where am I? In one second, I remember. But who in room with me? What is noise I hear?

Then it happen again and I laugh. My stomach so hungry, it sound like a dog. That what wake me up.

I look at alarm clock. It three in afternoon. Arre, Ram. That poor boy Kishore. What he thinking? What if he leaf? I goes washes my face second time, change into the short-sleeve kameez. I puts Sudhir babu's letter in the pocket of my tunic, and then I goes downstair.

"Hello, auntie." Kishore near me as soon as I there. Poor boy wait for me while I sleeping like a maharani.

"I's so sorry, beta," I say. "I so tired that—"

He shake his head. "No problem, auntie. I told you to take as long as you liked, remember?" He stop to look at his watch and then say in Hindi, "Kya khaenge? Indian? Chinese? Mexican?"

"Anything, beta. I wants to go see my friend soonly."

"Sure thing. I'll go get the car."

One thing about this California—all the peoples here smiling. Everything smiling. Even the trees. When Kishore come with his car, a young hotel boy run up to open the door for me. What this magic that I go from cleaning lady to rich memsahib?

Kishore take me to Thai restaurant. The red curry I eats so good, I wants to go for short walk and then eat it second time. But just then Kishore say, "So, auntie. You're meeting a friend? What time is she expecting you?"

Suddenly, all the happy go away. Now the pain come back in my heart. Maggie not even know that I coming. What if she get angry to see me? What if she not opening the door? What if she call the police?

"It a surprise," I say. "She not know that I here."

"Oh." He frowns. "Let's hope she's home, then." But he looking at me like I's crazy woman.

Now I thinks of new problem. I not wanting Kishore to be there when I meet Maggie. But he such a sweet boy. What if he feel insult?

"Kishore," I says. "I's meeting Maggie after long time. We—we have many thing to talk. What if I . . ."

"Don't worry, auntie," he say. "I wasn't planning on hanging out." He take out a small piece of paper and write. "Here's my phone number. You just call me when you're ready to be picked up."

Now I feels really bad. "But where you go, beta?"

"Oh, I'm not too far from where I'm dropping you off. I'll just go home and take a nap." He shake his head. "It's no big deal. Honest. You take as long as you want." He look at his watch. "But we should get going."

It is close to sunset when we get near Maggie neighborhood. I say goodbye to Kishore, who wait until I take the wood staircase that lead to the beach. Then he blow his horn and drive away.

I not knowing Maggie house right on the beach. I not knowing that when sun set over ocean, it look as if the whole world ending and being born at same time. In my whole life, I never see anything this much beauty. The sky so pink and orange, some of the color fall on my skin, making it look pretty. Even the sand change color. And the sound the water make. Even the bells the priest ring in the temple not sound so holy. It sound like the ocean giving birth to the whole world. It sound like the whole world breathing, in and out, in and out.

Sometime, when I use to walk alone in my father's field evening time, I feels such peace. Then I use to feel that I belong to more than Ma and Dada and Shilpa—that the trees, the earth, the sky, all my family. I not feeling such connection for many years. But today, in this California, I feels it. I's no longer the waterfall—it too small. I is the ocean. Its fishes, its stones, its waves, they all inside me.

I takes off my slippers and walks near the water on the cold sand. A small wave run up like a mouse and chews my feets. I feels like I could walk this beach for days, but I look left and I facing Maggie house. And then the tears comes to my eyes. Because I knows Maggie not coming back with me. How she can leaf this beach, this ocean, this sun to return to Cedarville? Although her house is far from the water and it sit up from the beach, I can see how sweet it is. All other house here are big. Hers look like little baby house, but it have flower and bushes around it. I stands near the water and look up. All the light is on. Maggie is home. I only little ways away from her. But now I cannot move. Now I see what husband see—I have no business to come here. I make big mistake.

Maggie is about to lower the bedroom blinds when she spots the lone figure staring at the house. The sky is darkening behind the figure; the beach is almost deserted. She is used to tourists gawking at the beach houses as they walk by, but something about the stillness with which the person is looking up arrests her attention. The person is too far away for Maggie to be sure if he or she is looking at her house or someone else's. She shrugs and continues with her task, but just when the blind is lowered all the way, she pulls it up a few inches. She sits on the window seat and looks out again. And is mildly irritated to see that the figure has not moved, is continuing to stand motionless and look upward.

As she watches, the woman—Maggie can see it's a woman; she's released her long hair—bends, as if she's touching her feet. And then she is walking into the dark waters of the Pacific. In January.

Stupid or not, I has to finish what I comes here for. I must to take Sudhir babu's letter to Maggie. If she not willing to see me, that God's will. But I must try.

Then I feels need to do the soo-soo. Urgent. All this water make me want to make my own water. I feel frighten. Kishore gone. If I wait till he come to pick me up, I will have accident. I cannot go to Maggie house all smelly. Then the idea come. When we children, we do soo-soo in my village river. Why I cannot go toilet in the ocean? Water will clean me up. Wind will make me dry.

The wind so strong, it untie my hair. I goes to where the sand is dry and put hotel key, cell phone, money, and Sudhir babu's letter under my slippers. Then I walks back to the ocean.

Arre, Ram. This not water. This is ice. How I can go inside this icebox? I stands still for a second, trying to fight with my body. Either way, I goes to Maggie wet. How this can happen to me at such important time? Ae, bhagwan, I pray. Please to help me.

Before God can speak, my body do. The soo-soo roll down my leg and into the sea. It feel so warm and good down my legs that I happy to lose this fight.

Now I having new problem: How I can show at Maggie home smelling like soo-soo woman? Nothing to do but walk into this icebox at least until the hip level, so water can take away smell. I bite my lip and walk in. If I can bear this cold, Maggie come home, I makes bargain with myself. If I can go two more step, Maggie not be angry with me. Slowly-slowly, I goes deeper.

Maggie hesitates, waits for the woman to turn back, not to risk hypothermia by wading farther into the water. Her eyes scan the beach for another passerby to notice what's going on, but there's nobody around. Watching the billowing clothes, she knows that the woman is not wearing a wet suit. The sun has set, and it is hard to see precisely what's going on.

She opens the blinds a bit more and waits, unsure of what's happening.

My both leg have no feeling. The waves hit my body like cricket bat. Thap, thap, thap. I know what I do is stupid and now I turn and begin to leaf ocean behind. It is hard to get to the sand but I keeps moving. Sometime the wave hit so hard I feels it push me forward. The whole time I keeps my eyes on Maggie house. How I going to show up, all wet like a dog, I don't know. The cold make my teeth shake, make it hard to think.

With one push, the ocean throw me out, like mother giving birth to a baby. But my legs too weak to stand. I falls on the sand. It no longer gold like jewelry but dark like stone. I feel hard to breathe. I not too far from my slippers but I cannot move. If I not call Kishore, will he come to look for me? Or will I sleep on this beach because my legs cannot make support for me? That way I be dry before I knock on Maggie door.

Sudhir babu's letter. I wants to make sure it safe. I talks to myself. "Move, Lakshmi," I say. "Nobody here to help you but yourself. And you here to do a job." I begins to crawl. I feels the sand cutting my hand but my legs and feets still no feeling.

I almost near the letter when I hears a faraway voice say, "Hello? Is everything all right?"

If I near dead—maybe I am?—I will knows this voice. It is Maggie. She coming down the wood steps from left direction. I stops crawling, happy that she find me but ashame that she see me like this.

"Hello?" she say again.

"Hello," I say. "I's here."

She fall silent. When she speak, her voice sound shock. "Wha—? Lakshmi? What the hell? I don't believe this."

I lift my head. The wind blow the shawl Maggie have around her. Her feets are naked. "I don't believe this," she say again, as she come closer to me.

Then I knows what I must do: I must make her belief it. Make her belief that Sudhir babu want her back. Make her belief he forgive her. Make her belief that although the California is where the God live, her place belong in Cedarville. Most of all, make her belief that for the sin that I make, I will always be sorry. That I willing to crawl for a thousand mile to get her forgiveness. Like those pilgrim who climbs on their knees all the way up Mount Kailash, our lord Shiva's birthplace, I willing to do the same.

I lifts my head. Maggie walking fast down the beach toward me. I am here to give her the letter from Sudhir babu. This is my duty. I knows that if I crawls quickly, I get to the letter before she reach me.

I moves quick on the sand, like the crab, but when I reaches the letter, she is there. I looks up and I sees the face that I knows as good as my own. Above Maggie head, the sky dark. Around us, the wind and the sea make their mischief music together, loudly, like naughty children banging on the drum. Maggie saying something and I tries to listen over their noise. "Lakshmi," Maggie saying again. "What on earth? What are you . . . ?" She look around. "Are you here alone? How'd you get here, anyway?"

"In aeroplane," I say. "I flies. All by myself."

The wind blow some of my word away and Maggie bend down to hear me. "What? But why?"

The letter from Sudhir babu under my hand. But I don't give to her. Instead I says, "I comes to beg your forgiveness, Maggie. For what darkness I puts in your life."

Maggie straighten up and look as far away as the moon. For long minute she not saying anything, and something cold make a shiver in my heart. "I can't . . . I don't know what to say," she whisper. And the cold become freeze in my heart.

She take a few step away from me. She look at her house, then at the sea, then back at me. I knows Maggie wanting to leave me on this beach like a dirty paper bag and go back inside her cozy house. I about to say, Please, sorry to disturb, you go inside your house, but something stop me.

It is how Maggie look at me. Even in dark, I see. No, I feels it. She take two step back and stand over me, and the look on her face, different. It is not the look of pity. It is not the look of wanting to help. It is look of—how you say?—curious. Maggie look at me curious. Like how Dilip use to look when he fix the motor of the car and he wait to see if it will start. She waiting to see the result of what she make.

The wind blow again and I shivers. Maggie notice. She shake her head one time, two times, like she having fight with herself, and then she say, "Good grief. You need to come inside and get dry before you freeze out here."

And then she putting her hand out for me to take. It reminder me of how many times this woman has give me her hand to get up. Even now, when she not knowing why I show up like the devil in the California, she pulling me up.

I don't take it.

I knows that if Maggie help me, I can stand up, but I not wish to. It is correct that I stay, animal-like, on this wet sand. It is better that I stays close to Maggie's feet, so that it easier to beg forgiveness. I knows that, for the sin I have done against the woman who has given me my life, my voice, my happiness, even this evening when I sees the face of God across the sky, only crawling will do.

"Please," I say. "You lead the way home. I follows." And I moves on the beach like the worm, like the snake, even though the sand cut my body.

"Lakshmi," Maggie say, and I hears a irritate in her voice. "What are you doing? Are you not able to walk?"

I starts to explain about Mount Kailash but then I sees me as Maggie do—a crazy who show up in the California, who walk into ice water for no reason, and who now moving toward her house like a half-dead fish.

"Sorry," I says. "I's okay." I puts one hand on the ground and slowly lifts myself up.

When we gets to her place, Maggie make me take off my wet pant to place in dryer and gives me a big towel to wrap. When I returns to living room, I hands her the letter.

"What's this?"

"A note. From Sudhir babu. For you, Maggie."

She look puzzle, then angry. "I don't get it. If he has something to say, how come he didn't just mail it?"

Before I answers, she get up and goes to the kitchen with the letter.

Maggie living room small and cozy, so different from the big house she live in with Sudhir babu. I sits here alonely while Maggie in the kitchen, reading Sudhir babu's letter.

When she finally come back, she holding two cups of tea. One she is putting down on the little table next to my chair. Then she sit down across from me but not saying anything. Her eyes are red. What Sudhir babu say in his letter to make her cry?

The silence between us louder than the noise the ocean make outside Maggie house. All this year, my head full of things I wanting to tell to Maggie, but now no words come.

"I's a masi," I say suddenly.

"A what?"

"An auntie. My Shilpa has a son. His name Jeevan."

Maggie look like she about to ask more question but then she remember how I destroy her life and she blow the questions out like the candle. She sit back in her chair and say, "What are you doing here, Lakshmi? What do you want from me?"

Nothing, I wants to say. I am wanting nothing more from you, Maggie. Except your forgiveness. But what I wants is to give you. Everything that I stole from you, I wants to return. I am not knowing if this is even possible. I am not smart like you, Maggie. I cannot tell if you is happy in your new life. The things I do not know bigger than this ocean outside your door. I am just an ignorant village woman who destroy the one good thing in my life. And the one good thing in Sudhir babu's life.

Maggie watching me, waiting for me to speak.

"One time I looks at your appointment book," I say. "In Cedar-ville, when you leaf the room for one minute. On Monday, for full month, at one-thirty, you write, 'Lakshmi's Hour.' "

She look annoy. "So?"

"That how you build me, Maggie. Hour by hour. Story by story. Day by day. That how you give me my whole lifes."

"And we all know how that turned out."

Maggie look as shock to have say those words as I look to hears them. "I'm sorry," she say. "That was—"

"No, no, Maggie. You's correct to be angry. That's why only I come."

Maggie give big sigh. She rise up and look down at me. "Lakshmi," she say slowly. "It's getting late. I have an early-morning appointment tomorrow. And I'm still not sure why you've shown up at my door."

I opens my mouth. I am not sure what will come out—words or crying, rats or flowers, light or darkness. I just knows that the next few minutes will decide whether Maggie's story will con-tinue next to Sudhir babu's or not, whether this will be the last time I see my best friend or the first of many more.

"How much more minutes in the dryer?" I say.

"What?"

"For my pant to dry. How much time?"

Maggie give the shrug. "I don't know. Maybe another ten min-utes?"

"Please, Maggie. Please to sit. I have one more story to tell. Just one more. And after that, if you say, I will leaf."

She look at me again, as if she trying to decide who this new, crazy Lakshmi is, and then she drop back in her chair. Her face is tired, her eyes blank. "Shoot," she say.

Maggie waiting for me to speak. I thinks of all the stories I have told her—about Ma and Dada and Shilpa and Munna and

Mithai and Dilip. Now I must tell her the story of Sudhir babu and me. How we both knows that Maggie is worth more than her one sin. As we hope we are also.

I close my eyes. In the dark, I hears the ocean banging its head against the sand. I have come as far as I can. What happen now is the job of the same God who made the small Lakshmi and the big ocean.

I begins.

ACKNOWLEDGMENTS

Thank you, Dad

For being that rare, beautiful thing—a genuinely good human being.

You were incandescent—a sight to behold

A gift to cherish

Always

Always

ABOUT THE AUTHOR

Thrity Umrigar is the author of five novels—*The World We Found, The Weight of Heaven, The Space Between Us, If Today Be Sweet,* and *Bombay Time*— and the memoir *First Darling of the Morning.* An award-winning journalist, she has been a contributor to the *Washington Post,* the *Boston Globe,* and the Huffington Post, among other publications. She is the winner of the Nieman Fellowship to Harvard, the 2009 Cleveland Arts Prize, and the Seth Rosen berg prize. A professor of English at Case Western Reserve University, she lives in Cleveland, Ohio.